STAR TREK: 6
BLOODTHIRST

D0318296

STAR TREK NOVELS

Coming soon:
STAR TREK:
THE NEXT GENERATION NOVELS

STAR TREK GIANT NOVELS

STAR TREK LARGE FORMAT

A *STAR TREK*® NOVEL

BLOODTHIRST
J.M. DILLARD

TITAN BOOKS
LONDON

STAR TREK 6: BLOODTHIRST
ISBN 1 85286 039 1

Published by
Titan Books Ltd.
58 St Giles High St.
London WC2H 8LH

First Titan Edition December 1987
10 9 8 7 6 5 4 3 2 1

British edition by arrangement with Pocket Books, a division of
Simon & Schuster, Inc., Under Exclusive License from
Paramount Pictures Corporation, The Trademark Owner.

Printed and bound in Great Britain by Cox and Wyman Ltd,
Reading, Berkshire.

Acknowledgments

Back in 1985, when *Mindshadow* was at the bottom of an editorial slushpile and *Demons* was a mere twinkle in my eye, I lived under the mistaken notion that I was the only *Star Trek* fan in the entire Washington, D.C., metropolitan area.

Hoo boy, was *I* wrong.

It was Liz Clark who got me (trembling and unsure) to my first *Star Trek* convention. Liz used to work at a local bookstore. It was she who introduced me to Ann Crispin at ClipperCon 1986. As Ann shook my hand, I think I stammered something about enjoying *Yesterday's Son,* but I don't remember much except that I was *sure* Ann thought me a total idiot. But to show you the type of person Crispin is, she went straight to the dealers' room and bought a copy of my book, and had me sign it for her.

What can you say about such a generous person? From there, Ann has helped me to get onto panels at other conventions, introduced me to publishers, and thrown out literally thousands of ideas when I was mired deep in a plotting problem. (As a mutual friend of ours says, Ann always has eleven ideas before breakfast.)

She also gave me advice on getting an agent. Hers was Merrilee Heifetz, and I'm glad to say that Merrilee is now my agent, too. Besides being an incredibly pleasant person, Merrilee is the type of agent who goes beyond the call of duty, and I'd like to thank her here.

But back to Ann Crispin. Not only did she introduce me

v

to Merrilee, she introduced me to all the wonderful members of the Whileaway Writers Co-op:

Debby Marshall, talented writer and quite possibly one of the most charming people on this planet;

Anne Moroz, author of *No Safe Place,* which deserved all the rave reviews it got;

Teresa Bigbee, talented reader and commenter, and

Kathleen O'Malley, not only a talented writer but the most inspired editor I've ever met.

These here are Good People, folks.

Other Good People I've had the pleasure to come into contact with since *Mindshadow* was published:

Dave Stern, *Star Trek* editor for Pocket Books. Luckily for us, Dave is a fellow fan who knows and respects *Trek;*

Bob Greenberger of D.C. Comics, and his beautiful entourage of wife Debbie and daughter Katie (who, we all know, is actually Saavik's child);

Dave McDonnell and Dan Dickholtz of *Starlog;*

My mother-in-law, Argyri Kalogridis, who is not only delightful company but absolutely the best public relations agent anyone could ever hope for;

Maritta and Faye, friends and fellow *Trek* fans, and the youngest Trekker of them all, Amanda Eileen;

Kum Ja and Chenda of the McLean Café, who deserve thanks for the most delicious sandwiches in McLean;

and last, but by no means least, all of you fellow *Trek* fans out there. Feel free to write to me at P.O. Box 7182, McLean VA 22106-7182.

Jeanne M. Dillard
May 1987

P.S. For the sake of our Vietnamese friends, please note that Ensign Lisa Nguyen's last name is pronounced almost exactly the same as the English word "when." Those of you interested in reading more not only about the rest of the *Star Trek* crew but also Nguyen and Tomson can find out more about them in *Mindshadow* and *Demons.*

Prologue

YOSHI AWOKE KNOWING that sometime in his sleep, he had made the decision to kill.

His eyes opened to the flickering yellow light of the half-melted candle in the hurricane lamp, and after a second of disorientation in which he feared he had awakened to the wrong century, he remembered he was in Lara's quarters. His jaw ached. He had been sleeping sitting up, with one side of his face flattened against the hard lap of the rolltop desk.

He had not been able to bring himself to sleep in her bed.

His tongue seemed fashioned of dry wool. It stuck to the inside of his cheek, and he winced as he tugged it away; bits of soft, membranous skin clung to it.

The pain awakened his anger. He had been dreaming just then of Reiko, and he could still taste the bitterness that had filled him in his dream: anger at her for leaving him, fury that she was not with him now, when he most needed her. Dying alone was a cruel thing. Of all times, he wanted her with him now, so badly that he saw her in front of him, there, in Lara's quarters, laughing, hair and eyes shining. Her eyes were clear amber glass, nothing hidden, so that he could see right down to the bottom of them, just as on their honeymoon he had looked down through the warm celery waters off HoVanKai and seen minnows nibbling his feet. He had always read those eyes: seen the joy in them each

1

day when she greeted him, seen the pain when their infant daughter died. He could bear his own sorrow, but he could not bear the grief in Reiko's eyes. Even then, it had seemed she still loved him.

Reiko's image stopped laughing. Against his will, he saw the time she had faced him with those sweet eyes—a memory more painful to him than the day the child died—and he had seen . . . nothing at all. Nothing for him, just a new, strange deadness that made him want to cry out when he saw it. *How have I failed you?* he asked. *What have I done? What have I forgotten to do?*

Nothing, the image whispered, and those beautiful crystal eyes generated cold so fierce it took his breath away. There was someone else, he knew instantly, someone else. *Nothing you've done.*

It had always been so with the evil in his life. Nothing he had done, and yet the evil never ceased coming. He had been a model son, a model student, a model husband and worker, for his own part inflicting grief on no one, yet it always managed to find him. First the loss of his mother, then a different loss in Reiko . . . and now, to be forced to kill—and die, all for nothing he had done.

His right hand gripped the scalpel so tightly that the skin above the knuckles paled to the color of the bone beneath. He hardly realized that he was still holding it, that he had clutched it tightly through the long fitful night. He was knotted with the need for revenge, for his mother, for himself . . . but there could be no retribution for him. For his mother, perhaps, if he died quietly. It was for her sake that he would consider it.

In his office there was an old holo of his parents, taken long ago when his mother was alive. He wanted to see it again so badly that he physically ached, but there was no chance of that. He stared at the dark red back of his eyelids and summoned it from memory as best he could. His father appeared first, olive-skinned and proud, back when he still had a full head of dark hair. Next to him stood his Japanese wife, as delicate and slender as her husband was thick-boned and coarse. Yoshi's father had changed when she died, become morose and brooding, and Yoshi had grown up constantly reminded of her absence. His father had never quite forgiven himself and Yoshi for living.

Now his father could only blame himself; now he was losing his only child. Yoshi thought unhappily of the added grief it would bring his father, and slumped over the desk again.

His hand touched the open page of a book he had been reading. Lara was an avid collector of antiques, including the paper books that lined the shelves. He had read himself to sleep the night before, a book chosen because he found the title vaguely familiar, but the choice had been poor and haunted his dreams. His eyes fell upon a line:

I was indeed awake and among the Carpathians. All I could do now was to be patient, and to wait the coming of the morning.

Yoshi closed the book and pushed it away. He had been patient, but morning for him would not come again. He drew a breath deep into his lungs to clear his head, but the air was stale and heavy and yielded little oxygen. He had cut off the circulation system to Lara's quarters. Any of the rooms could be sealed when containment was breached, but the system presumed that decontamination of the rest of the station would take only a few hours. Naturally, there would be no need during that time for food, or water, or fresh air.

No provisions had been made for the insanity that occurred here. He closed his eyes and saw the impossible: he and Lara in the stasis room, standing in front of the closed burial tube . . . and watching aghast, as the lid slowly rose because *it was being pushed open from the inside*—

Don't think of it.

He swallowed a sob of fear and calmed himself by listening to his stomach rumble hollowly. Without food it was not so bad—after the first two days, his hunger was replaced by a dull headache. But thirst tormented him unbearably.

It would be quicker, better, to go outside. It was no longer a question of surviving: it was a question of choosing how he was to die.

Yoshi rose from the desk too quickly, and had to clutch it to keep from falling. The worst thing was what the lack of water had done to his mind, making him the victim of his thoughts rather than the master of them. He could face dying, even killing, if his mind were clear.

He pushed himself away from the desk and walked unsteadily through the gloom. The lights had gone out some time ago, and he had groped, childishly frightened of the dark, and found the lamp, candle, and lighter in the old desk. Now he held the lamp in one hand and the scalpel in the other, moving past the bookshelves and the dusty tomes with cracked spines, past the picked-over display of antique medical instruments, to the great thick slab of metal that sealed him off from the outside.

For a time, Yoshi contemplated the door. Small beads of sweat stung his cracked lips and he savored them greedily with his tongue as he thought of what lay beyond: murder, followed by his own suicide.

He tried to swallow and could not, the muscles in his neck pulsing with the effort. He would not lose heart now. He would do it. Dying of thirst was worse . . . letting the evil live was worse. Killing had become an act of mercy. He leaned weakly against the cold metal and pressed the control. The seal slid upward with a whisper. The door opened.

The corridors beyond were draped in blackness. Yoshi held the lamp high and ventured tentatively beyond the threshold. The small stub of candle flickered, capturing at the far edge of its illumination a pale, indistinct shape. Heart fluttering, he followed that shape down the hall to sickbay, where he stopped, sensing a presence within. He leaned forward into the open door and raised the scalpel high, like a dagger at the ready.

"Lara?" His voice was low, scarcely audible, yet in the darkness it carried as if he had shouted.

And in the lampglow, Yoshi glimpsed straight to the

4

bottom of the eyes of death: the clouded eyes of his mother as she lay dead on the floor of the shuttle, the eyes of Reiko that spoke of betrayal, the wide, unseeing eyes of Lara Krovozhadny.

The light of the candle reflected the swift, downward glint of silver.

Chapter One

LEONARD MCCOY ABHORRED technology; in fact, it was his firm conviction that it would someday be the death of him. So when the transporter beam deposited him a half mile underground into total blackness, his heart skipped a beat at the prospect that his belief might suddenly be vindicated.

"God almighty!" McCoy reached out, unable to see anything but the faint glow outlining his hands. He waved them cautiously in front of him without touching anything. "Stanger, you still there?"

"Here, Doctor." The soft tenor voice came from a short distance away on his right. "We'll be okay in just a second—" and before Stanger finished, a focused beam of light cut through the blackness. Behind it, McCoy could just make out the security guard's brown features beneath the fleeting glimmer of his field suit.

McCoy felt for his communicator and opened it with an indignant flourish. "McCoy to *Enterprise*." He had to speak up to be sure he was heard. The suit muffled the sound of his own voice, rather as if he had a head cold. "Jim, how the hell do you expect us to operate in the dark down here?"

There was a pause at the other end, and he could picture the corner of the captain's mouth crooking up a half inch or so, but the reply showed no trace of it. "Don't tell me neither of you thought to take a flashlight."

"I did, sir," Stanger volunteered from a distance—a little

too eagerly, McCoy thought. He frowned at the transmitter grid before speaking into it.

"That's not the point, Captain. The point is that—"

"The point is inferred and noted," Kirk said, and now the smile was in his voice, too. "Next time, we'll warn you."

"Thanks," McCoy answered sarcastically.

"Everything else okay, so far?"

"How should I know? I just got here," McCoy said. "I'll yell if we need anything."

"You do that, Doctor. Kirk out."

Stanger had already made his way to the nearest wall and had located the control panel for the lights, but he was frowning. "Power source cut off. That's odd. Other systems seem to be working."

McCoy nodded. "What kind of place are we in, anyway?"

Stanger swept around with the flashlight at waist level. "Looks like some sort of lab . . ."

The beam swept over gleaming onyx counter tops and an elaborate assortment of Petrie dishes and vials—all encased in a pentagon of crystal. The entrance to the pentagon shimmered with the same type of field as Stanger and McCoy's suits. As they moved closer, the crystal threw the light back in their faces. "Looks like a medical lab," Stanger said.

"A hot lab," McCoy murmured, mostly to himself.

Stanger frowned. "A what?"

"A pathology lab, from the looks of their containment setup. An isolated disease control center. Reminds me of the one in Atlanta. Wonder why they'd have such a small setup in the middle of nowhere like this."

"Seems to me you'd want to keep something like this out in the boondocks," Stanger said.

"Maybe. But you'd think they'd have given some sort of warning. If we'd beamed down here without the precaution of the suits—"

Stanger's expression grew sickly. "You mean they didn't *tell* us anything?"

"Just a class-one medical emergency. But there's nothing to worry about. These suits are standard procedure. They'll keep us safe."

7

The guard grunted dubiously and started moving the light around the corners of the room. "Anyone in here?"

His voice echoed in the shadows of the empty chamber; no answer came.

"Guess we'd better take a look around," McCoy said, though quite frankly it was the last thing he wanted to do. He'd never been afraid of the dark, not even as a kid—well, not *really*—but the lab was giving him a distinctly uncomfortable feeling. He wanted to find whomever he was supposed to find and get out of there. "That was a class-one medical emergency signal. We can't afford to take our time."

In response, Stanger led the way to the door and glanced down at the tricorder. Its dials glowed feebly in the dark. "I'm getting a faint life-form reading coming from that direction." He pointed and started moving for the door. McCoy followed—perhaps too closely. At one point in the corridor, he stepped on the back of Stanger's heel.

"Sorry," he said sheepishly, feeling embarrassed.

"That's okay." Stanger swung around to look at him, politely lowering the flashlight so it didn't shine in the doctor's eyes. McCoy could tell from the sound of his voice that Stanger smiled slightly. "Place getting to you?"

"No—well, actually, yes. Don't you think there's something creepy about this place?"

"I find it all very appropriate." Sounding bemused, Stanger turned away from him and started following the tricorder again. McCoy tried this time to maintain a respectable distance. "You *do* know what day it is, don't you, Doctor?"

McCoy frowned. "Stardate . . ."

"No, I mean Old Earth calendar."

"Oh. Uh, October something . . . I think it's the last day. Is it the thirtieth or the thirty-first? I can never remember that damn poem—"

"The thirty-first," Stanger said helpfully.

McCoy grinned in spite of himself. "Well, I'll be . . . It's Halloween. I'd forgotten. Not many people celebrate it these days."

"A shame, too," Stanger said. "My folks did. It was my favorite holiday when I was a kid."

"Well, that explains it, then. These people are having a Halloween party, and they've invited us."

Stanger chuckled. "Thank God we remembered to wear our costumes."

McCoy smiled, feeling a little more relaxed. He liked Stanger. Personable, good sense of humor, and seemed to know what he was doing. But awfully old for an ensign. There was some sort of rumor going round the ship about him, something bad he'd supposedly done that Tjieng had been repeating to Chris Chapel, but McCoy had been too busy to stop and listen. Besides, he disapproved of gossip . . . in theory, anyway. "No wonder I was feeling a little skittish."

They inched their way along the corridor until Stanger planted himself in front of a closed door and gestured at it with the tricorder. "In there."

"What do you think we'll find?"

"Bats hanging from the ceiling," the ensign retorted, but his eyes were faintly anxious.

"Well, then, after you." McCoy gestured gallantly; Stanger turned to face him. "You *are* the security guard, after all."

Stanger's lip curled beneath the field suit, and he shot the doctor a sour look. "You know, that's the trouble with this job." But he went in first—not without resting his free hand lightly on his phaser. McCoy followed close behind.

The flashlight swept the room at eye level.

"Looks like their sickbay," McCoy said. And a small one at that, barely big enough to accommodate three or so people. "See if there's anyone on the diagnostic bed."

Stanger lowered the flashlight. "Funny, I'm not reading anything now, but I could have sworn the tricorder said in here—"

McCoy's communicator beeped, and he flipped it open. "McCoy here."

The ray of light shot straight up, painted an insane zigzag

9

on the ceiling, then disappeared as the flashlight rolled into a far corner. "GEEzus!" Stanger gave a muffled cry. The faint outline of his suit showed him sprawled across the floor.

"Stanger! Are you all right?" McCoy dropped the open communicator.

"What the hell is going on down there?" An angry voice emanated from the communicator on the floor.

Stanger emitted a small bleat of disgust and pushed himself away and up into a standing position. He was on his feet by the time McCoy recovered the flashlight and shone it on him.

"My God, Stanger—"

Deep red fluid beaded up and dribbled down the front of Stanger's suit, repelled by the energy field. McCoy grabbed his arm, but Stanger shook his head and pulled his arm away.

"I'm all right. Fell over something—someone. Feels like a body—still warm." He pointed at the floor.

The beam shone down into the dull eyes of a woman, beautiful, bronze-haired, dead. On top of her, face down in a gruesome embrace, lay the still, white form of a dark-haired man.

McCoy gave the flashlight to Stanger to hold while he bent over the man. The woman was cold, dead for a few hours at least, but the man's body was still warm to the touch. McCoy shook his head bitterly. If they had only gotten there a few minutes earlier . . . He gently rolled the body over, and started. "Will you look at that?" His voice was soft with awe.

The light shone on the man's neck, which had been slit from ear to ear in a hideous, gaping grin. An old-fashioned scalpel dropped from his limp fingers.

"I'm trying not to, thanks." Stanger averted his eyes quickly. "What about the woman?"

"She's been dead for some time. Both bled to death. You can see how pale they are. You probably were picking up a reading on him a half minute ago—if we hadn't spent so much time stumbling in the dark, I might have been able to do something—"

10

"Must have gone crazy." Stanger shook his head. "There's nothing we can do?"

McCoy sighed. At times like this, his medical knowledge seemed a useless burden. "I can beam him up to the ship, and by the time I get him pumped full of enough blood to make a difference, the damage to the brain—"

Frowning, Stanger interrupted. "Do you hear something, Doctor?"

McCoy listened carefully. The sound of someone talking, very far away . . . "For God's sake, my communicator—"

Stanger took the flashlight and retrieved it for him.

"Anybody there?" McCoy said apologetically into the grid.

"What the devil is going on?" The captain's voice had no trace of amusement in it now.

"We just stumbled over two corpses, Jim. Quite literally. They've been cut very neatly."

McCoy could hear the slow intake of breath at the other end of the channel. Kirk was silent for a beat, and then he said, "Doctor, I just got a message from Starfleet Command in response to my report that we were answering the distress call. It says that under no circumstances are we to respond. Unfortunately, we were too far out to get the message before we beamed the two of you down."

"But it's standard procedure—" McCoy began to protest indignantly. Behind him, Stanger had overheard and muttered what McCoy assumed was an obscenity.

"You don't have to tell *me,* Doctor," Kirk said dryly. "What interests me is that there is no explanation as to *why* we should not respond."

The thought did not strike McCoy as a pleasant one. "Did you tell them we're already down here?"

"Not yet. But if there's nothing you can do down there, we may as well go ahead and beam you up. I don't want you exposed to any unnecessary danger—"

"I'd just as soon not be exposed to *necessary* danger, either, if it's all the same to you."

Stanger interrupted, flashlight down, his eyes fastened on the glowing tricorder. "Doctor, I'm getting another faint life-form reading. . . ."

11

McCoy sighed. "Jim, someone else is down here. I just lost one person by a few seconds, and though I'd just as soon get out of here, I think we ought to stay a bit longer and see if there's something we can do." He and Stanger exchanged unhappy glances; it was clear that the security guard was just as displeased to have a reason to stay longer.

There was a second's pause, and then Kirk said, "All right. I suppose we can't disobey the order more than we already have."

"That's the spirit. I'll check back in if there's any problem. McCoy out." He snapped the communicator shut and looked up at Stanger. "Where's the reading coming from?"

Stanger nodded at the door just as it slid open in the dark. There was an instant of confusion before he got the flashlight aimed at the intruder's face.

The man in the doorway threw pale arms up to protect his face. "The light! Please, the light!"

There was honest agony in his voice. Stanger lowered the flashlight. "Who are you?"

Even the presence of the light near his feet seemed to dismay the man. Still shielding his face with his hands, he squinted at the others in obvious discomfort.

McCoy gave a small, involuntary shudder at the sight of the man's face. Maybe it was an illusion created by the shadows, but the man's skin was gray, the expression pinched—like a corpse, McCoy thought, like a med school cadaver that'd been taken out of stasis and left lying around the classroom too long.

"Adams. Jeff Adams." He did not move closer. The light at his feet kept him pinned in the doorway, unable to come any nearer, but drawn to Stanger and McCoy by some need. "I'm not used to the light anymore—it's been shut off for days."

"Mr. Adams—" McCoy began.

"Dr. Adams."

Good Lord, did titles matter at a time like this? "Dr. Adams, then, can you tell us what's going on here? We intercepted an emergency signal—"

"I broadcasted that signal, yes. Thank God you're here."

Although Adams' face was shadowed, it looked like the man was making an effort to smile.

"How many of you are there?"

"Three. Three of us."

Stanger aimed the beam on the faces of the dead. "Then would you mind explaining *this?*"

Neither of them made it to Adams in time before he fell.

Jim Kirk felt a headache coming on. At first he attributed it to the cumulative effect of several days' unrelenting boredom on a stellar mapping assignment. Such tasks invariably left the captain with nothing to do but fidget, so Kirk had jumped at the chance to respond to a distress signal. But the more he listened to what McCoy had to say, the less thrilled he was that the *Enterprise* had answered the call, and the more his head throbbed. He took a generous mouthful of chicken salad on rye, in the hopes that it would somehow help.

"Here's the thing that bothers me." McCoy leaned forward over an untouched plate of fried chicken and mashed potatoes. Normally, such a meeting would have taken place in sickbay or the captain's quarters, until McCoy put up a fuss about missing lunch and it already being past dinnertime. Which was no problem, except that McCoy had simply stared at his plate for the first five minutes.

Kirk finished swallowing. "You mean only *one* thing about this bothers you?"

"All right, then, the thing that bothers me the *most* about all this is—what happened to all the blood?"

"Please elaborate, Doctor." Spock sat opposite McCoy and next to the captain with his fingers steepled, having already silently and efficiently disposed of an unconscionably large salad.

"There just simply wasn't enough blood left in the corpses—"

Kirk had just taken another huge bite of his sandwich; he stopped chewing. He wasn't particularly squeamish by nature, but with the headache . . .

"Forgive me, but I believe you mentioned that the throats

of both victims had been slit," Spock said calmly. "Isn't it logical for significant blood loss to occur?"

"Yes, but Stanger and I examined the area around the bodies—with a flashlight, mind you; kind of spooky down there, in the dark—before we moved them, and there wasn't as much blood as there should have been. Yoshi—that's the man, Adams says—was face down with his carotid slit. Do you have any idea how fast blood would drain from a body under those circumstances?"

"Approximately—" Spock began. Kirk looked up from his cup of coffee in dismay, but McCoy came to the rescue.

"Chrissake, man, when are you going to learn to recognize a rhetorical question? Suffice it to say that there would have been enough blood to swim in."

"Doctor." Kirk set down his mug.

"At least to go wading," McCoy persisted.

"Do you *mind?*"

McCoy caught the look on the captain's face and a sheepish grin slowly crossed his face. "Sorry about that, Jim." His expression grew more serious. "But there are at the very least three or four liters total of blood unaccounted for, particularly in Lara Krovozhadny's—the woman's—case. She hardly had a drop on her—of her own blood, that is. Most of what was on her belonged to Yoshi."

Kirk looked disconsolately at his half-eaten sandwich. "Any ideas as to why that is?"

McCoy shook his head.

"Obviously, someone removed it," said Spock.

McCoy eyed him with disgust and brutally thrust a fork and knife into his chicken. "Well now, that thought occurred to me, too, Spock. But who would want to steal blood? Our friend Adams?"

"He *is* a likely suspect."

"Our only living one, actually. And, intriguingly enough, he's severely anemic. I've had to give him a massive transfusion." McCoy's expression became thoughtful as he speared a piece of chicken and chewed it. "It's a weird bug he has. I've never seen anything like it—and frankly, I have the gut feeling it's been genetically engineered. Stop rolling your eyes, Spock. The lab's running tests on it now. At first I thought his symptoms indicated porphyria, but they're not quite right."

Kirk frowned. "That's a new one on me. Por—what?"

"Porphyria. I doubt you've heard of it before. Of course, I'm sure Spock has—"

"Porphyria," Spock recited. "A genetic mutation affecting the production of enzymes required for the synthesis of heme—"

"Thanks, Spock, but that wasn't an invitation to lecture." McCoy shook his head and turned back to the captain. "Anyway, like Spock said, porphyria is caused by a genetic mutation, not an organism. An interesting disease, though. Explains how stories of vampires and werewolves got started. A person with porphyria is sensitive to light—so sensitive that it can literally burn holes in the skin."

"Vampires?" Kirk frowned. "I thought that was a sort of bat that lived in South America."

"I'll bet your mother never told you about Santa Claus, either," McCoy retorted.

The Vulcan explained. "A vampire is indeed a South American bat, but the term also refers to a legendary creature—a human who each night leaves the grave to feed on the blood of the living, employing similar methods to the vampire bat. At sunrise, the vampire must return to its crypt, or be destroyed by the light. Its victims in turn become vampires themselves." He paused. "Would you also like to know about Santa Claus?"

McCoy groaned audibly.

"No thanks. I appreciate the folklore lesson," Kirk said impatiently, "but what does this have to do with Adams?"

"He suffers from many of the same symptoms," McCoy answered. "Such as photosensitivity. The photochemical reaction of light on his skin literally burns holes in him—he has a number of lesions. The presence of light is excruciatingly painful for him. If exposed long enough, he would die. A porphyria victim is also extremely anemic—which Adams definitely is—and the disease makes the gums recede from the teeth. But Adams' disease seems to be much more insidious. I'm running some tests now to see what we can do to help his body produce its own heme—

15

because if the anemia worsens as its present rate, we'll be giving him a liter of whole blood every five minutes."

"What about his mental state?" Kirk asked.

"You mean is he capable of killing the others? I don't know, Jim, I really don't. He seems lucid one minute, disoriented the next, but I can't really say he seems violent. Of course, slitting one's throat is hardly a preferred method of suicide."

"Regardless, I'm going to question him," said Kirk. "This whole situation on Tanis smells too fishy."

"I don't deny that." McCoy put down the fork and knife. "What exactly *are* they doing on Tanis? What's the official word?"

"No official word at all," Kirk said. "I've advised them of the situation and I'm waiting to hear back, that's all. They aren't telling much of anything."

"The planet is charted, but listed as uninhabited. There are no records of a base being constructed," Spock said. "Yet the fact that a hidden underground laboratory facility exists indicates one of two things: either Starfleet purposely intended the facility's location to remain secret—which would explain why we were instructed to avoid contact with it, medical emergency notwithstanding—or the base was built without Starfleet's knowledge. Considering our orders, the first explanation is the most logical. Most probably, the base was built in order to do secret research."

"The question is, what type of research?" McCoy said. "They've got some sort of microbiological facility down there. And the fact that our boy Adams is infected with some type of bug that the computer is unable to catalog makes me very uneasy. Soon as I came up, I put Stanger and myself through decontam. Ran some blood tests, too. Both of us negative, fortunately."

"What's your point?" Kirk asked.

"My point is that Tanis is set up for work with microbes. Disease-causing organisms. I asked Adams what they were doing down there, and he handed me some cow patty about agricultural research—plant diseases and the like. But Tanis is a sterile, practically atmosphereless planet. Nothing grows on its surface, and I didn't see them cultivating

16

anything for testing purposes in the underground facility. And the containment procedures they're using strike me as being awfully elaborate for plant diseases on a planet that couldn't grow mushrooms in the dark."

Kirk frowned. "Would they be working on cures for diseases?"

McCoy shook his head vehemently. "Adams is infected with something so new, so unheard-of, that the computer can't even classify it, much less diagnose it. And explain to me why Starfleet would want to keep disease research a secret? That's public domain. Any news of a breakthrough is good news."

"Microbial warfare," Spock said softly. It was addressed to no one in particular.

"Exactly," said McCoy, apparently so intrigued by the subject at hand that he failed to realize he had just agreed with his adversary. "I'll bet you credits to doughnuts they're creating bioweapons down there, Jim."

Kirk shot an angry glance at each of them. "The Federation outlawed that a hundred years ago. And Starfleet Intelligence is answerable to the Council. If that's what they're doing, they're not working for Starfleet."

"The equipment I saw down there sure looked suspiciously Fleet issue."

"That doesn't mean anything," Kirk said. "Before you start making accusations, Doctor, let's wait until Spock takes a look at their records."

"Have it your way, Jim, but I think you're being awfully fair. It still doesn't explain why we were told not to respond to their distress call." McCoy gave a careless shrug and stabbed his chicken. "It's as simple as that."

"I don't know the explanation," Kirk said shortly. "But I intend to find out." He rubbed his temples and wondered why McCoy's statement made him feel so damned defensive.

Maybe it was because of the sinking feeling that the doctor was right.

Adams looked like a walking corpse.

Kirk repressed a shudder. Adams lay on a diagnostic bed

17

inside the pitch-black isolation chamber while the captain stood outside. It was small comfort that the sick man probably could not see him, was probably blinded even by the dimmed light outside the chamber. Kirk could see Adams perfectly well, thanks to the infrared visor McCoy had given him, although at the moment, he wasn't sure that constituted an advantage. The man's face was a death mask: pale skin stretched tight over jutting cheekbones, sunken eyes glittering above dark circles. He looked thin and wasted, as if he had been ill for months instead of the week or so McCoy suggested. The deep gray tones of infrared only added to the ghoulish effect. Kirk was uncomfortably reminded of Spock's vampire legend.

He reached out and pressed the intercom. At the sound of it, Adams struggled as if trying to get to his feet.

"Don't get up." Kirk gestured for him to sit, before he remembered that he was invisible.

The man squinted in Kirk's general direction. Around Adams' scrawny, corded neck was a chain, and he clutched the locket in his palm as if trying to draw strength from it. "Jeff Adams," he answered. The voice was warm and affable, the antithesis of shadow. Kirk found that he was smiling, and attempted to counter the effect by reminding himself that the man was quite likely a murderer, and even if not, at the very least was working on something the Federation looked on with revulsion.

"Captain James Kirk. I assume you were told you're aboard the starship *Enterprise.*"

"Yes, I spoke with Dr. McCoy earlier. Where are we? Still orbiting Tanis?"

"At the moment, but we'll be leaving shortly. Your signal pulled us out of our way. We were mapping in the Sagittarian arm a few parsecs out. Dr. McCoy's been taking care of you, but I presume we'll be receiving orders shortly to drop you at Star Base Thirteen."

"I'm very lucky you happened by."

"I can't say we expected to find anyone out here. It's *Doctor* Adams, isn't it? Are you a physician?"

"A microbiologist. Botanical diseases."

"Is that the type of work you're doing down there?"

18

"Yes, of course." Adams seemed puzzled. "Is there some sort of problem about the base?"

"As a matter of fact, yes. Dr. McCoy reported that you were using some sort of isolation method—"

"Containment procedures, yes." Adams nodded congenially. "I see. You probably thought we're doing work with life-form pathogens. I assure you we aren't. If you check Federation records, you'll find there was a tragic case of contamination from a base like ours near Deneb. A worker leaving the facility spread a plant disease that virtually wiped out agriculture in that system. Since then, containment procedures such as ours have been the law."

Kirk made a mental note to check it out, then said, "I see." He let the disbelief show in his voice to see what kind of effect it would have on his prisoner, but Adams only smiled, his eyes focused on a spot about six inches to the right of Kirk's ear. "Dr. Adams, Dr. McCoy tells me you've been unwell for some time."

Adams nodded. "I've never been robust, if that's what he was referring to, Captain. Shuttle accident. I suffered some internal damage—had most of it replaced without much problem, although the doctors had a devil of a time getting the small intestine to absorb nutrients. . . . Feel free to check that out with Dr. McCoy."

"Actually, I was referring to the infection."

Adams dropped the locket. "Infection?"

Kirk shifted guiltily. "You mean you weren't told?"

"No, I wasn't."

"McCoy says that the organism causing the infection seems to be very rare—the computer knows nothing about it."

"I don't understand," Adams said softly.

"I'd like to hear your explanation of how you could have become infected. You've been isolated for some time on that base. How could you have been exposed to a rare disease?"

Adams shook his head. "I'm not sure. . . . It's extremely unlikely that one of the organisms could mutate into something that could affect humans. And containment was never broken—that is, unless . . ."

19

"Unless?"

"One of the researchers down there—Yoshi Takhumara. He . . . he went insane."

"Why?"

Adams became suddenly irritable. "How should *I* know? Sometimes it happens, for God's sake. You obviously don't trust me."

"Sorry," Kirk said shortly, without trying to sound as if he meant it. "Keep talking."

"He murdered the other researcher there with us—" He stopped, as if unable to say the name, and then hurried past the thought. "I think it was a case of unrequited love. It would have been possible for him to sabotage the alarm and the instant seal-off of the lab that would occur in the case of a break in containment." He paused briefly, considering. "Yes, that would make sense. After all, he sabotaged the lighting system."

"I heard about that. No lights. Why would he want to do that?"

"So he could stalk us more easily, I suppose." Adams turned his head toward the wall. "Don't ask me what happened to him, Captain, because I don't understand it myself."

"The other researcher—"

"I assume Yoshi killed her. I stumbled over her body in the dark." He looked back quickly, his voice stronger and more passionate. "If you don't believe me, if you want to arrest me, go ahead."

"There's hardly any need for me to do that," Kirk answered. He had already decided that McCoy was right: the man seemed too lucid to be a murderer, but not too lucid to be involved in something illegal. "After all, you're confined to isolation until McCoy can figure out what's wrong with you." He paused. "What I'd really like to hear is your explanation of why your colleague suddenly decided to take leave of his sanity."

"How am I supposed to know?" Adams' voice rose in sudden anger, but he continued. "After I found Lara's body—"

"Another microbiologist?"

20

"Dr. Lara Krovozhadny, physician and microbiologist," Adams said miserably, in a way that let Kirk know she had been more than just a colleague. "The three of us had been working together for two years. After I found Lara's body I went to her office and sealed it off with the manual controls. Thank God Yoshi hadn't thought to sabotage those. . . . That's when I signaled for help. I left the intercom on so that when your people came, I heard and came out."

"I see. Would you be willing to tell all this to the computer?"

"You think I'm lying, don't you?" For the first time, Adams' tone hardened. "What do you want from me?"

"The truth."

"Did it occur to you that I might not know what the hell is going on myself?" Adams grimaced suddenly, so that Kirk could see his pale gray gums, so receded that the teeth appeared hideously elongated. "You think I'm lying, don't you?"

"I have no idea," Kirk said smoothly, though he felt repulsed by the sight of the man. "Would you be willing to tell your story to the computer?"

"Of course." Adams' head dropped back on the pillow as if he were suddenly weary from the outburst. "I haven't done anything illegal, Captain. I certainly haven't killed anyone, and as far as our research on Tanis, we were doing work approved by the Federation and Starfleet. Go ahead and check it out."

"I'll do that," Kirk said. "One last question. Can you explain why Starfleet told us *not* to respond to your distress signal? And why Tanis is listed as uninhabited—if you've been there two years?"

Adams did not reply immediately. "No. I can't explain that."

It was an ambiguous answer at best.

21

Chapter Two

ON THE TERMINAL screen in the conference room off sickbay, a man sat frozen at a cluttered Fleet-issue desk. His face was severe—but it was not so much his expression as the configuration of his features: ominous black brows and coarse, exaggerated lips and nose. He was stocky without being fat—muscular, with a short wide neck and powerful shoulders. He leaned forward over the desk, his thick fingers meshed together in a gesture of sincerity. Above the deeply carved lines in his forehead, his scalp was pink and smooth, hairless as a newborn's, and the surviving fringe of wavy black hair had just begun to silver.

Kirk had never met Mendez before, but he was struck by the strong physical resemblance the admiral bore to his younger brother, José. Jim Kirk and José Mendez had been on a first-name basis for years, since Commodore José Mendez was in charge of Star Base Eleven, where the *Enterprise* often took leave. Jim didn't know José all that well, but he thought warmly of the man. After all, it was José who had once convinced the brass to drop the charges against Spock for violating General Order Seven.

But there was something Kirk instinctively disliked about the brother . . . perhaps it was the intangible air of arrogance, or the fact that the elder Mendez had the look of a bully.

McCoy fidgeted in his swivel chair and peered impatiently at the screen. "What's keeping Spock, anyway? It isn't like him to be late."

"Blame it on me." Kirk stood next to the terminal, arms folded in front of his chest. "I've got him looking at their records. How's the lab coming on that virus?"

"They agree with me—the thing's been genetically engineered."

"Any way of proving that?"

"Not really, no. But I'd swear to it. We're all working on the vaccine—no harm in it."

"What about a cure?"

McCoy sighed. "We're working on that, too, of course. I've made it top priority for sickbay and the lab. But it doesn't look good for Adams." He looked up as the door to the conference room opened.

Spock entered and took the chair next to the doctor. "I regret the delay, Captain." The Vulcan's expression was typically inscrutable, but there was something in his tone that boded ill. "I'm afraid that I had some difficulty retrieving the records. Most of them were lost."

"Lost?"

Spock shifted almost imperceptibly in his chair. Anyone unfamiliar with Vulcans would never have noticed. "When I initiated a scan, it activated a virus program on the Tanis computers which immediately erased all records."

"A virus program." McCoy jabbed in Jim's direction with an elbow. "Get it?"

Kirk grimaced but otherwise ignored him. "No one thought to anticipate something like that happening?"

"Actually," Spock continued without gracing McCoy's remark with so much as a glance, "our computers are programmed to anticipate such a possibility—but the programming on the Tanis computers is extremely sophisticated. It was obviously done by a class-one expert." Spock paused, and this time Kirk was more certain that he caught a glimmer of disappointment on the Vulcan's face. "I was able to save some of the records which were not overlaid. It will take some time to reconstruct the data, since it is not in any coherent format. I'm afraid we were left with isolated

23

bits of information. As for the rest, the damage was irreversible."

"You did what you could," Kirk said, not quite able to keep the bitterness from his voice. "We still have Adams. He's scheduled for a computer verification scan. We can still find out what we need to know."

"Doesn't look too good for him, does it?" McCoy finally spoke up. "Wonder how he'll explain away that program?"

"I wonder." A muscle in Jim's jaw twitched; the doctor's suggestion that the Fleet might be involved in biowarfare research was becoming uncomfortably plausible. He pressed a control on the keyboard in front of the viewscreen and sat down.

The man on the terminal came to life. His eyes pierced intently from the viewscreen, as though he sought to catch the eye of the viewer, and when he spoke at last, the voice was as deep and authoritative as Kirk expected.

"Admiral Mendez responding to your taped message. It is unfortunate that your party beamed down. In response to your questions, Captain—yes, Tanis is an agricultural colony. However, the work being done there is classified; in light of the incident with the Klingons on Sherman's Planet, perhaps you can appreciate the need for secrecy. However, we found your report most disturbing—it indicates to us that the researchers were deviating from their assigned project. As you know, research on bioweaponry is expressly forbidden, and Starfleet upholds that law. From what you've told us, it sounds as if the researchers were infected with some type of madness-inducing illness, and Adams should definitely remain isolated. Those who beamed down to the surface, I hope, took the proper precautions upon their return. If not, they, too, should be isolated."

"Give that man a prize for stating the obvious," McCoy said, *sotto voce.*

"Hush," Kirk murmured. "It starts getting interesting about here."

". . . If in fact the researchers have been infected with a microbe of their own making, samples of it must no doubt remain on Tanis; you are to retrieve it and bring it aboard the *Enterprise*—under strict containment, of course—along with any other microbes in the lab, since it is essential that any virulent disease not be permitted to fall into enemy hands."

"I love these guys." McCoy was full of angry sarcasm. "Enemy hands. As if we were at war with somebody. What do they expect, that we're going to broadcast this to the Klingons and the Romulans and auction it off to the highest bidder?"

"Perhaps not intentionally." Spock's voice was barely audible. "But if there is in fact a microbe on the surface, it is a possibility that third parties might express an interest, should our transmissions be monitored."

". . . analysis, after which we will advise you as to the disposal of any harmful organisms," Mendez was saying. "As for Dr. Adams, he is to be placed under arrest and brought immediately to Star Base Nine for questioning in connection with the deaths of the other researchers."

"Star Base *Nine?*" McCoy complained. "Typically ignorant bureaucrat. Someone tell that man to take a look at a star chart—"

Kirk shot him a dangerous glance, and the doctor fell silent as Mendez continued.

"Since he is already in isolation, that should present no problem for you. In addition, you are to impound any and all computer records located on Tanis."

Kirk leaned forward to press the control, and Mendez's image, thick lips slightly parted, froze once more. "Well, gentlemen?"

Spock sat back in his chair, arms folded, frowning. "As the doctor pointed out, Star Base Nine is considerably out of the way of our present course. I fail to understand why the admiral did not direct us to Star Base Thirteen, which is far closer. I am not aware of any difference in containment facilities at either base."

"Is that all?"

"Not quite. I find it rather difficult to share the admiral's enthusiasm for bringing a dangerous microbe on board."

"My sentiments exactly," Kirk said.

25

"You heard him. He wants to keep the Romulans and Klingons from getting it," McCoy offered.

"Then why not simply destroy it on Tanis?" Spock asked.

Kirk shook his head. "I think Mendez is more concerned with recovering the *corpus delicti* than he is with the safety of the *Enterprise*. Otherwise, he would have no real evidence of what the researchers were really doing."

McCoy shrugged. "What's he need that for? Two of them are dead, one is sick and quite possibly dying, if they don't get him for murder first."

Spock turned and addressed McCoy with a considerable degree of condescension. "If the researchers were in collusion with others, Doctor—especially if they were working for someone outside the Federation—then it becomes imperative to find out *exactly* what they were doing."

"I suppose so," McCoy said. "And to find out how Yoshi and Lara really died."

"That's not my concern." Kirk stood up again and leaned over the conference table. "The civil authorities can investigate that. What bothers me is the chance of exposing my crew to an illness that we know nothing about."

"You *are* under orders, Captain," Spock said.

"The ship's already at risk," McCoy pointed out. "Adams is on board, and if he took a mind to break out of containment, he could probably do it; and Stanger and I were down there, albeit with our suits on, but with no harm done. It could well be that whatever Adams has isn't all that contagious."

Kirk's lips had tightened into a grim line. "What you're both telling me, then, is that you think I shouldn't try to buck Mendez's orders."

"Not at all, Captain," Spock replied. "But I do believe that someone should go down and ascertain whether the postulated microbe actually exists. And I believe that if it is indeed found to be dangerous, it should, despite Dr. McCoy's comments, be kept 'out of enemy hands.' The method for so doing I leave to your discretion."

"Thanks," Kirk said without enthusiasm. "I suppose you agree with him, Bones?"

"Much as I hate to admit it. We could go down there and

retrieve something. We've got trained people, and the risks would not be all that great, barring an unforeseen accident."

"Before I do that, I want to get as much information out of Adams as I can. Let's set him up for questioning ASAP."

McCoy nodded, "Makes sense to me."

"What puzzles me"—Spock chose his words deliberately —"is why Admiral Mendez has chosen to involve himself in this affair."

Kirk let out a deep breath. "I've been trying to come up with an explanation for that one myself. Could it be that intelligence has gotten wind of what was occurring on Tanis, and Mendez was keeping an eye on them?"

"Or," Spock countered grimly, "that Mendez himself is involved?"

"Wait a minute." McCoy frowned and swiveled in his chair to face Spock. "I have to admit, I don't keep tabs on everyone's duty assignment, especially when it comes to the brass. Why is it surprising for Mendez to be involved?"

He turned to look from Spock's face to the captain's, but it was the Vulcan who finally answered.

Spock's tone was one of exaggerated patience. "Admiral Mendez," he replied, "is head of weapons research."

"Here." McCoy handed Kirk an infrared visor and put his own on. They were seated at a terminal temporarily moved in front of quarantine and were peering into the dark chamber where Adams lay, wired up for questioning. The doctor had trusted the job to no one else, insisting on suiting up and doing the job himself. It was difficult to do detailed work in infrared, but Adams' illness made ultraviolet light impossible; McCoy completed the job with much swearing, and was in a very sour mood by the time he took his seat next to Kirk at the terminal.

"Why the visors?" Kirk asked. "Do we really need to watch him?"

McCoy scowled beneath his visor. "How the hell am I supposed to make a judgment on whether a man is telling the truth if I can't even see his face?"

"I thought the computer made that decision." Kirk had the feeling he was wading into dangerous waters.

McCoy rose from his chair and snarled. "The computer can make its decision if it wants, but *I'm* the one who interprets the results. And I might choose not to agree with it; interpreting a person's physiological response to questioning is still an art form, regardless of what the programmers would love us to believe. Of course, if you'd rather believe that pile of circuits than me . . ."

"Sit down, Bones," Kirk said, in a good-natured tone calculated to mollify. He was as anxious about starting the questioning as McCoy.

The doctor sat grumpily.

"Can he see us?"

"No. Even though I've dimmed the light out here for him, too, it dazzles him. He's pretty much blinded as to what's going on out here. And I doubt he suspects we can see him."

Kirk nodded, grateful for the advantage, and put his visor on. Adams lay, threaded to the diagnostic bed by a hundred tiny filaments. His face was still starkly gaunt, but the shock of seeing it a second time was less. In time, Kirk supposed, he could even get used to it.

McCoy held down a control and spoke into the terminal. "Dr. Adams, the computer will begin to ask you questions now." He released the button and turned to the captain. "We can't be heard unless we want to be."

"Please state your full name," the computer droned in its slightly bored, feminine voice.

"Jeffrey Ryan Adams," Adams answered. He appeared perfectly relaxed.

McCoy's eyes remained fixed on the terminal screen in front of him; Kirk's were fixed on Adams.

"Please state your correct age in standard sols."

"Forty-one."

"Please state your place of birth."

"New Orleans, North America, Terra."

"Thank you," the computer answered in flat tones incapable of expressing gratitude. "Please give incorrect answers to the following questions. What is your full name?"

"Vlad the Impaler." Adams smiled faintly, amused by his choice.

McCoy raised an eyebrow at that; his eyes darted from Adams to the readout.

"Age?"

"A thousand years."

"Place of birth?"

"Old Earth, Transylvania, outside the town of Bistritz."

"Thank you." The computer paused. "Please answer all the following questions correctly, to the extent that you are aware of the information. What is your occupation?"

Adams answered easily, without reflection. "Research microbiologist."

"What are the names of the other researchers who worked with you on Tanis?"

"Lara Krovozhadny and Yoshi. Yoshi . . . Takhumara, I think it was."

"Why is Tanis listed in Starfleet's charts as uninhabited?"

"For security purposes," Adams said shortly.

McCoy and Kirk looked at each other; McCoy pressed for the intercom. "Dr. Adams, please elaborate."

"We didn't want the Klingons or the Romulans to get wind of what we were doing."

Kirk could not restrain himself. "What *were* you doing on Tanis, Dr. Adams?"

"Agricultural research," Adams said agreeably, still perfectly composed, without a trace of defensiveness. "We're working on a new plant to be used as food. You'll remember, Captain, what happened on Sherman's Planet—"

"That's the second time I've been reminded," Kirk muttered, but McCoy had already switched off the intercom.

The computer stuck to its line of interrogation, unaware of the content of the interruption. "Did you do agricultural research on Tanis?"

"Yes," Adams said, with the barest hint of smugness. "Yes, I did. High security agricultural research."

"Did you do any other type of research on Tanis?"

"No." The answer came quickly. "I did not."

"Did you know Lara Krovozhadny?"

"I did."

"How did Lara Krovozhadny die?"

"She was killed." There was a hint of painful hesitation in the voice, but Adams' expression did not alter; it remained relaxed and agreeable, as if he were discussing something pleasant. "Her throat was slit, I think."

"Did you kill Lara Krovozhadny?"

"No," Adams said softly.

"The reading," Kirk hissed at McCoy. "Is he telling the truth?"

"Looks like it." But McCoy's expression seemed troubled.

"Did you know Yoshi Takhumara?" the computer asked Adams.

"Yes."

"How did Yoshi Takhumara die?"

"The same way as Lara. His throat was cut."

"By whom?" Kirk asked, but Adams could not hear.

"Did you kill Yoshi Takhumara?" the computer queried.

"No," said Adams. There was a pause, as if Adams found it too painful to answer. "Yoshi killed himself." And, clearly thinking himself to be invisible, he gave a wide, beatific smile.

"Good Lord." McCoy glanced down at the terminal screen.

"What does it say?" Kirk demanded, and, when the doctor did not answer immediately, asked again. "What does it say?"

"It says," McCoy said, his eyes now fixed on the still-smiling Adams, "that he's telling the truth."

The questioning went on for what seemed to Kirk an interminable period of time, with the computer asking the same questions over and over in a thousand different ways; through it all, Adams remained unrattled. At last, Kirk pulled off his visor and turned to McCoy.

"How did he do?"

"You want the official report?"

"Let's start with that."

McCoy set his visor down on the terminal console and

30

rubbed one hand over his eyes and face. "There were some hints of deviation around certain questions, especially the difficult ones, about the deaths and the nature of the research."

Kirk was irritated. "So you mean he actually failed, then. He's guilty."

The doctor shook his head. "Would that it were as simple as all that, Jim. Everyone assumes that the computer can tell who's lying and who isn't, without a shadow of doubt. But the problem is, not everyone reacts to lying in the same physiological manner. Some people are better at it than others. Now, the computer can pick out ninety-nine percent of the liars, as long as you feed it accurate data about the person's cultural background. That's because most people can't completely master their anxiety about lying, and the computer picks up on the physiological changes that go with that anxiety."

"Most people. What kind of people can outsmart the computer?"

"A Vulcan could probably get away with it, if he wanted to. Or a truly insane individual who didn't know the difference between reality and fantasy."

"I thought you said Adams wasn't insane."

"He's not. But he could be sociopathic . . . without any conscience or sense of morality. True sociopaths are pretty rare, these days. Of course . . ." McCoy frowned thoughtfully. "Maybe the disease could have something to do with it."

"Well, I don't understand," Kirk said, quite truthfully. "If there were deviations in the readout, why did the computer say he passed?"

McCoy looked down at his readout and sighed. "The computer will tell you that Adams' reaction was 'within the bounds of normal physiological response.' In other words, that he was just nervous about those few questions."

"Something in your voice tells me you don't agree with that."

"I don't . . . though if I can't come up with more conclusive results than a gut instinct, everyone will look at the computer readout and they won't give a damn about my

31

opinion." McCoy shook his head at the dark chamber in disbelief. "But you saw that smile, Jim. He's lying. And he's not insane—just the coldest, sickest devil I've ever met."

Jonathon Stanger stood, hands clasped behind his back like an attentive student, and attempted to keep the humiliation he felt from showing while Security Chief Tomson paced in front of him. A rush of blood warmed his face and pounded in his temples.

He had been three minutes late reporting for duty, the result of another near-sleepless night. When he did manage to drift off, his dreams were of the *Columbia* and Rosa, and so full of venom that he wakened, furious, his stomach in knots. Further rest was impossible. It had gone on, night after night for nearly a week now.

Last night, he could have sworn he'd given the computer the correct wake-up time, but it never signaled him. He'd wakened in a panic, some subconscious part of his brain alerting him to the fact he'd overslept. He had stumbled into the closet, synthesized a uniform, and slathered on some beard repressor so carelessly that now he feared he might have lost part of his mustache—from time to time, he touched it to make sure it was still all there. Then he'd staggered down to Security without breakfast. He could have tried to blame it on the fact that the *Columbia*'s circadian cycle was almost exactly opposite the one on the *Enterprise* . . . but after a week on board, he knew his insomnia had another, deeper cause. And he also knew that Tomson was not the type of commanding officer to listen to any excuses. He offered none.

Stanger's shame was doubled by the presence of a third party: Ensign Lamia, an Andorian female who stood shoulder-to-shoulder with him.

Tomson came to the end of the invisible line she was walking and turned on her heel to start in the other direction. Stanger took advantage of the break in eye contact to steal another glimpse of the Andorian. Like the other Andorians he had worked with, Lamia was narrower and longer in the torso than a human, and thus taller than most. Unlike the other Andorians he had worked with, Lamia was female.

Her coloring was quite striking: light blue skin against a silky cap of straight, silver-white hair. Not to mention those incredible celery-green eyes. All spring pastels, the colors of an Easter egg basket.

But the red security uniform clashed garishly with the delicate hues. *Should have gone into Science,* Stanger decided distractedly, in the midst of his suffering. *She'd look better in blue.* Or maybe the gold of Command . . . He pulled his tired mind away from the ridiculous train of thought—it was beginning to wander from lack of sleep—and directed his full attention to his wounded pride.

Besides, isn't this how you got into trouble the last time? Rosa's eyes had been the darkest shade of blue he'd ever seen. In a weak moment, he had lyrically compared them to sapphires. He looked away from the Andorian and forced himself to feel bitter distrust. *Competition, and nothing more.*

". . . won't give you a demerit *this* time, because you're new," Tomson was saying, towering over him icily. The first time he'd seen her, he'd mistaken her for an albino because of her milky complexion and white hair, which she pulled back in a tight bun. Then he'd noticed the pale, pale blue eyes and realized she must have been from one of the winter worlds. Certainly she had a personality to match. She was as light as Stanger was dark, and if the situation had not been so acutely painful for him, he would have perhaps found some humor in the trio's colorful contrast. He had had a good sense of humor, once. "But this is the first and only time I'll let you get away with it," Tomson continued. "By tomorrow, you'd better be completely adjusted to the new schedule. No excuses."

Stanger narrowed his lips and tried to repress the bitterness welling up in him. It wasn't a personal sort of hatred. To the contrary, he respected Tomson. She had a reputation as a good security chief, even if she exuded all the personal charm of an iceberg.

It was just that *he* should have been standing in her place, chewing someone else out instead of being chewed out himself. What Stanger needed, craved, more than anything was a promotion back to his former rank, and now here he was, late his first week of duty. And Tomson had no doubt heard every rumor about him. Stanger's tardiness had been all that was needed to convince her he was a screw-up. And she was letting him know it, in front of a third party, no less. Stanger felt his lips curl even more tightly.

"Yes, sir," he answered stiffly, keeping his eyes focused straight ahead so that they would not meet Tomson's.

"Now, I suggest you and Ensign Lamia report to the transporter on the double, before you're any later."

"Yes, sir." Stanger paused. "About the ensign, sir—" He nodded in Lamia's direction without looking at her. He wanted to make it clear to Tomson right away that he would not only make amends, he would go the extra mile. "I'm capable of handling this without any—"

"I said you're *late,* Ensign." Tomson's sudden sharpness made him close his mouth swiftly. "I can appreciate your desire to make points, but Lamia is going with you. Dismissed."

From the corner of his eye, he caught the Andorian looking at him and glowered at her without Tomson catching it. He was not aboard the *Enterprise* to make friends; and if he was going to admire her appearance, he would do so without her knowing about it. The Andorian looked away quickly.

It was not an auspicious start to his tour of duty aboard the *Enterprise.*

In the transporter room, Kyle stood ready at the controls. Kirk leaned against the console and drummed his fingers lightly as he frowned at the door. The landing party, with the exception of the doctor, had yet to arrive. And in the captain's mind, the sooner he was finished with Tanis Base, the better.

McCoy knew him well enough to interpret his stance. "It's okay with me, Jim," he volunteered. He wore a field-suit unit on his belt, but was waiting to turn it on. "I'm in no hurry."

Kirk turned his face toward him. "You'd do anything to get out of going down there again, wouldn't you?" He almost smiled, then frowned at the door again. "Maybe I ought to give Tomson a call—"

Stanger rushed through the door, which barely opened in time to avoid a collision. He was flanked by an Andorian whose name Jim tried to remember.

"Sorry, Captain." Gasping, Stanger came to an abrupt halt in front of Kirk. "I know I'm a minute or two late—and I have no excuse. I can only promise it won't happen again, sir."

Kirk eyed him narrowly. By the looks of him, Tomson had already probably already taken care of chewing him out, so there was no point in wasting any more time. "Ensign Stanger, isn't it?"

It was pure ruse for Stanger's benefit. Kirk remembered the man all too well. Who could forget, with all the rumors that had followed him on board? A month ago, ex-Lieutenant Stanger had been chief of cecurity on board the *Columbia,* but had subsequently been demoted to ensign. Kirk himself had read the charge: possession of an illegal firearm. A burning phaser, a particularly cruel weapon that was looked upon with such horror by the Federation that Stanger was swiftly and severely disciplined. Stanger did not contest his demotion. He applied for an immediate transfer, but it was almost three weeks before Command could find another starship willing to take him.

When Stanger's file came to him, Kirk had noted that other than the one incident, the man's record was unblemished. "Outstanding" was more like the word for it. Stanger was liked by his fellow officers, respected by his subordinates, given high ratings by his superiors. His psych profile indicated command material. But it was the interview that convinced Kirk that the man deserved a second chance. Stanger politely declined to discuss the incident . . . and convinced Kirk that the whole story had yet to come out. Something was eating away at Stanger.

Besides, there was something about the man Kirk liked—but at this particular moment, the captain wasn't about to

35

let on. It was still up to Stanger to prove Kirk's instincts right.

"Yes, sir. Ensign Jon Stanger." He winced visibly at the word "ensign."

"Ensign Lamia," the Andorian said boldly, thrusting a delicate blue hand at him. Her voice was whispery, the sound of the wind rustling through leaves, but she made an effort to project it so that humans could hear. She lowered her head and tilted her antennae toward the captain in a gesture of respect.

"I thought we were keeping exposure to a minimum." Kirk looked around to catch McCoy's eye.

"Yes, sir." Stanger straightened suddenly. "I'd be willing to go alone, Captain. After all, I've been down there before. There's no real need to risk the ensign, too."

"That's very noble of you, Stanger." There was a trace of irony in Kirk's voice. Stanger was trying much too hard to make points, though you could hardly blame the man for it. "But if only one of you were to go down, why wouldn't Ensign Lamia be the better choice?"

Judging from the ill-concealed irritation at Stanger in her eyes, the Andorian was more than pleased to agree with Kirk's line of reasoning. "I probably wouldn't be affected by anything down there, sir," she responded without an instant's hesitation. Stanger gave her a sharp glance, but she kept her eyes innocently fastened on the captain.

"It's true," McCoy piped up. He'd been standing silently, watching the exchange. "Her blood's based on cobalt. It'd be a rare bug that'd be dangerous to us and an Andorian." He paused. "But Captain, both of them ought to go. Stanger's already been down there once and knows where everything is, and chances are Lamia's immune. The faster we get this done, the better. The longer we're down there, the greater the chance of contamination."

"All right then," Kirk relented, but he was not pleased. He addressed the ensigns. "You both have your cameras?"

"Yes, sir." Stanger patted his belt as Lamia nodded in silent agreement.

"I want you to focus on their sickbay, where the bodies

were found. Get everything, whether you think it's important or not. And the staff's quarters, too. Under no circumstances are either of you to turn off your suits—"

"Understood, sir," the guards chorused.

Kirk thought for a moment. "And the lab. I want detailed pictures of everything in the lab facility."

"Yes, sir." Stanger ascended the platform, closely shadowed by Ensign Lamia.

McCoy turned to Kirk. "I know how worried you are about bringing a potential hazard on board, Captain. All I can say is that we're prepared and the chance of a breakage in containment is virtually nil."

Kirk sighed inaudibly as the doctor climbed the platform and the three of them turned on their suits. "It's the *virtual* part that bothers me, Bones."

Stanger was ready for the darkness this time. His flashlight was lit before they dematerialized on the transporter pad. Once they beamed down to the lab, he immediately began setting up a small floodlight to illuminate the containment chamber.

McCoy moved toward the chamber and began testing the controls. One neutralized the energy field; the entrance went dark. But the doctor frowned. "We've got a problem here. I can't get the seal to the chamber open."

"I could try to find the manual override," Stanger offered, knowing full well it meant a time-consuming search through the circuitry embedded in the bulkhead. But he was in no hurry to return to those dark corridors.

"That'll take too much time. I'll just cut a hole with the phaser."

"It'll take some time, too, to burn through that." Stanger nodded at the crystal casing. "I'll help. If we both do it at once—"

"I think I can handle it, Stanger. You kids run along and do what you're supposed to. If I need any help, I'll just holler."

Stanger shrugged. "Can't say I didn't try, Doctor." He managed to sound nonchalant instead of angry. *I'm not a* kid, *dammit, I was an officer. Lamia, here, she's a kid.* He stopped the thought immediately. *Keep it up, and you'll have the beginnings of an ulcer outside of a week.*

He turned and nearly ran into Lamia, who had been standing close enough to almost touch his right shoulder. The surprise of seeing her right there startled him. *Easy. It's a little early to start letting this place get to you, isn't it?* She moved with alarming speed to get out of his way.

"We'll start by searching the lab here," he told her.

She seemed surprised. "Look, the whole point was to split up so we could get the job done faster. That's why Tomson sent both of us down."

Are you going to question a direct order? He almost said it, but stopped himself in time. Trying hard not to sound aggravated, he said, "We could be more thorough if we both comb over an area. That way we can check each other, in case we miss something."

For no reason he could fathom, she took offense. *"I* don't intend to miss anything," she said coldly. Her sharp chin was tilted up, and he had met enough male Andorians to recognize the gesture of disrespect.

He looked down at the ground for a moment until he felt he could speak without sounding angry. His quick temper was his worst failing, and he'd always worked to keep it under control. Lately, though, it had been flaring up at the most trivial things. And it certainly didn't help matters that the ensign appeared to have her own private chip on her shoulder. "I tell you what," he said finally. "How about a compromise? We both go off in our own directions, but we each go over the lab and sickbay."

"I thought I should do sickbay by myself," she challenged, gazing at him steadily, chin still in the air.

"Why?"

"We know it to be a contaminated area. It's very unlikely that I would be affected by the microbe. It would be less dangerous—"

"Ensign—" He broke off, letting the frustration show in his voice. "I've already been to sickbay once. For God's sake, I *fell over* one of the bodies and I survived."

"So far," Lamia said softly, in a tone that made him nervous.

"All right, so far. Quite frankly, my guess is you're straight from the Academy, and this is your first deep-space assignment. Am I right?"

"Yes." She glowered at him defiantly. "And you're going to ask me how much violence I've seen, right? What do you think, that I'm going to faint when I see human blood on the floor of the sickbay?"

He didn't back down, but looked directly down into those green eyes. "How much violence *have* you seen, Ensign?"

"None. None at all. But I can handle it." She was truly angry now, clenching her fists and leaning forward. "Just because I'm young and female—"

"Female?" Stanger shook his head, truly puzzled. "For God's sake, what does being *female* have to do with our discussion?"

"Never mind." She dropped her eyes for a moment and then looked back up at him. "Anyway, you think I'm too young to be efficient. That's it, isn't it?"

He groaned loudly and shook his head without answering her.

"You can't say it isn't true. You try to get rid of me, then you act so superior—"

"How am I acting superior?"

"You keep calling me ensign. We're the same rank, in case you haven't noticed. People of the same rank call each other by name. Mine is Lamia."

He didn't say anything for a minute. He had thought that everyone on board knew about him . . . but she was new. She obviously hadn't heard. Finally, he said, "I'm sorry . . . Lamia. I will try not to call you ensign anymore. If I do, let me know."

"I will," she said frostily.

He raised his arms in a "what more can I do?" shrug and dropped them again. "Lamia, I wasn't trying to suggest that you were incompetent. I was trying to keep from making a mistake myself by having us check each other's work. Remember, the captain said he wanted us to go over

39

everything in the lab and the sickbay. Now can we stop arguing and get to work?"

"Amen," came a voice from behind them. McCoy's back was to them, and orange-red heat streamed from his phaser and smoked gently where it impacted with the crystal. He had heard everything, Stanger realized, and was fed up with listening to it. Embarrassed, he turned back to Lamia.

"Do we have a deal?"

"If you mean will I check your work, I suppose so," she answered stiffly.

"We'll save the lab for last, then," he said, and at her expression, added: "I just issued another order, didn't I?"

She nodded.

Fine. Let her stay mad. Why should I worry about her liking me? I should worry instead about protecting myself.
"Do whatever the hell you want, then," he said, exasperated, and stalked out the door of the lab into darkness.

Getting into the containment chamber was a task that reduced McCoy very nearly to tears and very definitely to curses. Once he had cut away a large enough square of crystal from the containment chamber, he slipped an arm inside up to his shoulder, only to find that the test tubes that sat on the glistening black counter were far beyond his reach. He spent a decidedly uncomfortable moment angling first his head and then his neck, left shoulder, and arm inside the chamber. It was at that inopportune moment that McCoy realized that the hole was not large enough.

He pulled himself out awkwardly, producing a crick in his neck, which in turn encouraged him to comment on the legitimacy of the person who had sealed the chamber.

It took him several minutes to burn away another piece of crystal, but this time he met with greater success. He managed to wriggle in both shoulders and arms, and finally his torso up to the waist. In an effort to reach the sample vials on the counter, McCoy stood on tiptoe, pressing his body as close as the field allowed against the sharp, unyielding edge of the crystal. It was still not close enough.

He leaned precariously further, his fingers and neck stretched out, standing so far forward on the tips of his toes that he was in great danger of falling forward. He strained just a little more. . . .

At which point he felt a tearing sensation in the muscles of his lower back.

His immediate impulse was to straighten himself, which of course so increased the level of pain that he bent forward again with a groan, supporting himself against the counter with both glowing hands. It took him five seconds to register the absolute futility of his situation, and less time than that to try to reach for his communicator. It was not a fun proposition—reaching backward with his arm dramatically increased the torment in his neck and back—but teeth gritted, perspiring, the doctor persisted until his fingers touched the hard edges of the communicator strapped to his waist. With a grunt, he triumphantly pulled it free.

The communicator slipped from his fingers and clattered on the shiny surface of the counter, well out of reach.

He decided that only one thing could have made the predicament any worse: Spock could have been there to see it.

It wasn't as bad inside the living quarters as Stanger had feared: he could rig the portable floodlights so that the rooms were blindingly bright, stripped of the eeriness that had so oppressed him in the dark corridor.

He wandered through the cabins, aided by the small sketch made by Adams—a dubious choice of informant at best, Stanger thought—and found little of interest in Yoshi and Adams' rooms: the former was spartan, monastic, consisting of no more than a bed, a chair, and a terminal; the latter was disheveled and littered with personal effects, but free of anything incriminating.

Krovozhadny's quarters amazed him.

It was like stepping into a different world, a different era. The ubiquitous colorless carpeting had been covered with a large oriental rug—not a real antique, but a decent replica. There was a heavy wooden roll-top desk, and a four-poster bed, along with tall wooden shelves that held the only true antiques: paper books. One of them had been pulled out and lay open on the desk, next to a brass lamp with a candle

41

inside it. The candle had been burned almost all the way down. Stanger reached out and closed the book gently, then grimaced at the title on the cover.

He felt very sorry that the occupant was now dead. He would have liked to meet her.

As in all the rooms, there was no sign of violence or a struggle. He was in the doorway when it occurred to him that he had forgotten to check the contents of the desk.

The top drawers contained female undergarments in neat piles. Stanger filmed them as instructed, not without questioning the investigative merits of so doing. The bottom right-hand drawer was deeper than the rest. It had been converted to a small refrigeration unit, and inside he found a half-full two-liter lab container and a used drinking glass. He pulled them out and set them on the desk to film them before he realized what was in the container.

Stanger's hand moved instinctively to his mouth.

The blood in the bottom of the drinking glass had long ago dried.

Chapter Three

McCoy REMAINED FOR some time in that unbearable and undignified situation until at last he heard a stifled chuckle behind him.

"Dammit, Stanger," he growled, recognizing the origin of the sound. "Laugh again and I'll see to it that your next checkup is a painful one."

The laughter stopped abruptly, but Stanger's voice kept its ring of good humor. "Sorry, Doctor. How did this happen?"

"You don't need to know. Just get me out of here!" Pain made McCoy petulant.

Out of the corner of his eye, the doctor saw Stanger and Lamia lean up against the crystal to study his predicament. "It looks simple enough to me," Stanger said. "You just need to straighten up."

"Don't you think I would if I could?" McCoy flared. "I've pulled my damn back! Of all the stupid things—"

Lamia interrupted him calmly. "Do you have any pain medication, Doctor?"

McCoy nodded, which made the pain shoot down his back. He clenched his teeth harder. "In the black kit, to the left of my waist."

The Andorian positioned herself just behind him, then slipped her thin arms inside the chamber and around the doctor's waist. In spite of his discomfort, the humor of the situation was not lost on McCoy.

"My dear," he murmured, "you have me at a disadvantage." She didn't answer, and McCoy dropped his lascivious air. "Inside . . . the hypo with the blue coding on it. Set the indicator to four cc."

He felt a slight tingling as she administered the spray to his backside. The pain eased. He sighed and sagged back into her arms. "Have you considered a job in the medical field, Ensign?"

She answered with a great tug; the doctor felt himself falling backward and slid out with a groan. Lamia staggered, still holding on to him, until the two of them finally regained their balance.

"Thanks," McCoy said sheepishly, rubbing the offended muscle in his lower back. He did a couple of test stretches. "It's much better."

Stanger narrowed his eyes at the hole McCoy had cut in the crystal, then glanced at the Andorian. "Do you think you could fit in there?"

"Probably," she answered, barely civil; apparently their feud hadn't been resolved. McCoy was going to protest until he realized that although she was as tall as Stanger, she was at least a third narrower. She put her long, slender arms through the hole at first, then ducked her head and pulled herself in, sliding on her stomach onto the counter with surprising ease.

McCoy shook his head. "Do you *have* to make it look so easy?"

Lamia was already completely inside the chamber, crawling on her hands and knees. She retrieved the doctor's communicator, clipped it to her belt, and then, with gentle deliberateness, began collecting the vials from the stand on the counter.

"They're not sealed," she said, looking up at the others. "If they contain samples, shouldn't they be sealed?"

"They *should,* but maybe these folks were sloppy housekeepers," McCoy said. "Try not to spill any of them."

Lamia peered down into the vials. "I don't think there's anything to spill."

"Of *course* there's something to spill," Stanger argued.

44

"You're not going to tell me that I came down here a second time for nothing."

Without saying another word, Lamia crawled to the opening in the crystal and thrust the vials at Stanger. He shied away involuntarily.

"Look for yourself, Ensign," she said, with a slightly nasty inflection on the last word. "There's nothing there."

Stanger stared. Stiffly, McCoy reached for his tricorder and passed it over the open vials.

"Well, I'll be damned," he said. "She's right."

"Nothing!" Mendez thundered on the viewscreen in Kirk's quarters. The admiral's heavy brows formed a threatening V above his eyes. The *Enterprise* was eight hours from Tanis, close enough at last for direct visual contact.

"Nothing, sir." Kirk felt only relief at McCoy's findings, but Mendez's reaction struck him as odd. The admiral was furious at the situation and not doing a very good job of hiding it. "Tests were run on all labware confiscated on the base. No organisms of any sort were found in the laboratory."

"Are you sure there wasn't some sort of mistake?"

"My people are extremely competent, Admiral. I trust their report."

Mendez hunched forward over his desk so suddenly that Kirk instinctively moved back, as though expecting him to come charging through the screen. "Did it occur to you, Captain, that it is a trifle odd to find a completely empty laboratory?"

"Yes, sir, it did." Kirk managed to maintain his composure, though he cursed himself for flinching. Mendez was bullying a subordinate for no reason other than the fact that the admiral was disappointed. He felt a surge of contempt: how was it possible that this man was José's brother?

"And what do you think that means?"

Kirk's expression was pleasant and respectful, but his jaw was clenched. "One of three things, sir. One, someone

45

destroyed the microbe; two, it has been stolen; or three, it never existed, in which case Adams caught the disease some other way."

"Tanis is extremely isolated, Captain. Don't you think that the third possibility is rather unlikely?"

"Yes," Kirk admitted. "Although it doesn't rule it out—"

"There *was* a microbe down there, Kirk. All the evidence points to it. And it was destroyed or stolen. And in that case, it was either one of your landing party or Adams."

Kirk felt his face redden in spite of himself. "With all due respect, Admiral, it was *not* one of my people. Such an accusation is unjustified."

"I tend to agree with you there, Kirk. I'm sure it was Adams."

"Or one of the dead researchers—"

"It was Adams. The man is obviously mad and murdered the others."

"He denies it, sir, and the computer says he's telling the truth." Kirk didn't mention McCoy's reservations. Something about Mendez's dogged insistence made him want to stick up for Adams and the concept of innocent until proven guilty. "And we have no evidence against him except for the fact he was the only survivor." He also didn't mention the drinking glass . . . better to wait and see what Forensics found before he gave Mendez more reason to condemn Adams.

"The two corpses—were they infected, too?"

"The woman was in the initial stages of infection, but the man was clean. Adams said the man went mad, attacked the woman—"

"Impossible," Mendez snapped. "Why would he kill her if he didn't have the illness?"

"Sir, you're presuming that the illness causes madness. My ship's surgeon claims that Adams seems fairly sane—"

"Then maybe you ought to get a new ship's surgeon. I'm not going to argue with you about this, Captain. You're to put Adams under arrest and turn him in to the nearest star base for questioning *now*. Tell them to arrange the proper containment methods."

The screen went dark, leaving Kirk to wonder exactly what Rodrigo Mendez had against Jeffrey Adams.

Through Kirk's infrared visor, Adams was beginning to look more and more like a doomed soul trapped in the gray shadows of hell. He was still lying weakly on his bed, thin filaments running from one arm to a container of blood above him.

Adams' face was turned to the wall, but at the sound of the intercom coming on, he turned his head and gazed listlessly in Kirk's direction.

Jim said it straight out. "Dr. Adams, I've come to tell you that we've found some evidence on Tanis that implicates you in at least one of the deaths."

He did not get the reaction he hoped for. Adams' eyes remained dull and uninterested, and he spoke with the faraway voice of a dying man as he fingered the locket around his neck. "What's that?"

"A drinking glass—with Lara Krovozhadny's blood in it. The computer has verified that your fingerprints are all over it."

Adams turned his gaze to the ceiling and said nothing.

That's it. I've got him, and he knows it. There was no question in Kirk's mind that Adams was guilty. He pressed his advantage, knowing that the man could not be far from confessing. "Dr. McCoy says you were lying when you said you didn't kill the others." No point in mentioning that the doctor disagreed with the computer results.

"That's one man's opinion." Adams turned his face away and muttered something at the wall.

"If you have something to say, you can say it to me."

Adams looked back at him, and this time there was more energy in his voice. "I said that this is ridiculous! What kind of accusation are you making, Captain? That I killed Lara so I could drink her blood out of a *glass*?"

The glimmer of hope faded. The man was actually going to continue to deny it; McCoy was right. He had to be a total sociopath. "You tell me, Dr. Adams. Is it so unreasonable to ask for *some* kind of explanation?"

"God." The sick man shuddered. "Who could explain

47

something like that? I don't know. Yoshi must have done it. I told you, he was mad."

"Then why does the glass bear your fingerprints and not his?"

"I don't know." There was a note of petulant desperation in Adams' voice. "Maybe he got it from her quarters after I left them—"

"I thought you never left her quarters until our landing party arrived."

"Look, I'm sick. My mind isn't clear. Why don't *you* figure it out?"

Kirk folded his arms. Mendez had a point—the man was probably guilty of murder, maybe more. . . . And yet, it was unfair to assume his guilt until he had a chance for a trial. "I suppose I should tell you you're under arrest. We're taking you to the nearest star base to turn you in to the authorities."

"Under arrest?" Adams looked at him with wide eyes. "You're arresting me because of a *drinking* glass?"

Kirk shook his head. "I'm not arresting you. Admiral Mendez gave the order. But it will hardly make any difference to you in your current condition."

"You're right," Adams whispebed, closing his eyes. "Any way you look at it, I'm a dead man."

If it weren't for Lisa Nguyen this first week, Lamia decided, she would have died of homesickness, or at the very least packed up her bags and hijacked a shuttlecraft to Andor. It had occurred to her more than once during her brief stay on the *Enterprise* that she had made a horrible, dreadful mistake, and that *Tijra* was right: she belonged back home instead of on a starship, sailing around the galaxy risking her life to protect strangers. Of course, she hadn't risked anything yet; her assignments had been more boring than anything else. And she comforted herself with the thought that she had felt exactly the same way her first few weeks at Starfleet Academy, yet she had grown to love it. In time, she'd feel the same way about the *Enterprise*.

In the meantime, thank the stars for Lisa Nguyen. Lisa

was a firm believer in the *Enterprise*'s "buddy" tradition—making sure that new arrivals didn't get too lonely their first few weeks out in space. Lisa was more than her roommate, she was Lamia's social director, introducing her to other crewmates, dining with her, showing her the ship's facilities. Lamia could have used someone like Lisa her first year at the Academy, back when she had to learn to sleep in a room with only one other person in it, instead of the thirty-odd bodies she was used to. It was tougher then, in a way.

Of course, there were new concerns now. Lamia's *Tijra*—her mother's sister, the most important family member to a female Andorian—had still not responded to her message that she had accepted a deep-space assignment aboard the *Enterprise*. *Tijra* had been furious at Lamia, of course, when she had gone to the Academy on Earth, but she'd never stopped communicating with her. *Tijra* had said that Lamia would come to her senses, would realize where her duty lay—with starting a family, as it did for all those who were fertile—when she was finally faced with the reality of going out in space.

Those were the old times, Lamia had answered. *Andor is populated again. Most children are born fertile, not scarred from dheir parents' disease. It's time for customs to change when they are no longer necessary for survival.* But *Tijra* was unconvinced.

Now Lamia was in space, and had sent word of it to *Tijra*. For weeks, there had been no reply. Of course, the *Enterprise* was very far from Andor . . .

"Cheers." Lisa Nguyen raised her glass of pineapple juice, interrupting Lamia's reverie. They'd just come from the gym, where Lisa had beaten her soundly in a wrestling match, and were now seated in the rec lounge enjoying a drink.

Lamia smiled and raised her glass of Thirelian Mountain mineral water in a token gesture. No matter that she'd had years of practice at smiling . . . to her, the expression was an unnatural one, and she always felt as if she were grimacing. But then, none of her human friends had ever complained.

"You're awfully quiet tonight," Lisa said, still smiling. She was pretty for a human, with Oriental features and dark, shoulder-length hair. Although she was rather short, her muscular body made Lamia feel weak and spindly. "Heard from your family yet?"

"Not yet," Lamia said into the bubbling glass of mineral water, but Lisa didn't hear the answer. She was busy waving at someone else.

"Jon!" She half stood from the table and smiled broadly. "Stanger! Come have a seat with us."

Lamia took a sip of water and looked up in time to see Stanger gazing around the room uncertainly, with a glass in his hand. Apparently he had been deserted by his "buddy" —that is, if anyone had been willing to volunteer for the job—and had been trying to slip unnoticed into a dark corner of the lounge. Now he was headed for their table. Lamia swallowed hard and imagined she could feel the water sink all the way down to her feet.

"Hello," Stanger said. He had spotted the Andorian, but he directed his attention to Lisa, returning her smile. "Are you ladies managing to keep the lounge secure this evening?" He asked the question with an easy good humor that surprised Lamia; he seemed altogether different from the irritable man who had beamed down to Tanis.

He pulled a chair next to Lisa's. "So," Lisa asked, "how's the first week on board going? Like it enough to stay?"

"It's going fine," he answered, without so much as a glance at Lamia. "There're some good people on board this ship."

Lisa dimpled again. "Glad you think so. I hope that applies to all of us in Security."

"It does," Stanger said gallantly, and raised his beer in a toast before taking a sip.

"Well, good for you. Not everyone hits it off with Tomson right away. She usually takes some getting used to."

Lamia waited for him to say something. Surely he wasn't going to claim he liked *Tomson,* not after what happened this morning—

"She's all right," Stanger said casually.

50

The Andorian could hold her tongue no longer. "You can't mean that." She leaned across the table toward him, and he was forced to meet her gaze. "Not after the time she gave you about being a minute late." She turned to Lisa. "He was *one minute* late, and for that Tomson spent five minutes lecturing him. If she were really angry and trying to run a tight ship, then give him a demerit and be done with it. But it's almost as if she were looking for a chance to unload on someone. I'd heard she was unfriendly, but she seems . . . well, almost hostile toward the junior officers."

Stanger's good humor vanished. His voice became quiet, but there was an undercurrent of anger in it. "It was more than a minute, okay? Besides, I'd rather not go into it, En—Lamia. Let's just say I deserved it. In Security, one minute can make the difference between life and death. The chief of security has got to be a stickler for details, and she's got to drum it into her crew any way she can. I damn well deserved a demerit. But I'll take a lecture any day if I can avoid—" He broke off. "Oh, the hell with it. Let's drop it."

But Lamia wasn't about to let it rest. How could anyone be so forgiving when their pride was at stake? "Instead she called you on the carpet in front of another officer. I thought it was cruel. I'm just trying to stick up for you—"

"I don't need anyone to stick up for me," Stanger snapped, so sharply that Lamia recoiled into her chair. "As long as Tomson does her job, it doesn't matter a damn bit whether her crew likes her or not, does it?" He took a savage gulp of beer and almost choked, but managed to swallow it.

"I suppose not," Lamia answered icily, her antennae flattened on her scalp in a gesture of disapproval.

Lisa squirmed uncomfortably in her chair as the others looked down into their glasses and sulked. "Hey," she said, with insincere brightness, in a pathetic attempt to lighten the mood. "Speaking of Tomson, I forgot to tell you both today's skinny—"

"Skinny?" Lamia was still sulking while counting the bubbles in the Thirelian Mountain water.

"You know. The lowdown. The latest gossip. I got it from Acker Esswein—you know him, he's security night shift—"

"We share quarters," Stanger said softly, in a way that let everyone know he wasn't pleased by the fact.

"Good." Lisa continued bravely. "Anyway, Acker overheard Lieutenant Tomson talking to the captain. It's been months since Tomson's had a second-in-command. They were going to bring someone in from outside because nobody on board was due for a promotion, but apparently Tomson is so picky that no one has suited her. So Acker overheard her saying to the captain that she's decided someone on board the *Enterprise* should be promoted anyway." Lisa leaned back with a satisfied expression. "How's *that* for news?"

"I suppose this means that everyone will be knifing his or her colleague in the back." Expressionless, Stanger rose, leaving his glass on the table. "If you'll excuse me, ladies." And without further hesitation he walked out of the rec lounge.

"Hey," Lamia said angrily. "What is *wrong* with that man?" What she wanted to say was: *Humans. What is wrong with them?* But for Lisa's sake, she held back.

Lisa seemed more sad than angry. She watched him leave, and her eyes lingered at the doorway for a moment before she spoke. "Don't be mad at him, Lamia; it's my fault." She stared disconsolately into her pineapple juice. "I always do this. I just ran my mouth off without thinking. I should have known it might upset him."

"What would upset him? About the promotions? Just because his chances aren't good? Well, mine aren't either, but you don't see me walking out. It's no wonder he's an ensign at his age."

"You don't know." Lisa looked up at her wonderingly. "I guess I never told you."

"Told me what?"

Lisa glanced around guiltily to be sure Stanger was gone, then lowered her voice, as if afraid he'd overhear anyway. "About Stanger. You didn't know he was the security chief on board the *Columbia?*"

Lamia's antennae surged gently in Lisa's direction. *"Chief?"* She brought a hand to her mouth. It certainly explained his behavior down on Tanis. "No wonder he kept calling me ensign—I just assumed he was pompous. But how—"

"He made a big mistake, that's how. The story I got from Acker was that they caught Stanger trying to smuggle illegal weapons onto the ship. Apparently, he didn't offer any sort of defense when they caught him."

"Smuggling?" Lamia gasped. "I'm surprised they let him stay in the Fleet!"

"I know, it's hard to believe, isn't it? Acker said his record was otherwise so good that all he got was a demotion." Lisa sighed. "And you know, it's really hard for me to believe, after meeting him."

Lamia shook her head slowly in disbelief. "No wonder Tomson yelled at him for being late."

"Everyone's been gossiping about him and avoiding him, so I felt like the least I could do was try to be nice to him. I really *was* trying to be nice when I asked him to the table." Lisa's expression was still one of remorse. "I shouldn't have mentioned the promotion. It was like rubbing salt in an open wound."

"Well, he'd have heard about it somewhere else, then." Lamia leaned across the table and patted Nguyen's arm. "Don't feel bad, Lisa. He's the one who made a mistake. If he can't handle being reminded of it, then he doesn't belong in Starfleet."

She was talking about Stanger, of course, but in a way, she knew the words applied to herself as well.

Christine Chapel adjusted her visor and gave a worried glance at the patient behind the crystal barrier as she lowered the tray into the vacuum lock. No matter that Adams was a suspected killer—he was a patient, first and foremost, a patient that had Chapel very concerned. There was a soft *swoosh* as the lock sealed itself and reopened inside the isolation chamber. Robot arms lowered themselves from the ceiling and deftly ferried the tray with the steaming bowl to Adams' bedside. Just as efficiently, they disappeared again.

"You'll feel better if you eat something," Chapel said into the intercom beneath the crystal. "I refuse to give you another IV. You're not sick enough. Now eat."

The man on the bed continued to lie with his face turned toward the wall.

"Don't make me have to sound like your mother." Chapel's tone was light but firm. "I'm not leaving until I see you eat something."

She amazed herself sometimes with her ability to put on a good show. Adams had gone into a sudden, rapid decline; within a matter of hours, he had deteriorated to the point that he looked—to Chapel, anyway—like a skeleton. He had the look of death to him . . . it was only hours away now, and Chapel was frightened for his sake. But she was too damn good a nurse to let on. She'd seen miracles before—people who lived, who had no business surviving. They just simply hadn't known any better. Hadn't realized they were close to dying.

But Adams realized it. He'd already slipped into a depression. If she could somehow convince him that he had a chance . . .

She cleared her throat and tried again. "I'm *not* leaving."

He sighed and stirred. Chapel saw him glance at the bowl next to the bed. After all that time in the unlit chamber, she bet he could see better than a Vulcan in the dark.

"What is it?" Adams asked feebly.

"Some nice chunky soup." She tried her best to make the words themselves sound delicious. "Or stew with broth. Whichever sounds best to you. Good and hot."

He raised his head and looked up in the direction of her voice. "Why should I eat? I'm just going to die." He said it with the simple, unself-pitying bluntness of a child.

"You're not going to die," Chapel answered with what she hoped was convincing exasperation. "You've stabilized. And our lab is very close to a breakthrough on this." Both lies, of course, but if it took a lie to help him, then she would never speak the truth again. Her tone became lightly teasing. "Besides, I wouldn't waste this good food on you if you were going to die. Now, eat up. You must be awfully hungry."

He was still looking in her direction, though she knew the light blinded him so that she was invisible. He seemed to be thinking hard about something; and then, his face relaxed.

"All right. I'll try to eat a little."

"Good." Christine smiled, wishing he could see it.

Adams picked up the spoon and leaned over the bowl. As the steam rose into his face, he looked so nauseated she half expected him to gag. But he dipped his spoon into the broth and took a tiny sip. "You still there?"

"I'm still here."

Adams took another spoonful of broth, then another. Then a spoonful of vegetables and meat. Christine felt pleased.

And then he stopped in mid-chew. His expression became very odd. The muscles in his neck pulsed once, twice, beneath the gold chain.

She leaned forward, putting a hand on the crystal. "Are you all right?"

Adams' eyes grew very wide. He put a hand to his throat.

"My God, you're choking!" Christine grabbed a field-suit unit from a nearby cabinet, strapped it to her waist, and fumbled for the control. Her hands were shaking. *Too long, it's taking too long.* At last she pressed the right control, and flinched as her ears popped painfully, the way they always did when the field first enveloped her. She ran to the entrance of the isolation chamber and pressed in the code that told the system to open the door.

It opened almost immediately. Chapel stepped into the airlock without a second's hesitation.

How could she have been so stupid, giving him solid food when he was so weak? She should have just given him the broth . . . .The door to sickbay shut behind her, and she punched the next code into the panel facing her. The panel rose slowly upward.

"Hurry, dammit!" She pounded it with her fists, realizing that her gesture was a wasted one. "Hurry!" How many seconds had it taken her to get this far? She had to get to him, soon. The panel was a third of the way up when she stooped down and crawled beneath it to get to the next stage.

55

A scan passed over her, and once it sensed that she was safely suited up, the door to the chamber rose automatically. *For God's sake, hurry!*

She stepped into infrared darkness. *Dear God, don't let him be dead. Don't let me have killed him. . . .*

The bed was empty.

"Adams?"

There was a noise behind her. She turned to look around, and for one brief second before she lost consciousness, she was surprised by the strength of the blow he delivered to her head.

Chapter Four

ADAMS' BREATH WAS coming fast as he bent over the blond woman. Sometimes the euphoria came over him powerfully, stealing air from his lungs and making his heart hammer against his chest, but it also made him strong. Still, as he studied her limp form, he was glad she seemed to be unconscious—she looked too capable of putting up a fight. He preferred to be sure, however; he searched for the control on her belt unit. The field tingled uncomfortably against his fingers, rather like a mild electric shock, but he forced himself to push hard against it and switched off the control.

No matter that it would cause her to be exposed to the microbe. There were far more important concerns on Adams' mind now. Like not wanting to die. And if he let them take him to a star base, death would come sooner than even he had anticipated. No, he wouldn't let them take him there. He was better off fighting the microbe.

It occurred to him, then, that he was not exactly sure how to know someone was unconscious without using a tricorder. On instinct, he lifted the woman's head in one hand and peeled back an eyelid with the other. The eye was rolled back, so that all he could see was the white and the merest edge of a blue iris. *Of course she's unconscious,* a tiny remnant of rational mind told him. *If it were a trick, she would have attacked you already.* And his new mind answered shrilly: *I have to know, I have to know . . .*

His fingers touched something warm and sticky. He pulled them away, startled, letting the woman's head drop back, and lifted his hand to his face.

Blood. The scent of it was heady, metallic, sensual. He touched a finger to his tongue and closed his eyes in ecstasy at the taste of iron, recalling with an odd nostalgia how it had been with Lara, and Yoshi. . . . For a moment, his head swam so he thought he might faint. And then he managed to collect himself. It was tempting, too tempting, to drop to his knees and lap up every drop that oozed from the small nick on the back of her head. Her head must have struck the table with such force that the field suit was an inadequate cushion.

Reluctantly, he stood up, leaving the woman on the floor. As painful as it was to pull himself away, he had to move fast. The lights outside the chamber in sickbay dazzled him, so that he could not see anything beyond the barrier. For all he knew, someone could be watching him right now, and he had no way of knowing. No, he had to leave her, and quickly, but he comforted himself with the thought that there would be others. After all, a ship the size of the *Enterprise* carried four hundred crewpersons. Adams smiled to himself. Yes, there would definitely be others.

He went over to the exit. When the doctor was leaving the chamber after preparing his patient for the computer verification test, Adams had been careful to memorize the code the doctor had punched into the panel to open the door. Apparently it hadn't occurred to the doctor that his patient's eyes had adjusted well enough to the darkness to make out the numbers.

Now Adams entered the code with trembling fingers and was rewarded when the door began to slowly rise.

The euphoria flooded him anew. He would make it. He wouldn't die. Mendez wouldn't have the pleasure of killing him. No, Adams would find a way to survive on the *Enterprise* until he could escape. . . . Suddenly, he felt better, stronger. Incredibly strong.

Yet as the door rose higher, he cried out at the pain. The passageway was filled with intense ultraviolet light that cut

58

through him like a thousand sharp knives. He raised his arms, shielding his eyes as best he could, but the agony engulfed his entire body. It was like being stabbed and burned at the same time.

Tears streamed down his cheeks, soaked the sleeves of his shirt; still, Adams managed to stumble forward blindly. He staggered on, unseeing, until he bumped into another door. He squeezed his eyes shut, gasping, and groped for the code panel. It took him several seconds to enter what he prayed was the correct code.

"Invalid entry," the computer said in a polite but unsympathetic tone. "Please reenter."

Adams made small, desperate noises in the back of his throat. He put his face right next to the panel and forced one eye open, gritting his teeth. Carefully, as slowly as he could bear, he punched in the same three digits as before, the ones that had opened the first panel.

At first, nothing happened. Adams fell shrieking and clawing against the panel. "Open, damn you! *Open!* I don't want to die . . ."

And then he could hear a muffled buzz outside, in sickbay, and the voice of the computer saying, in perfectly simulated alarm, "Unauthorized exit from isolation! Unauthorized exit!"

There was a *whoosh* as the panel behind him descended, cutting him off from the safety and darkness of the isolation chamber. He was trapped.

Adams sank to the floor, buried his head in his knees, and sobbed.

"Will she be all right?" Kirk asked gently. There were a hundred other questions he wanted answered as well, but now was not the time. He waited patiently as McCoy paced in front of the isolation unit across from Adams. This one was lit, and Christine Chapel lay unconscious inside.

The doctor's arms were folded tightly to his chest, and his blue eyes were shooting sparks. He was pacing back and forth so fast in front of the captain that Kirk was beginning to get dizzy from watching him.

"What, you mean the head wound?" McCoy responded irritably. "She'll be fine. A very mild concussion, a tiny laceration of the scalp. She ought to come to in a minute."

Kirk nodded silently. No point in pushing the doctor when he got like this.

"So don't you want to know what happened?" McCoy stopped pacing abruptly and glared at him. "Aren't you even going to ask?"

Kirk raised his eyebrows in mild surprise. "I was waiting for you to wind down a little."

"Wind down?"

"You seemed a little . . . upset."

"Upset?" McCoy snarled. *"Upset?* You're damn right I'm upset! When they string Adams up, I'll volunteer to supply the rope. He didn't have to expose her. He could have restrained her without turning off the suit, the son of a bitch." He kicked the computer console for emphasis.

"Any chance she won't come down with it?"

"Sure." McCoy forced himself to calm down a little. "There's always a chance. We ought to know something soon." He slumped into a chair next to the captain. "Sorry, Jim."

"It's okay. I might even help with that rope myself."

McCoy gave an unconvincing imitation of a smile that faded quickly.

"Now suppose you tell me what happened, Doctor."

McCoy sighed deeply. "I'll try to make a long story short. The alarm sounded in my quarters and Security. By the time I got here, Esswein had already turned off the alarm. The computer indicated that Adams was trapped in the exit." He ran a hand over his face. "How he could have gotten hold of the exit code is beyond me—"

"I thought you were going to make this short," Kirk said.

"Sorry. We suited up, Esswein took care of Adams, I took care of Chris. I reprogrammed the matrix to seal up the nick in her suit and got her to this other chamber. That's it. Adams was no trouble—the light had him in too much pain for him to put up a fight. Chris was out, so I couldn't ask her what happened, but it's pretty obvious. Adams tricked her inside somehow, then struck her so she hit her head."

"Did Adams have anything to say for himself?"

McCoy shrugged. "Not much that made sense. He was incoherent—and not just from the pain. The disease has affected his mind. He was manic, raving. I gave him a mild sedative."

"Is he still awake?"

"Yeah, if you want to question him. He's calmer now, but he still might be a little shaken up. Question at your own risk."

McCoy led him over to Adams' chamber and handed Kirk an infrared visor from the nearby console. "Here, take this. I'm gonna keep an eye on Chris, if you don't mind. I'd like to be there when she wakes up." The doctor went back to the other side of the room.

Kirk put on the visor and snapped on the intercom. Behind the barrier, Adams sat on the bed, hugging his knees to his chest and rocking himself gently. The pendant around his neck swung slowly back and forth. He was quite oblivious to the tubing attached to his arm.

"If you're an innocent man, Dr. Adams," the captain asked quietly, "then why were you running away?"

Startled, Adams stopped rocking and squinted toward Kirk. Something about his gaunt, shadowed face gave the impression he had been weeping . . . and for a moment, Kirk half expected him to burst into tears.

But Adams controlled himself. "You must believe what I tell you," he said with dignity. "Because if you don't help me, I'll die."

"The lab is working round the clock on a cure, Dr. Adams—" Kirk began.

"I didn't mean the disease." Adams hugged himself tighter and shuddered.

"What *did* you mean? I have no patience anymore—"

"Mendez," Adams answered abruptly.

"Mendez? Admiral Mendez? You know him?"

Adams nodded and looked away. "How soon will we reach the star base?"

"About ten hours. But what did you mean about Mendez?"

For a moment, Adams was silent.

"I can leave," Kirk said shortly. "You're the one who needs help." He took a few purposely loud steps away from the barrier.

"Wait!" Adams sat forward on the edge of the bed. "I need . . . your protection."

"Protection? From what—or whom?"

"Mendez," Adams said.

"Why?"

"I . . . work for him."

"You were working for Starfleet?" Kirk felt his body tense. He couldn't believe it, wouldn't believe it, even if the computer and McCoy both verified it.

"I didn't say that. I said I worked for Mendez. And . . . others."

"What others?"

"Even I don't know. I'm just paid to do my job. Mendez is my only contact. He's trying to set me up, don't you understand? Now that something has gone wrong with the project, he wants me out of the way so that there's no chance of my talking. If I'm turned over to Starfleet, I'll be killed before there's ever any trial."

"Biowarfare is illegal," Kirk said. "Why would a Starfleet admiral risk court-martial and criminal prosecution—"

"Ask *him*. I don't know." Adams drew his knees back up to his chest and huddled miserably on the bed. "If you turn me in, I'm a dead man. It's the same as killing me outright." His wild, pleading eyes looked out blindly at the brightness. "You could tell them I died. That's it; tell them I died, and I didn't talk—"

"I can't tell them that. Even if I wanted to—which I don't—they'd never believe it."

"You've got to—"

"Why not get to the bottom of this?" Kirk asked. "Why not find out who else is involved? Testify against Mendez. Starfleet will see that you're protected. I can verify your accusation."

"No," Adams almost sobbed. "Starfleet will see to it that I'm killed. Just say I died. Don't you understand? There's too many of them—and if you try to start an investigation, they'll kill you, too."

Too many? In Starfleet? "I don't believe you." Kirk turned away angrily.

It was not quite the truth. The truth was that he didn't want to believe.

The rec lounge was dimly lit and deserted except for two. For most it was late, and those who had to report early the next morning had already cleared out. The night shifters were on duty.

McCoy stifled another yawn.

"Go to bed, Doctor." Kirk took another sip of his brandy and set the glass on the table. "I'm keeping you up past your bedtime."

"Nonsense," McCoy lied, taking another sip of bourbon. He wasn't talking about it, but it was clear he was worrying about Christine Chapel, although he was doing his best not to show it. "I'll go when I'm ready, thanks." He leaned over the table surreptitiously, as if worried nonexistent others in the room might overhear. "Did I tell you I heard my first Iowa joke the other day? As a native, I'm sure you can appreciate—"

Kirk groaned and slumped lower in his chair, one hand firmly around his snifter of brandy, the other pulled wearily across his eyes. "You've had too much to drink, Bones."

"Not nearly enough," the doctor answered tartly. "You're just trying to get rid of me."

"You're still sober enough to be perceptive." Jim smiled faintly. "Spare me, Doctor. I heard 'em all when I was a kid."

McCoy dropped the facade of good humor. "All right, Jim, I'm just trying to cheer you up. Now, you can stay up all night while I go get some sleep, or you can spill what's eating you. I assume this has something to do with Adams?"

Kirk asked the question before looking up. "Do you think he's capable of telling the truth?"

"About the murders? No way."

"That wasn't exactly what I meant. Let me rephrase it. Do you think Adams might tell the truth in order to save his own skin?"

"Well, now, that's different . . . but I'd be tempted to take anything he said with a grain of salt. Plus the disease is beginning to impair him mentally. His lucid periods are becoming shorter. I don't think it'll be long before he's delirious." McCoy frowned at him. "But you didn't come here to talk to me about Adams' mental health. Out with it."

"I told Adams we were turning him in to the nearest star base." Kirk watched McCoy intently for a reaction. "He begged me not to turn him in. He said that Mendez would kill him."

McCoy snickered. "Come on. Paranoia must be a side effect of the disease."

Kirk didn't smile.

"Give me a break, Jim. Why would a Starfleet admiral like Mendez want to kill a small-time researcher like Adams?"

"So that word won't get out that Starfleet is secretly financing a biowarfare facility."

"Well . . . that's possible. I *did* see Fleet-issue stuff down there . . . but now that I think about it, almost anybody can get their hands on surplus Fleet equipment."

"I've been trying to dismiss it myself, but dammit, Bones, the man makes a convincing argument. Why do *you* think they told us not to answer the distress signal?"

McCoy's smirk faded; he became silent.

"I don't *want* to believe the man, Doctor. I'd like to believe that Starfleet would never get mixed up in something like this." He paused. "But if they wouldn't, then why would they order us not to go to Tanis? And why is Adams so terrified of Mendez?"

"Again, he's not the trustworthy—" McCoy began.

"Are you saying I should ignore this?" Kirk folded his arms. "Be a good soldier and not question?"

"Not at all. Don't ignore it." All trace of McCoy's sarcasm was gone. "You've got friends in high places—how about calling one of your old drinking buddies at headquarters? What's-his-name. Waverleigh. Call him and ask him to check it out."

"And what," Kirk said slowly, "do I do if Adams turns out to be right?"

"I don't have an answer for you on that one, Jim."

On the viewscreen, Quince Waverleigh looked a good twenty pounds heavier than he'd been during his Academy days, but he still looked every inch the ladies' man, with a headful of shocking red-gold hair, gray eyes, and even, white teeth displayed against a perfect tan. Despite his reputation at the Academy as a hell-raiser, Quince's grades were in the top percentile. He was three years ahead of Kirk, and decided it was his mission in life to teach his overly serious underclassman how to lighten up. To his frustration, Kirk staunchly resisted his efforts, but in spite of their differences of opinion as to life-style, they became fast friends. Later, when Waverleigh captained the *Arlington,* he'd raised hell of a different sort, receiving the Palm Leaf with Cluster twice. He was the youngest man in the Fleet to hold the rank of rear admiral—so far, at least, Kirk promised himself. Kirk took every opportunity to take shore leave at the same time and place as the *Arlington:* Quince's tall tales were not to be missed.

Quince's desk was cluttered, not with work, but with mementos: his medals, of course, prominently displayed with typical egotism; cat's-eye marbles; a nineteenth-century dueling pistol with inlaid ebony handle; a stuffed creature about the size of a large cat that looked to Jim like a cross between an opossum and a turtle; and a holo of Quince's family. The holo was a beach scene of mother and children. The woman was an exotic beauty, a blonde with Oriental features, the little girl strawberry blond like her father, the boy with platinum hair. He was throwing a ball into the air. His mother smiled broadly and the sister's mouth made an O as the three of them focused on the ascending ball. *The perfect family,* Kirk thought, and for only an instant, he felt a twinge of jealousy.

"Jimmy! What's up?" Quince's drawl was thick as taffy;

he was a west Texas native who managed to resist losing his regional accent.

"Hi, Admiral. You look like life's agreeing with you."

"It is, it is." Quince leaned forward and found a clean spot to settle an elbow on. "I take it from your use of rank this isn't a social call."

"I'm afraid not. I need a favor."

"I hope it involves something adventurous."

"Maybe," Kirk answered. "It's about Admiral Mendez."

"Rod Mendez? Head of weapons research? Huh!" Quince snorted contemptuously. "Another paper-pusher *par excellence*. Pardon my French, but you couldn't give me that ass-kissing job. He's pandering all the time to Command, to political lobbyists. . . . But enough of my opinion. What do you want to know about him?"

Kirk told him Adams' story. Somewhere in the middle of it, Waverleigh's expression sobered and he started tracing the holo with his finger. When Kirk finished, Quince said, "That's a mighty shaky charge, coming from a very questionable source. Adams' current predicament isn't going to help any charges stick. You have to admit, they're pretty outrageous. To accuse an admiral, especially one with Mendez's reputation . . ." He shook his head. "But I get the funny feeling you believe this guy."

"Enough to check it out."

"Well, that says something as far as I'm concerned. So you want me to stir up a little trouble, eh?" Waverleigh rubbed his hands together lasciviously. "Well, thank God. I'm tired of trying to create my own excitement around here."

"I thought driving a desk was exciting," Jim said sarcastically. From the moment Quince had been transferred to HQ, he had done nothing but complain long and loud of boredom to anyone who would listen.

The remark struck too close to home. Quince's lips twisted in a wry little grin. "Don't you ever let anyone talk you into a desk job, Jimmy. I'd give anything to be back out there again." He forced a less serious tone. "I've tried a dozen times to get myself busted back down to captain, but they're wise to me now. No matter what outrageous thing I do, they ignore me."

Kirk nodded at the holo. "That's because your captain's quarters would be a little crowded." He meant it as a joke, but for some reason the smile that stayed frozen on Quince's lips went out in his eyes.

"Ke opted not to renew our contract," he said shortly. "She's got the kids with her now. I get 'em in a few months."

"I'm sorry," Jim said, feeling like a fool. "I didn't know." He could think of nothing better to say.

"So'm I. But hey." Quince shifted in his chair and waved a hand at the stuffed animal on his desk. "Jimmy, you've met Old Yeller here, haven't you?"

Jim's discomfort eased. He grinned and shook his head, more in resignation than in answer to Waverleigh's question. Quince was famed as a practical joker, and once he got a notion in his head, it was best to play along. "Quince, where in the galaxy did you get *that?*"

Waverleigh looked scandalized. "Why, the folks back home sent him to me. Jimmy, I'm shocked. Haven't you ever seen an armadillo before?"

Jim shook his head. "I thought they were extinct. But I can't say that I've missed much."

"It's a good thing he can't hear you say that." He stroked the little animal protectively. "Actually, Yeller used to be a bit livelier, back before old age caught up to him."

"Or the taxidermist, from the looks of it," Jim said.

Quince scowled at him. "Yeller passed out of this vale of tears long before that, I'll have you know. But he's still pretty personable. Go on, say hello to him, Jimmy."

Knowing Quince, it was a trick, but Jim bit anyway. "Hello, Old Yeller."

At the sound of Jim's voice, Yeller's long head poked out of the shell and his narrow muzzle yawned open. "Hello, Jimmy," he said, in Waverleigh's voice.

Kirk started, then laughed. "Admiral, you are *weird.*"

"Yeah," Waverleigh answered smugly. "You should have seen the look on Stein's—that's my aide—face the first time Yeller said hello to her." He settled back in his chair. "Well, look, Jim, I've got to hop this morning, but I'll let you know what I can find out about Mendez."

"Don't get yourself into trouble," Kirk said seriously. "Just see what you can piece together about Tanis. Find out why we were ordered not to answer the distress signal. Find out who signed the order."

"Some orders are confidential. Does this mean I get to bend the rules a little bit?"

"For God's sake, the last thing I want you to do is get yourself into trouble. Don't do anything illegal."

Quince grinned wickedly. "Jimmy, I get the feeling you don't trust me."

"I don't. I know better." Kirk hesitated. "Just don't forget to consider the fact that Mendez just *might* be involved in something illegal, and be willing to do anything to protect himself."

"In other words, be discreet."

"In other words, don't do anything stupid. If you get too much heat about it, forget it. I'll find some other way."

"I promise not to get myself into trouble," Waverleigh said with a wink.

"You be sure and do that," Kirk told him.

Chapter Five

THE OBSERVATION DECK was silent and dark, its only source of light the stars that shone down through its invisible roof. Fierce, bright stars, undimmed by atmosphere or moons, rather like Andor's night sky, though the constellations were wrong. As a child, Lamia had thought it a great adventure to steal outside with one or two of the other children and sit in the open field gazing up at the star-littered sky. Sometimes, when she felt a need for it, she would sit alone.

She was alone now, and lonelier than she had ever thought possible; yet in the midst of her grief, she could not have faced another living being, not even Lisa Nguyen.

Thank the stars the deck was deserted, except for one or two shadowy figures, their faces turned up and reflecting starlight.

The message had been waiting for Lamia when she got off duty. The light on her terminal was flashing, and she keyed the message onto the screen. No face, no voice, no name. A written transmission that could have been sent by a stranger. And yet she knew immediately, crushingly, who had sent it.

You are no longer ours.

With that ritual phrase, she was cut off. No family, no tijra, no home, nothing to tie her to Andor or anywhere else in the universe, for that matter, save the small, impersonal cabin she shared with Lisa. She was free now, free to float among the stars . . . free to float aimlessly, outnumbered and alone.

Lamia crossed the deck quickly, her footsteps absorbed by the thick carpeting. She was intent on one thing: reaching a cubicle . . . reaching safety, privacy, darkness, so that she could properly grieve. She made it to a cubicle and reached for the door just as someone else did. She brushed against a warm hand and opened her mouth to apologize. . . .

And closed it again as she recognized Jonathon Stanger.

Well, hell, Stanger told himself pessimistically, *isn't that just your luck? Try to find a little privacy, a little peace of mind . . . only three people on the whole deck, and you get to wrestle with one of them for a cubicle.*

But the hand he touched was cool, inhuman. He gaped up at the Andorian. In the starlight, her hair shone like spun silver. "I'm sorry," he said softly. "Go ahead." And then berated himself for forgetting that he was supposed to be annoyed with her.

She had clearly not forgotten. "No, thank you." She turned away with a graceful, sweeping motion that also managed to express her disdain.

"Lamia," he began helplessly. He should have let her go, should have pretended to be disgusted himself, should have held on to the humiliated anger that had erupted in him in the rec lounge. But he couldn't. *You fool, why do you give a damn about what she thinks of you? Isn't this how it started with you and Rosa?*

He did not let himself answer his own questions.

She stopped with her back to him, breathing heavily as if she had been running, and he watched as her wide, triangular shoulder blades rose and fell under the red uniform. It made him think of an insect fanning its wings. "I'm sorry," he said at last. "I was rude yesterday. I wanted to apologize."

"It's all right," she said, without turning around. Her voice sounded oddly strained.

It was not the reaction he'd hoped for. This time he injected a little good humor into his tone. "I just didn't

70

want you to get the impression I was always so temperamental. I had a few things on my mind—"

She lowered her head, resting the fingers of one hand against the bridge of her nose. "Would you please just *leave?*"

He took it the wrong way at first and swung around, ready to stomp off in the other direction (not that stomping made any audible difference with the carpet). And then it suddenly registered . . . the way she'd really sounded when she said it. Desperate. Agitated. But not angry. He turned back.

"Hey, are you all right?"

Stop it, fool, this is how you got started with Rosa.

But she wasn't all right. She was fumbling blindly, trying to open the door to another cubicle . . . blindly, because she was upset. He knew Andorians saw very well in the dark. He came up behind her while she was still struggling with the simple latch. "Hey." He put a hand on her shoulder. No padding to speak of, bones so thin and fragile it made him afraid to press too hard. Ridiculous, of course; although she was thinner and leaner, the different muscle insertion actually made her race stronger. She was probably a match for him in hand-to-hand.

"Hey," he repeated. "Something happen today? Bad news from home?"

She faced him, her eyes wide with panic. "I don't *have* a home anymore."

You fool, his mind started up, and then melted away at the sight of the pain on her face. Distrust, suspicion, all of it melted away, except for the need to help her.

"Here." He pushed open the cubicle, helped her in, sat next to her, and put a supportive *(supportive, Stanger? or something else?)* arm around her narrow shoulders. He could feel the large, strong heart hammering against her back, could feel the huge lungs that took up most of her upper torso fill and empty themselves. She moaned for a while, but didn't cry, because she wasn't human.

Her hair smelled of grass and sun.

"Tell me," he said.

71

She told him. Some things he knew about, such as the plague that began centuries ago on Andor, that made most of the female babies sterile. About the great responsibility placed on fertile females to raise large families, and how the custom continued even after the plague had left and the population come back.

Some things he didn't know: about her thirty-eight *bezris,* a term that included all sisters, brothers, and cousins as equal, and how she missed them. About the horrible fight with *Tijra* when Lamia resisted the expected path and left for Starfleet Academy, about how certain *Tijra* had been that Lamia would surrender to loneliness and return home before she ever accepted her first assignment in space . . .

About how Lamia wished now she had waited for an assignment aboard an all-Andorian ship. About how humans disapproved of the Andorian need to discuss personal matters openly, how they seemed to feel emotional honesty was in bad taste. How cold they were to each other. How it was a form of hypocrisy, of repression, of not telling the truth . . . Of how nice Lisa Nguyen was, and how Lamia always worried Nguyen would think she was going on too much.

He said nothing; he just listened, and gave her thin shoulders an occasional pat. And wondered what the appropriate Andorian gesture of comfort was.

She fell silent after a while, so he talked a little bit about his own family. (As he recalled from a long-ago class, on Andor, one confidence deserves another.) He told her about his folks being doctors, about how scandalized they were to have raised a son who not only was a jock, but wanted to go into (horrors!) police work.

He had no intention of confiding anything to her about Rosa, or the *Columbia.*

At the end of it, she looked up at him and smiled, the first really convincing one he'd seen her wear, and he caught himself thinking how beautiful she actually was.

Dammit, Stanger, when are you going to stop being such a fool?

* * *

"Chris?"

She opened her eyes. On the other side of the containment panel, McCoy smiled at her.

A good sign, she thought. *I'm okay.* She returned the smile broadly and sat up. Until that minute, she'd convinced herself she had the disease. She'd felt dizzy and disoriented, growing weaker with each passing second. What an incredible hypochondriac she'd been! It couldn't have been the head wound. She touched her hand to the back of her head. McCoy had used the sonic adaptor on it—there wasn't even a tiny scar. She felt foolish, just like the proverbial med student who promptly came down with the symptoms of the latest disease being studied.

"You tested positive," McCoy said, and she suddenly realized that the hand that gripped the lab report was white-knuckled.

She slumped back on her elbows, the idiotic grin still on her face, and said the first thing that came to mind. "That's too bad. Airborne mode of transmission?"

McCoy shook his head. "Contact. Adams must have touched your head wound."

"So I'll wind up like him," she said, with sarcasm that bordered on bitterness. "Killing people and drinking their blood."

"Of course not," he soothed unconvincingly. "We're very close to a breakthrough on this, Christine. The lab might have a way to stabilize the anemia."

"Uh-huh," she answered automatically, barely hearing him. It was the same line she had tried to get Adams to believe. "Let me guess. The cure is a stake through the heart."

McCoy's smile sagged a bit at the corners. "Actually, it's filling your mouth with garlic and then cutting off your head. But we're trying to work the kinks out." The smile faded entirely. "Dammit, Chris, do you have to make jokes about it?"

"Look at you," she retorted. "Grinning like the cat that ate the canary. How am I supposed to react? Would you feel better if I yelled at you?"

"Probably." McCoy's face relaxed a bit; he put one arm

against the crystal and slumped. "I kinda feel like yelling at someone myself."

"All right, then. I think it stinks. If I could get my hands on Adams, I'd throttle him. So much for helping the sick."

His expression darkened. "Ditto."

Chapel sighed. "Don't look quite that sad, Leonard. It makes me feel like I ought to cheer you up, and I'm not up to it right now."

"Oh. I'm not permitted to smile *or* frown. Maybe I should have sent Spock in to tell you."

She smiled in earnest. "Now *that* wouldn't have been such a bad idea."

"Look, I was telling the truth about the lab. They're testing something right now. We could spring you out of here in a couple of days."

"That's good. I guess I can hang around that long." She tried to look convinced, but she knew her eyes were anxious.

Kirk snapped on the viewscreen in his quarters less than a split second after it whistled. "Kirk here."

At first the screen remained completely dark. He thought it was a malfunction until he remembered to key up the infrared filter.

"Spock here, Captain." The tall, slender figure of the Vulcan appeared in shades of black and white. "You asked me to contact you when the landing party was ready to beam down."

"Thank you, Spock. Could I talk to McCoy?"

The first officer stepped away from his viewer. Behind him, Kirk caught a glimpse of the group on the landing pad—Adams lying on a stretcher, wearing a field suit for the purpose of keeping the virus *in* rather than out. He was flanked on either side by two people from Security. Tomson had shrewdly sent the new Andorian and Snnanagfashtalli, since neither was likely to be affected by the virus if exposed, and both were able to get along in the dark. Still, McCoy had insisted on everyone suiting up, including Spock.

McCoy neared the viewer, blotting out the others behind

him. He was the only one wearing an infrared visor. "Yes, Jim?"

"How's the patient doing? Think he'll survive the transition?"

"He should. My only concern is that they have enough stores of O negative blood. They say they do. He's one tough customer, Jim. He's on continuous transfusions, but I think he'll make it."

"Is that your captain?" Adams said weakly off-screen.

McCoy paused.

Adams spoke again. "Tell him he's sending me to my death. I want him to know that. Tell him I warned him."

McCoy's visor shifted beneath the matrix as the doctor raised his eyebrows. "Well. I guess you heard that." He lowered his voice. "What was that all about?"

"Never mind," Kirk answered grimly. "Just get him set up and then get the hell out of there, Doctor. I don't want any of my people being exposed a second longer than they have to."

"Well, since I'm probably the only one affected"— McCoy turned his head to look at his alien companions—"I appreciate the sentiment, Captain. I promise not to hang around. McCoy out."

The doctor returned to his place on the transporter pad to the left of Snnanagfashtalli.

"Beaming down now," Spock said.

As the transporter hummed, Kirk signaled the communications officer.

"Lieutenant Vigelshevsky here."

"Get me the head of Star Base Nine, please."

"That would be Commodore Mahfouz, Captain. I'll have him right for you."

Vigelshevsky disappeared from the screen, replaced first by darkness and then by the hawkish face of Mahfouz.

"Commodore Mahfouz here."

"Commodore. This is Captain James Kirk. Did our landing party arrive safely?"

"All in one piece." Mahfouz was bronze-skinned and white-haired, with eyebrows so long they almost obscured his eyes. "Admiral Mendez is seeing to them now."

"Admiral Mendez is *there?*" What possible excuse could Mendez have contrived for coming? Or was he so arrogantly confident that he didn't care what suspicions he aroused?

"Yes, he has taken charge of transporting the prisoner. Would you like to speak with him?"

"Yes, thank you, Commodore." Kirk attempted to swallow his surprise.

Mendez appeared on the screen. From his expression, it was clear to Kirk that their dislike was mutual. "What is it, Captain?"

"Admiral. I just wanted to check on Adams' beamdown—"

"Your Dr. McCoy is getting him situated in the medical facilities down here." He scowled. "Anything else?"

"Well, sir, I'm surprised to see you here. Star Base Nine is a long way from Starfleet Headquarters."

"This is an important matter."

"Yes, sir. But I'm sure Commodore Mahfouz's security is adequate. Certainly there was no need to send an admiral—"

"Maybe I had other reasons for coming out to Star Base Nine." Mendez's swarthy face crimsoned. "I'm tired of listening to your veiled accusations, Kirk. The fact that I may be personally involved in this is none of your damn business."

Kirk drew in a breath. Was Mendez so casually admitting his involvement with Adams? "With all due respect, Admiral, I fail to understand your hostility toward this prisoner. I am curious as to why you are so intent on bringing him to justice. Frankly, sir, you seem to have already condemned him without a trial."

The color drained from Mendez's face. "Captain, if I seem hostile toward the prisoner, it's because I am. If I seem in a hurry to see that he is brought to justice, it's because I am." He said the next sentence abruptly, as if by speaking fast enough he could elude the grief that crossed his face. "Yoshi Takhumara was my son."

Kirk was still in his quarters when McCoy stopped by.

"That's that," the doctor said, rubbing his hands to show

76

he was finished with the matter. "Adams got down there without a hitch. No break in quarantine. He actually seems to have rallied once I gave him some packed RBCs. And I even remembered to scrub under my fingernails before I came here."

Kirk grunted. "That's that." Somehow he didn't believe it.

McCoy's expression lost some of its good humor. "At least, it would have been—if not for Christine."

"How's the lab coming on it?" Kirk asked in lieu of sympathy.

McCoy sighed. "They say they're on the verge of stabilizing the anemia—but I'd much rather they had a cure. The vaccine is the next priority."

"You'll come up with it," Kirk said, hoping he sounded reassuring.

"I just hope we're in time. . . ." McCoy's voice faded, then he said, "But it's amazing how long Adams has lasted. That man has more lives than a Terran cat."

"What do you think will happen to him?"

"If he lives, you mean?" McCoy frowned in thought. "I think he'll get himself a very shrewd lawyer, because if he gets better, he's still in a lot of trouble."

"Think he could get off?"

"Depends on the lawyer. There's no way he could convince me he was innocent now, though."

"Speaking of innocence," Kirk said nonchalantly. "Did you say hello to Admiral Mendez while you were on star base?"

McCoy's eyebrows rose to his hairline and hovered there for a minute. *"Mendez* is there? You're kidding!"

"I talked to him just a few minutes ago."

"Well, what the hell did you say to him?"

"I asked him what he was doing there."

"No demotion? Not even a demerit for a question like that?"

"No." Kirk paused. "I suppose you didn't notify Yoshi's parents when you filled out the death certificate."

"I have to do enough damn reports, thank you, without that unpleasant duty. I notified Command, and they're the ones who tell the next of kin. Is this leading where I think it is?"

"Maybe. Mendez was his father."

"Yoshi's father. Well." McCoy blinked. "I dare say he took after his mother more."

"Took her family name, at least."

"No wonder Mendez is hot to get his hands around Adams' throat. Can't say I blame him."

"I suppose not." Kirk could not bring himself to say it convincingly.

"Oh, come on, Jim, you're still not thinking—"

The whistle of the intercom cut him off. M'Benga's brown face filled the screen.

"I'm sorry to disturb you, Captain. I was looking for Dr. McCoy."

"He's here." Kirk turned the screen toward the doctor.

McCoy leaned forward anxiously. "What is it, M'Benga?"

"You asked me to keep you updated on Nurse Chapel's condition. She's just lapsed into a coma."

Adams lay in a room just like the one on the *Enterprise*—dark, quiet, oppressive—with a few exceptions. Instead of the elaborate containment procedures with three code checkpoints, the star base personnel had rigged a temporary quarantine (no computer codes, Adams had been sure to notice, although he had pretended to be unaware of his surroundings) behind a force field at the door.

He felt better after the last transfusion. Maybe he was recovering after all. His mind was certainly clearer. He spent his time fondling his lucky amulet and considering his best means of escape. All he had to do was get out of here, and then his lucky amulet would see him to freedom. He held the pendant up to eye level and studied it fondly. On the face of the locket, a bas-relief Amerind chief stared into a ruby sun. The necklace had belonged to Adams' grandmother, and he had worn it since he could remember. He had worn it on the *Brass Ring* and credited it with his survival. And it would save him again now.

In front of the force field, a security guard patrolled at all times. Adams supposed they would not be likely to fall for the choking routine again, since Dr. McCoy had warned them. He would have to think of a new way out.

He was on the verge of a solution when his concentration was disturbed by soft scratching on the other side of the room. Damn. The qefla trying to dig out of its cage again. Someone had smuggled it as a pet onto a starship, and no one had been the wiser until a mysterious outbreak of Rigellian fever. They had dumped it at the nearest star base, where it would sit in its quarantined, escape-proof cage. If it recovered, it would be inoculated and shipped back to Rigel, if someone here didn't adopt it first.

Adams grimaced in distaste. Qeflas reminded him of a cross between a cat and a rat. Why would anyone think a twenty-pound rodent cute? He forced his thoughts back to escape, thinking of what, if anything, in the room could be used as a weapon.

Scratch-scratch-scratch.

"Shut up, you stupid Rigellian rat!" But the scratching continued. Obviously the qefla did not speak Standard.

And then a chill passed over Adams. He could feel Mendez's eyes on him.

Since getting the disease, he could not explain how he had the ability to sense certain things, but now he could sense Mendez's presence. Mendez was here, watching him now.

But of course there was no one else in the room with him, except for the damn qefla. But it was possible that he was being watched. The doctor's patient monitor . . .

"You're there, Mendez. I know you're there. I know you're watching."

He waited in the darkness for a moment, and then he sat up slowly and pulled the bedside terminal over to him. He keyed in a few commands, trying to override security programs and find the controls for force fields. The computer did not respond to him. No matter what he asked for, the information had been closed off.

He laughed out loud in the darkness. Mendez *was* there. No one else would think to close down access to this terminal. What sick man would use it?

"Hello, Mendez," he said, in the most casual voice he could muster. Inside, he was trembling, but he would never let Mendez know. "Are you going to be a coward, or are you going to talk to me if you have something to say?"

There was no response. Just the *scratch-scratch-scratch* of the qefla seeking freedom.

When the terminal whistled at him, Adams jumped. The screen lit up, so bright in the darkness that Adams shut his eyes and turned his head away. He made himself look back, steeling himself against the pain so that he would not flinch. He forced a sardonic smile.

Mendez did not return it.

"I understand you're trying to pin a murder charge on me," Adams said. "You've got no evidence. It happened as I said. All Starfleet will be shocked when they hear how you've hounded me—"

The intense hatred in Mendez's eyes seemed to bore right through him. "I don't give a damn what anyone thinks. You and I both know you're guilty. I'll do whatever it takes to make it stick."

"Anything?" Adams forced the smile wider. "I told Kirk that you were out to kill me. If anything happens . . ."

"Kirk can think what he wants." Mendez's lips drew back to reveal large, uneven teeth, but he was not smiling. "Threaten all you like, Adams. No matter what you do, you're a dead man."

Adams cut off the communication before his expression revealed how much he feared Mendez was right.

Chapter Six

THE DOOR TO Kirk's quarters opened in response to Spock's buzzing. The captain had quite clearly not been sleeping—if anything, he seemed alert and anxious.

"Come in, Spock." Kirk did not smile in greeting; such an emotional display would have been wasted on the Vulcan anyway.

"Thank you, Captain." Spock stepped inside and remained standing while Kirk paced up and down on the carpet. Spock watched him go back and forth, reminded of the time on Earth he had sat in the Wimbledon stands during a tennis match. It had left him with a slightly stiff neck and no real enlightenment as to what humans found so fascinating about the sport. "I trust that everything with Adams proceeded smoothly." Although he anticipated it had not, judging from Kirk's behavior.

"Let's hope so. I talked to Mendez. He came to take Adams back to Federation Headquarters." He stopped for a moment to glance up at Spock. "He told me that Yoshi was his son."

Spock's expression remained bland. He had not suspected this, yet it made little difference as far as his conclusions.

Kirk eyed him carefully for a reaction. "I suppose it explains Mendez's hatred for Adams. I guess Adams' charges are beginning to sound pretty ridiculous."

"It *does* explain his hatred of Adams, if he indeed believes Adams to be his son's murderer. But it in no way makes Adams' claim any more or less credible. Yoshi and the others may well have been working for Admiral Mendez."

"Damn," Kirk said softly, looking vexed. "I was afraid you'd say that."

Spock opened his mouth to express his confusion, but Kirk waved him silent. "Don't respond to that, Spock. I just meant I wanted to hear your opinion . . . and I was hoping you wouldn't agree with me. But you came here to talk about something else."

Spock folded his arms behind him. "I was able to piece some of the data from the Tanis record banks together, Captain. The information I gleaned is extremely spotty—a few garbled data fragments from various documents. In some cases, it was impossible to match data to any file." It was illogical, Spock knew, to feel at fault simply because he had not met with success; failure in this case was unavoidable. His abilities could have made no difference in the outcome. And yet, for some reason, he found himself feeling personally to blame. "I have done what I could—"

"Enough disclaimers, Spock. Any conclusions?"

"Two rather surprising ones, sir. First, there is a strong likelihood that research was being done on *two* viruses. Second, a Vulcan researcher on Tanis died as a result of exposure to one of those viruses."

"What Vulcan researcher?"

"I told you the conclusions were surprising. Some of the data fragments were from personal logs. One of them was kept in Vulcan—by someone called Sepek. References to his death were made in what appears to be Lara Krovozhadny's log. Also, references in several documents were made to an R-virus, as well as an R-prime virus, which later came to be called the H-virus." A muscle in Kirk's jaw twitched; the captain clearly understand the implications of what Spock was telling him.

"So it's certain that the researchers were involved in biowarfare experiments."

It was not a question, but Spock had learned to recognize that particular human tone of voice as requesting confirmation. He phrased his answer carefully, though he knew humans often paid little attention to such distinctions of certainty, and Kirk was likely to take it as an outright affirmation. "At present I am unable to come up with a better explanation."

"If the Vulcan died, then where is his body? Back on Tanis somewhere?"

Spock nodded assent. "I have no data on it, but I would expect to find it in stasis."

"And why *two* viruses? Why one deadly to humans and one to Vulcans?"

"Unfortunately, all data relating to the researchers' purpose was destroyed. But there are three possible theories. One, the researchers were working for Starfleet. In that case, it would be logical for them to develop a germ harmful to the Romulans. That would explain Sepek's death, since Romulans and Vulcans are often susceptible to the same diseases."

"Then why develop a virus harmful to humans?" Kirk asked.

"An accidental mutation, perhaps. Or perhaps the same microbe proved to be more deadly to Vulcanoids than to humans, and the other was a harmless decoy. I can only speculate."

"Go on. Second theory."

"The researchers were working for an enemy of the Federation. The Klingons would have much to gain from acquiring weapons effective against humans, Vulcans *and* Romulans."

"But there was a *Vulcan* working on that base, Spock."

"I know, sir," Spock said quietly. The thought had troubled him greatly. What Vulcan would knowingly work to create weapons capable of causing such misery and destruction? It went beyond his normal curiosity; Spock felt a moral obligation to find out what role Sepek had played in the development of the viruses. "It is not logical, yet the fact exists. I have no explanation for it at present."

"Let's hear the third theory, then."

"The researchers were mercenaries, intending to sell their products to the highest bidder."

"That," Kirk said slowly, "is the one that frightens me the most."

"I find none of the theories to be particularly comforting, Captain." Spock hesitated, searching for the correct words to make his request. There was more he wished to discuss, but broaching the subject required delicacy.

It would not do to say, *Sir, I wish to recover Sepek's body and ascertain whether his* katra, *his spirit, survives, in the hope that spirit and body may be rejoined; or, failing that, that Sepek's knowledge may be preserved in the Hall of Ancient Thought.*

No, it would not do. For the prospect of recovering Sepek's *katra* was so dismal that Spock had little hope of success. He had heard of the rare instances in which *katras* were saved (usually those of Kolinahr High Masters), but they were always from those who sensed death's approach and had time to make the proper arrangements. The *katra* was then placed in the Hall of Ancient Thought. Spock knew of no successful attempts at rejoining, for the body was invariably too worn or diseased or damaged.

And even assuming that Sepek had had the time to make arrangements, the only possible receptacle for his *katra* was Jeffrey Adams.

Clearly, logical argument in favor of recovering the body was impossible. Even so, Spock was morally bound to try.

"Something on your mind, Spock?"

Spock cleared his throat, mildly disgruntled at his transparency. "I have a request, sir . . . regarding the Vulcan Sepek's body."

Kirk waited.

Spock continued rather uncomfortably. "It is extremely important for Vulcan families to recover the body of a deceased member. I respectfully request that we return to Tanis and—"

"Retrieve Sepek's body?" Kirk finished for him, and shook his head. "I'm sorry, Spock, but Tanis is out of our way. Not to mention that the whole base is contaminated. I refuse to risk any more people down there."

"Sir." Spock suspected from Kirk's expression that his was a losing battle, but conscience compelled him. "I cannot emphasize strongly enough the responsibility that I feel—that any Vulcan would feel—to recover another Vulcan's body to send it home. If we do not—"

The faint surprise on Kirk's face indicated that the captain had finally registered the urgency with which Spock made the request, but he held firm. "I'm sorry. I'll see to it Starfleet is notified of the body and also of your request."

Spock sighed and took his leave. There was no point in arguing once the captain had made up his mind. Unfortunately, Starfleet currently had no ships in Tanis' vicinity. Recovery of the body would be given low priority and take months. But there was nothing Spock could do. Further explanation would only bring charges of Vulcan mysticism and raised eyebrows. And Spock far preferred raising a brow to having one raised at him.

Adams had forgotten what color looked like. The world for him had become so many varying shades of gray. Yet he had learned to tell colors apart in the darkness—could recognize the red tunic of Security, the blue of Medical.

He had not slept at all, though he knew he had been awake more than twenty-four hours. How could he sleep, knowing that Mendez would be coming for him soon? He spent the day with his eyes open wide at the ceiling, seeing nothing, listening to the maddeningly patient scratching of the qefla and thinking of what to do.

And then, after he had lost all track of the time, over the sound of the qefla's pawing came a low hum, followed by a click. It was the sound of a force field being turned off.

They were coming for him.

Adams' heart pounded. Fear brought with it strength.

He had only a few seconds to cause a distraction. He pulled the tube from his arm, ignoring the droplets of blood rilling on his skin, and darted to the animal's cage.

There was a use for the Rigellian rat after all.

A man's form was passing through the second entryway into the room by the time Adams pushed the button that released the electromagnetic field around the qefla's cage.

A round, writhing disk of fur, the animal scrambled onto the floor, scratching Adams with its long claws in its desperation to be free. He scarcely felt it. He gave the qefla a push so that it skittered toward the man, and he dropped to the floor himself and rolled under the bed. It wasn't a particularly good hiding place and he would be spotted soon, but it would win him a few seconds.

The man had made it through the entryway and was followed by a female. Both wore Starfleet uniforms and visors beneath glowing field suits. Both carried phasers in their hands.

Mendez's people, no question about it.

The man surveyed the room. From where he stood, he didn't see Adams crouching under the bed. "What the—" As the woman came through, he turned to her. "He's escaped."

"That's not possible," she said. "It's a trick."

At that, they both turned and moved toward the bed. The qefla had joined Adams there, attempting to burrow beneath him. Adams gave the animal a pinch and a firm push, and sent it squealing toward the guards.

It skittered into the man, who dropped his phaser and scrabbled after the animal on his knees. The woman had knelt down with her phaser drawn and was a second away from seeing him, but could not resist turning her head first to watch the man. Adams only had to reach out to grab the wrist that held the phaser.

He fired it before she had a chance to cry out. For one beautiful, brilliant instant, she lit up the room, and then faded to nothingness. Adams turned pain-dazzled eyes to the man, who had dropped the struggling animal and was scrabbling for his phaser on the floor. Adams fired again, this time remembering to close his eyes first. Even so, he could see the blast through closed eyelids.

It had all taken only seconds.

He felt no remorse over their deaths. If anything, he felt triumphant and vindicated: they *had* been sent by Mendez to kill him. Why else had the woman's phaser been set on kill, and not stun?

His next concern as he passed through the doorway was light; if the corridor was still lit, he at least had to try. Better to die writhing in the halls of star base than at Mendez's hands. He grasped his amulet and stepped out of the room. To his relief, it was soothingly dark. They had planned to take him somewhere else to kill him.

Up to this point, he had not considered where escape might take him. He feared the brightness of daytime on star base. If he stayed, Mendez would search every corner until he was found.

What he needed was a starship.

Lisa Nguyen sat in a tourist bar on Star Base Nine, wishing she were anywhere else. Not that it was bad for a tourist bar, actually; she almost suspected it of being a local hangout. It was quieter and darker than usual, less crowded, and the furniture was new and kept clean. It lacked that musty, slightly unsavory aroma that seemed to cling to heavily populated bars. In fact, it was probably one of the nicest base bars she'd ever been in. But she was far from having fun.

She stared down once again at the painting propped against the wall near her chair. It was a scene of wild horses in the desert, rearing up against a sunset of iridescent purple and blazing orange gold. Normally, she would never have given in to impulse buying, especially not from anyone as disreputable as a star base street vendor, but the painting seemed to her to be a sign. Her purchase had caused some dissension; Lamia insisted the creatures were too delicate and spindly to be Terran, while Stanger took Lisa's part and said it was merely a stylized representation. The vendor was of no help in settling the argument; he barely spoke enough Standard to negotiate the cost.

She looked up at Stanger and Lamia, who sat across from her at the tiny round table, getting drunk. In the middle of the table were three shot glasses, each one filled with a slightly different shade of amber liquid. Stanger was expounding on each type of liquor with the earnestness of a lecturer, and Lamia was listening raptly, her cheeks flushed a bright shade of blue, her eyelids open a millimeter less than normal. She was already fairly drunk, not a particularly difficult accomplishment for an Andorian. She had only had three tiny swallows of alcohol, though if she slouched any lower over the glasses, she would have to worry about the effect of the fumes. With each sip, she leaned a little closer to Stanger.

Nguyen sat back in her chair, holding a glass of local juice whose name she had already forgotten. She didn't care for it, but the effort to send it back seemed too great tonight. Everything seemed too much of an effort. She would have refused shore leave if Stanger hadn't begged her to come along. She got the impression he wanted a buffer zone between him and the Andorian; now, at the sight of the two of them together, she decided that what he'd really wanted was a chaperone.

Can't the man make up his mind? One minute he acts like he wants to kill her, the next he acts like he's getting ready to ask for her cabin door code.

The change in Stanger and Lamia's relationship was hardly what she'd expected, after that incident in the rec lounge. Mutual throttling would have made more sense than their sudden peace treaty. But whatever Stanger had said to Lamia the night she heard from home had made a difference. Not only did Lamia have a newfound respect for him, she also seemed to have taken her *Tijra's* message extremely well. Deep down, Nguyen disapproved of Lamia's rapid emotional recovery. Lisa had never had a family, had spent her childhood shuttled from one distant relative to the next. It was one reason she found it important to make friends, and it made it impossible for her to think of anyone cavalierly giving up an immediate family of almost fifty members.

No matter how long Lisa had known Lamia, she was always amazed at the sudden swings of the Andorian's emotions. One moment intensely depressed, the next, cheerful; one moment ready to disembowel Stanger, the next, sitting beside him in a bar taking an alcohol appreciation course.

"Now this," Stanger said earnestly, pointing to the glass in the middle, "is sour mash. Take a small sip and see how it compares to the bourbon." He had had two drinks before launching the Great Taste Experiment and was not at all drunk, although Nguyen thought his eyes glistened a little more brightly than usual.

Lamia complied, blue cheeks pulsing as she swished it around her gums. She swallowed and gasped, sending a blast of whiskeyed breath in Nguyen's direction. Her eyes grew even rounder.

"I like it. There's a sort of sweetness to it, and it's smoother—"

Obviously pleased at her answer, Stanger showed a flash of teeth under his mustache. "Better than the bourbon, isn't it?"

"I think so." One of Lamia's antennae suddenly drooped at a cock-eyed angle to the other one.

Nguyen had trouble keeping her eyes off it. "I don't think you ought to swish it around your gums like that."

"Why not?" Lamia's tone was a little belligerent, but Nguyen took no offense. She was used to Lamia's moodiness by now.

"Your gums are permeable and let it pass through into the bloodstream faster. You don't want to get sick."

Stanger smirked. "Come on. You're making that up. I never heard—"

"I'm not going to get sick," Lamia said with swaying haughtiness. "Besides, if I do, I can always get a pill from sickbay."

"She's right, Lamia," Stanger chided with good humor. He alone had changed his uniform for civilian clothing before beaming down for six hours' liberty. Nguyen hadn't understood why anyone would take the time, until she thought about it from Stanger's point of view. He had put on a tight-fitting tunic that showed off the muscles in his arms and chest. Nguyen thought chastely of Rajiv and did her best not to notice. "We don't want you losing dinner right when we're all beaming up. I think I'll let you stand next to Lisa."

"What a disgusting thought," Lamia said unsteadily, but she giggled. "Okay, what's this last one?" She indicated the third glass.

"This really *is* the last one. Maybe you should skip it,"

Stanger said thoughtfully. "It's a blend. To my taste, the most inferior of the three. I should have had you try it first."

"I *want* to taste it. Here." Lamia picked the glass up and swallowed before anyone could stop her.

"That was a big sip," Nguyen said.

"But I didn't swish it around this time."

"Good for you." Stanger pushed the glasses toward Nguyen. "Go on, Lisa, why don't you give them a try? You seem like you could use a little cheering up. You've been awfully quiet."

She had hoped they wouldn't notice. Lamia was certainly too drunk to, but Lisa hadn't been able to fool Stanger. The last thing she wanted to do was to talk about it. She searched for a believable lie.

"I really don't care for whiskey, thanks." Nguyen forced a credible smile. "I guess I *am* a little down. It's been a long time since I had the chance for shore leave, and I was really looking forward to a blue, sunny sky—"

"The sky's blue here?" Lamia wondered. "How very *odd.*"

"Whatever. I was in the mood to stroll through a big, grassy field, maybe even find out how to get a soccer game together. I just wanted to feel sun on my face."

Stanger had thrown back the shot of bourbon and was fingering the sour mash. His face had that expression of attentive concern found on those just beginning to get tipsy. "You can do that on the ship."

"I mean *real* sun. I know it's supposed to be exactly the same, but I can tell it's not the real thing. I guess it's psychological."

"Well, that's too bad." Stanger put the glass of sour mash to his lips and drained it with a sharp flick of his wrist before setting it down on the table. "Tell you what, let's all go someplace fun. Like dancing. How would you ladies like to go dancing? I think Lamia needs to work the alcohol through her system."

Lamia smiled at no one in particular and hiccupped silently.

"I tell you what." Nguyen still wore the false smile. "Why

don't you go ahead and take Lamia? I think I'll take a walk. Maybe the sun's not out, but there's one hell of a moon. I bet I could even find some trees."

"We'll go with you," Lamia said unevenly. "Besides, I don't know how to dance." She leaned right up against Stanger, who smiled as if the contact made him pleased and uncomfortable at the same time.

"Yeah," he added. "A walk would be really nice. Besides, you don't want to go alone. What if you run into some unsavory, drunken types?" He looked at the Andorian. "Present company excluded."

But Lisa was too upset to worry about Stanger's problems tonight. "I have this." She patted the phaser on her uniform belt. "And actually I *do* want to go alone. If you don't mind."

"Oh." Stanger drew back as if slightly embarrassed. "No problem. If you'd rather be by yourself . . ." He nodded at the painting. "Leave that with us. We'll take care of it for you."

"That's all right," she said quickly, tucking it under her arm. It wasn't all that awkward, a half meter wide by a half meter long. And besides, in their current condition, she didn't trust them to remember it. "It's fine, see?"

"Suit yourself." Stanger shrugged and turned to Lamia. "You can learn to dance. After all, you didn't know anything about whiskey before tonight, but you learned, didn't you?"

The dawn of revelation lit up Lamia's face. "I suppose I did." She rose from her chair. Stanger put out a hand to steady her. "Let me pay for this, my friends. I insist."

"Of course," he soothed, winking at Nguyen, who understood from the gesture that he would take care of the bill and debts would be settled later. "We all appreciate that. I'll go tell them. Lisa, go on if you like. We'll catch up with you later."

Nguyen left. As she stepped outside, she could hear Lamia inside.

"What's eating *her?*"

* * *

91

Caught in the transporter beam, Adams was suddenly struck with terror. He was escaping one evil only to fall into the grasp of another. What if he beamed into an open field with the sun beating down on him, searing his skin until his body was one great oozing sore? With no one to help him, he would die in agony. He was no longer certain that anything was preferable to a quick death at the hands of Mendez's men.

At the moment of materialization, he felt disoriented. Something was wrong; choosing random coordinates had backfired. Something cold and wet swirled around his legs. He was not on solid land.

Eyes squeezed shut, he had steeled himself against the pain he knew would come the moment light touched his eyes and skin. But the pain was not at all what he expected —more like mild irritation than agony. Cautiously, Adams opened one eye.

There was a short dazzle of discomfort as his eyes adjusted, but again, nothing like what he had expected. He looked down at the water coursing around his legs.

He was standing hip-deep in a fountain in the middle of a park. Above, the sky was dark and starry, lit feebly by a thin slice of moon.

Adams threw back his head and laughed. Half a meter to the right, and he would have appeared in the middle of the spray that jetted up from the fountain's center. The amulet was protecting him so far. He sloshed carefully to the edge, mindful of the slippery stone floor, and crawled over the railing onto grassy turf. His skin felt less irritated; the water was illumined with a faint blue light.

He looked about. The park was a real one, not one of those artificial underground simulations (though he suspected the moon was the result of an engineering feat) and while the planet's surface had been terraformed, the atmospheric temperature was not carefully controlled. The night breeze was cold, and Adams was already becoming chilled. He stamped his feet, water squishing in his boots, then leaned over to wring water from his dripping pants.

The park was deserted. Maybe nighttime would work

against him after all. Everyone was probably crowding the bars; he ought to find a dimly lit one and find someone on leave from a ship.

"Whoever's manning your transporter must have already had too much fun on leave."

Adams started at the sound of the husky feminine voice. He turned to see a tall, cloaked figure behind him.

The style of the cloak was Vulcan, but the woman inside it was definitely not. She had light brown skin and hair the same color. Adams decided the hair was curly; certainly, it defied gravity, streaming in all directions like a medusa's. The woman wore a lopsided smile; obviously, she had already visited the bars.

Adams smiled back in the hopes there was a uniform beneath the cloak. A uniform meant a ship, and a ship meant freedom. He rubbed his arms and let his teeth chatter a little.

"You can say that again." He stamped his feet. He was still wearing his beige lab coveralls. Hopefully, she would mistake him for a technician or a maintenance worker. "They didn't tell me about the nights being so cool. Guess I ought to find someplace warm—"

"Guess you ought to beam back up and change your clothes." She had a smugly drunk expression on her face.

"If I beam back up, they'll just put me to work. I barely managed to get away as it is." He shivered in earnest. "I need to get out of this breeze."

She leaned closer and squinted at him. "You certainly look overworked. Here." Her shoulders shifted as she slid out of the cloak. Underneath, she wore a black satin tunic, black pants, and pearl-gray cowboy boots with pink handstitching. A matching belt that held a large, sheathed hunting knife was slung low on her hips. Hardly regulation. Adams felt a surge of disappointment until he realized that the black pants were Fleet issue, and the belt had a communicator and phaser strapped to it, along with a few other devices of questionable legality. Border patrol, then. He fought to keep his grin from inappropriately widening.

She held the cloak out to him. "Go on, take it." Even in

the faint light, it was clear the cloak was custom-made. The fabric was deep scarlet velvet that shifted to iridescent silver blue where the light caught it.

"I can't," Adams lied. "It's beautiful. I'd hate to get it wet."

She shrugged. "It can be dried. It's up to you."

He took it without further pretense. It was a little too long, since she was about two inches taller than he, but it was perfect. If he pulled the hood up, he could walk out in daylight, once he got his eyes accustomed. "Much better, thanks. It's very warm."

"You here for long?" She lowered her lids and glanced at him sideways with an exaggerated smirk. It was the standard pickup line. Adams abhorred drunks, but then, the woman was attractive. It wouldn't hurt to play along. He could get her alone, distract her enough to get the phaser from his pocket, and force her to take him up to her ship.

"Long enough," he told her.

"Good. I know a place where we could be alone for a little while. And it's warm." She smiled and patted one of the devices on the belt. "And I've got a little something to ensure some privacy. Even our ships couldn't track us down unless we wanted."

"That would be nice," Adams said, trying not to sound too eager. "Is that one of the sensor scrambling devices?"

She grinned affirmatively. "Comes in handy when you have to hide from the enemy . . . or your friends. Someone could walk right by you with a scanner and never know you were there."

He felt a rush of euphoria. The amulet had definitely brought him luck tonight.

They started walking; she was weaving a little. The fountain became open grassy field, turning into trees where the park bordered the city.

"What ship?" she asked finally.

He gave the first name that entered his head. "The *Enterprise*."

"The *Enterprise*," she repeated approvingly. "Well, if you're given to spit and polish, I suppose you could do worse."

"You?"

"The *Uncommon.* She's a small scout vessel." She said it with great pride. "I'm second-in-command of a crew of thirty-two."

Thirty-two. Adams' heart sank. Even with the scrambler, he would be too easily detected on a vessel that size. He needed something larger . . . a starship.

She was still talking. "Say, I don't even know your name. Mine's Leland. Red Leland."

"George Minos," he lied. There was no point in getting up to her ship. He would just as soon leave, but he had already decided to keep the robe.

"George. That's a nice name. I knew a man named George once, on Rigel Four."

She chattered on, Adams giving an occasional grunt or replying briefly. The night grew brighter as they moved toward the city. Adams began to think about pulling up the hood of the cloak to protect himself. Besides, the woman was beginning to stare suspiciously at him.

She laid a hand on his arm and moved her face closer to his. It was all he could do not to pull back from the overwhelming smell of liquor. "To tell the truth, George, you look kinda peaked."

"I told you I'm overworked." He turned his head in an effort to get fresh air.

"Now that I can see you better, you look sick. You don't have anything catching, do you?"

"Don't be ridiculous." He started walking faster, dragging her toward a copse of trees.

"Hey, slow down." She pulled her arm away and stood, swaying. "Look, let's just forget it, okay?"

He kept walking.

"Hey, I'm not going with you. And I want my robe back."

He stopped and faced her; he would have kept on walking if he hadn't feared she would draw her phaser and shoot him in the back.

"I need it just for tonight. I can return it to your ship tomorrow."

"We're warping out tonight. Besides, I'm not sure I trust you. How do I know you're really from the *Enterprise?"*

Her hand hovered over her knife. Adams was amused that she seemed to prefer it to the phaser on her belt.

"You don't." Beneath the cloak, he drew his own weapon. He barely had time to set it on stun before she had the knife in her hand. She would have thrown it at him if he hadn't fired first, and he had no doubts it would have killed him.

Red collapsed into a lanky heap on the soft grass.

Adams berated himself silently. Setting the phaser on stun was foolish; the second had nearly cost him his life. But he had his reasons for wanting her body intact. After all, there was the scrambler, and what looked like a small subspace transmitter attached to her belt. Perhaps the transmitter was strong enough to broadcast into the heart of the Romulan Empire itself.

And he could certainly use the knife.

Chapter Seven

LISA SAT ON the fountain's edge with the painting in her lap
and watched the iridescent blue water leap against the night
sky. The moon was false—too perfect a match for Earth's—
but the rest of the surroundings were authentic, which
soothed her. The grass was native and imperfect, growing in
irregular clumps, and the night air was a little too chilly to
be comfortable. She closed her eyes and felt the cool spray
against her face. Probably the best thing about it all was
being alone.

She had wanted to be alone ever since she'd heard from
Rajiv. Seeing him again, even in a taped message, had
brought on a sweet sense of melancholy. She wanted to sit
for hours thinking of what he had said. Thinking of him, of
his serene dark eyes, of the way he looked when he smiled.
Yet at the same time, the decision he had asked her to make
brought a sense of pressure and panic.

It was a decision she did not want to make. She felt both
touched and resentful that he had asked her.

The memory of him brought with it thoughts of Paolo,
Zia, and Rakel. The month in the Colorado mountains was
one of the happiest memories Lisa had of her life. Of trees,
and riding horses in the new snow. They had seemed like a
family then.

Lisa had never had a family. Her parents had separated
after their two-year contract expired. Lisa lived with her

father and never heard from her mother, a researcher who volunteered for a deep-space mission. When he died a few years later, Lisa was shuttled from relative to distant relative. If her mother had ever asked to see her in that time, Lisa was not told. Even now, she did not know if her mother was still living.

She had loved Colorado. She would have done anything to go back to it. Or so she thought, until Rajiv's letter.

He was leaving the Fleet, he said, to join the group, and he was asking Lisa to do the same. The others had consented to welcome her. Group marriage, a built-in family. Zia was expecting her first child in September.

Lisa was thrilled at the invitation—until she realized exactly what he was asking. He was asking her to come to Colorado, to the ranch, to live. Everyone had decided that the family would consist of permanent members, for the sake of future children. Surely Lisa of all people would understand that.

He was asking her to give up Starfleet.

He might as well have asked for an arm, or a leg. Starfleet had been more than a natural choice for those without families, or those who sought to be rid of what families they had. For Nguyen it was an opportunity to gain a sense of pride in herself. A chance to accomplish, to bolster self-esteem. And it had occurred to her that traveling across the galaxy might increase her chances of hearing news of her mother.

Lisa shivered. The combination of cold spray from the fountain and the night air chilled her. A walk would warm her up; perhaps she would walk through the sparse bit of forest, and pretend she was walking through tall mountain pine.

She stood up and sighed, putting the painting under one arm. There seemed to be no way of making a choice. She couldn't give up the family, and she certainly couldn't give up Starfleet. Any attempts to plead with Rajiv to consider letting her be an occasional member would be met with those quietly disapproving eyes. He was willing to leave the Fleet. He could ask no less of her. And surely she understood how unfair it would be to the others.

She started walking toward the trees, careful not to stumble over the uneven clumps of grass. Even though she was glad no one else was out enjoying the evening sky, she thought it odd that the park was deserted. Everyone else probably preferred the warmer bars. Since she wasn't going to come to a decision tonight, she might as well look for Stanger and Lamia. Maybe she should confide in the Andorian about it. Lamia seemed hotheaded and irresponsible sometimes, but that was just Andorian biochemistry and culture. She had a sensible head on her shoulders. But Lisa hadn't wanted to bother her, in her less cynical moments figuring that Lamia was just putting on a good show about getting over that business with her family.

The grass grew sparser near the stand of trees, and the light of the city filtered through, throwing long shadows. Lisa stopped and put her hand on the first tree she came to. The bark was rough and fibrous, and she leaned forward to smell it. A clean pungent scent, but nothing like Terran pine. She began to pick her way slowly toward the city. The patch of forest grew thicker, until she could not see her feet. The ground was still uneven, and she shuffled her boots so that she would not stumble.

Halfway through, her right boot struck something large and yielding. She threw an arm out to steady herself against a tree and winced at the *thud* as the painting hit the ground. Slowly, she prodded the object again with her foot. It moved a little, then fell back heavily against the soft ground.

It was a body. She almost panicked, but scolded herself back to rationality. Just a drunk, from one of the bars, passed out. She would have liked to ignore it and keep on walking, but the only right thing to do was to be sure that the drunk was all right. For all she knew, it could be Lamia or Stanger. She squatted down next to the body.

"Are you okay?" She would have felt better if she could have heard snoring, but there was no sound at all. She fumbled for a wrist. From the feel, she judged it to be human and female. But she could not get a pulse.

That did not frighten her particularly; she knew it was sometimes difficult to get a wrist pulse on a female. She crouched down closer and felt for the neck.

Her hand found the head and very gently followed down the side of the face, past the ear, under the jaw. When she got lower, she felt something warm and wet. She pressed down, feeling for the artery, and her hand slipped and touched something hard. A sensation of extreme cold traveled down her spine as Lisa realized she was feeling the woman's exposed trachea.

She drew her hand away, sickened. It was not the blood or even the gaping wound in the woman's neck that made her shudder; Nguyen was resolutely stoic about such things. It was the fact that someone had been able to do such a thing to another living being. In the feeble moonlight, she couldn't see what covered her hand, but she knew nevertheless. *Calm. Calm. Be calm.* She wiped it on the grass, stood up, and reached for her communicator.

A steely arm encircled her neck before she could flip the communicator grid open. She was too surprised to feel panic. She threw her arms up and tried to pry the arm away until something cold and hard was pressed to her temple: a phaser. Nguyen dropped one hand to her belt and realized the weapon against her head was her own. She stopped struggling.

The voice speaking directly behind her head was male, calm, not unpleasant.

"You're from a starship."

Nguyen moved her head up and down a fraction of a millimeter; the arm around her throat was too tight for her to speak. She slid one leg backward, cautiously. If she could just find one of his legs, pull him off balance . . . But they were hidden in heavy folds of velvet.

"Your communicator," he said. "Call your ship. Tell them you have a package you need beamed directly to your quarters."

"What package?" she asked, trying desperately to think of a way to stall him. "They can't be fooled into thinking *we're* inanimate—"

"The picture you dropped," the man said, pulling her backward so that she tottered. "Tell them you're tired of carrying it. You want it beamed to your quarters." He

100

nudged it with his foot, and she could hear it scraping across the ground until it lay at her feet.

If you hurt it, you son of a—The thought was interrupted by an eerier one: *How in the worlds did he know it was there? How could he see it?*

"Here." He loosened his grip just enough for her to raise the communicator to her face. "Call them."

Now I have him, she thought. *Give Vigelshevsky a Code Yellow and Tomson will have people waiting in the transporter room. If I can just make it sound casual enough.*

He ground the phaser hard into her temple as if he read her thoughts. "Say anything else, and you're dead. No codes, no dropping hints. Believe me, you are expendable. Just as the woman on the ground was."

Nguyen couldn't stop herself from looking down in the darkness, though she was grateful she could not make out the body.

He squeezed her neck so tightly she began to gag, then relaxed the pressure. "Call."

She flipped open the grid. "Nguyen to *Enterprise.*"

"Vigelshevsky here. Tired of liberty so soon, Lisa?"

"Not at all. Actually, I was just wondering if Kyle would beam a package up for me." She sounded stiff, unnatural, and wondered if her captor noticed. But the pressure around her neck did not increase.

"I'll notify Kyle. Vigelshevsky out—"

"Wait!" she almost shouted, then forced her voice to be calm. Certainly Vigelshevsky must have heard something odd in her tone. The communications officer did not terminate the link, but silently waited for explanation. "I—I have a special favor to ask. Could you ask him to beam it directly to my quarters?"

"That's a little unusual," Vigelshevsky answered quietly. He *had* noticed.

"It would save me a trip. Could you check with him?" Nguyen asked with forced joviality. *Please figure it out, Vigelshevsky, for God's sake, please read my mind.*

"Okay." The communications officer's tone was dubious. "Hold on."

She held her breath and waited. Good God, what if Kyle wouldn't do it? What then? Would this crazy scatter her molecules all over the park? She held her breath and waited. With each passing second, she imagined the pressure against her throat increased until at last she could bear it no longer.

"He'll do it," Vigelshevsky said at last. "Apparently there's no regulation against beaming objects intraship. But he said not to get mad at him if he loses it inside a bulkhead."

"Tell him I promise." She felt both relieved and disappointed by his answer. The arm tightened around her neck; time for the conversation to end.

"Thanks, Vigelshevsky. Nguyen out."

She shut her communicator and replaced it carefully on her belt. Within seconds, she heard the hum of the transporter near her feet.

"Pick it up." The man pushed her to her knees. She groped for the painting, found it, and wrapped both arms around it as he knelt behind her and circled his arms firmly around her waist. Together they were caught up in the beam.

A chill breeze sighed through the branches, carrying on it the smell of blood.

Kirk had finally drifted off to sleep when the intercom whistle wakened him.

"Sorry to bother, Captain, but Admiral Mendez is calling from star base. He says it's urgent."

Kirk sat up, made instantly alert by Vigelshevsky's tone of voice. Mendez's agitated face appeared on the screen.

"Admiral. Is there some problem?" Kirk's tone was far more civil than the last time; while he still disliked the admiral, he found it difficult to maintain his hostility toward him after learning of his son.

But Mendez seemed barely able to contain his rage. His huge shoulders hunched forward; his fists were clenched tightly. "More than a problem," he said through gritted teeth. "Adams has escaped."

"Escaped? But Dr. McCoy told me the containment methods—"

"Were foolproof, I know." Mendez waved Kirk's comment away impatiently. "He got away while my people were transporting him to my vessel. The area was closed off and darkened, so no one was there to stop him before he transported out of the medical facility." He stopped abruptly and lowered his voice. *"Two* people, Kirk. Two of my people were killed."

"I'm sorry to hear that, sir," Jim said. He knew what it was like to lose a crewperson: the feeling of ultimate blame, of helplessness . . . He found his dislike of the man easing.

Mendez did not seem to hear him. "I knew Jacobi's father. I have to call him and tell him." He stopped for a moment to gather himself, then continued quietly. "Are you still so willing to believe in Adams' innocence?"

"I'm truly sorry about your people, Admiral. But it wasn't so much that I believed in Adams' innocence, but in his right—"

"I know." Mendez half turned away in frustration.

Kirk was at a loss. "Is there anything I can do, Admiral? The *Enterprise* can help in the search."

The admiral shook his huge head, his anger turned to resignation. "No." He looked up at Kirk. "There's no reason for the *Enterprise* to be involved in this matter any further. Your people have already been placed at risk once, at my order."

"I appreciate that, Admiral," Kirk said, quite sincerely. "But we stand ready to help if you need us."

"Do you have anyone down on the surface now?" Mendez asked.

"A handful on leave."

"Get them aboard now. Adams is down there somewhere. If I were you, I'd get my people off star base before there's any chance of the disease spreading."

"I'll do that, sir," Kirk answered. "We'll warp out as soon as I can get all my people up."

He had no way of knowing that he was already too late.

"Are you feeling any better?" Stanger asked solicitously. He was feeling quite a bit of guilt by this time. He had not realized the effect such a tiny bit of alcohol would have on an Andorian's system, else he would not have encouraged Lamia back in the bar.

The attempt to find a dance hall had given way to a need to find Lamia some fresh air. She would not admit to feeling ill, but when Stanger suggested they take a stroll instead and try to find Lisa, she had jumped at the chance. They'd barely made it to the ring of trees when Lamia had made it clear she wanted some privacy.

Stanger rubbed his arms and steadfastly ignored the sounds of gagging that came from a few yards away. The night was colder than it was on most star bases, but perhaps that would help to clear Lamia's head. He felt dreadfully guilty that he didn't have an antihangover pill, not even an aspirin, to offer her. Not that it would stay down, anyway.

When she emerged from the shadows again, he could see even in the thin light that her face was a paler shade than usual, and that she was shaky. "Come on. Let's get you up to sickbay, or tomorrow you'll be even sorrier. Dr. McCoy can give you something to keep you from getting any sicker."

"No," she said, her voice thin but resolute. "Let's call Lisa first and tell her we're leaving. Otherwise, she might worry about us."

Stanger raised his eyebrows. "What could possibly happen to the two of us down here?"

"I don't know." Lamia closed her eyes and swayed where she stood; he went over to her and took an elbow.

"All right," he said. "I'll call her. But first, you sit."

He lowered her next to a tree before taking out his communicator and setting it to Lisa's frequency. "Stanger to Nguyen . . . Lisa, this is Jon. Come in, please."

A hailing override whistled shrilly in his face; he nearly dropped the communicator. "What the—"

"Vigelshevsky here. Sorry to interrupt your conversation, Mr. Stanger, but it's imperative that everyone get up to the ship right away."

Stanger frowned. "We've still got three hours of leave left. What's the rush?"

"The captain didn't tell me, but from the way he's acting, it must be pretty serious."

Stanger sighed. It was just as well; if Vigelshevsky hadn't

called when he did, Stanger would have called and requested a beam-up himself. The next three hours weren't going to be much fun, regardless of where he spent them. "Could you contact Ensign Nguyen for us? She's supposed to be with our group, but we got separated. Ensign Lamia here isn't feeling well and I'd like to get her up to sickbay ASAP—"

"Nguyen's already on board," Vigelshevsky answered, with such an odd note in his voice that Stanger immediately asked:

"Is she okay?" When no answer came, he added, "Lisa and I are good friends. If something's wrong, she'd want me to know."

"Well," Vigelshevsky answered reluctantly, "if you're her friend, you'd better talk to her. She's in trouble."

"*Lisa?* You're kidding. What for?"

"She tricked Kyle into beaming her directly to her quarters. They could *both* get a demerit for that."

Stanger shook his head in disbelief. "It's got to be some kind of mistake. That doesn't sound like Lisa at all."

"And—swear you won't repeat this, ever—"

"I swear," Stanger said indignantly. "Look, I said I was her *friend*. I'm not the type to talk behind someone's back."

"She brought an unauthorized person aboard." There was a meaningful pause. "If anyone finds out—"

Stanger's face grew hot. "Even if Lisa met someone interesting down there, she'd have the good sense not to take him up to her quarters. I think Kyle better calibrate his sensors."

"Let's hope so," Vigelshevsky said, but he sounded unconvinced. "In the meantime, Kyle would really like to hear from her. He doesn't want to have to put her on report . . . he's hoping it was some kind of mix-up."

"I'm sure it is," Stanger replied firmly, to let Vigelshevsky know the subject was closed. He eyed the Andorian, slumped against the tree, head resting on her knees. He'd have to deal with Lisa's problem later. His priority was to get Lamia to sickbay and get her treated for alcohol poisoning. *You're just as bad for her as she is for you. Why don't you break things off before it gets any worse?*

105

He would have to do it. It was time to stop indulging himself, time to stop pretending he didn't realize what was happening to him . . . just as it had with Rosa. In the bar, it was clear that Lamia was becoming attracted to him.

It was time to stop things before anyone had a chance to hurt anyone else.

(*You mean before she has a chance to hurt* you, *don't you, Stanger?*)

Yes, dammit, that's exactly what I mean.

He'd have to firm with himself—and with her. He'd have to let her know exactly the way things were going to be. Later, of course, when she was feeling better.

(Coward)

To Vigelshevsky, he said, "I guess we're ready to call it a night, then."

"I'll tell Kyle."

Nguyen and her abductor beamed into the quarters she shared with Lamia. The lights were dimmed, so that they stood in twilight.

"The lights," the man said, loosening his grip and pushing her forward, toward the panel on the wall. The painting fell from her arms; she barely avoided stumbling over it. "Turn them off."

She turned her head just enough to see who stood behind her: an anonymous figure in a scarlet cloak, waving a phaser at her. *Little Red Riding Hood,* she thought crazily. *The wolf can't be far behind* . . . . She moved toward the wall slowly. There was a connection her mind was trying to make out of all of this.

Adams. This man was Dr. Adams. Stanger had told her about the bodies on Tanis with their throats cut, just like the woman on Star Base Nine. Somehow, Adams must have gotten away . . . and back onto the *Enterprise.* Stanger had told her how the man screamed at the sensation of light on his bare skin.

"Now," Adams snarled. Even the dim light must have made him uncomfortable.

She pressed the wrong code deliberately. The room was flooded with bright light.

He screeched, covering his eyes, and ran at the wall, as if to turn off the lights himself. She stepped aside, and when he pushed on the panel, darkening the room, she tugged at his phaser. She wasn't able to wrest it from him, but forced him to drop it. She could hear it slide across the floor. Adams scrambled after it.

Lisa didn't follow. She wouldn't have been able to see it in the dark, as he could. Her only hope was to turn on the light and blind him again before he could fire.

She did so, and was almost successful. She pulled away from the direction of the blast as it came, but the edge of it struck her, knocking her to the floor.

She was conscious, but temporarily paralyzed. She watched as Adams turned off the light, listened as he walked toward her, felt his thin, strong arms lift her and place her on the bed. It was impossible in the blackness to see his face, but she could sense him near her.

And then she heard a very strange sound . . . the sound of polished metal being slid along a soft surface. It took her a moment to identify it as the sound of a knife being pulled from its sheath.

Adams made a sound of pure, sensual pleasure. She could feel the cold, sharp edge of the blade rest against the warm skin of her neck, just under the left ear.

Fear would have been the normal response. But she felt frustration to the point of anger: she could have missed all this. She could have left yesterday, for Colorado, where she belonged. Right now, she should be with Rajiv and Zia and Rakel, but instead she was on the *Enterprise,* having her throat cut. All because she thought she wanted a career. And now she would miss out on ever having a family.

The pressure against her neck increased gradually—

Why doesn't he just get it over with? What does he think he is, a surgeon?

—until she felt the blade break through the skin.

With all her mental strength, Lisa summoned back the image of horses in the snow. She closed her eyes to the pain and darkness, and tried not to feel what was happening to her.

"You could at least have come by sickbay if you knew you were going to drink." Dr. M'Benga's South African lilt had taken on a disapproving tone. He frowned down at Lamia, who was sitting up on one of the diagnostic beds. "Andorians have no business drinking alcohol anyway. You absorb it into the bloodstream too quickly. Do you realize all it takes to reach toxic levels?"

Lamia hung her head, which was just beginning not to hurt so badly after the injection M'Benga gave her. The room had finally stopped rotating, too. "Lisa was right. I shouldn't have swished it around my gums."

M'Benga stared, confused, and opened his mouth to say something else, but Lamia interrupted hastily: "I know. I should have come by for something. But I really hadn't planned on drinking anything until I got down—"

"Just a minute." M'Benga got up, went into the pharmacy, and reappeared with a small bottle of pills. "Here. If you ever go on leave again, take these with you. One of these taken before you start drinking will slow down the rate of alcohol absorption into your blood."

"I don't ever intend to drink again," Lamia said in a small voice. She was truly embarrassed in front of M'Benga and Stanger, who stood nearby. She slid off the bed onto her feet. "Thank you for your trouble, Doctor. Can I go to my quarters now?"

"Yes." The disapproval on M'Benga's dark face did not ease. "But you're taking the pills. Another ounce of alcohol without the proper precautions and you could have died, young lady."

"I'll take them," Lamia said, aware that she was flushing bright blue, "but I'll never do anything stupid like that again." At least, she thought morosely, not for a while. It was never long before she caught herself doing something irresponsible again.

"It's really all my fault," Stanger blurted, his voice strangely bitter. M'Benga and Lamia both frowned at him. "It really is. I encouraged her to drink. I was stupid. I didn't realize how little alcohol she could handle."

"That's not true," Lamia protested angrily. She didn't

need Stanger to take her blame, though she appreciated his offering.

M'Benga sighed. "Regardless of who's at fault, I just want both of you to promise me it won't happen again."

She and Stanger exchanged guilty glances. "It won't," Lamia said. She meekly took the pills M'Benga proffered.

Outside sickbay, she and Stanger walked the same way for a while, since their quarters were both on D deck. As Lamia began to feel almost herself again, she sensed that something was definitely wrong with Stanger. Nothing that she could put her finger on, but he walked silently next to her, his expression troubled and withdrawn.

Could it really be that he felt that upset about what happened? That he was really so worried about me? The thought brought with it a warm flood of gratitude. They stepped onto the lift, and she looked over at him and smiled.

"I really *am* feeling better."

He glanced at her and then dropped his gaze, his voice still sounding strained. "M'Benga said you could have died."

She was flattered by his apparent anguish over what she felt was a minor incident. "M'Benga was being dramatic," she said. It was partly true; she knew she hadn't had a fatal amount. She had gotten terribly ill back in her Academy days from too much beer at a party, and she knew this time she wasn't nearly as drunk. "I was just a little sick. I can be trusted not to kill myself."

"Well, I knew you were upset about . . . your family situation. I didn't know if that had clouded your judgment a little."

"Actually, I'm not that upset anymore. You and Lisa have been very nice to me. You've been a real friend." She reached out and stroked his hand.

Startled, he pulled it away as if her touch had burned him.

"Jon!" she cried, half angry, half cajoling, unable to fathom his reaction. He seemed almost . . . frightened. "What's wrong? What did I do?"

The lift door opened and he stepped out quickly and

started walking, so that she had to hurry to catch up to him. "It's not that you did anything, Lamia," he said darkly. "It's not you at all. It's me." He took a deep breath, tried to meet her eyes, and failed. "It's just that I don't think we should see each other . . . socially. My life has enough complications as it is right now."

"Complications?" In the rush of adrenaline, she entirely forgot about any lingering discomfort caused by the alcohol. She stopped in her tracks and stood seething, her fists clenched so tightly the knuckles seemed on the verge of popping through the skin. "Is that how you see me? As a complication?"

"Lamia, *please.*" He kept his voice low and glanced uneasily around as if embarrassed. "Don't make this more difficult than it has to be. Come on."

He reached for her arm, but she pulled it away angrily and started walking very fast. "You treated me like your friend, once, but when I try to be nice to you in return, you freeze up." She threw her arms up in total exasperation. "What is *wrong* with you?"

His mustache twitched, but he said nothing.

"Come on, did I violate some sort of Terran taboo?"

"No." He stopped abruptly as the corridor forked in two directions. "Look, I just don't want to talk about it, okay? It's late. I'm going to head for my cabin and try to get some sleep."

"You're going to leave it at this? After helping me about Tijra, you're just suddenly going to tell me you'd rather not be my friend?" She didn't, of course, believe it for an instant. He was acting strangely because she must have said or done something that so totally violated Terran custom that he couldn't even bring himself to tell her about it. Certainly it couldn't be the simple, cruel fact that he didn't want to be friends.

"Yes," he answered uncomfortably. "Look, be sure to buzz before you walk in on Lisa."

She stiffened. Was this yet another insult? "What do you mean by that?"

"Just be sure to buzz," he repeated, and disappeared in the direction of his quarters.

Humans! she wanted to scream in frustration, but she stood, stunned, and watched him go. No, it couldn't be as he'd said, it simply couldn't be. She'd had the strength to deal with the disowning because she'd found a new family of sorts in Stanger and Nguyen . . . and now for him to suddenly say she meant no more than a stranger to him was as painful as reading *Tijra's* message for the first time.

You are no longer ours.

Don't think about it, don't . . . At least you've still got Lisa. She's your friend. There's always Lisa . . .

She held on to the thought. She could always talk to Lisa . . . and maybe this was for the best. Lamia had become so caught up, first with *Tijra's* message and then with Stanger, that she'd been ignoring how quiet Lisa had been for the past day or so. She would show her friendship by trying to get Lisa to talk about what was bothering her. And in that way, Lamia could forget her own pain. She headed in the direction of their cabin.

The corridor lights were muted in deference to the concept of night. Lamia stopped at the door to her cabin and buzzed first, to permit Nguyen a second of privacy, then punched in the code that unlocked the door.

It slid open. At the same time, a cloaked figure pushed past her, causing her to stumble in the doorway.

"Hey!" she yelled, more from indignation than surprise. Humans on starships had impeccable manners; she had not been pushed so rudely in years. She recovered her balance and wheeled around, intending to pursue the unknown offender. Perhaps it was a thief—but then, why would anyone steal anything aboard the *Enterprise*? And why was the room behind her pitch black?

A low, soft moan caused her to peer back into the room and fumble for the light.

It revealed Nguyen, lying sprawled across the bed with blood on her throat.

Chapter Eight

KIRK WOKE IN the middle of the night, feeling unrefreshed after an uneasy sleep. Mendez and Adams had been foremost in his thoughts. While he still instinctively disliked Mendez for being a bully, at least now he understood the admiral's desire for revenge. For all intents and purposes, Mendez was in the clear, and Adams had quite obviously demonstrated himself to be a cold-blooded murderer.

So why couldn't Jim dismiss Adams' accusations against the admiral?

It was still hours before he was scheduled to go on duty, but he rose from the bed and took a uniform from the closet. He stepped into the pants and pulled them up. Two of Mendez's people, dead. Two researchers, dead. And how many more during the night on Star Base Nine?

Why are you still worried about anything that murderer said?

He was glad to have left Star Base Nine and Adams behind. He would like his involvement with the Tanis affair to be finished.

The intercom whistled. Kirk pulled the tunic over his head and punched the control. Vigelshevsky appeared on the screen, looking haggard.

"Still on duty, Lieutenant?" Kirk asked.

"Yes, sir," Vigelshevsky answered listlessly. His pale beige eyes were bloodshot. "But Lieutenant Uhura's scheduled to replace me in another half-hour." He cleared his throat and made a bleak effort to sound military. "Message for you from Fleet HQ. On a scrambled channel. I was going to apologize again for waking you, but I can see there's no need—"

"Thank you, Lieutenant."

Vigelshevsky's pale image faded away, replaced by the tanned, hearty one of Quince Waverleigh.

"Quince." Kirk couldn't help returning Waverleigh's smile. Talking to Quince cleared his head like a gulp of fresh air. "What news have you got for me?"

"Hot stuff, Jimmy. Hot stuff." Waverleigh's gray eyes sparkled. It was impossible to tell if he really had news or if he was just pulling Kirk's leg for the hell of it. "But if you're looking to lynch Rod Mendez, you may consider it disappointing."

Kirk sighed. "Don't count on it. I'm beginning to reconsider my opinion of him. He told me one of the researchers killed on Tanis was his son."

"Dang it all!" Quince feigned exasperation. "You've gone and stole my thunder. *I* was supposed to say that."

"Sorry."

"Well, at least you can understand now why Mendez was hot to bring Adams to justice. Rod had no living family, outside his son. He took advantage of his rank and came to bring Adams back. None of the brass raised a stink about his going to Star Base Nine, since he's considered pretty responsible. They knew he wouldn't try anything stupid like getting even with Adams on his own terms."

"Adams has escaped on Star Base Nine," Kirk said shortly. "I take it you haven't heard yet. He killed two of Mendez's men."

Quince's gray eyes dulled and became serious. He considered what Kirk had said for a moment. When he spoke, his tone was no longer breezy. "They never tell me anything here." He paused. "That's a lot of people to expose to Adams' illness. They'd better get a vaccination program together ASAP."

"There *is* no vaccine. But our people are working on it."

Quince shook his head. "I wish them luck, then. But there's more news, Jimmy. I do have a few tidbits, mostly about Adams."

"Let's hear them."

"First off, Adams has a criminal record. Fraud, embezzlement, that sort of thing. Nothing violent like murder, though. He operated under a couple of aliases. He was on the lam from the Denebians when he disappeared, apparently to go to Tanis. The Ph.D. in microbiology is no joke. Most of his scams involved convincing prospective investors that he'd just made some kind of biological breakthrough—some new cure or bioproduct—and he happens to be a whiz at computers to boot. Your basic criminal genius."

"So maybe he was working with honest researchers on Tanis," Kirk said, "and something went wrong." He paused. "Can you think of any reason why Adams would want to develop a virus harmful against either Vulcans or Romulans?"

A curious expression passed over Waverleigh's face. "Funny you should say that. One fact I uncovered about his past is that he was on a ship that made the mistake of stopping for repairs on a planet too close to the Neutral Zone. The Romulans disputed ownership of the planet, and said so by way of attack. As a result, Adams has artificial intestines. I suppose he wouldn't be kindly disposed to Romulans."

"Quince. I don't know how to thank you. Could you relay that information about Adams to whoever handles his case?"

"Will do." Waverleigh shrugged. "No problem, Jimmy. I'm just disappointed that I didn't dig up anything more exciting. I was hoping for some intrigue. There *is* that Starfleet file on Tanis, but it's probably just some intelligence on Adams' latest scam. Admiral Tsebili has clearance to look at the file, so I've turned it over to him."

Kirk's stomach knotted. "Are you sure that's wise? I don't think this should go any further than the two of us."

"Relax." Quince snickered at the implication. "Adams really got you paranoid, didn't he? You know you can't trust anything he's told you. Besides, I've known Bili for years. We can trust him to be discreet."

"I hope so." There was no more time to worry about it; Kirk's eyes were drawn to the message flashing at the bottom of the screen. "Is that everything, Quince? I've got to go. My sickbay's trying to get through to me with an urgent message."

"That's everything. Bili should have something for me by the end of today, maybe tomorrow. Translated into your time—between six and twenty-four hours. You'll hear from me as soon as I know something. Old Yeller says hello. Waverleigh out."

His image faded to dark. Kirk pressed a control and McCoy's face appeared, covered by a glittering energy field.

"My God, Bones. What's happened? A break in decontam?"

McCoy did not answer the question. "We've got a big problem here, Jim. Give me five minutes to disinfect the place, then get down here."

"I'm not waiting five minutes without knowing what's happened."

"All right, then. Ensign Lisa Nguyen of Security was attacked and almost bled to death. We think Adams did it."

"Adams?" Kirk repeated, trying to make sense of what the doctor had just said. He saw a flash of an image—Lisa Nguyen on Star Base Nine, lying bleeding in an open park. . . . "Who found her?"

"The Andorian security guard—uh, what's her name?"

"Lamia," Kirk said intently. "She got her to sickbay?"

"Yes, but don't worry about contamination." McCoy put a finger to the tip of his nose in an attempt to scratch it, realized it was a useless effort, and tried gently rubbing it instead. "Lamia called sickbay immediately. M'Benga took the proper precautions. The medics who brought Nguyen here wore field suits, and we closed off the affected corridors. They're being decontaminated now."

"And the transporter room," Kirk said automatically. Of course.

McCoy blinked at him. "Why the transporter . . . ? Oh, I think I see what you mean. The transporter room wasn't contaminated. Nguyen and Adams were beamed directly up to her cabin. That's how he managed to get past Kyle and everyone else."

Kirk frowned. For a moment, his mind refused to register what the doctor was saying; and then, instantly, he understood . . . and was not at all pleased with the conclusion. "You're telling me Adams attacked Nguyen *here?* On the *ship?*"

McCoy seemed honestly surprised. "I thought I told you. Nguyen was attacked in her quarters."

"No, you didn't."

"I could have sworn—"

"It hardly matters, Doctor. Is Adams still on board the *Enterprise?*"

"It certainly looks that way," McCoy said, looking decidedly uncomfortable. "I'm sorry if I—"

"Has Security been notified?"

"No, that's why I was calling you, Captain, as soon as I could leave Nguyen—"

"How is she?"

"Unconscious. She lost a quarter of her blood volume. But she ought to be all right . . . as long as Adams didn't infect her."

"I'm calling Security," Kirk said. "Let me know when she's up for questioning. And the other—Lamia—"

"We're holding her here for a while, until we can check her blood test. Like I said before, she's probably immune, but it doesn't hurt to be safe."

"I'll want to question her. And Tomson will, too, probably. I'm calling Security to institute a search. I'll be sending them your way for briefing as far as quarantine precautions."

"We'll be here."

"I'll be there in five minutes. Kirk out." He punched a code into the screen: a priority override message directly to the security chief's quarters, and forced himself to ignore the fury that was growing inside him. He had no use for it now; it could only interfere with his efficiency.

"Tomson here." She answered the page immediately. Kirk flinched slightly as Tomson's image formed in front of him. He had expected her to block the visual for privacy's sake, since it was the middle of the night and she had no doubt been asleep. But she seemed wide-awake; in fact, she wore her uniform, leaving Kirk to wonder if she ever took it off. The only hint that she was off duty was her thin lemon-platinum hair, which streamed down her shoulders. It had never occurred to the captain that the tight bun was not its natural incarnation.

"Lieutenant," he said, "I have a job for you to do." It seemed to him that her cold eyes brightened.

He briefed her, and then he notified Spock. When he was finished, he snapped off the screen and let the anger take hold of him. He suddenly felt a great deal of sympathy for Mendez's position. If Adams were to suddenly appear before him, Kirk felt quite capable of strangling him with his bare hands.

Ten minutes later, McCoy sat calmly at his desk watching the Andorian security guard pace back and forth in front of him. *One more time,* he thought. *Let her pace in front of me just one more time, and I'll put her in an isolation booth and slap some restraints on her.*

She passed in front of him, one more time. McCoy did nothing of the kind.

This particular shift, McCoy could tell, was starting none too auspiciously. Chris Chapel's condition was worsening. It made absolutely no sense. Adams was running around the ship, killing people, and Chris lay in isolation, dying. He tried not to think the word, but it lingered unspoken in his mind nonetheless. Her physiological functions were weakening across the board. Her body was shutting down. She was dying.

McCoy could not accept it. She would get better . . . she *had* to get better. Adams had gotten better, and he was a psychopathic killer. Chris was one of the finest people McCoy had ever known; her recovery deserved to be resplendent.

Then, on top of everything, there was Nguyen. Thank God M'Benga had been the physician on duty and had insisted on doing the surgery. McCoy didn't have the heart for it today. Tonight. Whenever the hell it was. It wasn't even morning yet, but he had sent M'Benga to bed out of gratefulness, and M'Benga hadn't argued.

The doctor watched the Andorian pace back and forth one more time and tried as best he could to sound kindly. It wasn't easy; like all Andorians, her emotions were on the surface, and she saw nothing wrong in letting them show— though she tried to keep something of a handle on them for her human shipmates' sakes. *If she paces one more time,* McCoy thought again; and then he said, "Lieutenant Tomson has already been notified, Ensign. She'll understand if you aren't able to make it on duty—"

"Not go on duty!" Lamia sounded horrified at the thought. She was about to say something else, but broke off suddenly and snapped to attention at the sight of Kirk in the doorway. "Sir."

The captain gave her a perfunctory nod. "At ease, Ensign."

It was clear she was not; she began pacing nervously again, hunched over with her hands behind her back. McCoy shuddered.

Kirk took the seat across from McCoy's. "How is she?" McCoy realized he referred to Nguyen.

"She's all right." The doctor glanced in Lamia's direction. "The ensign here saved her life. Lamia notified sickbay immediately, but suspected Adams might be involved, so we were able to take the proper precautions. Lamia kept Nguyen from bleeding to death by following M'Benga's instructions." It was true, but he said it loudly so that she would hear and be cheered.

"Good work, Ensign," Kirk said softly, but she seemed too agitated to hear. "What about Nguyen? Is she conscious yet?"

"Just coming around." McCoy anticipated where the captain was leading. "I doubt she'll be able to positively identify her attacker as Adams, though. According to the ensign here, he wore a Vulcan robe with the hood up, and the lights were out."

"What about contamination?" Kirk asked.

McCoy felt the slightest glimmer of amusement threatening to break through his depression; the captain had obviously become uncomfortably aware of the fact that everyone else in the room was suited up. "Relax, Jim. I'm still wearing a field suit because I had it on when Lamia and Nguyen got here. Just haven't thought to remove it yet. All of sickbay's been decontaminated, so you don't have anything to worry about." To reassure Jim, McCoy pressed the control on his belt and winced as the field disappeared with a *pop.*

Jim seemed noticeably relieved. "How soon will Nguyen be up for questioning? Tomson's probably on her way to talk to you about search precautions."

"She's still weak and shaken up. It must have been a hell of a shock."

"How about the disease?" Kirk lowered his voice as if he didn't want the Andorian to hear.

"We won't know for a few hours yet. It takes time to know how the immune system will react."

Lamia had started pacing again. She wheeled around to face McCoy with the slightest air of defiance. "I'm sure I don't have the disease, Doctor. After all, you were the one who told the captain it was okay to send me down to Tanis, weren't you?"

McCoy felt gravity pulling at the corners of his mouth. "I said that you were *probably* immune, Ensign. The virus is *probably* less of a threat to you than it is to us." He changed his tack as soon as he realized her expression was becoming more defensive. He forced himself to smile. "Ensign . . . the effects of Nguyen's sedative should be wearing off by now. It'd be best if a friend were there when she woke. Would you like to see her?"

It was true, after all, McCoy thought. No harm in killing two birds with one stone. It would be best for the patient, and it would get the anxious Andorian out of his office for a little while.

Her face brightened. "Yes . . . yes, please. I promise, I won't say anything to upset her."

McCoy glanced at Jim, who shrugged. "If you think it's

best, Doctor. Tomson and I can probably wait two minutes." But there was a light in the captain's eyes. He knew what McCoy was doing.

"All right," McCoy said. "You can go see her."

They both watched her leave. "They must be very good friends." Kirk's voice sounded grim and distracted.

"Let me guess." McCoy finally got up out of the chair and stretched, feeling stiff and old. "Thinking about Adams."

"Aren't you?"

McCoy grunted. Thinking about Adams . . . and what he'd done to Chris. And wondering how many others would follow.

"What precautions can we take?"

"Not that many." The doctor shrugged. "Let's be honest with ourselves, Jim. If Adams has free run of the ship, no one can know where he's been. Any area could be contaminated." He had a sudden, ridiculous image of four hundred people jammed into isolation. "If Adams is sighted, we'll have to quarantine the area immediately, decontam it, and hope for the best. But there's no real way to ensure against someone getting infected without knowing it . . . and infecting others before he even realizes he's ill."

"There's got to be more we can do."

"Everyone can't go around wearing field suits indefinitely." McCoy sighed. "Other than that, there's not much more we can do, except tell folks to sleep with their doors locked. That rules out Mr. Spock, of course, but then, I don't think he's Adams' type."

Kirk did not smile. "How's Chapel?"

"It shows, does it?" McCoy folded his arms and looked down at a corner of the room. "Not well. Not well at all, Jim. It doesn't make any damn sense."

"I'll find Adams," Kirk said, in that very quiet tone that McCoy found frightening. "And when I do, I'll *force* him to make sense out of it."

The lights in the isolation unit were slightly dimmed. Inside, Lisa lay on the bed with her eyes closed. Awake and on her feet, she had impressed Lamia as being strong and sinewy; now, she seemed small and frail. Her normally almond skin was ashen, and there was a seam under her right jaw where M'Benga had sealed the wound.

The sight of her friend so close to death pained Lamia greatly; yet, at the same time, she could not look at her without a sense of joy. Lisa would live because of what she, Lamia, had done. It was an act as worthy as bringing a new life into the universe. Even her family on Andor could not disagree. Lamia wished there was some way to share this with *Tijra.*

"Lisa?" Lamia said softly, and tapped the window. Then, feeling foolish, she saw the intercom below the glass and switched it on. "Lisa?"

Lisa opened her eyes. She had not been asleep.

Lamia smiled brilliantly at her. She had come very close to total despair at the thought of losing Lisa, so close after losing *Tijra,* and Stanger. *Not so. You didn't lose Stanger. You never had him. . . .*

But Lisa would live. Lamia still had a friend aboard the *Enterprise.*

"Lamia?" Lisa whispered hoarsely. Her eyes were dark and frightened. "Where am I? Is this sickbay?" Her fingers went to her throat, to the cut that was already healing and would leave no scar. Without warning, her face crumpled and she burst into heaving, voiceless sobs.

The Andorian's antennae drew back in sorrow. She pressed a hand against the glass, unable to comfort with a touch. "Lisa. Poor Lisa, don't cry. You're all right. Dr. McCoy says you're going to be just fine."

"Then why am I in *here?"* Huge tears ran down her face, unsettling her friend greatly—on Andor, no creature wept. "It was Adams, wasn't it?"

"Yes," Lamia said.

"Then I've got his disease. Don't lie to me, Lamia. You're a terrible liar."

It was true. It was simply not in her nature to lie. Nguyen wouldn't have believed her if she did, so Lamia told her the truth. "We just don't know, Lisa. Dr. McCoy doesn't have the lab results yet. We both might have it." She kept her glowing hand next to the glass while Lisa wept silently.

121

"I'm sorry," Lisa sobbed. "You helped me, didn't you? If you get sick—"

"They're almost positive I'm immune. If I did get sick, it probably wouldn't be serious. It's going to be all right, Lisa. I have a feeling, I really do, that you're going to be okay. And Stanger and I will come visit you until you're well enough to go back on duty." Stanger. Why did she bother to mention him? He would probably decide that it was too inconvenient to visit Lisa . . . *too much of a complication,* Lamia thought bitterly. "I'm your friend, and I'll take care of you." She had said it to make Lisa feel better, but it only seemed to make her cry harder.

Lisa managed to stem the flow after a bit, and wiped her eyes with the back of her hand. "Thank you. You've been so good to me."

"You'll be back on duty before you know it," Lamia prattled on, "wishing for shore leave again. You'll see."

Lisa tried to shake her head, but the discomfort made it impossible. "No," she whispered, and closed her eyes.

"You don't mean that, Lisa. I care about what happens to you. You've got to get better. You can't . . ." Lamia's voice caught. "You can't leave me."

"No," Lisa said again. She closed her eyes and would say no more. Lamia was uncertain whether the pain reflected on her friend's face was emotional or physical, or both.

The Andorian took her hand from the glass. "You'll feel differently soon. You're in pain and frightened now." She said it to reassure herself as much as Nguyen. "When you feel better, I'll come see you again."

Lisa still did not answer. Lamia turned and left, telling herself that her friend was still hysterical from the trauma of what had happened. Lamia would be patient, would visit Lisa every day, would show her that she had people who cared for her on the *Enterprise.* She refused to lose Lisa now, because if she lost her, there would be no one left.

After the captain and Tomson had left and gotten what information they could from Nguyen and Lamia, McCoy confined the Andorian to a corner of sickbay and then shut himself in his office to reflect on his particularly foul mood.

Maybe he'd caught it from Jim, or maybe it was just the fact that they both realized that as long as Adams was tiptoeing around the *Enterprise,* there was the very real chance McCoy might run out of empty isolation units. Then there was the fact that he'd checked on Chris again and found that her pulse was inexplicably slowing. Stimulants seemed to help somewhat, but there was nothing he could do for the bizarre changes in her brainwave pattern. He turned on the alarm system so that if there were any changes in her life functions at all, he would be summoned from his office.

He huddled over his desk miserably and thought of how he missed her. He kept half expecting her to walk by so he could say: "What do you think is holding up that lab report on Lisa Nguyen?"

Or he could talk to her about the astonishing development of coma in the early stages of the disease. But she wasn't there. If he just had more knowledge of the early symptoms—if there were just some way to question Adams about it . . .

His lip curled sourly. He ought to go to the lab and help with the blood tests or the vaccine—he'd had word they were within hours of coming up with something—but he felt like staying at his desk and moping.

Nguyen's reaction to her attack and possible infection was another good reason to feel mean. The woman was completely dispirited and broken, sobbing before McCoy even got the words out of his mouth. Her tears rendered McCoy helpless. She even refused to listen to his upbeat lecture about how the lab was *this* far from a miracle cure.

He struck the intercom with his fist. "Lab! How long before that report on Nguyen and Lamia?"

Tjieng answered. Her voice sounded very tired. "It'll be a few hours, Doctor. We're pulling double shifts today; the vaccine is top priority. Or would you rather everyone got a toxic dose and be done with it?"

"Sorry, Chen." It was as close to the proper pronunciation as he could get. He propped his head on an elbow, slumped on the desk. "I don't mean to be such a pain. Maybe I'll be over in a bit and give you guys a hand—"

"I know what you're like when you get this way," Tjieng

continued wearily, but he heard the undercurrent of teasing. "Maybe you'd better stay and take care of your patients. If they can survive your mood."

"Well, I'll only come if I cheer up, okay? Keep me informed."

"You know I always do."

"I know," McCoy said, sounding conciliatory. It paid to stay on Tjieng's good side. "McCoy out."

He looked up to see Spock standing outside his door. And that, he decided, was just one more reason to be in a sour mood. "Come in," he said, feeling wary.

The Vulcan stepped inside, his expression composed but his tone hesitant. "Dr. McCoy, I have come to ask for a favor."

"Well! A historic occasion," McCoy said, aware that his sarcasm was quite lost on Spock. He motioned with his arm. "Come in and take a seat."

Spock entered, but he said, "Thank you, Doctor. I prefer to stand." And then he said, "An."

"I beg your pardon?"

"The correct phrase is 'an historic occasion.'" The Vulcan's expression was completely serious; McCoy glared at him, searching for a glimmer of humor beneath the mask.

Unable to find one, he said, "Forget I ever said it. Just get to this favor, will you?"

"Very well. I would like you to run some lab tests."

McCoy raised a brow. "You feeling poorly?"

"Not at all. I'd like for you to culture the virus in my blood to see how it affects Vulcans."

"I assume you're talking about a sample of blood, not what's circulating around your body at the moment."

"Precisely."

McCoy leaned back in his chair. "Chances are, even if Vulcans aren't affected, you might be. After all, you're half human." He expected Spock to take mild affront at that, to point out that the doctor never missed a chance to remind him of that fact; but the Vulcan took no offense.

"That is a fact. But what I'm suggesting is that you filter

124

out the human elements and test the virus on the Vulcan elements in the blood."

"I don't get it." McCoy frowned. "Isn't the point to find out whether you're immune, whether you have to take precautions—"

"Actually, I am somewhat curious, of course, but that is not the reason for my request." He paused, and the way that he paused made McCoy brace himself for a surprise. "After piecing together the data recovered from the Tanis computers, I have learned that a Vulcan researcher was the first to die on Tanis as the result of a mysterious illness."

"A Vulcan researcher . . ." McCoy was aghast. "But Spock, aren't you fairly certain that they really were working on bioweapons down there?"

Spock nodded.

"Well—excuse me for mentioning it, but don't Vulcans consider it a tad immoral to create the means by which others kill?"

If Spock felt any discomfort at considering this, he failed to show it. Calmly, he answered, "I do not know. I prefer to think he was somehow . . . uninvolved with what went on."

"Uninvolved? What was he, a casual observer? If he didn't tell anyone, then he's as guilty as the rest."

Spock folded his arms behind him. "Possibly. Regardless of his degree of involvement. Dr. McCoy, would you be willing to run the tests for me?"

McCoy waved his hand in a whatever-I-don't-care gesture. "You don't need me. You could ask the lab to do this."

"I did. They informed me they're too busy developing the vaccine."

"Well, that's a fact. But there's a logical gap, here, Mr. Spock. You haven't finished explaining what the Vulcan researcher has to do with any of this."

"Oh. I presumed the connection was obvious."

"Maybe it is. Maybe I'm just stupid and you have to explain it to me," McCoy retorted, and then felt like biting his tongue off for saying it. Spock gazed calmly at him, and

125

though his expression did not change, there was an unmistakable flicker in the dark eyes.

"I see," the Vulcan said, and though he did not say, *as I had always suspected,* McCoy understood it. "Records seemed to indicate the Vulcan's body is still in stasis on Tanis. He may have died from the same virus that infects Adams, or he may have died from an entirely different microbe."

The doctor leaned forward suddenly over his desk. *"Two* viruses? Isn't *one* bad enough?"

"Certainly. But if we want to understand what happened on Tanis, the logical thing to do is to recover the Vulcan researcher's body and ascertain what virus killed him. If the two viruses are related . . ." Spock stopped abruptly, as if unwilling to take the idea any further.

"If they're related, then what?" McCoy pressed.

"Then we have more reason to believe that Starfleet is involved."

McCoy started to open his mouth to ask how the hell Spock had come to *that* conclusion when a sharp beeping came over his intercom. He leaped from his chair, ignoring Spock's quizzical look.

"Doctor?" the Vulcan asked, but McCoy was already out of his office and passing through the quarantine entrance to Chapel's isolation unit. The fact that he was still wearing his field unit on his belt saved him several seconds; he switched it on, then entered the proper codes with furious haste. It took him less than fifteen seconds to don an infrared visor and arrive at Chapel's side.

Chris lay silently in the darkness, as she had for the past eighteen hours. Above her head, the function monitors glowed brightly.

Every one of the indicators had dropped to zero.

"No," McCoy whispered vehemently, with only himself to hear. It was not happening. Adams was alive . . . Adams was strong enough to kill people. It was not right that the virus could kill someone like Chapel and leave Adams alive. He keyed up more stimulants from the pharmacy, pounding softly on the wall slot until they arrived. He administered the drugs, and when each of them failed, he summoned the

life-support complex from the ceiling and lowered it over Chris' chest.

It worked, sort of. It provoked Chris' heart into beating again. It filled the lungs with air and emptied them, and removed waste products from her blood.

But it could not produce brain waves for her. And Chris' brain was dead.

Chapter Nine

ADAMS LEANED AGAINST the wall of the darkened turbolift and felt the strength bleed out of him. He slid, trembling, until he half sat, chest level with his knees. He did not understand this sudden surge of weakness; he had fed off the security guard only a few hours before, and before that, off the border patrol officer. Perhaps he was finally dying.

At the thought, he was filled with terrible fear. He felt as if he were drowning, like a fish out of water, starving for air in the midst of an ocean of oxygen.

The angry buzz of the intercom made him cringe. They had caught him; they would bring him out into the light to die. But no, it was only a recorded message that directed him to start the lift moving again, before the alarm was tripped. Adams grabbed the railing, pulled himself unsteadily to his feet, and started the lift in motion without any clear idea where he should go.

And then an instant of clarity descended on his hunger-fogged brain. "Sickbay," he told the lift's computer.

It deposited him on the proper level. The bright lights in the corridor pained him; he drew the hood forward so that it hid his face and followed the markings along the top of the bulkheads to sickbay. To his amazing good luck, he ran into no one along the way, a fortunate thing since they had probably already alerted the crew. He was within sight of

128

the entrance when it opened, and he fell back, flattening himself against a bulkhead.

From where he stood, he saw the back of the captain's head, and next to him, almost a foot taller, a pale, thin woman. They walked away, their backs to him, and he waited until they had gone.

It occurred to him then, in another rare flash of lucidity, that it made no sense to enter sickbay without a plan. He had a phaser, but it would be better to know where he was going.

Down the corridor he found an empty conference room; he sank into its darkness gratefully, settling in front of the computer terminal. He put his thin arms on it as if embracing an old friend and asked it a question. Many questions. The blood type of Jeffrey Adams. A listing of those with the same blood type and the location of their rooms.

The medical banks complied graciously with his request. Adams watched longingly as the list of names rolled past.

> STANGER, JONATHON H.
> YODEN, MARKEL
> TRAKIS, EVANGELIA
> ESSWEIN, ACKER M.

He memorized the first two names and then keyed up a schematic of the entire ship, and then a detailed schematic of sickbay, showing where equipment was stored.

Adams smiled to himself. Enthusiasm shored up his weakness. He had found a place to hide, and with Red's sensor-neutralizer, they would never find him. With her subspace transmitter, he would be able to call for help. And soon he would have a place to feed.

He began the more delicate work of overriding the computer security program that protected the locks on the cabin doors. Stanger's seemed as good a place to start as any.

That afternoon, McCoy sat mourning at his desk. If the night and morning had been a disaster, the afternoon had turned into a living hell.

Nguyen was still in isolation, awaiting test results. But the Andorian's questions had so irritated McCoy that he had sent her to her quarters. The field suit was enough protection against the virus . . . but not against his fingers around her throat. As soon as he realized what was happening to Chapel, he sent the Andorian away.

He had lost patients before. But when he had lost them, it had been because of life-threatening illness that had advanced too far, and McCoy and the patient had both known it. Or it had been an injury so extensive, so mutilating, that even modern medical techniques could not have restored a life worth living. And again, both McCoy and patient had been prepared for death, had seen it coming.

Chris had simply slipped away. She should not have gone into a coma; and once in the coma, she should not have died. For some inexplicable reason, the virus had acted on her system in an entirely different way than McCoy had observed in Adams. It had shut down Chris' systems, one by one. And McCoy had no way of stopping it, no way of explaining what was happening.

And since Chris had never wakened, he'd never even had the chance to say good-bye.

Oh, he'd managed to get her lungs breathing again, managed to keep her heart beating . . . but the brain wave stayed flat. In some strange way, he felt that he had been through this before, tried to argue for this before . . . and knew that he was wrong to keep Chris alive. She was gone. And yet, he could not quite bear to let her go.

He left her there on life supports and went into his office, where he did something he had never done before. He drank bourbon while on duty.

The problem was, he couldn't get drunk enough for it to help. He didn't want to get too drunk, because of Nguyen. She had recovered beautifully from surgery, but Tjieng had promised to have the lab results any minute now. It wouldn't look good for him to be passed out at his desk.

After two shots of whiskey, McCoy came to the conclusion that Chris simply couldn't be dead. He needed her. He had started missing her back when she went into the coma, and already sickbay seemed terribly empty.

130

The simple fact of the matter was, he loved her. Not romantically, of course; both of them had been hurt too much for that. But he cared about what happened to her. He loved her like family, and God knows, he didn't have much family to lose. No, Chris simply couldn't be dead. McCoy decided against taking her off life support. Adams . . . Adams knew what had happened to her. Security was bound to catch him soon, and when they did, he would be able to clear up the mystery.

McCoy heard steps outside his door. Tjieng? Had she come to bring the results in person? He opened a drawer with the thought of hiding the whiskey glass inside. But the steps faded away, and McCoy forgot them. If he could just get his hands on Adams for a few minutes . . .

The intercom buzzed jarringly at him.

He snapped it on. "McCoy here." Saying just those two words required a supreme effort.

"Tjieng here, Doctor." He could hear the sympathy in her voice, the unspoken apology for disturbing him, and he thought of the old saw that bad news travels fast. Hesitantly, she asked, "Is it really true . . . about Chris?"

"It's true." His voice sounded harsh and bitter to his own ears. "It's true . . . but she's still on life support. I keep thinking maybe Adams—maybe there's something about the disease, about the coma, that we don't know."

McCoy sensed implicit disapproval in her silence. *Go ahead,* he thought savagely. *Go ahead and say that I should just let her go.*

"It doesn't seem right somehow." Tjieng's voice was sorrowful. "But I have some good news."

McCoy did not even lift his head.

"Nguyen and Lamia. The two people from Security. Both tested negative."

"Negative," McCoy repeated. His mind registered the fact as a good thing, but it did not penetrate the layers of grief.

"You can release them from isolation. From what we gather, the virus is spread through contact, just as you suggested. Exchange of body fluids—blood, saliva—increases the risk of infection. But Nguyen has a strong

131

immune system. She managed to fight off the infection. She's a real survivor."

"So it's not that highly contagious." McCoy struggled to make the connections. "That's good. I'll relay that to Security. McCoy out." He started to close the channel.

"Doctor, there's more. We're distilling a vaccine for use now. I'll call when it's available for distribution."

"Good," McCoy said. He switched the intercom off before Tjieng could protest and leaned forward in his chair until his forehead rested against the cool, hard surface of the desk.

He ought to go tell Nguyen the good news; after all, she'd seemed so depressed. But he remained where he was, exhausted from grief. He heard someone outside the door again, and argued with himself to get up. Maybe someone was looking for him.

But at the moment he really couldn't give a damn.

Nguyen lay in the loneliness of the isolation unit and forced herself, once and for all, to stop weeping. The tears had been almost steady since she regained consciousness, and they both surprised and embarrassed her. She had always been an optimist, the type of person who overcame hard luck and never let it get her down, and the overwhelming depression that enveloped her now had so taken her off guard that she was quite unable to deal with it.

After an initial flurry, sickbay had become empty and quiet. McCoy had disappeared after showing her how to signal him, and she'd had a chance to think, to try to understand her reaction.

She had been horribly, terribly frightened, beyond all ability to reason. The fear still oppressed her: it hovered in the background, waiting for another chance to surface.

She'd been ashamed until she realized it wasn't the fear of Adams, or the dreadful fact of what he had done to her. Not at all.

It was the nearness of death, the realization that her life might be no more than what it had already been. That this was all there would be for her, and there was no more time for anything else.

132

When she'd first come to, she'd cried, from shock and sheer relief that she'd survived. The relief faded quickly, as soon as she'd realized that Adams had probably infected her. A lingering illness, with no cure, no certain fate in sight. It was not a cheerful prospect, but it brought with it the chance there might be time . . .

Then, this morning, Chapel had died. Nguyen tried to remember when Chapel had gotten sick so that she would know how much time she had left.

Her thoughts strayed again to Rajiv and the others. She wanted to write back, to let him know what had happened to her, to let him know that if she lived, she would do everything in her power to join him. But each time she tried to begin a letter, it came out sounding too melodramatic. *(Dear Rajiv, by the time you receive this, I will probably be dead. . . .)* And the glowing screen pained her eyes until she finally leaned back and closed them.

Outside her unit, the door to sickbay *swooshed* softly. She didn't open her eyes; whoever it was, she didn't care. While she knew that someone would be coming soon to tell her the test results, she had already convinced herself they would be positive so that when she was told, the disappointment would be less.

Light footsteps paused for a moment in the outer room, went past the isolation units, back into the storage areas. There was the sound of someone carefully going through equipment. Something surreptitious about the noise made Nguyen open her eyes.

The sound stopped. Whoever it was had apparently found what they were looking for. The footsteps headed back toward Nguyen again.

The man in the cloak paused. In the light, Nguyen could see the cloak's color for the first time—how opalescent quicksilver shimmered over the deep red velvet. As her mind registered its beauty, her body registered fear.

Her first response was to press the alarm on the side of the bed, but she stopped herself in time. If McCoy came immediately, Adams might kill him outright—or at the very least, the doctor would be exposed to the infection. If

133

only she could press the intercom next to the bed and whisper into it without Adams noticing . . .

But Adams stopped and turned slowly until the front of the hood faced Nguyen's isolation unit. She froze, motionless except for the insane beating of her heart.

Fingers emerged slowly from under the bell-shaped sleeve, touched the intercom, disappeared again.

A cold-hot thrill passed down her spine. If he came inside, there was nothing she could do now to stop him. He couldn't know the code, she repeated to herself like a prayer. There's no way he can know the entry code. . . .

"Care to join me?" Adams invited, and laughed weakly. He knew she would not summon McCoy. And then, smoothly, he swept out of the room. The door closed behind him.

Nguyen pushed herself up on wobbly arms and hit the intercom. "Dr. McCoy! No, don't come. Adams was just here—"

You're probably wondering why I've called you all here, Lieutenant Ingrit Tomson thought as she stood in the Security briefing room and stared at the eighteen faces— half of them sleepy, half of them not—that comprised the entire Security squadron. Of course she did not say it. Natives of her frozen home world, Valhalla, were supposed to be a cold and suspicious lot, even more humorless (some said) than the Vulcans. Tomson was indeed suspicious by nature—a definite advantage in her profession—and as far as humor was concerned, she kept hers in check. Especially at the moment; no point in causing these people any more cognitive dissonance than was necessary. Those who had been wakened in the middle of their night—Snarl and a handful of others—already looked confused enough. Except for Stanger. He gazed expectantly at Tomson.

She cleared her throat and stepped to one side of the podium, resting a milk-white hand on it. "The captain has informed me that we have an intruder on board. The evidence indicates that it is Jeffrey Adams."

She let the murmurs stop before she continued. "Adams attacked Ensign Lisa Nguyen and then fled. The transporter room and hangar deck have been alerted, but so far he has made no attempt to leave the ship." She paused for a moment to let the information sink in. Stanger made a move as if to stand up and say something, but held himself and kept his eyes focused intently on her. "Nguyen is all right. Her injuries were serious, but she was saved by the appearance of Ensign Lamia. Both Nguyen and Lamia are in sickbay, where they will remain until it is determined whether or not Adams infected them."

Tomson's voice was without inflection, but she said the words with true regret. She'd been watching Lisa Nguyen for a couple of years now, and of all her people, Tomson trusted Nguyen the most. She'd been planning to have her promoted to lieutenant, junior grade, to her second-in-command. It was not a decision she had made lightly. She liked Nguyen, and was sorry to see this happen to her.

Adams' appearance brought with it an additional problem: who was to assume command of the night-shift search. While Tomson was tempted to extend her own shift to twenty-four hours a day, she realized she would have to delegate. But Nguyen was the only one she trusted enough to delegate anything to.

"As usual, we'll split into two shifts. I'll be coordinating the first one. Those of you on duty will be assigned a specific area to search. First, though, you will report to sickbay for a briefing by Dr. McCoy on the necessary precautions." She paused. "That's it. Those of you not on duty are dismissed —but I want you here fifteen minutes before your shift so you can report to sickbay first."

The audience rose; the night shifters lingered for their assignments; the day shifters began shuffling out. All except Stanger. He stood off to one side of the podium. She stepped over and narrowed her eyes at him.

"Do you have a question, Ensign?"

"Yes, sir." His voice was lowered so that the others, who were speaking softly to each other, could not hear. "Who's coordinating the search for the night shift?"

Tomson let her lips press tighter together. She resented the question; she'd been hoping against hope that McCoy would call to say Nguyen had had a miraculous recovery. As

135

it was, she was forced to choose from among a bevy of junior-grade ensigns, none of whom had the seniority aboard the *Enterprise,* much less the experience. "I haven't made that decision yet."

"I'd like to offer myself for consideration, Lieutenant." If Stanger was still smarting from being chewed out the other day, he did not show it. *Handsome,* she caught herself thinking, looking at his dark, broad features, smoothly arranged in a display of respect and responsibility. For an instant, the face of al-Baslama flashed in front of her. She canceled the image immediately, but was left with an odd sense of hatred for the man standing in front of her. *You'd like to take Moh's place, wouldn't you, Stanger?* she thought with sudden resentment.

"I realize I haven't made a very good impression, Lieutenant, especially being late the other day," Stanger continued. "But in spite of any rumors you may have heard, I'm very competent. I've organized a number of searches in my day, and I'm damn good at it. I've been trying to think of a way to show you that, sir."

She gazed at him without answering for a moment. She often used silence as a means of unsettling people, but Stanger did not squirm. He simply stared right back at her.

"I need someone to supervise evening shift," she answered finally. "You're day shift." He started to say something and she silenced him with a look. "I need everyone on day shift I can get, with Nguyen and Lamia out indefinitely."

"Then let me do the next day shift, and the following evening shift. I'll take Esswein's place. He can rest up, and then take my place tomorrow morning."

She approved inwardly of his determination, but did not show it on her face. "You're either very sincere or very slick, Mr. Stanger."

"Both, sir," he said, straight-faced. "And determined. Nguyen and Lamia are my friends. I want to find Adams. Will you consider it?"

She used silence again, but again it failed to ruffle him. When she finally did speak, she was thinking more of Mohamed al-Baslama and his spotless record than she was

136

of Stanger and his feelings. "Acker Esswein will be temporary second-in-command," she said abruptly. "Quite frankly, Mr. Stanger, I can't trust you not to screw up again."

His expression did not change, but as she turned away, she thought she saw a shadow fall over his face.

Sulu settled in his chair at the navigation console on the bridge and tried to keep his mind on his work. It wasn't easy; Chekov had already laid in the course, and there was very little for a helmsman to do except sit and make sure that nothing went wrong with the equipment. And once they arrived at their destination in the Sagittarian arm, Sulu's greatest challenge would be to slow the ship to sublight speed in order to facilitate star-mapping. Such uninspiring work was bad enough on an ordinary day, but today there were other factors working to increase Sulu's restlessness: the shipwide alert in the middle of the night about the intruder on board, and the rumors about the attack on Nguyen and Chris Chapel's closeness to death. The truth was impossible to get. McCoy was talking to only a few, and those few weren't telling.

Sulu would have liked to discuss all this with Chekov, who sat next to him at the console, to see if the navigator had any insights or new information on the rumors. But the captain's dark mood had kept both of them silent.

And then McCoy had called the bridge. Sulu heard enough of it to know that Adams had been spotted in sickbay. Kirk left the conn in Spock's hands. The impassive Vulcan remained at his station, gazing serenely into his viewer at things Sulu could only guess at.

With the captain safely gone, Chekov shot Sulu a sideways look that the helmsman took as an invitation to talk. Sulu glanced apprehensively at the science officer's station. The Vulcan's hearing was sensitive enough to overhear them, no matter how softly they whispered, but Spock seemed far less likely to be irritated by it than the captain.

Sulu turned to face his friend. "So. Looks like we have an uninvited guest aboard. How long before you think we'll be turned around and headed back for Star Base Nine?"

The corners of the Russian's mouth crinkled upward,

giving his broad, boyish face an impish look. "Five credits says I'll have a new course laid in before lunch."

The helmsman considered it. "Why not?" He shrugged. "I've got nothing more exciting to look forward to."

"Except maybe a visit from our friend Dr. Adams," Chekov said mysteriously, his dark eyes acquiring the glint Sulu knew so well. Another Muscovite legend would soon be unleashed on an unsuspecting public. . . .

Sulu smirked skeptically. "I keep my door locked. Besides, what would Adams want with me?"

"The same thing he wanted from the people on Tanis, the same thing he wanted from the security guard." He leaned closer to Sulu and hissed, "Your blood."

"Come on, Pavel." Sulu laughed aloud in spite of himself, then looked guiltily around to see who had heard. Spock ignored them steadily, face still buried in the viewer; but Uhura glanced up from her communications console and gave Chekov a dirty look.

"Sorry." Sulu smiled at her. She looked back down at her board without returning the smile; she was probably worried about Nurse Chapel and, like the captain, didn't appreciate humor at this particular time. Sulu forced the smile from his face and turned his attention back to the navigator. "For God's sake, Pavel, don't be so theatrical. We all know Adams is psychotic, but Security will find him—"

"Security can do nothing about it," Chekov intoned. It seemed to Sulu that his Russian accent was growing thicker by the second. "Security knows nothing about dealing with"—he paused for effect—"wampires."

"Wampires?" Sulu felt entirely ignorant.

Chekov shook his head, irritated. "No, no, a *wam*pire."

"Oh. You mean a vampire." Sulu frowned. "I think I've heard of them. Isn't that a type of Terran bat that lives in South America?"

The stocky young man turned away, disgusted. "I'm not talking about bats." Then, with sudden inspiration, he fumbled under the collar of his tunic. "Here. *This* is what I'm talking about." He drew out a gold crucifix on a heavy chain.

"Pretty." Sulu gave a soft, low whistle. "But not exactly regulation. Where'd you get that?"

"A family heirloom." Chekov held it up by the chain so that the cross dangled hypnotically in front of the helmsman. "Very useful against wampires."

"Bats?"

"The undead. Creatures who return from the grave to drink the blood of the living."

Sulu shook his head and grinned broadly down at his console. "Pavel, I swear. Sometimes you're too much. I can never tell when you're serious."

"I *am* serious," Chekov said, slipping his crucifix back under his gold tunic, but the storyteller's gleam was still in his eyes. "Whoever is bitten is doomed to become a wampire as well. You'll see, Sulu. You'll come back to me for help."

Sulu just shook his head and grinned. Behind them, Uhura made a clicking sound of disgust. Spock continued to stare impassively into his viewer.

"Adams stole one of these portable transfusion units and some drugs." Hands trembling slightly, McCoy displayed the object to Kirk and Tomson in the outer room of sickbay. "Don't worry, we're safe in here. The lab report says the virus can only be spread through direct contact."

"That's a relief." Kirk studied the doctor with concern. It hadn't really been necessary for the captain to come down to sickbay for the second time that day—but Kirk wanted to see how McCoy was holding up after Chapel's death. The doctor looked as if he had barely managed to pull himself together, and exuded a faint aroma of bourbon. In the next room, the life-support equipment hummed softly in Chapel's darkened isolation unit.

"It should facilitate the search," Tomson said. "I'll let my people know they can forgo the field suits."

"Oh." McCoy rubbed his face as if trying to wake himself up. "By the way, I got the lab results on Nguyen and Lamia. They've both got a clean bill of health. Lamia's probably reporting for duty right now."

139

"Great." For a moment, Tomson seemed on the verge of smiling—but the uncharacteristic surge of warmth soon passed. "What about Nguyen? How's she recuperating from the wound?"

McCoy released a bone-weary sigh. "Physically, she's doing quite well. By tonight, she'll be able to return to her quarters. But she needs at least three days off duty . . . especially considering her poor emotional recovery. The attack seems to have taken all the spirit out of her. Even after I told her the good news, she—well, she seemed relieved, but it didn't seem to cheer her up all that much. She's still depressed and I'm not sure what's at the bottom of it." McCoy didn't seem to be doing all that well himself.

"Could I see her?" Tomson said suddenly. "I might be able to cheer her up some."

The disbelieving look McCoy shot Tomson would have struck Kirk as amusing under less disheartening circumstances. Tomson, with her forbidding exterior, seemed more likely to depress the most manic of optimists. "All right," McCoy said at last. "Guess it couldn't hurt." He motioned Tomson to the back room. "She's through here. You can go on in—she's awake."

Tomson disappeared through the doorway and McCoy turned to face Kirk. "That's all I know, Captain. I'll call you if anything happens."

"What about that vaccine?"

McCoy shrugged as if it were just another nuisance to attend to. "We should be distributing it to the crew by tomorrow afternoon."

"Good." Kirk did not turn to leave, but stood and stayed his ground, trying to think about how to broach the subject of Chapel.

The wall intercom whistled. "Bridge to Captain Kirk."

He walked over to the bulkhead and answered it. "Kirk here. What is it, Lieutenant?"

Uhura's voice sounded perplexed. "Something strange, sir. Just a second ago, I picked up an unauthorized transmission from within the ship."

Adams! But who was he trying to contact? "Location?"

"Tracing it now, Captain. But transmission has ceased. Whoever sent the signal may very well have moved to another part of the ship."

"Nevertheless, call me here as soon as you have the location. Kirk out." He switched off the intercom and turned back to McCoy.

"I guess you'll want to talk to Tomson about this." McCoy turned, swaying a bit unsteadily, and began moving away. "I'll be in my office."

"Bones—"

The doctor stopped, keeping his back to the captain. "What is it?"

"I think you know."

"I have no idea," McCoy said hostilely, without turning around.

"Christine Chapel. Has there been any change?"

"Not yet." McCoy tried to get past, but Kirk stepped forward to block his way.

"Doctor . . . I hate saying this as much as you do." It was true. Maybe he wasn't as close to Chapel as McCoy, but he felt her death keenly nonetheless. "Don't you think you owe it to her to let her go?"

He waited for the arguments McCoy would throw at him. That perhaps Adams could tell them something about the symptoms, that there were more tests to run on the virus. That perhaps it was some bizarre new effect of the disease they hadn't anticipated. Kirk had heard them all; he also knew the doctor didn't believe any of them himself.

But McCoy did not protest. Hoarsely, he said, "Just give me a little time, Jim."

Kirk hesitated. "All right. A little time." He let McCoy retreat to the dark safety of his office.

Lisa was riding a horse. She leaned forward in the saddle and put her hand on the animal's chestnut coat, feeling its strong, solid muscles rippling beneath her, breathing in its warm, dusty smell, along with the clean scent of Colorado air.

"Ensign?"

141

The horse stumbled. At the sound of Tomson's voice, Nguyen started and opened her eyes wide. She attempted to scramble to her feet, but gave it up quickly for an upright sitting position. Her head began spinning and she put a hand on it to make it stop.

"As you were, Ensign. Don't try to get up."

The dizziness began to recede. "Lieutenant," Nguyen said. "Sir. I didn't know you were coming."

"I didn't know myself until a second ago." Tomson found a chair and pulled it next to the bed. Seated, she was as tall as Nguyen was standing. "Dr. McCoy says you're recovering very rapidly."

"Yes, sir." Nguyen could hear the hesitation in her own voice. She was recovering, and it was a relief to be out of the isolation chamber . . . but she could not bring herself to think about going back on duty. She wanted to stay alone, in sickbay forever, to daydream about Colorado. She didn't want to have to make the choice.

"He also says that you seem . . . very troubled since the attack." Tomson shifted in her chair as if what she were about to say made her uncomfortable. "I hope it's nothing serious, Ensign. I need you back."

Nguyen did not answer. She did not want to come back. To say it was not serious would be lying.

"I've been watching you since you first came on board." Tomson folded her long thin arms in front of her, forming a protective barrier against what she was saying. "I'll be honest. I didn't expect much from you at first. But you've turned out to be a fine officer. I've recommended you for a promotion. I don't do that for very many people. When it comes through, I'm going to make you my second-in-command."

My God, Nguyen thought with an overwhelming sense of revelation. *You mean she likes me?* Suddenly, the lieutenant's expression assumed a whole new meaning. Nguyen could actually see the concern hidden in those pale, narrow eyes. She'd always assumed from Tomson's demeanor that the lieutenant despised her. But then, the indications were that Tomson despised everybody. "Thank you, Lieutenant," she stammered. "But there's something—something you ought to know. I'm thinking of leaving the Fleet."

"Oh?" The warmth fled from Tomson's expression, making it cold and mistrustful again.

Tell her you didn't mean it, her mind argued. *Don't be stupid. Just wait till you're sure.*

Nguyen was sure. She took a deep breath. "No. Not thinking. I'm positive. I'm leaving the Fleet."

"When did you come to this decision?"

"A little while ago."

"Nguyen . . ." Tomson's voice was actually gentle. "The attack shook you up. That's pretty normal. I'm sure you'll feel different later. You just need to give it some time."

Nguyen shook her head and was surprised to find that her voice did not shake at the thought of contradicting her superior. "No, sir. I've been thinking about it for a while. I—I've been invited to join a group marriage. I'm very fond of the people, but the rules are that I would have to leave the Fleet." Immediately, she felt embarrassed. Tomson would not understand something like that. Tomson could understand nothing but duty and career. She braced herself for the ridicule that was sure to follow.

It did not come. "Ensign." Tomson fixed her ice-blue eyes on Lisa's. "Do me a favor. Give it a week. Then tell me this again."

"Sir, my mind's—"

"Give it a week, Ensign." Tomson's gaze was piercing.

Nguyen sighed meekly. "Yes, sir." But, she reassured herself silently, it wouldn't make any difference.

"The time is 0610." The computer paused to raise the volume of its feminine voice by a decibel and then repeated its message: "The time is 0610."

Stanger opened one eye a slit and fought to extricate himself from a confusing tangle of dreams. 0610. That meant that the computer had been trying to coax him from the bed for the past ten minutes, its volume steadily increasing until now it thundered in his ear.

"The time is 0611."

"All right," Stanger croaked, and the computer stopped, satisfied. His mouth seemed incredibly dry, as if he were hung over, but he had not been drinking. He pulled himself slowly to a sitting position on the edge of the bed. It took an exquisite effort: his arms and legs felt heavy, too heavy to move, and for a second he thought he was back on Vulcan for special training, in the extra gravity and thin air.

Once up, he sat on the edge, his heart pounding with the exertion. Bits and pieces of the dreams began to come back to him: the darkness that was Tanis, the eyes of Lara Krovozhadny that stared up blindly at him, her body draped with another corpse as if with a blanket. And then her face wavered and became Lisa Nguyen's. Startled, Stanger directed his flashlight up into Jeffrey Adams' pale, desperate face. . . .

The dreams had exhausted him. He sat with his head cupped in his hands and tried to decide if he were late. He wasn't; since the run-in with Tomson, he had taken care to set the alarm a half hour early. He was still twenty minutes ahead of schedule. From the way he was feeling, he needed it.

He staggered off to the bathroom. The flu, maybe . . . perhaps he was coming down with the flu. He would go by sickbay before going on duty and get something for it. He could tell he already had a bit of a fever, because the light hurt his eyes.

He went to the toilet and then closed himself in the shower stall. A water shower, this time . . . he indulged in them only rarely, since they wasted time, but today it was therapy. And he *was* twenty minutes early. He stood under the hot water spray for a long time, letting it run directly on his face, to clear his head.

It did, a little. He began to feel more himself, to remember the day before, though the weakness stayed with him. More than just a rough night. He was definitely getting a cold.

He hoped to be out of the cabin before Acker got off duty. There was still a good chance he'd make it. Certainly, it wasn't Acker's fault; Acker hadn't done anything, but Stanger still was in no mood to talk to him this morning. He could still see Tomson's mistrustful expression, could hear her saying, *I can't trust you not to screw up.*

No, you can't, he told her, silently, angrily. *I'm too damn much of a fool not to. Too damn gullible, too damn willing to trust people I thought I knew.* Tomson had the right idea, after all. Why trust your underlings? Why give them the chance to turn on you, to damage your career when you weren't looking?

He made himself stop the train of thought immediately. He'd gotten very good at that lately, to keep from getting too bitter about things. He was very conscious of the fact that he was *not* thinking about Rosa. . . .

He turned off the water spray and pressed the control for dry, starting just a bit as the warm blast of air touched his skin, evaporating every last bead of moisture.

He stepped from the shower feeling tired and defeated. Tomson was not going to give him any kind of chance to redeem himself. And maybe she was right; maybe he didn't deserve one. Maybe he had to learn his lesson the hard way.

He squinted into the mirror. He was not looking all that well, either; the skin beneath his eyes was gray. He decided against using beard repressor and went over to the closet to pull on a uniform.

He refused to feel guilty about breaking it off with the Andorian. (It was easier to think of her that way . . . if he thought of her by name, it was somehow harder to maintain his distance.) It simply wouldn't do. There was no saying how long he'd be able to stay aboard the *Enterprise,* the way Tomson felt about him . . . or even, for that matter, how long he'd be able to stay in the service. Because if the *Enterprise* refused to keep him, he might as well just get the hell out. It was actually kinder to Lamia this way. (Damn. He'd let himself think her name, which always evoked her face. . . .)

It was stupid, damn stupid to let himself get involved with someone else, even if it was as platonic and one-sided as his friendship with Rosa. Besides, she wasn't even human. It was rough enough trying to work things out with your own species, without all the added intercultural headaches.

You fool, you miss her, don't you? Then it's a good thing you stopped before it got any worse.

He dressed, pulled on his boots, and left feeling very weak. On the way out, he noted with distracted curiosity that the electronic door lock had been canceled. He reprogrammed it in before he left and reminded himself to ask Acker about it.

Chapter Ten

QUINCE WAVERLEIGH PASSED through the anteroom to his office with barely a glance at the aide already seated at the terminal. He was nursing a spectacular headache this morning, no doubt due to the tequila he'd consumed the night before and the fact that he hadn't taken anything to prevent the hangover. It'd gone this way the past several days, each time with Quince telling himself that he wasn't going to be drinking that night, ergo the pills were an unnecessary precaution. And each night he drank anyway, punishing himself for it by not taking the pills.

He might as well admit that he needed to talk to the staff psychologist about Ke. Maybe this morning he'd get Rhonda to make an appointment for him. She'd been after him for weeks to quit pretending it had been a breezy transition.

"Morning, Rhonda," he croaked without looking at her. He'd ask for the appointment later. First, to the synthesizer outlet in his office for a cup of coffee. Rank, after all, had its privileges.

"Good morning, Admiral."

Quince stopped and turned his head—slowly, to keep the pain to a minimum—to stare. Rhonda had just answered in an uncharacteristically baritone pitch.

"You're not Rhonda."

The man in Rhonda's chair swiveled to face him. "Ensign

147

Sareel, Admiral." A Vulcan male, young—at least as far as Quince could guess; they all looked young to him until their hair began to silver—with a broad, square jaw and pointed chin. He had the typical Vulcan coloring—dark brown hair and eyes. "I am Lieutenant Stein's replacement."

"What, did she call in sick?" She'd seemed fine the evening before.

"It is my understanding that Mr. Stein was transferred."

"Transferred? Are you sure?" Now, what kind of major screw-up had Personnel pulled *this* time? Rhonda had been on temporary assignment, but he'd made it clear that she was to stay with him until his regular aide returned. "I want her back in this office immediately!"

He realized he was yelling and stopped himself. The Vulcan blinked twice, his face absolutely devoid of expression, and said, "Perhaps you should take this up with Admiral Tsebili."

"I'll do that." Quince stomped into his own office. The rise in blood pressure did nothing for his mood or his headache. He slumped into his desk chair and swiveled to one side to unthinkingly punch the code into the synthesizer.

Great. Just great. As if things weren't rotten enough, now he was going to lose Rhonda, too. The synthesizer panel rose and he picked the coffee up, cradling it in both hands. He let the steam rise into his face before taking a reverent sip.

Rhonda was one of the most efficient aides he'd ever worked with. Hell, after a month here she was as efficient as his regular aide, Bazir-om the Aurelian, had ever been. Quince had been sorely tempted to ask her to stay on permanently—but that wouldn't have been fair to Baz. Every officer had the right to take parental leave and come back to the same position, even if Baz *had* been sitting on those damn eggs for three months now.

Still, Quince wished he could figure out a way to keep her. It was more than just her efficiency. He got along with Stein. He could *talk* to her, and God knows he didn't have anyone to talk to, these days. Damn Personnel! He turned in his chair toward the aide's office.

"Ensign . . ." He'd already forgotten the man's name. "Do you know if Admiral Bili's in yet this morning?"

"Yes," the Vulcan answered clearly.

Wait a minute . . . Quince paused to rub his temples. Vulcans were so confounded literal-minded. Did that mean yes, Bili was in, or yes, he knows whether Bili's in? He couldn't deal with a hangover *and* a Vulcan aide in the same morning.

The ensign apparently picked up on his dilemma. "Admiral Tsebili is in this morning. Shall I raise him for you?"

"I can do it myself." God, he hated the kind of coddling that some brass insisted on. Bili was a good man, but he loved that sort of pomp and circumstance. Maybe Quince could find out where Stein had been transferred and talk Bili into taking this joker.

"Get me Admiral Tsebili," he said to the dark screen.

Bili's round head and shoulders appeared almost immediately on the terminal in front of him. It was still early enough for the admiral not to be tied up.

"Admiral Tsebili," Quince said respectfully, since Bili was a full admiral, two grades above him. It was an act. Bili had a pudgy, pink face with three chins, a thick crown of silver hair, and innocent blue eyes. He looked more like an aging infant than head of star base operations, and because of it, people had a tendency to forget his rank and not take him very seriously. But Bili had ways of making them do it. He earned his reputation as a stickler for regulations. Just last week, he had fired his aide for bringing Romulan ale to a staff party.

Quince learned early on that if he reminded Bili once a day of his superior rank and otherwise knew when to defer to Bili's opinion, he could generally get away with murder.

"Quincy. You seem to be moving slowly this morning."

"Got one whale of a headache. And the fact that a stranger is sitting in Rhonda's chair isn't helping. You know anything about that, Admiral?"

"Lieutenant Stein, yes." Bili brushed a hand against one plump cheek as if stroking his memory. "The aide in your office. She asked for a transfer."

"She *asked* for one?" His voice came out harsh, and he

149

softened it and added the rank so Bili would not be offended. "Admiral, are you *sure?* Rhonda said nothing to me—"

"Positive. I'm the one who put it through for her. She's starting in Personnel this morning."

"Personnel," Quince repeated, dumbfounded. He knew he'd been terribly moody since Ke and the kids left, but he'd thought Stein understood. He'd thought they were friends. Had he misread her so completely? Yesterday, she'd said good night same as always, in a perfectly cheerful mood. If she'd been hiding something, he would have known. Surely she knew how impressed he was with the job she'd been doing. In fact, just last week, didn't he say to her that if Baz didn't hurry up and hatch those eggs—

"Don't let it worry you, Quincy. Lots of temps request transfers. Speaking of temps, I was wondering if you'd mind if I borrowed your Vulcan from time to time. They're awfully efficient, you know—"

So was Rhonda.

"—and I haven't been able to find a replacement for my aide yet."

"Sure," Quince said unenthusiastically. "Use him all you want. Something about him gives me the willies." That was typical of Bili, taking forever to find a replacement. He would interview for weeks until he could find someone who would be able to put up with his compulsion for detail. "Say, have you interviewed him?"

"Oh, I couldn't take your aide, Quincy."

"Well, he's just a temp, Bili." Quince tried to sound altruistic. "I'm used to having them in and out of here, anyway. Baz will be back sooner or later."

"I appreciate that. Maybe I will." Bili's cheeks rose upward as he smiled, hiding all but a narrow slit of his eyes. "By the way, I'm glad you called. I had meant to tell you—that symposium set up for this weekend has been canceled."

"Oh." Quince felt mildly disappointed. Before Ke had left, he'd hated weekend symposiums. Now, they gave him something to fill the empty time with, something to keep

150

from being alone, even though they were generally boring at best. What was this one about? Something to do with Mendez, in fact. That's right . . . the installation of a new sensory and weapons system for star bases. Protection, of course. God forbid Starfleet should ever admit to designing offensive weaponry. "Why's that, Bili? Some glitch in the design?"

"Actually, no. We wanted to give it a test run somewhere. Rod's going to give me a demonstration."

"Well, that ought to be interesting. Why doesn't the symposium just take place out there, on the base?"

"Too late to reschedule. And we do, heh-heh, want to be sure it works before we get too many brass out there."

"Makes sense. Where you headed?"

"Star Base Thirteen or thereabouts." Bili smiled again. "Look, give the Vulcan a fair shake, will you? You're lucky to get one."

In his mind's eye, Quince saw the pleasurable but unlikely image of himself grabbing the ensign by his gold tunic and giving him a good shake. "Yes." He suddenly thought to ask if Bili'd had a chance to look at the Tanis file; but Bili was the sort who would have mentioned it if he had. He wouldn't take kindly to nagging from a subordinate, and besides, he'd been working hard to prepare for the symposium. Now that it was off, maybe he'd have a chance to glance at it today. "Yes, I guess I'm lucky. Well, thanks anyway, Admiral."

He let Bili close the channel first, and then he called Personnel.

Just as he suspected, Stein's face came on the screen first. "Personnel. Admiral Noguchi's office."

That made it easy. At least he wouldn't have to get switched through half a dozen morons who'd never heard of Stein and didn't know she was working there. He opened his mouth to say something and realized he had no idea what to say. He stared.

She stared back guardedly. "Admiral," she said. She was terribly young, probably twenty-four at the outside, attractive, dark hair pulled back with a clip at the nape of her neck and no makeup. Innocence and youth personified. Had they gotten to be *too* good friends? Had he said something she had misinterpreted to mean he was attracted to her?

Seeing her, it occurred to him that maybe he *was* attracted to her.

What the hell are you doing there? he wanted to ask. *Why didn't you tell me?*

"So, Lieutenant," he said. "You're in Personnel now, I see."

"Yes."

"Don't you think you're a little overqualified for reception?"

"Yes." Stein opened her mouth just enough to form the answer and then pulled her lips back into a thin line. Her expression reminded him of the Vulcan back in his office.

Damn it. Enough tiptoeing around. He'd never had the patience for it, anyway. "Stein, you're mad at me. Why?"

"Isn't it *obvious,* Admiral?" Her voice rose with barely controlled anger.

In the midst of his hurt feelings, he felt a twinge of admiration for her. Only Stein had the guts to let a superior officer know outright what she thought of him. She was wasted in a bureaucracy; what a hell of a starship captain she'd make. "I guess I'm a little thick. What exactly did I say?" Quince asked, eager to make things right. Whatever it was, he'd apologize.

"It wasn't what you *said.*" She looked and sounded disgusted at his obtuseness. "It's what you *did.*" She glanced around her as if worried someone might overhear, then her image on Quince's screen grew larger as she leaned closer to her own terminal. "I thought you were happy with my work. You never said anything about being displeased with it."

"Of course I'm not displeased with your work. I told you how very highly I thought of it." He was becoming thoroughly confused.

"Well, then why am I in Personnel this morning?" She looked ashamed, angry, and near tears all at the same instant.

"Well, dammit," he answered, exasperated at trying to

152

figure out what she was getting to, "that's what *I* called to find out. What the hell *are* you doing in Personnel, Stein?"

They glared at each other for a minute, Stein apparently every bit as frustrated as he. Her eyes grew larger and larger, and when he thought they couldn't widen another millimeter, she burst out laughing. *"You* didn't request the transfer?" she finally managed to gasp out.

"Hell, no, of course not," Quince said vehemently, and then it struck him what she was saying. He began to laugh with her, not out of a sense of amusement—the situation did not seem the least bit funny—but out of sheer relief. "You mean, you didn't ask for it yourself?"

"No." Stein was grinning from ear to ear. "Does this mean I can come back?"

"Consider it an order." For the first time in weeks, Quince experienced hope. "But first, let me check around and find out who's responsible so I can skin the varmint. Who told you that I wanted you out?"

"Admiral Tsebili."

"That's impossible," Quince began, without thinking. "Bili told me—" He stopped abruptly and closed his mouth. It would do no good for him to accuse Bili of lying to a junior officer.

"Told you?" Stein prompted helpfully.

"Never mind," he said, looking at her curiously. Stein wouldn't lie to him. She might lie *for* him—little white lies, of course, to protect him from too many calls when he was busy—but the expression of absolute relief on her face was not feigned. She was telling the truth, and that meant that Bili was lying.

But why in hell would Bili lie to get Stein out of his office? There'd been no hint of impropriety between them. Bili obviously didn't even know he was attached enough to Rhonda to call her and find out her reason for leaving. And it wasn't that Bili wanted Stein's efficiency in his own office . . . he outranked Quince enough to steal her with impunity, without shuttling her through Personnel.

"Look, Lieutenant," he said finally. "You stay put, and don't worry. I'll pull a few strings and get you back here—just as soon as I find out what happened. Understood?"

She gave him a smart, military nod, and then another one of those beautiful wide grins. "Thanks, Quince."

"You're welcome, darlin'." He cut the channel and asked the screen for Bili again. By God, he was going to get to the bottom of this—but he'd have to watch his temper. He was too close to a promotion to the vice-admiralty to blow it with a careless, angry word to a superior.

The screen stayed dark. "Admiral Tsebili is unavailable at this time," the computerized voice told him.

Damn. Bili hadn't even bothered to tell the computer how long he'd be gone, and without a living aide there to talk to—

He turned in the direction of the anteroom. *Confound it, what was that Vulcan's name again? Sal something. Saloon. Saleen.* "Ensign," he called.

"Yes, Admiral." The young Vulcan appeared in the doorway. Sareel. That was it. Sareely glad to meet you.

"Sareel, do you know where Admiral Tsebili has gone?"

"Yes, sir. Perhaps I should route the admiral's calls through my terminal, since there is no aide—"

"That would be a jim-dandy idea, Ensign."

The Vulcan blinked at him. "I take it 'jim-dandy' is a synonym for 'suitable'?"

"Something like that." Would he ever survive this man's literal-mindedness? Sareel obviously thought he had already answered Quince's question. Why couldn't they require all Vulcans to take a course in figurative speech? "Where has the admiral gotten to?"

"To a meeting, Admiral. However, he left no word as to when he can be expected to return."

"I see. Thank you, Sareel, that will be all."

Sareel nodded and retreated back into his office.

Quince stared at the dark terminal screen. Curioser than hell, this business with Stein.

He got busy after a while, too busy to have time to call Bili, too busy to remember. The delegation from Znebe, a new admission to the Federation, showed up, ready for their tour of Starfleet Headquarters. They were pleasant enough, although as a race they shared certain physical characteristics with Hortas, and he had difficulty figuring out which end he was supposed to be looking at when he talked to them. The tour took the morning and the early part of the afternoon.

After that, he got tied up working on a proposal to turn Star Base Twenty into an agricultural warehouse and granary. Twenty had originally been a sentry outpost; now that that area of the galaxy was colonized by Federation members and the border moved parsecs out, it was time to adapt. Since several planets in the area were subject to periodic famine, why not change Twenty to an agricultural outpost?

He worked longer than he realized on it. When he looked up to rest his eyes, he noticed the time in the upper right corner of the screen. He blinked in amazement: it was already after 1900. The evening shift had started. His new aide must have slipped out a couple of hours ago; Bili was no doubt gone, too. *Damn.*

"Close file," he yawned, and the data on the screen in front of him faded. A message took its place:

REMINDER TO ALL PERSONNEL: CENTRAL TRANSPORTERS WILL BE CLOSED FOR MAINTENANCE TOMORROW BEGINNING 0100 HOURS. PLEASE SEEK ALTERNATIVE TRANSPORT HOME.

He rubbed his face and repeated the message silently to himself so he wouldn't forget to drive the skimmer in tomorrow morning. The message faded, and was replaced by another one.

QUINCE: YOU'RE BRINGING THE SKIMMER TOMORROW, AREN'T YOU? CAN I HITCH A RIDE HOME TOMORROW P.M.? TSEBILI

Still no mention of the file, Quince noted with disappointment. He was going to have to remind Bili of it tomorrow—though Bili was not the type to forget things. Especially something as memorable as finding out whether a colleague is involved in illegal research . . . And then

155

there was the strange business of Stein. He wasn't sure at all how to approach the admiral about that.

Why would you lie, Bili? What do you have to gain by having Stein out of my office?

Nothing, probably. It had to be some kind of mistake, something one or the other of them had said that Bili'd misinterpreted. It would all be set right tomorrow.

He rose from his chair and stretched. Time to go home, though there seemed to be little point in it these days. The apartment was oppressively silent lately. God knows he'd complained about the ruckus when the kids were there. Now, he'd give anything for a little noise. He reached absently for the holo, wanting to stroke Nika's silken hair, but his fingers passed through her.

Miss you, kid. He knew that in four months, he'd have Nika and her brother back again, for half a year, but it didn't help the loneliness any now. The contract he and Ke had stipulated that Nika and Paul would always be together, even if their parents weren't.

If it weren't for the fact that the kids were coming to stay, he'd get himself busted down to captain and back out in space so fast . . . He stopped the guilty thought. Nika and Paul were worth any price to him, even that.

He sat down in his chair again. He couldn't face going home just yet. Now that things were quiet in this department, he could do a little snooping about Mendez.

Something had been simmering in the back of his head all day, some piece of information Jim had sent along about Tanis.

He glanced in the direction of the aide's office. It was completely quiet. No telling when the Vulcan had gone home, but rather odd that he hadn't bothered to tell Quince he was leaving.

"Computer," he said. "Access to star maps, one square parsec, center reference Star Base Thirteen."

The neatly labeled charts showed up on his screen and he stared at them uncomprehendingly for a moment before speaking again. "Highlight location of Tanis base in relation to Star Base Thirteen."

The two bases glowed at him in bright, blinking white.

Tanis was less than one hour's journey from Star Base Thirteen at warp speed.

This was getting interesting. Mendez could go to Thirteen under the pretext of demonstrating the new system to Tsebili, then slip away to Tanis without anyone being the wiser. Quince smiled grimly to himself. So Mendez could recover the incriminating microbe, or destroy evidence. . . .

And there was something else. He called up Adams' bio, scrolling through pages of useless information about the man's schooldays (brilliant kid), his career as a genetic microbiologist, the emerging pattern of minor offenses, fraud, financial irresponsibility. History of ill health and debt. Quince waded through Adams' life until he sat staring at his medical history. He'd almost died in a Romulan attack on a passenger ship that'd strayed too far into the Neutral Zone. Quince vaguely remembered the incident himself, though it had happened almost twenty years ago. There'd been a huge outcry, he remembered, and the Romulans finally agreed to amend the original treaty, adding the clause about not attacking if it could be undeniably shown to be an accidental intrusion on the part of the ship. What was the name of that ship? He scrolled down a few lines. *Brass Ring,* that's right. The *Brass Ring* Incident had brought the Federation and the Romulan Empire to the brink of another war.

And it was setting off another alarm in Quince's subconscious. There was a connection with Mendez somehow. He directed the computer to close Adams' file and show him Mendez's.

He remembered before he even found the information. Mendez's wife had been one of the casualties aboard the *Brass Ring.* Quince went through the file, swearing softly as each page lingered a second longer than usual after his command. What was making the machine so damn slow tonight? Were they maintenancing the computers, too? He found that the admiral's son, Yoshi Takhumara, had also been a passenger, but had survived. Yoshi, the man Adams was suspected of killing.

He felt a ripple of excitement at the discovery. Mendez, Yoshi, Adams. There was a connection between the three, a connection based on more than blood kinship or accusations.

All three had good cause to hate the Romulans.

And out of the blue, Quince thought: *Bili fired his aide last week for . . .* No, it was too ridiculous. He shook the thought away, but it left him feeling clammy.

He wanted to look up Lara Krovozhadny's file, too, but his terminal was molasses-slow. He decided to try the terminal in Stein's office—that's Sareel's office, he corrected himself, but not for long—to see if the slowdown was system-wide or affected only his screen. Intrigued, excited, Quince pushed himself away from his desk and moved with light, quick steps into the outer office.

Sareel apparently did not expect him. The Vulcan was still seated at the desk, and as Quince stepped up behind him, he snapped off his own terminal and turned quickly to face the admiral.

But Quince had already seen enough to recognize Mendez's file. The slowdown on his own terminal had occurred because it was first being routed through Sareel's machine.

"How long have you been monitoring my terminal?" Quince snapped.

Sareel said absolutely nothing.

"You work for Mendez, don't you?"

The Vulcan remained silent, which Quince took as an affirmative. *He can't say no,* Quince thought; *being Vulcan, he doesn't want to tell an outright lie.* "You're fired," Quince told him.

Sareel studied him with dark, impassive eyes. If he felt shamed at being caught spying, he did not show it. *What lies must Mendez have told him to convince a Vulcan to spy on a superior officer?* "You cannot fire me, Admiral. You do not have the authority."

"Get out," Quince nearly shouted. "That's an order, Ensign!"

Sareel apparently considered him capable of ordering him to leave the office, for he walked past without further comment. Quince sank, shaking, into Rhonda Stein's chair.

158

In a clear flash of insight, he understood why Bili had lied about Stein's transfer.

He went home with Old Yeller tucked under his arm. Lately, he'd taken to carrying the critter around with him. At least there would be someone to talk to at home—or rather, at the apartment. He couldn't really call it home anymore. It was too neat, except for the gathering dust, no children's toys strewn all over the carpet, nothing out of place. He transported into the living room, in front of the window overlooking the bay. The fog was rolling in, pea soup from the looks of it, but through the mist he could see the black, choppy water beneath a darkening purple sky.

He was still stunned from the encounter with Sareel, but he was certain of one thing: he wanted to contact Jimmy Kirk. Not direct contact, since he doubted it was safe. But a message, at least some sort of way to warn him of Quince's growing suspicions without letting Mendez know. He walked into his study, sat Yeller down on the desk, and began to speak to the terminal screen before he stopped himself.

That was particularly stupid of him. If they could monitor his terminal at HQ, why wouldn't they monitor it here? "Help me, Yeller," he said absently. "Tell me what to do."

The little animal wriggled at the sound of his voice. "I love you too, Quince." A damn shame Yeller spoke with Quince's own voice. He would have liked to hear a different voice saying that right about now.

And then it struck him. Could he program Old Yeller with a new message and send him to Jimmy? It might work.

His hope faded. It would take several days for Yeller to catch up to a starship, especially one as far out as the *Enterprise*. No, he had to warn Jim a lot sooner than that.

He needed a public comm. He walked as if guided by some higher consciousness out of his office, through the living room with its huge window. The fog was blinking with skimmer lights and the lights of sailing vessels on the dark water.

"Open," he told the front door. It opened at the sound of his voice, closed, and locked itself after him.

He walked directly into the street. Their apartment—*his* apartment—was a separate building on the bay, not a cubicle in a hive. He refused to live like an insect. The air was fresh, but damp with fog. It drizzled softly on his face.

It was cool enough to go back for a jacket, but the chill helped him think. The nearest pubcomm wasn't far, down a rolling hill in Old Town San Francisco, on the treacherous original preserved sidewalks. The comm was at the bottom of the hill, where the fog had gathered so thick that Quince would not have found it if he hadn't known exactly where it stood.

He stood for several minutes before speaking into the comm to select the form and content of his message; and as he stood, a grin spread over his features.

Well, hell, he'd been looking for some excitement to alleviate the boredom, hadn't he? And this was just the ticket. Yet as he leaned closer to speak into the waiting computer, he hesitated.

Was he letting himself be paranoid over nothing? Would he feel like a fool tomorrow when Bili explained it to him? And then how would he explain this message to Kirk? God knows, he hadn't been on an even keel since Ke and the kids had left. Could all of this be a product of his wishful imagination?

Well, what's the worst they can do to you, old boy? Court-martial you? Maybe that's not such a bad idea.

The Vulcan *had* been monitoring his terminal. Someone was watching him, whether Bili was involved or not. Imagination had nothing to do with what was going on.

"Subspace radio," he told the computer, and let it take his retinal scan before he gave it the call letters of the *Enterprise*. A written telegram, no voice, no video. But he had to phrase it so Kirk would know who sent it.

JIMMY: WHERE THERE'S SMOKE, THERE'S FIRE. GETTING TOO HOT TO BREATHE ROUND HERE

He didn't sign it. The computer would give the message's origin as a public comm in San Francisco, and that was incriminating enough. Besides, how many people got away with calling Kirk Jimmy?

Just so Mendez and Bili couldn't trace it. If he was right, he didn't want them going after Kirk, too.

He walked for a while in the fog, not wanting to go back to the apartment. He knew it was going to be a bad night. If he went back to the apartment, he would drink, and he wanted to stay sober tonight, to try to figure the damn thing out. Could it be a string of coincidences?

But who had sent the Vulcan to spy on him? Why hadn't Bili looked at that damn Tanis file? Something like that would have piqued the interest of a whistle blower like Bili. No, too many damn coincidences, one right after another. The Vulcan. Bili's lies to him, to Stein. Bili and Mendez, headed for Star Base Thirteen. The *Brass Ring*.

It was all true. He'd gone to Bili unsuspecting . . . but how could he trust *anyone* at HQ? Who could he go to for protection?

An involuntary shiver passed through him. *Someone walking on my grave . . .*

By the time he got back to the apartment, the fog had begun to lift, and he was drenched in a cold sweat. He had an unshakable premonition that he was about to die . . . yet at the same time, he felt oddly exhilarated. And he had a plan.

Even assuming his home terminal was monitored, maybe he could get away with it. He'd access the Fleet computer, ask it to list those with clearance to the Tanis file.

Anyone without clearance obviously knew nothing about it. If he could find a high-ranking admiral without clearance, that would just about clinch his case. It would prove that rank did not necessarily clear you to know about Tanis—only complicity did.

He'd call that high-ranking admiral and go to him with the information. Now, in the middle of the night, before Mendez would have a chance to react. He'd beam over to the admiral's before they'd even have a chance to realize what he was doing.

161

But first, another matter to take care of. If his instincts were right and something did happen to him, Jimmy would feel awfully bad about it. And if he didn't die, no one would ever know, anyway. He took the required few minutes to reprogram Yeller. He'd willed him to Jimmy anyway, so his lawyer already had the instructions.

When he was finished, he went to the terminal in his study and stood in front of it for an instant, catching his breath. He'd have to do this quickly, to give them as little time as possible to react. He grinned suddenly. If he was wrong, he'd get into more than a little bit of hot water, waking an admiral up in the middle of the night with outrageous accusations of conspiracy within the Fleet.

They could just bust him down to captain for being such a jackass, then.

"Computer. Names of those with access to Tanis files."

Not very many names at all. Mendez, of course, and a few other admirals. Some of the names he recognized, some he did not. Tsebili's was among them.

Admiral Noguchi's was not. He called Noguchi's house, tried not to smile nervously at the admiral's petulant, sleep-drugged expression.

"Waverleigh? This had better be good."

"It is, sir," Waverleigh said seriously. "I need to talk to you, Admiral, about a conspiracy within the Fleet."

Noguchi blinked at him for a moment, and then he said: "Come on over. Wait a minute—the transporter's not working. You know how to get here by skimmer?"

"Yes, sir. It's on the program." The transporter. *Damnation!* He'd forgotten about the maintenance. That put an extra element of danger into this. *All the better then,* he told himself dryly. *You've been waiting for some excitement to come along, haven't you? Well, now you've got it.*

Let them come after him. He'd outrun them any day.

He took the elevator to the roof and slipped into the skimmer. She was fast and sporting, not by any stretch of the imagination a family machine. Ke had so disapproved.

He put the controls on manual, and took her up into the night sky.

Try and catch me, you sons of bitches!

He laughed out loud. For the first time in two years, he felt alive.

Good God, was he finally doing something that made a difference?

He rose out over the bay. The fog was clearing away rapidly now; if he wanted, he could have put the radar on manual, too, but decided to let the computer take care of it. If someone was tailing him, he wanted to know from the very first second.

But the skies around him were clear. He asked the program for the location of Noguchi's house; it was on the other side of the bay, barely a minute away.

As he drew closer, he felt his exhilaration fade into an odd sense of disappointment. They weren't even going to try to chase him. It was all going to be too easy.

He slowed his acceleration in preparation for landing. Already he could see the outline of the landing lights blinking on the roof of Noguchi's complex. The smile on his face began to fade. He was safe. "So much for excitement," he said. The sound of his own voice surprised him.

He was still over the bay, but it was time to start descending. He eased up on the throttle to start bringing her down.

Still no one in pursuit.

The skimmer descended gently, gracefully, ready for the approach. And then the throttle shivered, began to move under his hand. He stared at it stupidly, then looked up at the control panel. She was still on manual.

The throttle was definitely moving now . . . the skimmer shuddered and began to lose speed, and then altitude. Quince wrestled with the control, cursing the machine as the skimmer began its descent into the bay.

There wasn't much time to react, really. He felt a curious mixture of exhilaration and frustration instead of the fear he would have expected. Exhilaration that he had been right after all, that the danger had been real; frustration that he would not be able to warn Noguchi. There was just enough time to think two things: first, that he was glad he'd gone ahead and sent that message to Jim; and second, that there was gonna be one hell of a shake-up at Starfleet Headquarters, and he was sorry he wouldn't be there to see it.

Chapter Eleven

In the dim light of the isolation unit, McCoy stood over Chris Chapel's body, trying to gather his courage to do the unthinkable. There was no shimmer from a field suit to intrude on his vision; Tjieng had made good on her promise to have the vaccine ready today, and McCoy was one of the first to receive the untested inoculation. Since his blood was now producing the correct antibodies, he'd ordered the vaccine administered to the rest of the crew.

For Christine, it was a day too late. Her brain waves had remained flat for twenty-four hours. He tried not to notice the gentle, unbearably regular rise and fall of her chest as the life support unit breathed for her; it made her seem all too alive, and McCoy couldn't afford to think of her that way.

But he couldn't bear to think of her as being dead. She looked too alive, too beautiful.

Funny, he'd never let himself notice how really very beautiful she was. A classic, elegant beauty with her face in repose, flawless translucent skin framed by dark ash-blond hair. There was even a faint flush of color on her cheeks. *The bloom still on the rose,* McCoy thought painfully, knowing full well it was the result of a recent transfusion. The computer monitored her hemoglobin level, and the moment it dropped, blood was automatically delivered into Chris' veins.

Her body had been fooled into thinking her brain was still alive. It accepted the blood without complaint; the heart, artificially stimulated, pumped it through the veins.

But McCoy could lie to himself no longer. Christine's essence was gone, and he was doing her no favor by keeping the empty shell alive.

Nor was he doing himself a favor. He'd drunk enough to feel like hell today, but it hadn't been enough to make him sleep. He'd lain awake all night in a stupor, unable to push back anymore the realization that tomorrow he would have to let her go.

He'd thought a lot last night. Curious thoughts, like why he'd never bothered to fall in love with her. Why he'd never let himself register how beautiful she was . . .

He had remembered the first and only time he'd invited her for a drink in his quarters. It was shortly after he'd come on board the *Enterprise,* and he'd decided it was a good way to get to know his staff. Only most of his staff hadn't been able to make it that night, and he'd wound up, to his discomfort, alone in his quarters and drinking with an attractive woman. It suddenly occurred to him, as he sat at his desk and poured her a shot from his coveted flash of Old Weller, that she might be expecting him to make a pass at her. The thought almost paralyzed him with fear, and led him to drink far more than he would have, especially when he was trying to make a good first impression.

Chris got a little drunk, too, probably because the exact same thought had occurred to her. He'd never even seen her drink before or after. She arrived looking tall and attractive but very cool, and, thank God, in uniform. If she'd worn anything else he probably would have dropped his glass.

They drank the first shot much too fast, but by the time McCoy was pouring the second shot, they'd relaxed. Something about the way Chris handled herself, even tipsy, made it clear she wanted nothing more from him than friendship . . . something in the eyes, the tone of voice, the way she sat . . .

By the third drink, he'd learned that she'd been engaged, but her fiancé was missing, presumed dead. She couldn't bring herself to believe it, still held onto the hope that he would be found. McCoy felt sorry for her, but at the same time, he felt incredible relief: so they had both been bitterly hurt, and neither was looking for another entanglement. He relaxed and told her a little about his divorce from Jocelyn, about his only child Joanna and the great sense of guilt he felt about not having had more of a hand in raising her.

Later, he was surprised at himself for confiding so much to Chapel, but she never made him regret it. She was not a lover, she was something McCoy needed much more at the time: a friend, a close-mouthed confidante. There were things he could tell her that he could never talk to Jim about. And things she, in turn, told him.

McCoy was not the type of person who opened up easily about his personal problems, and the ease with which he spoke that night to Chris amazed him. He must have somehow instinctively known that it was safe to talk to her; maybe he had recognized her need to do the same.

At some point that evening, they got to talking about the outbreak of infectious madness from Psi 2000 that had recently affected the crew. Blushing, Chris confessed that she'd been responsible for infecting Spock. The Vulcan had stumbled into sickbay, searching for the captain . . .

"And I grabbed his hand and confessed my undying love for him. Isn't it horrible?" She gave a short laugh, the corner of her mouth quirking up in that self-deprecating way she had. "Frankly, I was as surprised as he was. I've been too embarrassed to look at him since then. I suppose he thinks I meant it. I'm surprised he didn't request an immediate transfer."

"*Did* you mean it?" The bourbon had warmed McCoy to the point where he dared to ask.

Chris was swallowing a gulp of her drink. It went down the wrong way, and she started coughing. "That's— ridiculous," she gasped, between coughing fits. She wiped her eyes and held out her glass to McCoy. He filled it from the flask of Old Weller on the desk. "Why on earth would anyone fall in love with Spock?"

McCoy shrugged. "I've heard a lot of women on board

say they thought he was attractive. You would hardly be the first to nurse a passion for him."

Chapel groaned, a little too loudly because by that time she was definitely drunk. "'Nurse a passion.' I ought to push you out the airlock for that." She screwed up her face. "I don't think he's particularly attractive. Certainly not anything to write home about." She gulped more bourbon, this time managing to avoid choking on it. "Be reasonable, Leonard. Why would anyone choose such a—a cold person as the object of their affections? It'd be impossible for a human and a Vulcan—"

"Impossible?" McCoy waggled his eyebrows. "Hardly impossible. Spock's mother is human."

"Well, that's her business. Though, poor woman, I can't see how she bears it."

"*In vitro,* actually."

"You're *terrible,*" Chris said with disgust, but smiled in spite of herself.

He grinned back. Why *would* she choose an unfeeling person like Spock as the object of her affections, indeed? He had the beginnings of a theory: falling in love with Spock was her way of remaining faithful to the lost fiancé. After all, fixating her feelings on someone who couldn't return them protected her from getting involved with someone who *could.*

Like McCoy. Was her hopeless devotion to Spock another reason the doctor had talked himself out of falling in love with her?

But that night, he'd been wise enough to keep his theories to himself. Still, he couldn't resist saying, "The lady doth protest too much." He filled his own glass again without watching, listening to the sound the liquor made as it sloshed into the glass, and stopped pouring when the pitch rose to a certain level.

Chris made a disgusted sound, and changed the subject.

She *had* protested too much. Later, his suspicions would be confirmed. Chris was good at hiding her feelings, but she wasn't *that* good. There were times he caught her looking at Spock in a certain way . . . and the time she had taken

Spock soup when he'd quit eating. He'd teased her then, in front of Jim, grinning smugly at her. ("And I'll bet *you* made it, too.")

He felt sorry now for embarrassing her. He could see her flushed face, hear her stammer, "Well, Mr. Spock hasn't been eating, Doctor."

McCoy waited for the memory of her clear, ringing voice to fade. As it did, he shuddered and drew in a breath, seeking strength . . . or if not strength, at least resolution.

He put a hand on Chapel's arm and steeled himself to pull out the transfusion needle. As he leaned over her, a tear rolled down his cheek and splashed unceremoniously across the bridge of her nose.

He thought of a story he'd been told as a child, of a princess brought back from the dead by the touch of a loved one's tears.

McCoy glanced hopefully at the monitor, but Chris' brain waves stayed flat. He reached out and gently wiped the tear from her face. At least he could touch her now; he could not have stood it if he'd had to do this by computer, on the other side of the glass wall. Her skin was warm and incredibly soft.

He set his jaw and drew the needles from her arm. Tears were streaming down his face now. A blur moved on the other side of the glass. Suddenly, angrily, he realized that someone was watching them.

He looked up, furious that someone would dare violate the intimacy of this moment.

Spock stood at the glass wall of the chamber, watching.

McCoy wiped his eyes carelessly with the back of his hand. "What do you want?" There was far more grief in his voice than he had intended the Vulcan to hear.

Spock was silent for a moment. He gazed beyond McCoy at Chapel's body, his expression carefully somber. "I'm sorry, Doctor. I did not mean to intrude." There was an uncustomary softness in his tone that made McCoy think the Vulcan understood what was happening here. Spock lingered for a moment, as if the gravity of the situation were too great for him to simply turn and walk away.

And then he moved to leave.

"Wait," McCoy said raggedly. His fury at being interrupted had suddenly vanished; he felt he could not bear what he had to do alone.

A glimmer of surprise crossed Spock's face, tilting one eyebrow upward. "My question can certainly wait, Doctor." He glanced pointedly at Christine.

"Spock . . ." McCoy stepped hopefully toward the glass, hanging on to Spock's presence as if it were a lifeline offering escape from the encroaching blackness. "Spock, you knew how Christine felt about you?" He let the intonation rise to a question. He would not betray Chris' trust by letting on she had told him about the Psi 2000 incident.

"Yes," Spock answered, composed but guarded.

There was no point in explaining to Spock what was going on here; he had already indicated that he had seen and understood. "You're immune," McCoy told him. "I got your test results today. The virus doesn't care for Vulcan blood." He paused. "Would you . . . come inside? Just . . . stay for a minute, while I do this?" The back of his throat tightened painfully. He had to swallow hard to keep the tears from coming. "Christine . . . Chris would have liked that."

Spock looked intently at him for a moment, and then he said, "Certainly, Dr. McCoy. Nurse Chapel has done the same for me on more than one occasion."

McCoy coded the doors open, glad that the second's pause while Spock entered the chamber gave him a chance to wipe his streaming eyes. Damn that Vulcan . . . McCoy would have been able to keep from weeping if Spock had typically said something aggravatingly logical.

Spock entered the chamber and stood next to the doctor in an elegant posture of restraint, hands clasped behind his back. With surprise at his own steadiness, McCoy removed the connections that kept Christine's heart beating.

Chris' heart should have kept on pumping for a while, but instead it gave three irregular beats and then stopped altogether, as if it had no will to continue on its own. The clinical part of McCoy's mind made note of this as odd, but

170

for now the agony of what he had to do kept him from mentioning it to Spock.

He turned off the respirator. Chris' lungs caught a final breath and deflated with a gentle sigh. Her chest did not rise again. Together, Spock and McCoy watched the monitor as each of her life signs stabilized at zero.

They stood for several moments in silence, McCoy no longer ashamed of the tears that coursed down his cheeks. The Vulcan finally spoke.

"She was a highly competent officer."

He said it reverently, but still McCoy turned on him in fury. *Competent!* Was that all he had to say? That this beautiful, intelligent woman whose only failing was to love him was *competent?* McCoy choked, trying to speak, but one look at the compassion on Spock's face stopped him. He stared, dumbstruck.

And then he understood. Spock was only trying to give Chris the highest form of praise he knew. "Yes," McCoy whispered. "She was that, and more."

"I grieve with you, Doctor," Spock said quietly, and walked away to leave McCoy alone with his sorrow.

That same morning, Tomson called while Kirk was still in his quarters, getting dressed. He pulled on his shirt before he snapped on the viewscreen.

"Kirk here."

"Tomson here, Captain." Tomson's voice was a shade flatter than usual, and her ice-blue eyes were bloodshot, the only bright spot in an otherwise colorless face. Kirk decided that she had not slept the night before. "I called to update you on the search, as you requested."

"I take it there's been no progress."

Tomson actually sighed. "I'm afraid you're right, sir. However, we did get a report last night that Adams was spotted on D deck, near the junior officers' quarters."

"Oh?" He reached at a small thread of hope.

"It turned out to be a false lead." Tomson seemed too tired to hide her disappointment. "I promise you, sir, that if he's here, we'll find him."

"Any chance that he might not be on the ship?"

She shook her head wearily. "Very doubtful, Captain. The transporter and the shuttlecraft have not been used. There's no other way he could get off the *Enterprise*."

"He's got to be found, Lieutenant." It was a ridiculous thing to say; as Spock would put it, he was stating the obvious. But he was too frustrated and angry to care at the moment. "One crewman is dead, another almost killed."

Tomson's small eyes widened; if possible, she turned one shade paler. "Someone died, Captain?"

"Possibly." Damn. Here he was, adding grist to the rumor mill. He didn't feel like explaining about Christine Chapel right at the moment, so he changed the subject. "When did you last get some rest, Lieutenant?"

"Sir?" She blinked at him, surprised.

"When did you last get some rest?"

He could see on her face that she first considered lying to him, but honesty won out. "Two days ago, sir."

"All the officers on board this ship are competent. Why don't you turn the night shift over to someone else?"

"Sir . . ." She sighed again. "My choice for second-in-command is Ensign Nguyen. Nguyen was injured, you recall. Dr. McCoy has ordered her to take another day of rest."

While he sympathized with her devotion and fear of screwing up, if she didn't hurry up and delegate soon, she'd become worthless. "I see. Well, what about your choice for third-in-command?"

Her thin lips twisted wryly. "Sir . . . it isn't much of a choice right now."

Kirk ran through Security's hierarchy in his mind. "Stanger's a good choice. He has experience." *And*, he thought silently, *now is as good a time as any to see if he deserves a break.*

"Sir." She seemed shocked. "Stanger would be my *last* choice."

"He's got more command experience than the rest of Security put together," Kirk answered, and at the frown on her face, added: "Present company excluded."

"He's got a *reputation—*"

He looked at her slyly. "You don't listen to rumors, do you, Tomson?"

She crimsoned, the color starting at her neck and spreading rapidly to her scalp. Mildly fascinated, Kirk watched it rise. "No, sir."

"Then give Stanger command of the night shift, Lieutenant. And get some rest. Part of the art of command is knowing when to delegate."

"I take it that's an order," she said stiffly. He could see he had made her angry, but at the moment he had better things to worry about.

"Take it any way you like, Lieutenant," he said, and closed the channel.

He had started for the door when the intercom whistled again. *Damn.* If this kept up, he'd never make it to the bridge. He punched the control. "Crisis Center."

McCoy's image materialized on the screen. The doctor's weather-beaten face was composed in a bland expression. He seemed peaceful, resigned, unlike the bitterly angry man Kirk had spoken to the day before . . . but McCoy's red-rimmed eyes glistened with unshed tears.

"Good morning, Captain." His voice was calm and lifeless.

"Good morning." Kirk said it with a sense of dread, knowing full well what the doctor was about to tell him.

"I called to let you know that three-quarters of the crew have been vaccinated. We're finishing up with the rest this morning. Hopefully, no one else will become infected." He paused to catch his breath, as if what he had just said had exhausted him.

"You called to tell me about Christine, didn't you?" Jim asked softly. He hoped like hell he was wrong, and knew just as certainly that he wasn't. He had half shared McCoy's stubborn delusion that Chapel would miraculously come back to life.

McCoy let go a long, shaky sigh. He nodded.

Kirk felt tears sting his own eyes. His relationship with Christine had been purely professional, but he had always liked her personally. And he knew how close she had been to McCoy. His tears were as much for the doctor as for

Christine. To lose a crewmember was always bad, no matter how you looked at it. To lose someone like Chapel was devastating.

"I understand," Jim said, so that McCoy would not have to say anything.

McCoy nodded, causing a tear to spill down his face. "I'll be in sickbay if you need me." The screen went dark.

Kirk made it to the bridge this time, though he was not in a particularly good mood by the time he got there. The crew deserved to know about Chapel's death, but he hated the thought of making the announcement.

He stepped from the turbolift onto the bridge. Uhura swiveled in her chair from the communications console. "Good morning, Captain." She greeted him with a musical lilt, a smile across her brown face. "I was just trying—" She broke off at the sight of Kirk's expression.

"Good morning," Kirk said shortly. The question in Uhura's dark eyes made him feel guilty about what he had to do. Sulu and Chekov, seated at the helm, turned to murmur greetings and looked curiously at him. Had they heard? Spock was already on the bridge with his face buried in his viewer. He did not look up when Kirk entered.

Jim stepped to the conn and sat down.

"You have a priority message waiting, Captain," Uhura said behind him. Her tone had abruptly become somber.

Kirk swiveled to face her and lifted his eyebrows.

"From San Francisco, sir."

"Starfleet Headquarters?"

"No, sir." She sounded genuinely puzzled. "From a public comm. A civilian frequency."

"A public—" Kirk frowned. Who the hell would be calling from— Of course. Quince. The announcement about Chris Chapel would have to wait for a minute. If Quince were calling on a public channel, it meant there was trouble. Kirk tried to ignore his quickening pulse.

"It's a written message, sir."

Good, then he could take it on the bridge without anyone hearing. Not that he had the slightest doubt about any of the bridge crew; but the fewer who knew about this, the better.

"Switch it over to my screen, Lieutenant." He pulled the viewer closer to him and after a second's pause as Uhura relayed the message, read:

JIMMY: WHERE THERE'S SMOKE, THERE'S FIRE. GETTING TOO HOT TO BREATHE ROUND HERE.

It was unsigned, but there was no question it was from Quince. For a moment, Jim stared at it, stunned. Good God, Adams was right. There was a conspiracy in the Fleet. . . . And now Quince was in trouble on Jim's account. He felt a sudden chill, though the bridge was perfectly warm.

He repeated the message to himself silently, then erased it and stood up. "Uhura, relay a scrambled channel down to my quarters."

"Yes, sir. Who can I raise for you, sir?"

"I'll do it myself." He rose and hesitated at the look in Uhura's eyes. *But what about Christine, Captain? Don't we deserve to know?* Or was it just his guilty imagination?

He went to his quarters, thinking of Quince the whole way. If it was getting too hot for him to breathe, it meant that Quince had uncovered something incriminating, something so incriminating that he felt unsafe using Fleet channels to contact Jim.

Good God, could it mean that Mendez is only one of many? The thought make him weak. *And Quince is right in the middle of them. . . .*

If anything happens to him, it's your fault.

Don't be ridiculous. Nothing's going to happen to him. You know Quince has a great sense of drama. He probably found out Mendez cheated on his income taxes years ago and has already reported it to Admiral Farragut.

Uhura relayed the channel to his private terminal. He had to ask the computer for Quince's home code, it'd been so long since he'd used it.

What if they'd found out that he was behind Quince's snooping? Of course, Mendez would suspect Kirk's involvement immediately, even if Quince said nothing. It was a scrambled channel, but surely someone with Mendez's resources would be able to monitor it and decode what was said.

It didn't matter. Let Mendez find out, then. He had to know what was going on with Quince.

It took several minutes' delay before the terminal informed him that no one was answering the summons at Quince's apartment. Had Jim misfigured the time back in San Francisco? He verified it with the computer: it was four A.M. in northern California.

Don't jump to conclusions. Quince is unattached these days. He could be spending the night somewhere else.

Or maybe he had changed his duty shift. Kirk got his nerve up and called Starfleet HQ and asked for Admiral Waverleigh.

The signal came back, slightly broken up and two minutes after he had asked the question. Admiral Waverleigh was not expected on duty for another five hours.

Kirk closed the channel. There was nothing to do now but wait until Quince came on duty, and somehow let him know he had gotten the message . . . and then hope that Quince would find some safe way to contact him again, and tell him what was going on.

Until then, he would try to be patient and not jump to conclusions about what might have happened to Waverleigh. The best thing was to stay busy.

Unfortunately, that included returning to the bridge and informing the crew about the death of Christine Chapel.

Earlier that morning, Stanger was having another dream. It was a bad one, of course, the only kind of dream he had these days. Lieutenant Ingrit Tomson was in it, towering over him like an evil ice queen while he hung his head like a naughty six-year-old. He was very impressed by the fact she was not in uniform: she wore a long, flowing cape. One long arm, draped in dark velvet, was extended, an alabaster finger peeking out and pointing straight at him.

Quite frankly, Mr. Stanger, I can't trust you not to screw up.

He was so agitated that he dropped the bag he was

holding. The contents spilled out: some rare Aldebaran statuettes he'd found down on shore leave, a scattering of local coins, a jacket he'd bought for Rosa. And a Klingon burning phaser. It slid across the floor, hit a table (Stanger suddenly realized he and Tomson were standing in the middle of the crowded officers' mess) and fired, scaring right through the bulkhead to expose the circuits underneath.

Stanger gaped.

Just as I suspected, Tomson said.

I—I don't know where that came from, Stanger said. And then he closed his mouth and let his lips tighten. He knew exactly where it had come from.

I always knew you were a screw-up, Tomson said. The dark cape loomed over him. *But I didn't realize what a fool, too.*

A fool. He was a fool. He only had to say *one* word, and be done with it.

Rosa.

Can I put something in your bag? I should have thought to bring one myself.

Bazaar shopping. Shore leave on . . . God, he couldn't even remember the name of the planet. Didn't want to remember the name.

He had loved Rosa enough to cover up for her, enough to keep their relationship low-key so she wouldn't be transferred. She was under his command, and it wouldn't have been seemly.

He had loved Rosa enough not to say, *That's not mine. Rosa must have put it in there.* It would have been his word against hers, and they would have believed him, because he was the superior officer.

Instead, he kept quiet, let them assign him the blame. And all the while, he kept waiting for Rosa to come up and say, *It's mine. I can't let him take the blame. I put the weapon there. He didn't know anything about it.*

He waited till the very end for her to come, till the day he packed up his things and left the *Columbia*. When she didn't, he had found it remarkably easy to stop loving her. He knew he should have turned her in at that point. Obviously, she was reselling black-market weapons at a high profit. He knew her well enough to know she was not a weapons collector.

He also knew her well enough to know that she was probably sending the money back home. Rosa came from a large family.

Tomson was right. He was a fool.

Slowly, threateningly, Tomson moved closer in the cape until she loomed huge in his field of vision. Something cold and metal brushed against his face . . . a necklace. Stanger blinked, and her face shimmered, changed. She became Jeffery Adams.

Stanger tried to struggle, tried to cry out . . . but he felt drugged, unable to move. And then the dream faded to black.

He woke the next morning and decided he definitely had the flu. Or maybe it was the vaccine. He'd had one yesterday afternoon . . . that was it. A mild reaction to the vaccine. At least that meant it was working. He sat on the edge of his bed for a long time, trying to gather the energy necessary to stand up. The energy never came, but he stood up anyway. With the search for Adams still going on, Tomson would never forgive him if he called in sick. She'd made it clear enough that no one could be spared.

Quite frankly, Mr. Stanger, I can't trust you not to screw up.

The unpleasantness of last night's dream came back to him all at once, but he forced the memory away. Bad enough he should dream about Rosa . . . no point in dwelling on it while he was conscious.

Slowly, painfully, he forced himself to get dressed and head for the door.

He didn't even notice that it wasn't locked. But when it opened, he did notice the corridor lights, and squinted painfully. He hadn't realized that he had dressed himself in the dark.

Somehow, he managed to make it to Security. The whole way, he felt as if he were waiting for his knees to give out, as if they had suddenly lost their ability to support him. He felt as though the air around him were thick as sludge, and he had to fight his way through it.

Maybe not the vaccine at all. The flu . . . some strange new form of flu. Maybe he had caught it down on Star Base Nine. He wondered how Nguyen and Lamia were feeling

It was a miracle that he reported for duty on time. Tomson scowled at him from behind her desk, as though displeased with him for not being late again.

She rose and came around the desk to talk to him. He stood at attention, listening very carefully, because listening had also become very difficult, demanding his whole concentration. He looked up at her pinched face and felt as if he were going to fall backward any second.

"I've talked to the captain," Tomson said listlessly. She looked tired, though not as tired as Stanger felt. "He suggested that, since you have the most experience, it makes sense for you to be temporarily appointed my second-in-command. I'm taking his advice against my better judgment. I want you to be aware of that. The new assignment is effective immediately."

"The captain," Stanger said slowly. In some distant part of himself, he felt a deep sense of gratitude and wonder.

"Yes." Tomson looked down at him, her scowl deepening. "Are you feeling quite all right, Ensign?"

"The captain," Stanger repeated. He started to roll backward on his heels.

Tomson leaned forward and caught him, somewhat awkwardly because the only way she could do so was to hug him to her chest. She corrected the inappropriate embrace and scooped the unconscious man up in her arms.

Oh, hell, she thought. *Now who am I going to get as my second-in-command?*

Chapter Twelve

LAMIA'S UNIVERSE WAS collapsing in on her like a black hole. First, the loss of Tijra and the family, then the very different sort of loss in Nguyen. A wall of depression had erected itself around Lisa ever since Adams' attack, and though she spoke to Lamia, and listened to her, she remained subtly withdrawn, as if in spirit, at least, she were already in Colorado. Lisa was talking openly about resigning and would be gone within a week or two. Lamia could no longer claim her as a friend.

Then the awful announcement about Nurse Chapel had come on the shipwide intercom, followed by the grapevine news of Stanger's illness. Lamia knew she had already lost Stanger's friendship, but to hear that he was sick and probably dying was no less painful. Oddly enough, Stanger —and the entire ship, for that matter—had been vaccinated as of yesterday afternoon. The rumors were flying fast and furious.

The vaccine doesn't work. And here we are, looking for the man without our field suits.

Did you hear? He passed out right into Tomson's arms. She's next. . . .

Lamia walked down the corridor and paused at the door to sickbay. She was still on duty for another three and a half hours or so, but sickbay was included in her assigned search area. Of course, she had already secured the area and should be proceeding down another level to continue the search, but she had sent Snarl on without her. Snarl rumbled about it a bit, but Lamia knew she could trust the feline. Snarl would say nothing, even if questioned. Tomson would never know.

She *had* to find out about Jon.

She drew a deep breath and walked in. At first she was confused; Stanger was not where she expected him to be, in one of the diagnostic beds used for less serious cases. An organ in her midsection fluttered as she realized where he must be: off to the left, in one of the isolation chambers.

She took a few steps to the left around the bulkhead and found McCoy and Tomson engaged in serious conversation in front of one of the chambers. The lieutenant had her arms folded over her chest and was hunching down so that she could better hear McCoy. The doctor was talking earnestly, face tilted up toward Tomson's. He was saying something about cabin locks.

Lamia knew that Stanger was inside the chamber even before she walked up to see. There was no point in trying to leave; Tomson had already seen her.

So the rumors about the worthless vaccine were true. She felt like screaming with anger and disbelief. If Adams had stood in front of her now, she would have killed him with her bare hands. *You can't have him too,* she wanted to cry. *Not him and Lisa both. Not him.*

But outwardly she remained as impassive as any Vulcan. She marched up next to the chamber, right next to Tomson. It took no courage. She was too grief-stricken to be afraid of anything so meaningless as a demerit.

The chamber was dimmed but not completely darkened, and inside Stanger appeared to be unconscious. His skin had changed from a warm, deep brown to a sallow grayish color, and there were tubes going into the crook of one elbow. He looked as if he were dying.

Tomson directed her gaze from the doctor to Lamia. For once, her tone was not imperious. She seemed chastened, shaken. "Ensign," she acknowledged softly, as if Lamia had every right to be there. Perhaps she had forgotten Snarl's call to say that sickbay had been secured.

181

McCoy stopped talking. He looked beaten.

"Lieutenant," Lamia said. "Does Ensign Stanger have the—the sickness?"

"Yes," McCoy answered. He did not ask her to be more specific.

She had known it the moment she'd seen him behind the glass, and so she was able to keep from crying out in despair. She glanced at him, then looked up at Tomson. "Request permission—" She stopped. She was not exactly sure what she was requesting permission to do. "Ensign Stanger is my friend, sir. I'd like to stay with him for a minute or two, if I could." Not military at all. She waited for Tomson's face to start turning pink, as it always did when her sense of protocol was violated. She waited for the lecture on how every warm body was needed for the search—especially now that Stanger was out of action.

She didn't get either. Something strange and fleeting crossed Tomson's face. Compassion?

"Report back to your station at 1300 hours." For some reason, the lieutenant did not meet her eyes.

In a half hour. Lamia consciously kept her mouth from dropping open. A half hour? She hadn't dared hope that Tomson would let her stay a minute. In that instant, she radically altered her opinion of the lieutenant.

Tomson glanced quickly at McCoy. "We'll continue this conversation at a later time."

McCoy nodded back, and Tomson left.

"Not really such a bad sort, is she?" he said to Lamia. She did not answer him; she was too busy staring at Stanger.

"How is he?"

McCoy did not answer for such a long time that she turned away from Stanger to look back at him. For an instant, his professional facade vanished and nothing but pure grief showed on his face. She knew then what he was going to tell her, and she was furious at him because she did not want to hear it. She clenched her fists until her nails dug into her palms, and raised them up as if she were going to strike McCoy. She was very close to killing him.

He saw it and did not flinch, but put his hands on her

upraised arms and gently lowered them. She fell against him, too grief-stricken to make a sound.

How could this happen? She wanted to scream again, but all she could choke out was the angry word, "How . . . ?"

"From the level to which the infection had progressed, I would say he was infected the day before he was vaccinated. The vaccine only served to speed things up a bit." McCoy paused, as if speaking was a great burden for him. "He's in the chamber because at first we were afraid there was some problem with the vaccine. There wasn't."

"So everyone's safe," she said softly, her eyes on Jon's still, gray form. Everyone else, that is. It wasn't fair; but then, nothing seemed to be fair anymore. The universe had become a dark and unjust place.

It struck her that for the first time his face was relaxed and free of bitterness. She sensed very strongly that he had carried with him a secret that had distanced him from her, and she was sorry now that he had not known her well enough to trust her with it.

"I'm sorry," McCoy said gently.

She straightened. She had been angry out of pure selfishness, out of concern for what would happen to her now that her family and friends were gone. It wasn't fair to Jon. She stood very still watching him and thought about him instead of herself. What happened to her was no longer important. She held herself back from traditional mourning; the wailing sounds would probably bother McCoy, and she guessed that Jon would have found them embarrassing. He would have preferred that she act reserved, so she stood woodenly, staring at his body. Her knowledge of Terran beliefs about death was vague, but she hoped that wherever Jon's human essence had gone, it was an easier place for him.

She was not aware when McCoy left her alone. She stood watch at the foot of Stanger's bed until 1300 hours, and then she went back on duty.

An hour later, McCoy called a medic and had Stanger taken down to stasis. He had sincerely liked the man, in spite of the rumors he'd heard about his background, and simply wasn't up to seeing him there in sickbay. If the medic hadn't arrived when he did, McCoy thought grimly, he would have gone stark, raving mad.

He would have sent Chris' body down, too—there was no point in letting the decay process take hold, and the mere presence of her body was a reproach—but he kept telling himself that he was going to make himself do the autopsy. Chris would not have wanted anyone else to do it.

Besides, there was his medical duty. They needed all the information they could get on this disease. Vaccine or not, they obviously didn't have enough knowledge of how the virus behaved in a human host. Studying it in the test tube could tell them a lot . . . but not enough. Had Chris known, she would have volunteered for the autopsy. It was the one last medical contribution she could make in her life, and it wasn't fair to her to deprive her of that chance.

It took him several hours to get up the courage to go into the room where Chris' body lay covered by a sheet. He pulled it back. Chris was still beautiful, still pink-cheeked from the recent transfusion. Amazingly, her skin had not acquired the pinched, waxy look of death. He had thought that looking at her body would help him to accept her death; instead, it only made it harder to believe. He started to sway on his feet, on the verge of sobbing again. He wanted to gather her in his arms.

Instead, he called the medic and had her body taken down to stasis.

Five hours after his last attempt, Kirk went down to his quarters and tried again to contact Waverleigh.

For the past five hours, he had waited for Quince to get in touch with him. Surely he wasn't going to send a titillating message like that and then just let Kirk stew?

Quince had to be in big trouble. So much trouble that he didn't dare attempt to communicate with the *Enterprise* again.

Jim argued with himself: was it brash of him to contact Waverleigh directly at Fleet headquarters? He might be getting him in even more trouble.

But he wanted Quince to know he got the message. And if Quince was already in trouble, it wouldn't matter whether Jim spoke to him now or not. There had to be *something* he could do to bail Quince out.

Uhura relayed the channel. Instead of Quince's broad, smiling face, a uniformed Andorian male appeared on the screen. "Admiral Zierhopf's office." The *Enterprise* had moved closer to Earth, so that the delay was now only a few seconds.

"Zierhopf? I was trying to contact Admiral Waverleigh's office."

"No one seems to be answering there yet." The Andorian smiled an unusually unnatural smile, showing yellowed teeth. "When the admiral and his aide are not in their office, communications are routed through this terminal. Could I take a message?"

Kirk squinted at the insignia on the aide's gold tunic. "No, thank you, Lieutenant. I'll try back—"

"I do know one office where he's very likely to be this time of day. Hold on one moment."

The screen flickered and changed. "Admiral Tsebili's office," the young man said. He looked the quintessential Vulcan: long, sharp nose, pointed ears, and perfectly straight, even bangs framing a high forehead. His youth did nothing to soften the severity of his features; his brows arched upward at an even sharper angle than Spock's. He reminded Kirk of a primitive painting of Surak the Reformer he'd once seen in a museum. "My name is Sareel. May I be of assistance?"

"I'm looking for Admiral Waverleigh," Kirk said, relieved to be in the competent hands of a Vulcan.

"This is Admiral Tsebili's office. I will connect you with Admiral Waverleigh's."

"No," Kirk said, but the Vulcan was too fast, too efficient, and had already cut him off. He stared at the gray screen and felt his frustration mount as Waverleigh's viewer signaled its owner in vain. God, how he hated bureaucracies!

And what was he going to do if Waverleigh wasn't there? Dear God, had Quince fallen off the face of the Earth? Or was he merely playing one of his practical jokes?

He was about to close the channel when a figure appeared on the screen. "Admiral Waverleigh's office. Lieutenant Stein here." The aide who answered was female, human, with a demeanor far older than she appeared to be. She was answering at Quince's terminal, standing hunched over the desk, as if worried that by sitting in the admiral's chair, she would commit the ultimate sacrilege.

"Thank God," Kirk said fervently. "You wouldn't believe what I've been through trying to get here. Is Quince in?"

"No," Stein said. Her hollow brown eyes regarded him strangely, as if she had trouble making sense out of the question.

Kirk felt another urge of irritation. *What kind of rejects do they have working at Command?* "Lieutenant, I need to speak to the admiral *now.* How can I get in touch with him? Surely someone must have some idea where he is."

Her mouth began working, but no sound came out. She closed it. He got the impression that she was trying hard to surpress a case of the giggles.

Not the giggles . . . something else. Suddenly, he understood. He jolted forward at the screen, knowing without believing. "Stein, what's happened? What's happened to Quince?"

Her entire face quivered. "There was an accident, sir. He somehow lost control of his skimmer over the bay. I just . . . I just . . ." Her voice trailed off and she swallowed hard. A fat tear fell from one eye and dripped neatly onto the desk without ever touching her cheek. "You'll have to excuse me, sir. I just found out myself a few minutes ago." She collapsed into Quince's chair and put her head on the desk and sobbed. Her elbow struck the gold frame that generated the holo of Ke and the kids and knocked it down.

It was in the later part of the evening when M'Benga buzzed McCoy.

"Doctor? Hope I didn't wake you. I know you sometimes turn in early." His voice was slightly higher-pitched than normal, as if something had him totally baffled.

"It's all right. I was up," McCoy answered. He had been lying on his bunk, staring at the ceiling, from time to time

186

letting a stray tear run down the side of his face and into his ear. He did not expect to sleep at all tonight.

"Look, I know this sounds crazy, but . . ." M'Benga hesitated and gave a short, embarrassed laugh. "We seem to be a little confused up here. Did you decide to go ahead with an autopsy on Stanger?"

"No. I was going to do one on Chris today, but . . ." McCoy trailed off. He was still in no mood to think about it. Blessedly, M'Benga did not pursue it.

There was an awkward pause, and then M'Benga said, "Well, did you order the body moved for any reason? I was going to take a tissue sample."

McCoy was beginning to be irritated. "I had Kenzo take it down to stasis if that's what you mean." Wasn't it bad enough that Stanger had died without having to go through the third degree on what he had done with the body? Why the hell couldn't M'Benga just go down and check stasis himself, without rubbing McCoy's nose in it?

"I knew it was supposed to be in stasis, Doctor. I asked you as you were going off duty—" M'Benga stopped and suddenly changed his tone. "I'm sorry, Leonard. I'm sure you don't remember. I know how you must feel about Chris. I miss her, too."

It took some time for McCoy to bring himself to reply. "Maybe if you checked with Tjieng—"

"I already did," M'Benga answered emphatically. "Leonard, you're not going to believe this, but I've checked with the microlab, everyone in sickbay, the medics, and stasis. Everyone insists the body has to be in stasis. You're the last person I called. In all my years on this starship, I've never heard of a body being misplaced."

McCoy frowned, for the time being ignoring his sorrow. "You went down to stasis yourself?"

"I did. The chamber with Stanger's name on it was open, as if the medic had taken it down there and intended to put it in but never finished the job."

"Did you check with Kenzo?"

"Yes. He said he put Stanger in the chamber around 1700."

"Well, he didn't just get up and *walk* out," McCoy said

tartly. "Obviously, someone in another department has taken him and forgotten to report it."

"I can't imagine who that would be." M'Benga's tone was dry. "Think we ought to let the captain in on this?"

"What's the point? Give it till morning. If we haven't found it by then, I'll tell him. But there's no point in getting someone in trouble unless we have to. Can your culture wait until tomorrow?"

"I suppose so." M'Benga sounded dubious. "But doesn't this strike you as rather *odd?*"

McCoy sighed. "Quite frankly, everything on this ship strikes me as odd these days, Geoffrey."

It was very early in the morning when Tomson decided to contact Lisa Nguyen, so early that the ship's corridors were still darkened. Still, she'd had a hunch that Nguyen would be up, and, as usual, her hunch was right. Nguyen answered the signal looking drawn and tired, but very conscious.

Tomson hated small talk, so she got right down to it. No point in asking if she'd wakened Nguyen, since she obviously hadn't. Even if she had, it was not in her nature to apologize for her actions. "Ensign. Dr. McCoy tells me that you're able to report for duty today."

"Yes, sir."

"I understand that you're still talking about resigning. But for the time being, I am in dire need of someone to coordinate the night-shift search." Especially with Stanger gone; but then, she had promised herself she wasn't going to think about Stanger—

he practically died in your arms

—anymore. She had spent most of the night doing just that, and fighting back a rare emotion for her: guilt.

Nguyen turned even paler than before, making the dark circles under her eyes look huge. "Sir, I couldn't—"

"It's not a question of could or couldn't, Ensign. It's a question of need. I am hereby appointing you my second-in-command."

Nguyen stared at her uncertainly, then finally swallowed whatever it was she had really wanted to say, and said: "Yes, sir."

Tomson was going to cut the conversation off right there, but she surprised herself. "I need you, Nguyen," she said suddenly, without changing her tone of voice. "You're good with people. I'm not. I need a second-in-command my people feel comfortable with, one they can trust. A go-between. One who can see my orders are implemented without antagonizing everyone."

"You don't antagonize people, sir." Nguyen's voice had changed, become concerned; she was thinking about Tomson instead of herself. "You're just abrupt, that's all. And we trust your judgment."

"I wasn't asking for your opinion, Ensign. I was telling you the way things are."

"Yes, sir."

"I'd like to see you in my office a few minutes early, to brief you on the search for Adams."

Nguyen blanched visibly at the name. No matter. The best way to get her over it was to put her in charge of finding him. It was no wonder the woman couldn't sleep, with him running around the ship. And Tomson couldn't sleep herself. Going on the third day, and her security team still hadn't found Adams! They should have found him within three hours, not three days, and Tomson had been going over and over in her mind how she had failed. It would never have occurred to her that she was not somehow personally to blame.

"Yes, sir," Nguyen whispered.

"Tomson out." She thumped the control with a fist and swiveled sideways in her chair so that she could stretch out her long legs. Fleet-issue furniture was too small and confining, but she refused to ask for anything custom-made.

It was ridiculous, feeling guilty about Stanger. How was she supposed to know the man was going to die?

You didn't. But you broke your own rule; you listened to the rumor mill.

Maybe. But the plain fact is, the man was demoted. People don't get demoted without cause.

No. But you had to rub it in.

Enough. The man was dead, and there was nothing more

189

she could do. Of course, there was always a posthumous commendation.

What for?

It took a lot of nerve for him to come up to you and ask to be in charge of the night-shift search. He offered to pull a double shifter, remember?

She remembered. Before she could change her mind, she swiveled back to face her terminal, typed up the order, and verified it with a retinal scan. She had just finished when there was a buzz at the door. Esswein, perhaps, with news of Adams' capture? "Come," she said, and turned off the lock. The door slid open.

Jonathon Stanger stood in the doorway.

"Stanger," she said with enormous relief, and stood up, vaguely aware that she was grinning hugely. "Stanger, they said you had died."

Stanger stared up at her with wild, feverish eyes. His skin was as sickly gray as it had been when Tomson last saw his corpse, and his uniform was disheveled. "Please . . ." He stepped inside. The door closed behind him, and he moved forward until he stood in front of the desk.

Tomson stared back. The reality of the situation passed through her with an ugly shudder. "You *did* die," she said softly. Repulsed, she stepped away from the desk until her back was pressed against the wall.

It was then that she made out the small utility knife clutched in Stanger's right hand. His eyes were insane with need. "I don't want to hurt you," he said earnestly, and raised the knife.

Tomson tensed, ready to defend herself. "Damn right you don't," she said.

Chapter Thirteen

McCoy GOT TO sickbay just as M'Benga finished sealing the cut on Tomson's hand with synthetic. M'Benga had not explained the crisis, had only promised that it was urgent, though Tomson seemed in fair shape. She'd obviously been in some sort of struggle; besides the cut, there was a rip in the shoulder of her red tunic that revealed skin so translucent, McCoy could see the blue-green blood vessels pulsing beneath.

"Don't worry," M'Benga was saying to her. "The hand'll be good as new in a couple of days."

"That's a pretty deep cut." McCoy peered at Tomson's wound. The lieutenant held her injured hand out in front of her and gazed at it critically, as if inspecting a fresh manicure.

M'Benga looked up from his work. "Doctor. Sorry to bother you twice, but it's been some night."

"No problem." McCoy had lain awake, just as he'd expected, running over in his mind what he might have/could have/should have done differently for Chapel and Stanger. "It's almost time for my shift anyway." Which was a gross exaggeration.

M'Benga glanced meaningfully at Tomson. "The lieutenant here has quite a story to tell. It explains that little problem we discussed earlier."

Stanger's body. "My God." McCoy was sickened. "Adams *stole* it? Then Chris—"

"Relax." M'Benga put a gentle hand on his arm. McCoy thought he spied a quirk tugging at one corner of M'Benga's mouth, as if the man were trying not to smile. "Adams didn't steal anything. And I've got stasis locked up tighter than a drum. Chris is safe."

Chris is safe. Something about the way he said it—*Chris, not Chris' body*—caused an irrational hope to surface in McCoy.

"Tell him." M'Benga turned to Tomson.

She focused small, humorless eyes on the doctor. "You're not going to believe this."

"For God's sake, just tell me what happened," McCoy snapped, desperate to know.

"Ensign Stanger attacked me." She said it soberly, with total and irrevocable certainty, so that no one could have doubted that it was the truth. "He's alive, Doctor. I am not insane, I have not been drinking or taking any type of drug. He seemed—desperate. As if he felt compelled to hurt me but, at the same time, didn't want to. I tried to restrain him, but he had a knife and managed to get away." Anyone else would have simply been glad to have survived. Tomson, of course, felt she had to explain why she had not personally delivered the prisoner to the brig. "My people are looking for him now."

Speechless, McCoy gaped at her. It didn't make any sense. Didn't make any sense at all. Stanger was *dead*. McCoy had watched each life function indicator on the man's monitor plummet to zero. Just as he had for Chris . . .

M'Benga was quite obviously fighting back a grin. "Know what I think we should take a look at? The waste products in Chapel and Stanger's blood. I bet we'd find some mighty interesting ones . . . like maybe some high serum magnesium levels."

"My *God*," McCoy cried, jubilant. Of course! Tjieng had said tests indicated it was a smart virus. It could be— He grabbed the now-smiling M'Benga by the shoulders, afraid to have hope and at the same time reveling in it. "My God, Geoffrey, I should have run a blood chemistry—"

192

"How were any of us supposed to know? That's not done on a corpse until the autopsy."

"My God!" McCoy repeated, holding his reeling head. "I've got to see Chris!"

"I was thinking you might say that." M'Benga cackled and gave him a joyful thump on the back. "Why don't you go down to stasis? I'll give you the code to get in. You've got a whole hour before your shift, and I can easily stay over if you need."

But McCoy was out the door before he finished talking.

"Excitable, isn't he?" Tomson observed.

He had to go back for a tricorder and medikit and the code, of course. By the time he got down to stasis, he was trembling.

What if I'm wrong? Dear God, what if nothing happens? Don't think about. Do what you have to do, and just don't think.

He coded the door to stasis open. Imagine, locking the doors to stasis!

To keep people out, or in?

Inside, two of the units had recently been put to use. One of them, the one marked STANGER, JONATHON, ENSIGN, had been opened. It was dark and empty. Next to it, Christine Chapel's unit glowed faintly.

McCoy stopped breathing. He stepped next to Chris' unit and stood there until he got up the nerve to open it.

She was enveloped from head to foot by the stasis field; its soft blue light gave her a distinctly ethereal beauty. Trembling, McCoy switched the unit off. The field melted away. Under normal lighting, Christine looked very much alive.

He picked up the tricorder that dangled by a strap from his neck and calibrated it to do life function readings. He directed it at Christine.

Nothing.

It was not unexpected. Remembering something he had studied long ago in a now-forgotten zoology class, McCoy leaned over the unit and, with one eye on the tricorder, screamed into Chris' ear.

"CHRISTINE!"

The tricorder gave a small *bleep* as it registered brain function. Chris was alive.

Sobbing with joy, McCoy buried his face in her shoulder.

Quince Waverleigh was dead, and Jim Kirk was to blame. At least, that was the way Jim saw it. It had been a bad afternoon, and an even worse night. For the past several hours, he had been staring at the expanse of white ceiling above his bunk.

Getting too hot to breathe.

He could have forgiven Quince if it were all just another one of his practical jokes. But he could not forgive him for dying.

Nor could he forgive himself.

If only I hadn't been so stupid. Mendez must have been waiting to see if I were going to follow up on any suspicions.

If only I'd sent the first message on a public channel . . . and to Quince's apartment . . .

The rational part of his brain knew that if Mendez wanted to monitor transmissions to and from the *Enterprise,* there was nothing he could have done to prevent Mendez·from finding out.

Then why did you have to call Quince? You should have suspected you were marking him for death.

Because he trusted Quince, that was why. And at the same time, he had no idea what was at stake. *Would it really have been any better if it'd been someone else?*

Yes. If it'd been me . . .

He decided to get up and start his duty shift three hours early. He pushed himself to a sitting position and swung his legs around. He felt stiff, as if he had grown very old in those few hours of lying still. It would be good for him, would force him to function, albeit in a haze of suppressed pain. The grief had begun to funnel itself into a stronger, darker emotion: revenge.

He rose and dressed himself. He could no longer see Mendez as the grief-stricken father. That perception was gone, replaced by that of Mendez, the cold-blooded killer. Whatever personal tragedy the man had undergone did not give him the right to inflict the same on others.

At the same time, fully aware of the contradiction, Jim wanted Mendez dead. Part of his bitterness stemmed from the knowledge that he would never bring himself to fulfill that desire. Still, he was going to bring Mendez and his associates down.

The question was, *how?*

There was time. Mendez might be plotting to silence Kirk even now, but wiping out a starship like the *Enterprise* would take considerable planning. There was time to get even.

And revenge is a dish best served cold . . .

Jim glanced into the mirror over the dresser and tried to smooth the angry grief from his face before heading for the bridge.

At the navigation console, Lieutenant Sulu suppressed a yawn. Anything that suggested relaxation would have been out of place; since the announcement of Chapel's death, the bridge had been a tense, unhappy place.

Even more so today. The captain had already been on duty when Sulu got there—fifteen minutes early—sitting in the conn with a stern, forbidding scowl on his face. Gods knew, they were all upset about losing Christine, but Sulu's instinct told him that the captain had suffered an even greater loss.

And so the day-shift bridge crew reported one by one for duty, murmuring hushed greetings to those they replaced. *As if we were at someone's funeral,* Sulu thought. He sneaked a sideways glance at Chekov, but the navigator stared somberly ahead at the viewscreen full of stars.

This is going to be an awfully long day. Sulu sighed and glanced down at his panel. Everything normal, everything as it should be. Except that Christine was dead and something was eating the captain alive . . .

The bridge was so hushed that when the captain's intercom whistled, Sulu gave a start. He didn't intend to eavesdrop on the conversation; after all, it was none of his business. But the bridge was so quiet, it was impossible not to overhear. He could tell from the way Chekov tensed next to him that the Russian was listening, too.

Kirk punched the intercom with his fist and grunted into it. "Kirk here."

"McCoy here. Jim, you're not going to believe this." McCoy's voice was trembling with such strong emotion that Sulu could not tell if it was grief or joy.

"Try me," Kirk said dully.

"Ensign Stanger attacked Lieutenant Tomson early this morning."

Kirk sat up very straight in his chair. His voice became more animated. "Stanger is *dead*, Doctor. Is this your idea of some sort of bad joke?"

"Stanger *isn't* dead," McCoy said, with maniacal good cheer. "Neither is Chris."

Christine was *alive?* Sulu no longer pretended not to be listening. A broad smile on his Asian features, he swiveled in his chair to face the captain. So did Chekov. So did Uhura. Even Spock glanced up from his viewer.

"It's true, Jim," McCoy raved on. "It only makes sense. We knew it was genetically engineered. It's a smart virus. It does whatever's necessary to keep the host alive for as long as it can. Adams probably never even remembered! Of course he didn't tell us! How were we supposed to know? It was hibernation, Jim. I should have guessed from the very beginning. I guess I subconsciously knew all along."

The captain's frown faded somewhat. "Doctor, you're babbling."

"Babbling?" McCoy laughed. "Babbling! You're damn right I'm babbling! And I intend to babble the rest of the day."

Kirk gave a small smile. "Why don't I come down and see if we can figure out what you're trying to tell me?"

McCoy cackled. "You do that, Jim. You just do that! McCoy out."

Kirk stood up, his mood apparently somewhat improved. "Mr. Spock . . . if you would accompany me to sickbay."

The Vulcan turned to look at him, the barest ghost of a questioning look crossing his face and then disappearing. "Yes, Captain."

"I need someone to protect me from Dr. McCoy," Kirk

said, as if an explanation were expected. "Mr. Sulu, you have the conn."

"Yes, sir," Sulu answered, already routing it through to his own station at the helm. Odd, for the captain to ask Spock to go with him. There was no need Sulu could see to have the Vulcan along . . . but then, command had its privileges. And it would give those on the bridge the opportunity to talk freely.

The turbolift doors closed over the captain and his first officer.

"Christine's *alive!*" Uhura exclaimed, and everyone laughed delightedly and began talking at once.

"But what . . . ?"

"How could it be . . . ?"

"Maybe she's not really alive," Chekov intoned solemnly. "Maybe she's just come back from the dead."

"Don't be morbid," Uhura scolded him. "Dr. McCoy said something about hibernation."

"I'm happy for Christine," Chekov said. "But the other— Stanger. McCoy said he attacked Lieutenant Tomson." His lips curved in a wicked smile. "And *I* know what he was looking for."

Sulu snickered. "In Lieutenant *Tomson?* You must be kidding."

"Not *that.*" Chekov looked vaguely disgusted. "Don't you remember what I told you?" His voice took on an exaggeratedly dramatic tone. "The wampire comes back from the dead to drink the blood of the living."

Uhura sounded insulted. "How can you tease about something like that, especially after we thought Chris had *died?* Why can't you just let us be happy?"

"Who's teasing?" Chekov said, but he turned back to his station and smiled. "At least, *I* have protection. At least, *I* don't have to worry while Stanger and Adams are free to attack innocent wictims."

"The only wictim around here"—Uhura's brown eyes narrowed—"is going to be *you* if you don't—"

"Don't listen to him," Sulu soothed. "He's just teasing because he's embarrassed to admit how happy he is about Christine."

But he found himself wondering if Pavel had an extra crucifix. . . .

In sickbay, McCoy clutched the lab report on Chris Chapel to him like a coveted trophy and beamed broadly at Kirk. Kirk forced a weak grin. He was happy for McCoy, for Chapel, for Stanger, for the fact that he had not after all lost two crewmembers. But he didn't feel much like smiling. Quince Waverleigh was still dead, and there was no chance of bringing him back to life.

But McCoy seemed too wrapped up in his own joy to notice the captain's reticence. "I should have run blood tests before declaring them dead!" he said raptly, without any sort of introductory remarks. "The serum magnesium levels in their blood would have tipped me off right away."

"Doctor," Spock said in his deep, quiet voice, "perhaps it would be less confusing if you began at the beginning."

"Oh. Well, it seems our smart virus is really smart, all right. I'm running tests on both Stanger and Chris right now. Chris is still unconscious, though she seems to be coming out of it. Her brain tissue is saturated with a hypothalamic neurosecretion, remarkably similar to a chemical normally found in hibernating mammals. Think of it, Jim! The virus works to keep itself *and* its host alive by causing the human host to hibernate."

Kirk frowned. "But if they were hibernating, why didn't they show any brain waves? I thought—"

McCoy interrupted gleefully. "That's just it, Jim! In some hibernating animals, brain waves slow to virtually nil, with maybe one barely measurable burst of activity every twenty-four hours or so. Of course, a strong stimulus—a loud noise, say—would cause measurable cortical activity. But the problem with Stanger and Chris was, once brain function appeared to cease, I turned the monitors off. If I'd just left them on for several hours . . ."

"I still don't understand," Kirk said. "Why did the virus cause hibernation in the first place?"

"Okay. Um . . . the virus is like a parasite. A symbiotic one. In other words, it keeps the host alive for as long as possible so that the virus can multiply in the host's body as much as possible. This also allows the host to infect more people with the virus."

"Uh-huh."

"One thing we'd already known about the virus is that it requires heme—that's the iron compound in hemoglobin—to reproduce. Now, every time we're active we use up our stores of hemoglobin in the blood."

"That's fourth-grade biology," Kirk said. "Go on."

"Sorry. The results haven't come back yet, but here's my guess: when the host's heme levels are high, the virus shuts the body down via hibernation. More heme for it, you understand, if the host is motionless. The more it can reproduce within the host's body."

"But Adams didn't go through a coma," Kirk protested.

"We don't know that. Maybe he did, before he sent the distress signal, before his heme stores became depleted. Maybe he killed Yoshi and Lara because his heme levels dropped."

"But you just said he was in a coma."

"Hibernation, actually. Two very different states. Anyway, maybe what brings the host *out* of hibernation is the heme level dropping *too* low. The virus wants survival, so it wakens the host to go and search for more heme."

"By killing someone else and drinking their blood," Kirk said distastefully.

"But drinking it would not have the same effect as getting a transfusion," Spock pointed out.

"Well, you're right there, Spock." McCoy was still cheerfully smiling, as if too happy to be aware of the gruesome turn the conversation had taken. "That's a strange little side effect, that craving for blood . . . a type of pica, an abnormal craving, caused by the anemia. I suppose that if the host is too stupid to figure out that just drinking blood won't help him, then he'll go the way of the elephant. Sure, it would raise his iron stores some, and help in the production of hemoglobin, but not at all like a transfusion would."

"And someone," Kirk said heavily, not wanting to believe the obvious, "Adams, perhaps, *designed* this virus to do what it does?"

McCoy stopped smiling and nodded.

"Elegantly insidious," Spock said. "The work of a darkly creative mind. The virus promotes its spread by driving the victim to search for heme. Thus more victims are infected. The craving ensures the necessary physical contact to spread the disease."

McCoy nodded. "As in Adams' case, there is some dementia. The pica tends to cause bursts of irrationality. But personality seems to be a factor."

He's hoping that because of Chapel, Kirk told himself.

"Tomson said Stanger seemed to be fighting the urge to harm her," the doctor continued. "Obviously, he's in need of another transfusion. We need to find him soon. Without a transfusion, the disease is ultimately fatal."

"Then Adams could be dead by now," Kirk said.

McCoy's expression soured. "Adams seems to be taking care of himself all right. Stanger got the disease because Adams was transfusing blood from him."

"How could he get away with that?" Kirk was puzzled.

"Beats me." McCoy shrugged. "I figured he must have overridden the cabin locks somehow. I asked Tomson to look into it. She said if that's how Adams did it, Stanger will be his first and last victim."

"Now that Stanger is infected, Adams will no doubt seek healthier prey," Spock added. "But I think it extremely unlikely that Adams overrode the lock. Very few people possess the ability *and* the security clearance—"

"And I'm sure you're one of them," the doctor interrupted. "But the fact exists that Stanger was infected."

Kirk ran a hand over his forehead as he strained to remember. "Wait a minute. He could have done it. Waverleigh said something about his being a computer expert."

"There you go. I just outlogicked Spock." McCoy smiled sweetly. In spite of the seriousness of the conversation, it seemed hard for him to control his elation about Chapel. Kirk wanted to smile, but found it still too difficult.

Spock sighed and gazed briefly heavenward, as if he were going to roll his eyes but, on reflection, considered the gesture beneath his dignity. He did not reply to McCoy. "Will there be anything else, Captain?"

"As a matter of fact—" Kirk stopped. His guilt over Quince's death made the matter too painful to go into, but he had to force himself. *If you want to get Mendez . . .*

Some of the happiness faded from McCoy's watery blue eyes, replaced by a look of somber curiosity. "Something's eating at you, isn't it, Jim?"

Spock waited. The Vulcan had probably known all along, and simply bided his time until Jim could bring himself to talk about it.

Jim took a deep breath. "You know that I contacted Admiral Waverleigh at Starfleet and asked him to check into the matter about Mendez."

"My God." McCoy leaned forward. "He came up with something, didn't he?"

"He sent me a message," Jim said. He wished he had been able to forget it, but he had thought it through a thousand times in the past day, analyzing each word. He repeated it for them.

Spock said nothing, but McCoy's expression was skeptical. "I've heard you talk about Quince, Jim. You sure he isn't just pulling your leg?" He looked at Spock. "Quince Waverleigh has a bit of a reputation as a joker."

Spock digested the information without comment; his eyes were watching Jim, as if he already knew what the captain was going to say next.

"Bones . . ." Jim began helplessly, and broke off. He tried to just say the words, and ignore the image he knew would come with them: *Quince's skimmer breaking up as it impacted with San Francisco Bay . . .* It came out harsh and bitter. "Quince Waverleigh is dead."

Spock's expression did not change.

"Dear God." McCoy blanched. "Jim . . . when did this happen?"

"Yesterday. His skimmer went into the bay." It was out. Jim took a deep breath to steady himself. The rest would be easy. "Gentlemen, Quince was my friend. I would appreciate some unbiased interpretation of these events."

"I don't know if I'm unbiased," McCoy said. "I knew Waverleigh, though not all that well. Better to say I knew *of* him, I suppose. But it seems very obvious to me that there's a direct connection between the message and his death. I hate to say it, but Adams must have been telling the truth."

"Spock?" Jim asked softly. He valued McCoy's opinion, but it was the Vulcan's he was really waiting to hear. "That's why I brought you along."

Spock nodded somberly. "I'm afraid I must agree with Dr. McCoy."

"You think Mendez had him killed?" Kirk asked.

"Likely. And if not Mendez, then someone else put at risk by the investigation." Spock paused. "But Captain, it is likely that Mendez is by now aware that you were in touch with Admiral Waverleigh. And certainly he knows that you will attempt to avenge the admiral's death."

Elegantly put, Kirk thought. *That's exactly what I intend to do—avenge Quince's death.*

"I don't like where this is heading," McCoy muttered.

Spock continued, ignoring him. "It is only a matter of time before Mendez decides to silence you. Or better, if he could arrange it, to discredit you."

"I've been thinking about that," Kirk said slowly. "My main concern is protecting the *Enterprise.*" *Bad enough that I've killed Quince . . .*

"I would be surprised," Spock said, "if Mendez has not already acted. The sooner you are silenced, the better."

"Mendez would like to have me out of the picture, of course," Kirk said. "But not necessarily at the cost of his own skin. Let's not forget that it's more than a little difficult to blow a starship out of existence without explaining why. I doubt Mendez has the power to commandeer another starship to attack the *Enterprise.*"

"But he would have far less difficulty focusing his attack on you personally, Captain," Spock said, with a quiet certainty that made Jim shudder. "Just as he did with Admiral Waverleigh. It might be best at this point to force his hand, in light of the fact that he may be aware of your contact with Waverleigh."

"How?" McCoy interjected. "What do we do, call him up and say, 'Look, we know you're guilty'? What sort of proof do we have against him?"

"None, at the moment," Kirk said. "Just Adams' word

against his. And we haven't even got our hands on Adams yet."

"Mendez need not know that," Spock said calmly. "It might be possible to convince him otherwise. Perhaps we have nothing incriminating against him now, but it might be possible to encourage him to act in such a way that we get it."

McCoy frowned at him. "You mean, call up Mendez and say that we have evidence against him?"

"That we have access to such evidence. For example, that evidence existed on Tanis. As it very well might . . . in the form of Sepek's body."

"Say who?" McCoy looked puzzled.

"The Vulcan researcher I mentioned to you before, Doctor, who died of the original R-virus."

"Then what?" Kirk asked. "Lure Mendez there and try to get a confession?"

"Let the admiral's own actions incriminate him. If he believes that there is incriminating evidence on Tanis base, he will find some way to get there quickly. And if he cannot locate any evidence by himself, he will be forced to take some sort of desperate action to find it."

McCoy looked unconvinced. "But how do we know Mendez hasn't already removed Sepek's body?"

"We don't," Spock told him. "That is why we make no mention of the type of evidence we have."

"And hope he doesn't decide to come after Jim."

"It's a risk I'm willing to take," Kirk said, "if it will help to incriminate Mendez."

Spock stroked his chin thoughtfully. "Perhaps less risk would be incurred if you were to tell the admiral the evidence implicated someone *else* in Starfleet."

Kirk nodded. "Tell him I think, for example, that Quince's boss Tsebili is to blame and that there's evidence on Tanis that should clear everything up."

"Precisely."

"And then what?" McCoy persisted.

Kirk turned to look at him. "And then, Doctor, we hope like hell we get to Tanis first."

Chapter Fourteen

AT THE VIEWSCREEN in his quarters, Kirk composed his features into an expression of respect. It took every ounce of his latent acting talent to keep his hatred from showing.

Behind his desk at Starfleet Headquarters, Mendez was looking unusually haggard, as if he had spent a sleepless night.

Guilty conscience, Admiral? I hope it eats you alive.

"What is it, Kirk?"

"Admiral," he said smoothly. He was quite surprised at his own ability to be pleasant to the man. "I take it Commodore Mahfouz informed you of Adams' escape onto the *Enterprise*."

"He told me," Mendez said tiredly. The folds under his eyes reminded Kirk of a bloodhound. "I assume he's been captured, or else that you're looking for a new security chief."

"The first," Kirk lied. Lying to this man was somehow gratifyingly easy. "Adams has decided to cooperate. He's told me some pretty interesting things about Tanis base. As we suspected, it's an illegal biowarfare base. Apparently a secret group within the Fleet is funding it."

He stared at Mendez, waiting for a reaction; the admiral's brow wrinkled slightly, distastefully, but the expression in the eyes never wavered. "Rather a ridiculous charge, don't you think, Captain?"

"I'd prefer to think so, of course, Admiral, but Adams says that he has the evidence to prove it on Tanis base."

"I see." Mendez nodded. "I'm not surprised. We've been doing our own investigation for some time, Kirk, but frankly, I'd be surprised if anyone other than private citizens are involved. We'll check out Adams' claim. All that remains for you to do is to take him to Star Base Nine."

A consummate actor, Kirk thought. The idea that Adams might have been lying all along occurred to him, but he dismissed it without a second's consideration. Instinct told him that Mendez was the liar here. He made himself smile slightly. "Actually, Admiral, I was offering to collect the evidence for you. We're probably the closest Fleet ship out, and we may as well find the evidence before someone has the chance to destroy it." *Such as yourself, sir . . .*

"It's a hot lab, Kirk, and while we're aware you're equipped, I'd rather not risk the *Enterprise* again. I'd rather send in some specialists."

"With all respect, sir, by this time we are experts on dealing with this particular virus. And my entire crew has been vaccinated." He let the smile widen a bit more. "I can't think of a better—"

Mendez rubbed his hairless temples with thick fingers as if the exchange was giving him a migraine. "Kirk, you have your orders. Proceed immediately to Star Base Nine and have Adams put in Mahfouz's custody. Mendez out."

The screen darkened. Jim swiveled in his chair to face Spock and McCoy.

The doctor spoke first. "Well, what now?" There was disappointment in his voice. "What are you gonna do?"

Kirk was still wearing the artificial smile. "Follow orders. Take Adams to Star Base Nine." He paused and let the smile fade. "Via Tanis base."

Stanger was sliding toward madness. Most of the time, he couldn't remember why he was no longer Ensign Jonathon Stanger, serving aboard the *Enterprise,* but a shivering creature who hid from the light.

The hunger was the worst part. Not a real hunger, for

food, but a horrible craving, like a drowning man's need for air. And in his desperate, blind thrashing, he would pull anyone down with him to get it.

He had wakened and opened his eyes to glistening black awash with a faint blue glow. Initial calm curiosity had given way to mindless panic as he realized he had been interred in a stasis tube. A vivid image tore at him: the prematurely buried victim, struggling with his last breath to push open the nailed-down coffin lid.

His terror was short-lived. The blue field parted to let him through; the lid to the tube opened without effort. Gasping, he clambered out. The tube next to him was glowing in the darkness, even its faint light making him squint painfully. Chris Chapel. He thought of opening it and saying, *Did they make a mistake with you, too?* but a vaguely superstitious discomfort at the thought held him back. Chris had really died. He hadn't . . .

Or had he? He could not think clearly, because of the monstrous ache that consumed him. He escaped into the corridor, sobbing as the light pierced him.

The craving had pulled him so hard he'd gone to the first person he could remember: Ingrit Tomson. Even then, he hadn't been sure of what he sought from her until he drew the knife. Perhaps the few remaining shreds of the real Stanger had known all along . . . and had chosen Tomson out of a deeply harbored desire for revenge.

Or perhaps he had meant to turn himself in, and in the end, had been too weak.

Weak. Too weak. Quite frankly, Mr. Stanger, I can't trust you not to screw up.

Either way, he hadn't killed her. He felt satisfaction at that—and a growing need as well. He was insane, he was diseased, but he would not sink to what Adams had become.

From Tomson's quarters he had thrashed deliriously through the halls, remembering enough to avoid the security checkpoints.

He found peace and darkness on the observation deck, though the hunger still gnawed at him. It was at an hour between shifts when the deck was silent, deserted. The weak light from the stars was unpleasant, but tolerable enough. He collapsed next to one of the meditation booths and rested, gathering the strength to open the door and go in. Perhaps he would find what he needed here, if he had the patience to wait.

At the other end of the deck, there was movement. Stanger hid himself behind the booth so he could watch without detection. Oddly, he could see quite clearly in the darkness.

A figure in a deep-colored cloak glided fleetingly across the deck. Stanger suppressed a gasp and leaned forward for a better view, but he couldn't see the face. Even so, he knew it was Adams, clutching a portable transfusion unit in his bloodless white hands. The cloaked figure stooped down and disappeared into a cubicle, closing the door behind him.

Adams was holing up on the observation deck.

Impossible. Stanger himself had been through the observation deck twice in the past few days. The tricorder had revealed nothing.

Of course, the tricorder only worked if the man had life-sign readings.

Stanger, they said you had died. . . .

He swallowed hard. The action was distinctly unpleasant; his mouth was dry as a bone.

As a bone, get it?

Dear God, he and Adams were walking corpses. Stanger shivered.

Suddenly, the security chief surfaced in him. *Wake up, you fool!* Here was Adams, the prey he'd been stalking the past few days, the man who had done this unspeakable thing to him. *Done an even more unspeakable thing to Lisa Nguyen,* he thought, with an odd mixture of titillation and revulsion. Here was one chance in his life to get even. Fear and need were eclipsed by an overwhelming fury, a desire for revenge on the man who had taken his life, however bitter, from him.

And he would not let Adams do the same to anyone else.

At the same time, Stanger licked his cracked lips at the

thought of the portable transfusion unit. He caught himself and tried to direct his confused whirl of thoughts back to Adams.

I'm your last victim, Stanger promised silently, and sat back on his haunches to gather the strength needed to kill.

Security-second-in-command Lisa Nguyen stood in front of the portal to the observation deck, rubbing the back of her neck and frowning. She felt a headache coming on, and it was not helped by Ensign Esswein's resentfulness. *It's not my fault Tomson chose me instead of you. Believe me, you can have the job. Maybe you will, as soon as I'm gone.*

Esswein shrugged in the direction of the deck. *Bright blue eyes adrift in a sea of freckles,* Nguyen thought. Acker's wiry auburn hair was the same shade as the freckles that covered most of him. "How many times are we going to comb through that? For that matter, how many times can we comb the entire ship before we find him? I think he's made it off the ship."

Lisa sighed and squinted down at her tricorder dial rather than face his accusing stare. "Then how do you explain what happened to Stanger?"

She didn't like talking about it. She was glad that Jon was still alive, but for him to become what Adams had become . . . the thought for her was somehow more painful than if he had died. At least that way, she could have remembered him as the good person he was—instead of a monster.

"He could have gotten infected two days ago," Acker persisted. "I still say Adams made it off the ship."

How? she almost asked, then stopped herself from falling into an exact repeat of last night's conversation. There was no point in going through it all again. She was not up to dealing with what had happened to Jon, and Acker's subtle defensiveness, too. She turned to him. "No point in you walking through this with me. Go ahead and secure the cargo hold."

"Wouldn't it be safer to stick together?" Acker said, his impossibly blue eyes all innocence.

What are you afraid of, if you're so sure Adams is already off the ship? Lisa thought, but didn't say it. She would not grace such a bold attack on her authority with a response. She composed her features into the coldest possible approximation of Tomson, looking displeased, and turned them full force on Acker.

"Do it, Esswein." She narrowed her eyes until they were slits.

"Yes, sir," he said, but there was a trace of defiance in the "sir." She ignored it and gratefully watched him leave.

She walked through the doors onto the deserted observation deck and sighed when she heard them close behind her. The room was blessedly dark and quiet. She would have given anything to crawl into one of the meditation cubicles and close the *Enterprise* out. The day had exhausted her with its continual barrage of strong conflicting emotions: her unhappiness at staying in Starfleet, her unhappiness at leaving, her terror of finding Adams.

It was dark, but she did not turn on her flashlight. Between the starlight and the glow from the tricorder dial, she could see well enough to keep from stumbling. Besides, the darkness seemed to help her headache.

She began to walk up and down the rows of cubicles, keeping her eyes on the tricorder dial. She was not afraid; she had been through this room yesterday with Acker, and no one had been here. Maybe Acker was right. Maybe Adams *had* gone. Even if someone were here, she had her phaser, and her communicator to call for help.

She walked to the end of one row. She was tempted to close her eyes, to lie down on the cool floor. Acker wouldn't know. No one would know. There was no one in here. *Besides, you're leaving in a week. What are they going to do, demote you?*

Of course, she had too much self-discipline to do it. Instead, she walked to the end of one row of cubicles and started scanning another, her concentration firmly on the tricorder readout.

When she got a reading, she nearly stumbled. She looked up, but it was too dark to see anything. She fumbled for her flashlight.

Take it easy. It's nothing. Someone just came here to relax. For God's sake, ask first and shoot later.

209

She turned on the flashlight. "Who is it? Who's here?"

No answer. And then, in the darkness, a shadow moved. She directed the beam at the crouched form of Jon Stanger.

The light made him scream in real anguish, until Lisa lowered it and the pain faded enough for him to be uncomfortably reminded of another encounter, with Adams on Tanis base.

I'm just like him now, Stanger thought miserably. He cringed at the edge of the light.

"Jon," Lisa said dully. Her expression as she clutched the flashlight was one of concern mixed with loathing, the way Stanger's must have been when he'd first seen Adams. "It'll be all right. Just stay there. Don't come any closer." Without taking her eyes off him, she took the communicator from her belt with her free hand and spoke into it.

She took a few steps toward him, past the cubicle where Adams was hidden.

Her tricorder did not signal. It was true, then: Adams had no life-sign readings. *Then why,* Stanger asked himself, *is the tricorder detecting* me?

She was close enough now so that he could see her clearly, even the faint traces of the seam where M'Benga had sealed her neck wound. Stanger closed his eyes and shuddered, the sweet, seductive call of blood thrumming in his ears. His fingers dropped to his belt, to his utility knife.

He opened his eyes and moved toward her, unsure what he was going to do. He was almost close enough to touch her.

"Stanger," Lisa whispered. She was near sobbing. He could not tell if it was from grief for him or fear.

Behind her, Adams floated silently from his cubicle. The velvet cape spread out behind Lisa like dark, ominous wings.

"Lisa! No!"

She followed his terrified gaze and dashed to one side as Stanger rushed forward into the cape and took the blow intended for her. The knife ripped across both his arms.

Fighting the frenzy evoked by the scent of his own blood, Stanger ignored the knife in Adams' hand and grabbed his throat. Insanity and rage filled him with strength. With his hands still around Adams' neck, Stanger pulled his enemy off his feet and dashed his head against the wall of the cubicle.

The thud of Adams' head against the wall gave rhythm to Stanger's thoughts.

I'm your last victim, understand? Your last victim, your last victim.

His head slammed once, twice, a thousand times, while Lisa and Acker yelled and waved their phasers, and Adams screamed . . .

Until everything went beautifully, blissfully dark.

Infrared visor in his hand, Jim Kirk walked over to the darkened section of sickbay where Adams and Stanger were being held. There was no longer any reason to keep them in an isolation unit, especially since McCoy believed in the value of hands-on treatment. But both were strapped onto the diagnostic beds with restraints, and a visored Ensign Nguyen stood over them.

Almost Junior-Grade Lieutenant Nguyen, Kirk corrected himself. Tomson had asked him for permission yesterday to put through a rush request for Nguyen's promotion. Evidently, Nguyen was shaken by her near-fatal run-in with Adams and was thinking of leaving the Fleet. Tomson was not above using bribery to keep a good officer; neither, Kirk decided, was he. He had forwarded Tomson's request with his approval.

But he was surprised to see that she had put Nguyen in charge of her former attacker. He supposed that the point was to get Nguyen to confront her fear and master it; but one look at Nguyen's eyes made Kirk doubt the wisdom of the idea. Maybe it wasn't fear so much that Nguyen needed to overcome, but hatred.

He put on his visor and smiled at her.

"Captain," she said. She did not smile back. Beneath the filter, her eyes were somber.

Kirk walked to the side of Adams' bed. Three beds down, Stanger writhed under the restraints and moaned softly, as if he were having a bad dream.

Both were being transfused, but Adams seemed spiritless after Stanger's violent attack on him. He rolled his head on his pillow to look at Kirk. His expression did not change.

It was more than recuperating from the concussion that had weakened him. McCoy had said that Adams' illness had advanced to a new stage, that the virus could no longer maintain stability. Adams was dying, and Kirk looked at him without the slightest sympathy.

"Mendez knows you're on board." Jim said it not as a threat, but a simple statement of fact. "Unless you tell me what I want, I'll turn you over to him as soon as we arrive at Tanis."

"Tanis?" Adams' eyes widened, half hopeful, half afraid. He turned his head back to stare at the ceiling and said, "What do you want to know?"

"I need . . . evidence. Evidence to convict Mendez. Unless you'd prefer to take the fall alone."

"No," Adams whispered. He closed his eyes. "I wouldn't."

Kirk waited for a while for the man to speak, but Adams remained silent. "Spock thinks there's a body still down on Tanis, a Vulcan who died of the original virus."

Adams was silent for a long time. At last he said, as if remembering something very unpleasant, "Sepek. The first to die. By that time, the virus had already mutated."

Kirk leaned over the bed. So it was true. Spock was right after all. "Two forms still exist?"

"They did. I don't know if the R-form—"

"Effective against Romulans," Kirk said quickly. No doubt certain members of Fleet brass had not been content with conventional weapons against their enemies.

Adams did not contradict him. "I don't know if it still exists. Sepek is dead, and the lab is decontaminated. All samples were destroyed—though I suppose recovering Sepek's body would show dead organisms and traces of the disease."

"That will have to do." Kirk said.

"As long as you have me," Adams added, with a hideous grin that made him look like a skull. "You need me, don't you?"

Kirk stared at him with open hatred. "Not quite as much as you need us. But I have more questions. It strikes me as rather odd that a microbe should mutate from a form deadly to Romulans into a form deadly to humans."

Adams shook his head weakly, his tone suddenly that of the scientist. "No. Such a rapidly proliferating virus can go through a hundred generations in a day. It wasn't surprising that an alternate version was dangerous to another life form."

Kirk listened, unconvinced. "And most importantly, how can we recover Sepek's body? We didn't pick it up during our search."

"That's because it's hidden in a specially sealed stasis tube on the base. We couldn't have a regular stasis room like you have on the *Enterprise*. The assumption was that a corpse was likely to be contaminated, given the nature of our business."

"Odd," Kirk said, more to himself than to Adams, "that a Vulcan would be involved in illegal research."

"Sepek . . . misled Mendez. He pretended to be a rebel Vulcan, an outcast." He looked up at Kirk. "They *do* happen, you know."

"So I've heard," Kirk said dryly.

"But after a while it became clear he was working for Starfleet after all, trying to stall our project. When Mendez found out, he had us arrange an 'accident.' It was easy enough, since at the time, the R-virus was dangerous only to Vulcanoids. Unlike the mutated form, it brings death swiftly." Adams paused soberly. "It could decimate the Romulan population in a matter of months."

Kirk shook his head. What kind of man was Mendez, that he would risk everything—his career in the Fleet, his son, his freedom—to get revenge against the Romulans? "Is there anything else we could use as evidence? Anything at all?"

213

"Showing that a Vulcan died of a genetically engineered virus doesn't prove much, does it?" The death-mask grin crossed Adams' face once more. "I guess that's all you have . . . except for me."

Stanger cried out in his sleep again, and Kirk turned away. They had said that Stanger had come very close to strangling Adams, that he had grabbed Adams by the neck and pounded his head against the wall.

Kirk felt envious. He walked past Ensign Nguyen and nodded. She nodded back politely, but beneath the visor, hatred smoldered in her eyes, and he knew it matched his own.

After Kirk left, Lisa stood silently in the darkness and watched her prisoners.

Adams closed his eyes and seemed to sleep, but even so, it was hard for her to look at him for very long. She hated him with a bitterness she had never known before. He had made her think she was going to die, and she could not forgive him for that. She was young, too young to have to face that yet. Adams, no one, had the right to make her face up to anything as terrifying as her own mortality.

At the same time, the experience had made her think, and she was glad of that. Otherwise, she would not have accepted Rajiv's offer.

Of course, up until tonight, Lisa's mind had been made up to go to Colorado. Now, she found herself wavering again, and it was all Lieutenant Tomson's fault. It was Tomson who had put Nguyen in charge of the search, Tomson who had assigned her (over Lisa's loud protests) to watch over Adams. It was Tomson who had forced her to face up to what had happened to her.

And the most infuriating thing about it was, Tomson's strategy was working. Lisa was still full of venom for Adams and what he had done to her, but she found she could control herself. She could stand guard over him and not strangle him with her bare hands. The fear was there, too, but becoming more manageable with each moment's passing. True, she had almost died . . . *almost,* but she hadn't.

214

She was alive, and the encounter she had feared most of all had occurred, and she had survived again.

She was beginning to remember why she loved the Fleet.

"Rosa," Stanger cried out softly. He had grown so violent at the sight of Adams in the nearby bed that McCoy had sedated him, but he was beginning to come out of it.

Lisa glanced at Adams: still sleeping. She took a sideways step toward Stanger, careful to keep Adams in the periphery of her vision. "It's all right, Jon." She said it low so that Adams wouldn't hear.

Stanger stared up at her, his eyes wild, lost, and struggled against the restraints to sit up. The sight of him broke her heart. Jon was a good person; even in the throes of the disease that had turned Adams into a killer, he had saved her life. He didn't deserve what Adams had done to him. Lisa blinked back tears, grateful that Adams was not watching.

"Rosa," Stanger repeated piteously.

She placed a hand on his arm and said, "I'm here."

Her touch seemed to calm him . . . for a moment, at least. Then his face contorted as if he were going to cry. "Rosa . . . why didn't you tell them?"

"Tell them what?" She humored him.

"That the phaser was yours." He started tossing from side to side. "But you didn't even *tell* me. Fell out and blew the damn bulkhead right out. Everybody there. And I never even *knew.*"

Blew the bulkhead out—what were Acker's exact words? She could see him sitting in the security lounge, scanning the room with his bright blue eyes to make sure Stanger wasn't nearby, and saying: *Fell out and blew the bulkhead out in the officers' lounge, right in front of the first officer! Talk about bad luck.*

Lisa's mouth dropped open. "Jon . . . are you saying the phaser wasn't *yours?*"

"I waited for you," Stanger whispered hoarsely. "I took the blame and I waited for you to come forward. I thought you cared about me, Rosa, but you never came."

"Hush." She put a pale hand to his dark forehead and

215

found it moist and warm to the touch. She marveled: all this time, and Jon had silently swallowed the blame for someone named Rosa, had given up his rank . . . .

And suddenly there was no longer any doubt in her mind about Colorado. It was quite clear what she had to do.

"You never came," Stanger moaned.

Lisa stroked his forehead again. "I'm here now," she said, and actually found it in herself to smile.

Chapter Fifteen

CHRIS CHAPEL STRUGGLED against encroaching consciousness. She'd been floating peacefully . . . for how long? Forever. A long time, but it didn't matter. She was content to
sleep, and didn't want to wake up, ever, ever, ever . . .

She fought it as long as she could, but the mist began to
lift, and as it did, her senses slowly returned. Feeling was
first: the sensation of breathing, the rise and fall of her chest,
the slightly cool temperature of the room, the yielding
support of the diagnostic bed beneath her. Hearing was
next, the sounds muffled and indistinct to start, then all at
once sharp and clear. She listened with her eyes closed,
staring into gray velvet nothing, and heard a baritone lilt,
one she recognized. The face came to her immediately, but
not the name.

*Her vital signs are stabilizing. Heme level rising. She's
coming out of it. Tell Tjieng it works!*

She understood each word by itself, but together they
made no sense at all. Reluctantly, she opened her eyes and
stared into the very face she had just conjured. "M'Benga,"
she remembered. Talking was difficult. Her mouth was very
dry.

M'Benga's smile spread from one corner of his dark face
to the other. "Christine! You have no idea how glad we are
to see *you!*" He handed her a glass of water without her even
asking.

"Bless you," she croaked, propping herself on one elbow. She took a small sip and swished it over her parched gums before swallowing. Not too fast, don't want to get sick. There was an odd taste in her mouth, metallic, like iron. As if she had bitten her tongue . . .

A horrible thought occurred to her. "Did I—" she stammered, hardly able to imagine it, much less say it. "Did I turn into another . . . Adams?"

M'Benga's smile broadened. "You never got to that stage, Chris. Besides, you're just not the type."

She smiled weakly at that. "Have I been out long?" So many questions. If it were just easier to talk . . .

"A few days."

"Wow." No wonder she felt weak. She looked around, and noticed with incredible relief that the lights were *on* . . . and they didn't hurt. But something was wrong. Someone was missing.

"Where's Leonard?" she asked, trying not to sound hurt. Certainly, if she'd been that sick, McCoy would have been here to see her the instant she woke up.

The smile faded. M'Benga sighed. "Christine, you're not going to believe this. . . ."

How do I keep getting into these messes? McCoy asked himself, opening his squeezed-shut eyes to darkness overlaid by the glimmer of his field suit. It was a rhetorical question. He knew full well how he had gotten into this particular mess: he had volunteered. And it made perfect sense for Jim to take him up on the offer. After all, he had been down to Tanis twice before and was most familiar with the layout.

A light flared in the darkness next to him and he could just distinguish the shimmering outline of Spock's form. It had made absolutely no sense at all for the Vulcan to go, but apparently he had said something to the captain that convinced Jim to send him. Some mumbo-jumbo about Vulcan burial rites and responsibility, McCoy perceived, though he knew better than to try to ask Spock about it when the Vulcan got that inscrutable look.

The beam from Spock's flashlight swept the room in a slow, steady arc, across bare walls, across the containment chamber with the hole McCoy had burned in it.

"This is it," McCoy said. "The lab." The field suit muted his voice and made it sound faraway to him, as if he had stuffed cotton in his ears. In spite of being vaccinated, he had decided to wear it; no telling what other sorts of surprises down here Adams might have forgotten to tell them about. For Spock, the danger of exposure to the R-virus made the suit mandatory. McCoy sighed and wished he were anywhere else at the moment. If he could have his choice, he would be in sickbay, where M'Benga was watching Chris Chapel right now. Tjieng's lab had come up with something to stabilize the anemia, and before he left, the last thing he had done was to convince them to try it out on Chris. She was part of the medical staff, after all, and it was more ethical to use her as a guinea pig than Adams or Stanger. Besides, Chris would have volunteered.

It was true, and no one disagreed. Still, Tjieng smirked at him knowingly when he suggested it.

Maybe that's why I feel so damn skittish. Worried about Chris. No reason for this place to still give me the willies.

Of course, they *had* come down here to recover a body. Spock motioned with the beam. "The vault would be this way," he said. McCoy followed, staying just a little behind the Vulcan as the light cut a path before them. They walked slowly out of the lab, into the narrow, claustrophobic corridor McCoy remembered all too well.

Now that the doctor understood how the virus worked, he knew that the deceased Vulcan they were recovering could not have survived indefinitely in stasis. If Adams' R-virus worked anything like the mutated H-virus, poor Sepek would probably have come out of his coma anywhere from ten to forty-eight hours after he was in stasis. How long depended on how severe his anemia was when he went into the coma. At a critical level, the virus would "waken" him to search for blood, preferably transfused. But Sepek had been sealed into the vault without any hope of escape. McCoy flinched mentally at the vision of the man, clawing at the sealed lid of his tube with his last shreds of incredible Vulcan strength. . . . He had no doubt died weeks ago.

Assuming, of course, that the R-virus works similarly to its mutated form. The alternative made McCoy shudder.

They passed sickbay, the flashlight skimming over the open door, the dark stains on the floor. A few paces beyond sickbay, Spock stopped. McCoy just caught himself in time to avoid running into him.

"The vault," Spock said. The light focused on a heavy metal panel built into the bulkhead. Next to it was a code panel.

Talkative, aren't you? McCoy suddenly missed Stanger; at least the joking would have helped to ease the tension. And no point at all in teasing the Vulcan when he got this way. He stood silently while Spock punched in the code, and tried to prepare himself for the rumble as the seal opened and the heavy metal wall slid upward.

Nothing happened.

Are you sure you entered the right code? McCoy almost said, but stopped himself in time. Ridiculous question to ask a Vulcan.

But it must have occurred to Spock, too. He entered the code again, then turned, frowning, to the doctor.

"Either Adams gave us the incorrect code, or—"

"Or the computer system is down, for some reason," McCoy finished helpfully.

Still frowning, Spock took the communicator from his belt. "Spock to *Enterprise.*"

"Enterprise. Kirk here. Any problems?"

"Apparently so, Captain. The vault refuses to open."

There was a pause as Jim considered the same possibilities McCoy and Spock had. "Any chance of getting through it with the phasers?"

Spock studied the wall thoughtfully, then answered, "Possibly. The metal appears to be a beryllium alloy, though it is impossible to estimate its thickness. I would expect, however, that burning through it would take considerably more time than we had planned."

Great, McCoy thought dismally. *Just great.*

Another pause. "We're keeping an eye out for anyone,"

Kirk said finally. "If anyone approaches, we're beaming you up immediately. Is that understood, Spock?"

Without the body, McCoy understood, and looked up at the Vulcan's face. But Spock remained impassive. "Understood, sir."

"Kirk out."

Spock put the communicator back on his belt.

"Well," McCoy said with asperity, "I suppose it could have been worse."

Spock raised his eyebrows questioningly.

"At least one of us wore a phaser." The doctor spread his hands out to show his belt, on which there were various medical items, but certainly no phaser. He hated wearing them, and certainly had no intention of using one.

Besides, who was he going to shoot at down here? The corpse? *(Don't even think it—)*

"It will slow us down somewhat," Spock admitted, "but will not prevent success."

"Strange definition of success," McCoy muttered under his breath. Spock opened his mouth to say something and closed it again. A curious expression crossed his face.

McCoy frowned, puzzling over what had distracted him, until he heard it, too: the sound of footsteps coming down the corridor.

Good God, Sepek made it out.

But it sounded like more than one person.

Next to him, Spock tensed, his hand reaching for the phaser on his belt. McCoy would have liked to screw his eyes shut at that point, but instead they opened wider and wider until he could make out two figures in the shadows. Human men, apparently very much alive, and wearing Fleet uniforms. McCoy did not recognize the tall blond one. The other, dark and stocky, he had seen before, and he tried to place him.

The viewscreen in the conference room. McCoy gulped.

"Admiral Mendez," Spock said politely, nodding as if he had just been introduced at a brass cocktail party. His hand stayed on his phaser.

But the blond man wearing a gold tunic already had his drawn.

"Please take your hand off your phaser," the admiral said conversationally. He shone a flashlight inconsiderately in their faces. "Or I will give the lieutenant here the order to kill you. I take it you are Commander Spock, Kirk's first officer. We've been waiting for you gentlemen for some time."

Spock slowly removed his hand from his belt.

"Well, isn't this all very cordial," McCoy said nastily, squinting into the light. He'd been looking forward to the chance to be nasty to Mendez for some time, but had never expected to get the opportunity. "So you're the man responsible for the deaths on Tanis and for infecting our crew with the plague."

He was too blinded to see Mendez's face, but he could hear the quick anger in the voice. "You have the wrong man, Doctor. Jeffrey Adams is the only person to blame."

"You set him up," McCoy countered.

"It was Adams who developed the R-virus," Mendez answered invisibly, his voice ringing with hate, "and Adams who developed the H-virus."

"The H-virus"—Spock's deep voice was as calm and rational as if they were debating theory—"was an accidental mutation."

"No. Adams developed it to sell it to the Romulans."

"That's *your* opinion," said McCoy.

"Yes, that's my opinion. And I know Jeffrey Adams well." Mendez's tone abruptly shifted to indicate that any discussion was at an end. "Your communicators, gentlemen. And your phaser, of course, Mr. Spock."

Spock handed them over without protest, while the doctor scowled at him disapprovingly.

"You're going to give them over just like *that?*" he hissed.

"Do you have a better suggestion?" Spock asked mildly.

McCoy squinted blindly into the light. At the moment, he did not. Sighing, he held out his communicator. The blond lieutenant snatched it from his hand and began to frisk him.

"Hey," the doctor complained, as the search proceeded roughly up his leg. "What is this? I'm not in the habit of carrying concealed weapons."

Mendez did not answer. The lieutenant finished with McCoy and turned his attention to Spock. At the end of it, he reported back to the admiral. "They're not carrying anything, sir."

It was definitely not what Mendez wanted to hear. He turned impatiently to his prisoners. "All right, where is it?"

Was he asking about Sepek's body? McCoy glanced sideways at Spock. The Vulcan wasn't answering, so the doctor kept his mouth shut.

"The R-virus. Where is it?" Mendez took a threatening step towards them. "I assure you, I will do whatever's necessary to retrieve it."

McCoy frowned. Maybe he wasn't looking for Sepek's body, but for something *else*.

He nodded to his aide, who raised the phaser and seemed to be very serious about firing it.

"There *isn't* any virus," the doctor blurted. *Fine prisoner of war* you'd *make, McCoy.* "If there is, we don't know where—"

The admiral's voice was filled with sarcasm, but beneath it, McCoy sensed, was desperation. "Then what are you doing on Tanis? Sight-seeing?" He nodded at the blond man. "Go ahead, Jase. Kill them."

"Wait!" McCoy raised his hands in a don't-shoot gesture, aware of Spock's disapproving gaze on him. "We were looking for a body—a Vulcan researcher." Hands still in the air, he turned to Spock. "What was his name?"

"Sepek," Spock answered in a quiet voice, looking mightily disgusted at the doctor's cowardice.

"I'm afraid you're rather late for that," Mendez said matter-of-factly. "His body has been destroyed."

Spock closed his eyes.

Mendez moved closer. "The R-virus. This is the last time I'll ask."

"But there isn't—" McCoy began.

Angered, Mendez cut him off. "Do you think we're stupid? Adams is a sick and desperate man; I have no doubt that he told you about our agreement that if anything went wrong, he would preserve a sample at any cost and hide it on Tanis so that it could be retrieved. But he's hidden it too cleverly; we haven't been able to find it. And *you* know where it is."

Spock and McCoy simply stared at him, unable to answer.

"We have weapons down here, do you understand? You both are willing to die nobly to protect your ship and your captain, but if you don't give me the virus, I'll blow the *Enterprise* out of orbit before I kill you both."

"My *God,*" McCoy whispered, paling. There was no way to warn Jim. . . .

"We came to retrieve Sepek's body," Spock said calmly, "and nothing more."

The lieutenant glanced at his superior. "It almost sounds like they're telling the truth, Admiral."

Mendez scrutinized them both for a moment, then an odd expression—regret? McCoy wondered—crossed his face. "I had hoped to avoid this," he said heavily, and flipped Spock's communicator open. "*Enterprise,* come in, please."

Kirk's voice, hot and strident. "Admiral, if anything has happened to my people—"

"A commendable attitude, Kirk," Mendez answered, quite serious. "Nothing has happened to your people. Nothing *will* happen to them if you do as I say."

"Just like nothing happened to Quince Waverleigh."

"I don't know anything about that," Mendez snapped. "If you want your people to live, you'll stop with the accusations."

There was a pause, and then Kirk said, grudgingly, "What do you want me to do?"

"The R-virus," Mendez said. "You have it. I want it."

"You're wrong, Admiral. The R-virus was destroyed by the decontamination system on Tanis."

"You're a bigger fool than I thought if you believe that," Mendez snarled. "And if you expect me to. You have Adams. By now, he's told you about the hidden sample. He knew I'd come looking for it *and* him, and he's told you where it is to try to protect himself."

There was a pause on the other end of the communicator.

McCoy resolved never to volunteer for anything again . . . that is, if he made it through this one. "Admiral," Kirk finally said. His tone had changed abruptly, acquired a negotiating wheedle. "I have no way of knowing if that's true . . . unless you give me five minutes to question Adams."

"Take six," said Mendez. "After that, your men are dead."

How very generous of you, McCoy wanted to add, but decided it would be better to hold his tongue.

"Captain." Sulu in the background, his voice clear and urgent. "I'm picking up a slight distortion on the screen."

"Magnify viewscreen." A pause, then, in clipped tones, "Red alert. Shields up, helmsman."

The klaxon sounded. "Aye, sir."

"Kirk," Mendez thundered. "Don't try it if you want your men to live."

"I'm not trying to pull anything, dammit," Kirk answered hotly. "We've got a visitor here. Expecting anyone?"

There was a snap as Mendez closed the communicator and lowered his light, and McCoy, the beam's image still imprinted on his retina, blinked sightlessly while a strong arm circled his neck and someone shoved a phaser into his back.

The doctor heard the whine of a transporter. *Well, hell, this is it.* Jim was taking an awfully big chance and beaming them up to the ship . . . a bigger chance than McCoy would have taken. Mendez was certain to make good on his promise to kill them. McCoy braced himself and wondered detachedly what being dissolved by a phaser blast felt like. For that matter, could one be dissolved while caught in a transporter beam?

A technological double-whammy. *I always knew that damned transporter would get me someday.* He scrunched his eyes shut, rather uselessly because he couldn't see anything anyway. Either he would feel the phaser blast first, or the unpleasant moment of dizziness he always felt in the transporter beam. He was betting on the phaser.

But the dizziness swept him. *Bad enough to die without having to do it in the middle of a transporter beam.* He waited for the blast sure to follow, but none came. The whine reverberating in his skull ceased, the bright aura dissipated. The phaser was still pressing against his spine. The doctor tensed, expecting full well to find himself smack in the middle of a standoff, with himself and Spock the most likely losers. He expected to see the familiar interior of the *Enterprise*'s transporter room, lined with the red tunics of the entire security force.

The room was crowded with security personnel, all right. But the uniforms were the wrong color, a matte silver mesh. McCoy blinked, stunned. By no means had he expected to find himself in the transporter room of a Romulan ship.

The grip on his throat loosened as the blond lieutenant fired his phaser, almost hitting one of the Romulan guards. It took McCoy less than a second to realize that every Romulan in the room was aiming a phaser directly at the lieutenant. What did it matter to them if McCoy accidentally got in the way? He took a deep breath and pulled down with all his strength.

It was enough to break free of the distracted lieutenant's grip. McCoy threw himself onto the floor and rolled. Even with his eyes screwed shut, he could see the blinding blast from the Romulan weapon, could feel the searing heat down the length of his back. He heard an excited yelp: Mendez. McCoy lay there, too stunned to move, until an incredibly strong grip pulled him to his feet. Spock, he thought at first, then opened his eyes to a collarbone covered by dull silver metal.

He almost looked behind him for the lieutenant, but stopped himself. There would be nothing left to see.

The man on the bridge's main viewscreen was long-faced, dark-haired, elegant. It was not just the upswept brows and ears that reminded Kirk of his first officer. There was something about the eyes, the bridge of the nose; he could have been Spock's second cousin.

"Captain Kirk," he said politely and with supreme confidence, without the help of the universal translator. His accent was near-perfect; only a trace of too little aspiration in the *k* sounds, too much trill in the *r,* gave him away as

Romulan. That, and the dull silver mesh uniform with the black sash at the shoulder. "I am Subcommander Khaefv."

Kirk wasted no time on diplomacy. His heart was still hammering in his chest from the sudden realization that McCoy and Spock were on board the Romulan vessel. It took all his self-control not to immediately ask whether they were all right. "Subcommander, you have violated the Neutral Zone Treaty, committing an act of war. You have kidnapped my men, showing that your intent is aggression. If anything happens to them, the Federation—"

Khaefv smiled, unaffected. "No one has been harmed, Captain. We could certainly debate ownership of this particular area of space with you, but in any case, we have not violated the spirit of the treaty. Our mission is one of rescue, not aggression."

Kirk's scowl deepened as he tried to second-guess Khaefv's motivation. Obviously, Romulan intelligence must have heard that the Federation had developed a bioweapon against them. Despite his outer calm, Khaefv was probably on a suicide mission to recover or destroy the microbe at any cost. "We have detected no other Romulan vessels in this area. Certainly no crippled ones. There's no one here for you to rescue."

"On the contrary. We have come to free a political prisoner from the oppressive Federation regime. Someone on board the *Enterprise* . . . a Dr. Jeffrey Adams."

Kirk laughed out loud. "A political prisoner? Dr. Adams is accused of murder. That's hardly a political charge. And I seriously doubt he'll go with you."

"I regret having to contradict you again, Captain. Dr. Adams contacted us to request the rescue."

"I refuse to believe it."

"There is one way to find out. Why don't you ask Dr. Adams?"

In the outer office of sickbay, M'Benga was incredibly ecstatic, so much so that the flashing yellow alert beacon and the scowl carved into Kirk's forehead failed to discourage him.

"Captain." His tone was one of delight at serendipitous

227

coincidence. "I was just about to call you again. I tried during the red alert, but the board was jammed. We gave Christine Chapel the serum, and it's stabilized the anemia."

"A cure?" Kirk was still frowning. Certainly he was happy for Chapel, for Stanger, maybe in some distant humanitarian part of himself happy for Adams—but right now he couldn't afford the time to show it.

"Close to it. They'll need regular doses of the medicine for a while . . . not a one-shot cure, but an eventual one. It definitely suppresses the virus' action." M'Benga rattled on happily.

"The Romulans have got McCoy and Spock," Kirk said. "Adams signaled them to come here. He's trying to cut a deal."

It worked. M'Benga stopped smiling, closed his mouth, and stared at the captain. Kirk felt bad doing it this way, but it was fastest—and there was very little time. He hadn't known exactly how he was going to get Adams to cooperate until this very moment.

"Have you given it to Adams yet?" he asked M'Benga.

The doctor shook his head. "Not yet. But I was just about to administer it to him and Stanger. It won't interfere if you want to question him."

"Give it to Stanger. I want to talk to Adams first."

M'Benga's reaction was swift. Kirk had never seen him in anything but a pleasant mood, but now something hard crept into the doctor's expression. "The man is dying, Captain. He's dangerously ill. It would be unethical for me to withhold treatment."

"Let me talk to him first," Kirk repeated. He held back his growing frustration. *He's as bad as McCoy.*

"I'd rather not." A muscle under the smooth skin of M'Benga's jaw twitched.

"I could order you," Kirk said, without emotion. He did not like having to say it, but there was no time for a discussion of ethics.

"And as acting chief medical officer, I could override your order."

"Five minutes," Kirk said in a humbler tone. "Do you

228

think he could make it five minutes? Especially since we're talking about saving two lives?" He didn't count Mendez.

M'Benga sighed and stroked his jaw as if to soothe all the tension from it. "You have a point there, Captain. But only five minutes. Then I go ahead and administer the serum to him."

"One last thing, Doctor. I promise not to physically harm Adams, but I'm going to have to use scare tactics on him." He looked intently into M'Benga's black eyes. "Spock and McCoy's lives."

M'Benga sighed. "I won't interfere unless you hurt him, Captain."

He put on an infrared visor and gave one to the captain. Kirk followed him from the office to the darkened corner of the treatment area where Stanger and Adams were held. The Andorian ensign was standing guard this time, anxiously watching Stanger, who seemed to be resting more calmly now. *The man has a lot of friends,* Kirk thought.

Adams lay on his bed looking gray and shriveled.

"Adams," Kirk said softly, as M'Benga went a few beds over to Stanger. He could hear a delighted exclamation from Lamia as the doctor explained the drug.

Adams opened one dull eye and glanced up listlessly, then closed it.

"Dr. M'Benga is administering a cure to Mr. Stanger," Kirk said in an exaggeratedly pleasant tone. "It stabilizes the anemia."

Adams' eye opened again. "A cure?" he whispered.

Kirk grabbed a handful of fabric on either side of Adams' neck and pulled him to a sitting position. It was cathartic, pleasurable, good to be able to scream with hatred at the man. "Your ride is here!"

Adams made a small squeaking sound.

"You miserable liar!" Kirk thundered. The others in the room had grown very quiet. "They're *here,* just like you've always planned it! *Where* is the R-virus they're asking for? *Where is it?*" He shook until he could hear Adams' teeth clicking together.

"Stop it!" Adams moaned.

"Go to the Romulans, then! Sell them the R-virus. Sell them the H-virus, too—why not? You're a walking lab culture. Because it doesn't matter! We've got the cure for it right here. Too bad you've got to leave with the Romulans. Let's see if they're in such a hurry to find a cure just for *you!*"

Adams was making a strange gasping sound, somewhere between a groan and a sob.

Kirk lowered his voice. "You'll be dead by morning, Adams."

The terror in Adams' eyes gave him a twisted pleasure. "No . . ."

He forced himself to speak calmly, though it was difficult. He didn't want to stop shaking the man; it would have been so easy just to raise his hands to the thin throat and squeeze. "The Romulans have two of my men. And if you don't do everything I tell you to *now,* I'm going to send you to them without the drug and let you die." He paused. "If they don't kill you as soon as they get a blood sample from you."

That much was true . . . and surely Adams must have considered it himself. Kirk glanced to one side and saw M'Benga frowning, his arms knotted in front of his chest. It was probably all the doctor could do to hold himself back. *As bad as McCoy.*

Shaking weakly with dry sobs, Adams pulled the amulet from his neck and handed it to Kirk. "Take it. *Take* it."

Kirk stared. "What's this?"

"The R-virus," Adams whispered. "Sealed inside. It's what you want, isn't it? Take it. Give me the drug."

M'Benga rose, but Kirk shook his head at him and handed him the pendant. To Adams he said, "I need you to talk to the Romulans for me. They say you want political asylum in the Empire. Tell them they've made a mistake. Tell them to leave."

"All right. Just give me the shot."

"You killed them, didn't you? The other researchers?"

"Yes," Adams hissed through gray, cracked lips. "I killed them. Lara first, and then Yoshi. In arranging the 'accident' for Sepek, I inadvertently exposed myself to the mutated form of the virus. Sepek died quickly, but I wasn't as lucky. The hunger . . ." He twitched painfully. "When they were all dead, the hunger stayed. I realized I would starve to death alone, so I sent the distress signal. I couldn't help it. Give me the shot."

Kirk leaned closer. "And what you've said about Mendez . . . is it all true?"

"All true." His head lolled weakly on his neck. "Please . . ."

Kirk looked at him without pity, thinking of Yoshi, of Lara Krovozhadny, of Lisa Nguyen, of Chapel and Stanger. "*After* you do as I say."

They used the viewscreen in the doctor's office and had Uhura relay a channel down to sickbay. Adams was so weak that his head fell back against the headrest of M'Benga's chair. The doctor stood to one side with the hypospray ready.

Adams was desperate enough to do a convincing job. Subcommander Khaefv listened expressionlessly and said, "This is all very interesting. However, we feel that Dr. Adams has been coerced into a change of heart, if I am using the idiom correctly. Since you clearly have no intention of turning him over to us, I have no choice but to order the execution of the prisoners." He signaled to his communications officer to close the channel.

"Wait!" Kirk leaned toward the screen. "There's no longer any point in trying to play games, Subcommander. Why can't we bargain truthfully?"

Khaefv folded his hands patiently and said nothing.

"We have the R-virus," Kirk said, hoping like hell he wasn't getting in over his head. Khaefv seemed young for a subcommander, so it was a safe bet he got there by being shrewd. "That's what you want, isn't it? So you can develop a cure, neutralize the threat? Although"—he swung the pendant in front of the screen—"I guarantee this is the only live culture remaining."

Khaefv's placid expression didn't even flicker. "We want that, and Dr. Adams."

231

"Because he harbors the mutated form deadly to humans. But as a bioweapon, its use is now limited. We've found a cure."

"Dr. Adams," Khaefv remarked dryly, "does not look very much to me like a man who has been cured."

"It's true," Adams croaked haggardly. "He's withholding it so I'll talk."

Khaefv glanced from Adams to Kirk with an expression very like admiration for a worthy opponent.

"I'm sure you realize by now that Adams is a criminal. The Federation hasn't broken its own laws on biowarfare. The R-virus was developed illegally, and I'm trying to repair the damage." Kirk gazed intently at him with what he hoped was his sincerest expression; if there were only some way to reach inside Khaefv's skull and show that he was telling the truth . . . "Believe me, Subcommander, we both have the same aim: to destroy the threat posed by the R-virus."

"How very interesting," Khaefv murmured, trying to seem disinterested, but Kirk caught the glimmer of curiosity in his eyes.

"Suppose we compromise and meet someplace neutral to destroy the R-virus?"

"We can just as easily destroy it aboard our ship," Khaefv countered.

Kirk half smiled and shrugged apologetically. "Subcommander, you can appreciate the Federation's concern about a virus that affects Vulcanoids." Surely he was giving nothing away; the Romulans no doubt were planning to test whether Vulcans were affected by the virus. And Vulcan was the backbone of the Federation. "A neutral area would be best."

"I suppose you consider your ship a neutral area," Khaefv said acerbically.

"I was thinking of Tanis base."

Khaefv considered for a moment. "Frankly, Captain Kirk, we have absolutely no way of knowing whether the sample you bring us contains the R-virus. And certainly no way to be sure that it is the only sample left in existence. There could be hundreds of vials of it on your ship . . . or

232

anywhere else in Federation space." He smiled humorlessly. "I would be very foolish to accept your offer."

"Dr. Adams and I would be willing to submit to a verifier scan," Kirk said, desperate, but he knew from the cold in Khaefv's eyes that the matter was closed.

"I am sure you are a man of honor"—there was not a trace of sarcasm in Khaefv's tone—"but as you mentioned, Dr. Adams is a criminal, and may have misled you. And verifier scans are not one hundred percent conclusive, especially with certain . . . personality types." He paused, and a subtle hardness crept into his expression. "No, Captain, I cannot agree to your proposal. The prisoners will be questioned, then executed. I regret that we could not come to an agreement." He signaled again to his communications officer, and this time, Kirk's protests did not prevent the screen from going black.

Chapter Sixteen

SPOCK LAY STRETCHED out on the cold floor. The cell was apparently designed for sensory deprivation: no furniture, bare walls and floor an unbroken gray. Intended to cause boredom and anxiousness, perhaps, but Spock found it restful.

He was concentrating on one of the two burly Rihannsu guards just beyond the force field that held him captive. Their brains were structured almost exactly the same as his own, although Rihannsu minds were undisciplined by Vulcan standards. Still, it was more of a challenge for Spock to implant a suggestion in the guard's mind than in a human's.

Spock chose to concentrate on the less intelligent of the two; it would increase the chances of his plan's working. Certain Vulcans would say that what he was doing to the guard was immoral, yet Spock was firmly convinced that, in light of the threat posed by the R-virus, what he was doing was justified. Better to use what methods he could, if it would help to save lives. Besides, he was not technically violating the guard's mind. He took nothing from it, only planted an image.

A vivid one, at that: Spock, dying on the gray floor of the cell. He concentrated on the image until it became so real in his own mind that he did not doubt it . . . and then he directed it to the mind of the guard.

Outside, the guard began to squint through the force field

at his prisoner. Spock's eyes were closed, but he knew it just as surely as if he had seen it. He concentrated harder on the image of death; the muscles in his face sagged.

After a few minutes, the guard could resist no more. He called to his companion to say he was going to examine the prisoner. Spock listened to all this without losing the image or the anxiety he projected. It was easy enough to understand, since the language was derived from Old Vulcan.

The hum of the force field stopped. Footsteps. Spock knew the other guard would be standing watch by the door. He held a phaser, and Spock split his concentration for a precarious moment, long enough to plant the suggestion that both guards put their weapons on stun. Then, quickly, he returned his full attention to the guard bending over him.

He had already put the image in the first guard's mind: bending down over the prisoner, just so, to check the pulse in the Vulcan's neck . . .

And very conveniently exposing the sensitive area at the juncture of the neck and collarbone. Spock reached out and pressed, hard. The Rihannsu toppled over on him, conveniently falling so that Spock had only to pluck the phaser from his hand, and use the unconscious man as a shield so that the other guard hesitated before firing. Spock did not. The second guard slid to the floor. Spock carefully propped the first guard against the wall, then relieved the second of his phaser.

Up to this point, it had all been quite simple, but Spock knew that the difficult part was just beginning.

"How can we get to them?" Kirk spoke quickly; there wasn't much time. *How long does it take to turn someone's mind inside out?* Instinct said: *Relax. Khaefv's playing a waiting game. He dare not go home without the virus.* But the stakes made it impossible to relax. He sat in the conference room nearest the bridge, drumming his fingers lightly against the polished tabletop. The situation made him feel Spock and McCoy's absence all the more keenly; they were precisely the two people he would have turned to for advice at a critical time like this. He glanced at the faces across the table from him: Uhura, Scotty, Sulu.

235

"We can't beam them," Engineer Scott said in clipped tones, having picked up on the captain's sense of urgency. He rested his arms on the table and folded his hands. "The Romulans have their deflector shields up, and as long as that's so, there's no beaming anyone off their ship."

Uhura's voice was composed and even. "Even with the deflectors down, you couldn't beam them aboard." She tilted her dark face gracefully from Scott toward the captain. "Wouldn't the holding cells be equipped with a jamming device to prevent that means of escape?"

"Aye." Scott shot her a critical glance, as if to say he was just getting to that. "If we tried, all we'd get would be bits and pieces."

Kirk immediately stifled the image conjured by Scott's words and said, "One thing at a time. First, let's worry about getting their deflectors down."

Scott looked pessimistic. "Well, the only way to do that would be to give them an occasion to use their transporter."

"But, sir," Sulu protested, "if Dr. McCoy and Mr. Spock are still in their cells—"

"Don't forget Admiral Mendez," Uhura said gloomily.

"Then we convince the Romulans to use the transporter *and* remove all three of them from their cells." It sounded impossible, but the captain's tone was matter-of-fact. It had to be done, and therefore would be.

"A pity we have to bring the admiral back," Scott said bitterly.

Kirk sighed; he'd been over this with himself a hundred times since talking to Khaefv. "I know, Scotty. But Mendez is head of weaponry design. He has too much valuable information that the Romulans would love to get their hands on."

"Aye." Scott shook his head. "A damn shame, too. I'd just as soon leave him and Adams with 'em, and good riddance."

Sulu leaned forward excitedly. "Captain, there *is* a way to get them to use the transporter . . . *and* remove the prisoners from their cells."

Kirk understood before the helmsman had a chance to finish. "Give in to their demands."

Uhura frowned. "Tell them we'll cooperate, turn over Adams and the virus if they give us our people back? You mean, have everyone beam down to Tanis?"

"Close." Kirk looked at Scott. "They'd have to lower their shields right before they transport down. Could you get a fix on two humans and a Vulcan and beam them onto the *Enterprise* while they're still in the Romulans' transporter room?"

The crease in Scott's forehead deepened. "It would be very dangerous, Captain. I'd have to time it to the nearest millisecond, because if they were caught in two beams at once . . ." His voice trailed off ominously.

Glum silence.

"Does anyone have a better idea?" Kirk snapped.

No one did.

McCoy lay with his stomach against the cold floor and waited. His backside was still throbbing enough to keep his mind occupied—at least, from time to time. He had spent most of his time in the cell not thinking about what he was waiting for. When he did let himself think about it, he figured his prospects were limited to:

(a) the Romulans releasing him because Jim had struck a deal; or (b) the Romulans killing him because Jim had *not* struck a deal. Either way, the thing that bothered him most was (c), the Romulans questioning him. Very little was known about their methods, except the fact that no one had lived to tell about them. That in itself sparked McCoy's imagination.

Of course, he was hoping against hope that before (c) occurred, (d) Jim would find some way of tricking the Romulans and rescuing them.

Oh, hell, quit being so damn logical about your situation. Do you want to spend the end of your life sounding like Spock? Admit it. You're scared to death, and thinking isn't going to make it any better.

He was fairly certain that Spock and Mendez were in cells on either side of him, and he wondered if the Vulcan were scared. *Ought to be, if he has any sense at all . . .*

McCoy concentrated on not thinking about what sort of

237

torture the Romulans would employ when they questioned him (let's face it, they would probably get to it before much longer) and closed his eyes. He tried to concentrate on the pain in his back, on each dying nerve ending to distract himself, but it backfired. *Enjoy minor pain while you can. This will seem like a pleasant memory when they question you.*

The sound of footsteps in front of his cell made his heart beat faster. *Relax. The guard's just pacing. He's not coming for you.*

He kept his eyes closed and took deep breaths. *Don't think about anything. Concentrate on your breathing.* After a few seconds, his pulse began to slow. The footsteps ceased, and McCoy sighed, relieved.

And then someone turned off the force field to his cell. McCoy's heart thumped wildly against his chest. He felt paralyzed; it took all his strength to force an eye open.

It took him one terrified instant to realize that the Romulan guard coming toward him was actually wearing Starfleet blue.

"Spock!" McCoy opened the other eye and grinned so hard it hurt. "How in God's name . . . ?"

Unmoved, Spock motioned for quiet. "Contain yourself, Doctor," he said, in a barely audible voice. "We need to move swiftly if our attempt is to be successful." He placed a strong hand on McCoy's arm and effortlessly pulled the doctor to his feet. "Are you able to run?" He glanced uncertainly at McCoy's back.

"No problem," McCoy whispered enthusiastically. "It's more aggravation than anything else."

In response, Spock handed him a Romulan phaser. The doctor grasped the weapon awkwardly. Starfleet medical personnel were not required to learn to handle weaponry. McCoy had fired a phaser a couple of times in his life, and then only out of necessity. He looked down at it with distaste. He didn't like it, to be sure, but at the moment it seemed a very bad idea to refuse it.

"Where're we headed?" he asked quietly, but Spock was already moving to the next cell.

Mendez's cell. He was going to let the admiral out. "Hey,

238

wait a minute!" McCoy hissed indignantly. The very notion made him furious. "How the hell are we supposed to escape *and* keep an eye on Mendez at the same time? Have you forgotten that he just tried to kill us?"

They were standing in front of the cell now; behind the glowing field, Mendez sat in the corner, his arms tucked around his knees. He looked up at them. If McCoy had been surprised to see his rescuer, then Mendez seemed doubly so. Other emotions flitted across his face: distrust, relief.

Spock reached out to press the control. "If we leave him, Doctor, then the Romulans will have access to every bit of intelligence on Starfleet weaponry. They will still possess the ability to bargain." His tone made it clear that the argument was closed.

"He's a criminal," McCoy said angrily. He knew that Spock was no longer listening, so he said it loud enough for Mendez to hear. "He was going to kill us and destroy the *Enterprise,* remember? He deserves to be left behind." Mendez's expression of relief began to change to one of outrage.

Spock touched the control; the field collapsed into nothingness, and Mendez rose quickly to his feet and joined them. He and McCoy glared at each other.

"You disgust me," Mendez said, in his deep, authoritative voice. "You and Kirk. You think you know everything about the situation. So quick to judge." He shoved his face in McCoy's until they were toe to toe.

McCoy did not back down. "I have this funny belief," he said, with as much coldness as he could muster, "that there can be very little justification for murder."

"I've killed no one."

"Ordering it is just the same as doing it yourself."

"*Gen*tlemen," Spock said, with an uncustomary lack of patience, "now is not the time. The Romulans will discover our absence in a very short while."

McCoy and Mendez parted grudgingly, and turned to face the Vulcan.

"Our communicators should be nearby, in the security office. We'll need them. Afterward, I will need your help in getting to their engineering room, to the manual override."

239

"What for?" McCoy asked.

"If the Romulans' deflector shields are up, and we must assume they are, they will have to be lowered before we can beam onto the *Enterprise*. I intend to signal the ship as soon as I lower the shields. Hopefully, they will be able to lower their shields and beam us aboard before the Romulans catch up to us."

"Then let's get moving," Mendez said, in a tone suspiciously like that of a command.

Spock paused. McCoy fancied he saw a hastily erased flicker of stubbornness in the Vulcan's eyes. "And just so you understand, Admiral," he said quietly, "you are now *my* prisoner. I am therefore in command here."

"You tell 'im, Spock." McCoy nodded approvingly.

Mendez's face darkened with rage. "On what grounds, Commander?"

"You have violated Federation Code I-745.G2, engaging in illegal biowarfare research. However, any argument on your part now is moot. You have no weapon, and we do. I suggest you do not attempt to hinder our efforts at escape." Spock leveled his phaser directly at Mendez's chest. "And I suggest you keep an eye on him as well, Doctor. You're quite correct in assuming that he would kill us, given the chance."

McCoy cheerfully followed suit and aimed his phaser, waiting for the admiral to splutter something about coercing a superior officer, the penalty for kidnapping, Spock's certain and imminent court-martial . . . But Mendez did none of that. He swallowed his fury and, with an intense look at Spock, said, "We'll take this up later."

"Very well." Spock motioned with his phaser. "To Security, gentlemen."

Kirk had always taken a certain amount of pride in his skill at bluffing; in fact, it was difficult to get anyone to play poker with him more than once. But at the sight of Khaefv on the bridge's main viewscreen, his confidence fled. Bluffing for credits was one thing; bargaining for his friends' lives was quite another.

He's got to know I'm lying.

"Subcommander Khaefv," he said smoothly; or at least,

he hoped it came out that way. He was in no condition to judge.

"Yes, Captain?" Khaefv smiled; smugly, Kirk thought.

"I've been rethinking your offer."

Khaefv waited.

Kirk shifted uncomfortably in his chair. "I'm willing to make the trade."

The young Romulan's right eyebrow rose a few millimeters. "The R-virus *and* Dr. Adams in exchange for the three prisoners?" He was not altogether successful in keeping the surprise out of his voice. He had probably been agonizing over whether or not to bother returning to the Empire without the R-virus.

Kirk nodded. "My conditions: the exchange takes place on neutral territory, on Tanis base."

"Of course," Khaefv said. "A transporter exchange would too easily permit duplicity on either side."

God, he sounded like Spock. Kirk sat forward hopefully. "Then you're agreeing to the exchange?"

Offscreen, the voice of Khaefv's communications officer. He spoke Romulan, but the screen's built-in translator interpreted: "Subcommander, urgent news from the head of security. The prisoners have escaped."

Khaefv turned away from the screen, toward the officer, but not before Kirk caught the anger in his eyes, not so much at the news, but at his officer, for letting the information slip into the enemy's hands. He muted the screen so that Kirk could not hear his furious reprimand, and then turned to face the captain again.

"Captain Kirk." He struggled to regain his composure. "Apparently you have heard. If your men survive this attempt, then perhaps we will talk again." His image disappeared.

If your men survive . . . "Mr. Chekov," Kirk barked.

"Yes, sir." The Russian sat up straight in his chair at the navigation console. Next to him, Sulu started.

"Keep an eye on the Romulan ship's deflector shields. The instant they're down, I want you to try to locate our people—that includes Mendez—and notify the transporter room of their coordinates."

"Yes, Captain."

Kirk punched the intercom toggle with his fist. "Transporter room."

"Transporter room. Kyle here."

"Stand by to beam three aboard. It may take some time."

"Aye, sir."

He hit the toggle again and sat back in his chair, feeling particularly helpless. There was nothing more he could do, except hope like hell that Spock was able to get to the Romulans' deflector shields before the Romulans were able to get to him.

McCoy shut his eyes and fired.

"You can open them, Doctor," Spock said next to him. "And, in the future, it might be better for your aim if you keep both eyes open."

McCoy looked. The two helmeted guards in the small (compared to the *Enterprise*'s, anyway) security room lay on the floor, unconscious. "Don't complain, Spock. It worked, didn't it? Besides, I have no intention of ever using one of these again, once I get off this ship."

"Why, Dr. McCoy." Spock's tone was as close as it ever got to human sarcasm. "I never suspected you were a pacifist."

Now is scarcely the time for insults, McCoy was about to say, but Spock had already located their confiscated communicators and phasers. The doctor turned and gestured Mendez into the room. The admiral was being extremely cooperative, and that made McCoy even more distrustful of him. Mendez moved with interest over to where Spock stood.

"Doctor." Spock handed McCoy his communicator and ignored Mendez's longing glances at his own weapon. "And I shall keep the admiral's phaser and communicator." He snapped them onto his belt.

"Which way now?" McCoy asked, glancing anxiously over his shoulder.

"There should be a manual override in their engineering room," Spock answered.

"Yes," Mendez spoke up. "Engineering. But it's on a

lower deck. The safest way to get there would be to use the emergency shaft."

Spock gazed at him sharply, then murmured, "Yes, of course."

"That's *it?*" McCoy blurted, amazed at the Vulcan's acquiescence. "You're going to trust him, just like that?"

Mendez's bushy brows rushed together in a scowl. "Do you really think that I'm stupid enough to lead you someplace dangerous?"

"The admiral has a vested interest in us if he is to get safely off this ship," Spock said to the doctor. "Up to that point, I am willing to trust him. And because of his position in the Fleet, he has the most recent information about the layout of Romulan vessels."

McCoy felt his lips tightening disapprovingly. "Maybe. But I still don't like it."

"Nor do I, Doctor, but we have no choice at the moment." Spock turned to Mendez. "You lead, Admiral."

Mendez peered around the open door and pointed left with a stubby finger. "That way."

They walked three abreast, with Spock slightly in front. Both he and the doctor held their weapons at chest level. Mendez, weaponless, walked between them.

"The shaft isn't far," Mendez assured them, but the wide-open corridor made McCoy feel exposed.

And with good reason: before they went one hundred meters, a uniformed Romulan centurion appeared in front of them. He stopped and gaped for a moment before reaching for the weapon strapped at his side. He never reached it; simultaneously, Spock and McCoy fired their weapons. Hit by a double blast, the centurion crumpled into a heap on the floor, his phaser still clutched in his outstretched hand.

Sickened by what he had just done, McCoy ran to the fallen guard's side and dropped to his knees. *My kingdom for a medikit. . . .* He lifted the man's eyelid gently. "I don't like the looks of him. A double stun like that could be serious."

Mendez squatted next to him. "Don't be ridiculous! Let's get out of here before someone else comes."

McCoy felt his ire rising. "He could die."

"Does it matter?" Mendez's voice was heavy with hatred. "Don't for a minute believe that he would be as concerned about you. Death and killing mean nothing to them. They have no regard for life, especially not human."

McCoy's voice rose. "Neither do you. But I'm not going to leave any man—"

"He's not a man, he's a *Romulan*," Mendez hissed, with more bitterness than McCoy had ever heard concentrated in one single voice.

"Nor am I a man." Spock's voice was velvet-soft, but his eyes had taken on a veiled look that spoke dangerously of Vulcan's savage past. "So I do not share the admiral's prejudice. But I am afraid, Doctor, that we have neither the time nor the means to tend to him."

"At least let me check his pulse." McCoy felt the man's neck and tried to guess if the racing heartbeat beneath his fingertips was normal for a Romulan. Spock sighed and turned his back to the corridor to watch.

What happened next, happened quickly.

Behind Spock, another Romulan appeared in the corridor. She too wore the uniform of a centurion, and she shouted an alien phrase at them. McCoy cried a wordless warning to the Vulcan, but realized that there was no chance either he or Spock could fire in time. The doctor fumbled helplessly for the phaser he had put down on the floor.

The blast lit up the corridor for one brilliant instant. McCoy held his breath and closed his eyes. But when he opened them, Spock was still standing. The female guard was gone.

Next to the doctor, Mendez clutched the phaser he had taken from the unconscious guard's hand. His eyes were wide.

McCoy was suddenly consumed by a sick, hot rage. "Feel better?" he spat sarcastically. His voice shook. "Here!" He grabbed Mendez's hand and pointed the phaser at the male guard still unconscious on the floor. "Why don't you kill him, too?"

Mendez stared blankly at him.

"Why don't you just kill them *all!*" McCoy railed.

"Doctor," Spock's voice warned, somewhere in the background, but McCoy was too angry to see.

Stunned, Mendez looked down at the weapon in his hand as if he had no idea where it had come from. "It was set on kill," he said, sounding surprised. "I didn't know it was set on kill."

"Does it matter?" McCoy flared, rising up on his knees and shoving his face into the admiral's. "The woman is dead—although I'm sure you don't consider her a woman. Something less than that, no doubt."

Mendez shrank from him. "They killed my wife," he whispered.

"So that gives you the right to kill *her.*" McCoy gestured at the now-empty space in the corridor. "Tit for tat, is that your philosophy? Or isn't that enough? You want them *all* dead, right?"

"Enough," Spock said, taking the phaser from the admiral's hand. Mendez did not resist. McCoy fell silent and got to his feet.

"The man will live," he said quietly to Spock, as the first officer helped the admiral to his feet. Mendez seemed greatly shaken. He headed to the end of the corridor and, by pushing on a nearly invisible seam in the bulkhead, opened a hatch.

"The emergency shaft," Mendez said tonelessly, and started to crawl in. Spock followed and grabbed him by the arm.

"I'll go first, Admiral." He gestured to McCoy to follow last and climbed in, heading down.

Mendez followed. McCoy got in last and shut the hatch, sealing them in darkness. Like a Federation vessel, the shaft consisted of a metal rung ladder that led either up or down to the different levels of the ship; unlike the *Enterprise,* however, the Bird of Prey's shaft was completely enclosed by a metal tube. It was hot inside, and stuffy. McCoy felt as if he couldn't get any air into his lungs. He began to find it difficult to catch his breath.

Just a touch of claustrophobia. Don't let it get to you.

He stepped down blindly, the heel of his boot just grazing Mendez's head. He murmured an apology and listened to it

245

echo along with the sounds of their boots ringing against the metal ladder. Mendez did not answer.

If anyone else is in here, we're all dead men.

They seemed to crawl down forever. Far away, muffled, an unfamiliar siren wailed. The search for them was beginning.

McCoy nearly put his foot on Mendez's bald pate again as their pace slowed abruptly. He found himself fighting panic.

A scraping sound . . . Spock opening the hatch. They moved down again, and suddenly McCoy moved out into light. He put an arm up and squinted as he stepped out into the corridor. Mendez and Spock were already fifty meters ahead of him. McCoy ran after them as fast as his still-sore back and legs could carry him.

The corridor came to an abrupt end at a large doorway.

"This is it," Mendez gasped. His broad face was mottled dark red. "Engineering."

Spock nodded silently. He raised his phaser, set it on blanket range, and gave McCoy a significant glance: they were going to storm the engineering deck. McCoy leaned back against the bulkhead, his knees suddenly refusing to support him. *Suicide. No choice. What's the point in thinking about it? What are you gonna do, go back to your cell?* He swallowed hard, set his own phaser on blanket stun, and nodded at the Vulcan. *Ready.*

It was, of course, far from the truth. The only thing McCoy felt ready for was slinking off into a very safe corner until it was all over.

Spock nodded back. Intuitively—or was it Spock's telepathy—McCoy found himself counting:

One . . . two . . . THREE!

The two of them rushed toward the door, causing it to open. Two Romulan officers, both male, were seated at the main terminal and looked up in mild surprise as Spock and McCoy entered. Spock fired; the blanket range stunned them both, causing them to slump forward onto the terminal. McCoy looked around desperately until he saw a third Romulan, frowning curiously as she came around the anti-matter reactor chamber (or what McCoy presumed was their version of it); teeth chattering, the doctor closed his eyes and fired his weapon. When he opened them again, the officer was on the floor. He was vaguely aware of Mendez cowering behind him.

"Is that it?" McCoy asked incredulously, surprised to find himself still alive. "Is it all over?"

"Not quite." Spock was already at the terminal. He gently lifted one of the Romulans from his seat and leaned him against the bulkhead, then sat down in the vacant chair. The unconscious officer next to him apparently did not bother him in the least. "The deflector shields must be lowered. To do that, I must route them through this terminal, and once that occurs, the Romulans will know our exact location. I suggest you stand by to contact the *Enterprise*. The sooner we leave, the better." Spock suddenly looked up and frowned. "Where is the admiral? It's imperative we watch him carefully from now on."

McCoy looked around. "My God, I didn't think—"

But Mendez had apparently tripped over one of the unconscious bodies on the floor and was dusting himself off. He struggled gracelessly to his feet. "I could help you if you'd give me a weapon, Commander. Believe me, I don't want to stay here any more than you do."

Spock's voice was far away; the Vulcan was distracted as he focused on the terminal before him. "Admiral, your disregard for my intelligence is most annoying. I have no intention of permitting you to arm yourself in order to make some sort of—" He broke off and looked up at McCoy. "Make an attempt to contact the *Enterprise*, Doctor."

McCoy felt an odd, tingling rush of exhilaration as he took his communicator from his belt and opened it. *If this doesn't work, this is it.* "McCoy to *Enterprise*. *Enterprise*, come in please. McCoy—"

"Bones!" Jim Kirk's voice, taut with excitement. "Is that you?"

McCoy grinned broadly at no one. "I don't suppose you could get us out of here, Jim."

"You've got it. Hang on."

Footsteps, somewhere down the hall . . . or was McCoy imagining it? *We're going to make it,* he thought wildly. *We'll be gone by the time they get here.* Amazingly, it was true. He felt the familiar light-headedness that marked the beginning of dematerialization. It was going to be all right.

The scene shifted, changed in front of his eyes. With near-tears relief, McCoy saw the *Enterprise* transporter room. Lieutenant Kyle stood behind the console, tanned and blond in his red tunic. Kyle flashed a white grin at them, and with his Aussie accent said: "Good day, sirs. Welcome back." He pressed something on his console. "They're here, Captain." McCoy did not hear the reply.

McCoy smiled and took a step forward. There was an earsplitting rumble, and he was thrown off balance as the room lurched to one side. He fell, between Mendez and Spock, into a tangle of legs and arms.

The Romulans had noticed they were gone.

The doctor tried to push himself to his feet, but too late remembered the weapon knocked from his hand. Crablike, Mendez scrambled across the platform and retrieved the phaser before Spock and McCoy could find their weapons on the floor. "Sit back down, Doctor." He waved the phaser in McCoy's direction.

"Well, *damn*," McCoy said, bitterly disappointed. He was weary to the bone of excitement, and had half a mind to take the phaser from Mendez's hand and give him a good whacking with it to show him what he thought of him. But the instinct for self-preservation won out over his irritation, and he sat back down next to Spock. "I knew it was all going too easily."

"One move and I'll fire," Mendez said. The entire transporter room seemed to vibrate, and then gravity pressed down on McCoy. They were moving, he guessed, trying to outrun the Romulans. He tried to keep his eyes focused on Mendez, in the hopes he would be distracted and lose his grip on the phaser, but Mendez somehow held on. When it was over, he was still holding the weapon on them.

"Call your captain," Mendez said to Kyle, whose tan had just faded by several shades.

"They're here, Captain," Kyle said through the intercom.

"Good," Jim Kirk answered. He closed the channel and leaned forward in his chair to give the order to Sulu.

The bridge convulsed, heaving him from the conn. He landed very unceremoniously on his backside. But there was no time to worry about the loss of dignity; besides, everyone else on the bridge was far too occupied to notice. Another blast like that without the shields up, and the top of the bridge would be sheared off.

Sulu had recovered from the shock of the blast and sat at the helm, facing the captain and calmly awaiting the order.

"Sulu," Kirk gasped, struggling to his feet. "Deflector shields up. Return fire. And stand by for evasive maneuvers."

"Aye, sir." The helmsman's Oriental features remained impassive as he took in all three orders without flinching. On the screen, the port side of the Bird of Prey flared in space as Sulu's barrage struck home. "A hit, sir. Minor damage."

Uhura had crawled back to her station after being knocked halfway across the bridge. Now she swiveled in her chair toward the conn, a model of composure except for her decidedly rumpled uniform. "Damage reports, Captain. One of the pods damaged, no estimated repair time yet. Engineering reports serious damage to one of the lower decks."

"Is that Scott? Let me talk to him."

"Aye, sir." She turned back to her board. "On audio."

"Scotty?" Kirk sat in his chair and leaned to one side, toward the intercom. "What's the situation down there?"

The engineer's tone was, as usual, gravely pessimistic. "They knew right where to hit us, Captain. A few meters more to the left, and they would have taken out the reactors completely. As it is, we've lost some power."

"How much? I want to get her out of here as fast as we can."

"Well . . . I suppose I could give you warp eight."

Kirk breathed a sigh of relief. To Scott, even a microscopic loss of power was a tragedy. "Give me warp nine and I'll put your name in for a commendation."

"You're on." He could practically hear Scott grin.

Kirk looked up at the helm. "Mr. Sulu. Implement evasive maneuver at warp nine . . . *now.*"

He braced himself against the conn as the bridge trembled and bore hard to starboard . . .

And then righted itself. Kirk glanced up at the main viewscreen. The Bird of Prey was gone, and in its place, stars. In a way, he couldn't help feeling sorry for Khaefv, a shrewd young commander who deserved better than whatever fate awaited him in the Praetors' Empire. The Romulan system had little tolerance for failure.

He stood up and waited for the adrenaline rush to fade. It was over . . . really over. All that remained now of the Tanis affair was to see to it that security escorted Admiral Mendez to the VIP quarters and kept him confined there.

His intercom whistled again. "Kirk here."

Kyle sounded puzzled. "Kyle again, Captain. I'm afraid —I'm afraid Admiral Mendez is making demands, sir. He says that if you don't bring Adams to the transporter room now, he's going to kill Dr. McCoy and Mr. Spock."

"He's coming," Kyle said.

"I heard," Mendez growled. "You'd all better hope he's bringing Adams with him."

"Your attempt to escape the consequences is illogical," Spock said, as if he were engaging in a friendly debate of only mild personal interest to him. "Even if you were able to avoid incriminating yourself in Admiral Waverleigh's death, Dr. McCoy and I will testify that you threatened us with physical harm here, and down on Tanis."

"Don't remind him of that *now,* Spock," McCoy hissed, exasperated. Sometimes the Vulcan could be incredibly naive when it came to his own welfare.

"I don't give a damn about logic." Mendez raised the phaser. The beginnings of desperation shone in his eyes, making McCoy distinctly nervous.

"You should," Spock answered pleasantly. "If you could have removed the evidence against you on Tanis—i.e., the R-virus—before the doctor and I arrived, it would have been to your benefit. You could have claimed that Tanis base was working on any number of different secret projects, but a germ so obviously engineered against Romulans is damning evidence.

"And, once we arrived, if you had located the virus and then killed us before anyone else on the *Enterprise* knew of your presence, it would still have been possible to avoid having your involvement with Tanis revealed. Unfortunately, once you decided to contact the *Enterprise,* secrecy was no longer possible. From that point on, you were bound to destroy an entire starship in order to protect yourself—"

McCoy interrupted, frowning. "What are you doing, giving him ideas? Whose side are you on, Spock?"

Spock paused. Mendez's expression was becoming increasingly desperate, but he did not tell the Vulcan to be quiet. Spock continued. "Your attempt to avoid arrest and prosecution is rather hopeless at this point. Even if you find a way of destroying the *Enterprise,* there is no way you can be certain that the captain has not already informed Starfleet of the current situation. With this last desperate action, you are only proving your guilt and aggravating the situation."

Mendez was considering all this; as he did, McCoy could tell out of the corner of his eye that Spock was almost imperceptibly moving toward the admiral. It took Mendez a full minute to realize what the Vulcan was up to.

"Go to hell." Mendez clutched the phaser more tightly. "I don't need you to tell me what the situation is."

They all turned their head as the door opened, though Mendez refixed his gaze on his prisoners quickly, before Spock could make a grab for the phaser. Just outside the transporter room stood a row of red security uniforms, headed by a tall, pale figure in red: Tomson.

"Keep them out!" Mendez barked.

The door closed over them as Kirk entered, flanked by a man outlined by the near-invisible glow of a field suit. Adams, McCoy marveled . . . while he had regained some color, he was still unhealthy looking (probably his normal state), but walking without assistance. The doctor felt a surge of wild hope: *That means Chris must be all right.* "What—" he began, then bit his tongue. *Is he doing in a field suit?* he had almost asked. With the exception of Mendez, they were all immune, and Adams was probably no longer contagious. But he knew the captain well enough

251

to suspect that Jim was up to something. Besides, there was something strange about Adams' attitude. He didn't seem at all frightened, like a man who is about to be traded as a hostage should. He seemed almost . . . *smug.*

Kirk and Adams stood in front of Kyle's console. The captain was no longer making no effort to hide the contempt in his eyes and voice. "All right, Admiral. Here he is. But before we let the two of you off the ship, there's something you should know."

"Whatever it is, I don't give a damn." Mendez gestured, a little crazily, with the phaser. "Send him over here and beam us down to Tanis."

But Adams remained where he was. "I think you *will* give a damn, Admiral," Kirk said. "You're right, Adams knows where the R-virus is. That's why you want him, isn't it? But you're making the wrong assumption. It's not down on Tanis base. It's here, on the *Enterprise.*"

"I don't believe you," Mendez said, but he was beginning to look agitated. "Send him over."

Kirk nodded to Adams, who took a careful step toward the transporter pad. Jim kept talking. "Even if there's no evidence to connect you to Waverleigh's death, Admiral, even if you somehow manage to convince Starfleet that you had nothing to do with the creation of the R-virus, I and my crew will testify against you.

"Of course, it occurred to me that you're resourceful and you could find a way to get rid of an entire starship. After all, you're head of weapons development. So just as a precaution, I'm having the computer logs of what is happening here now transmitted directly to Starfleet Headquarters. Even if the *Enterprise* is destroyed a short time from now, Starfleet will still see exactly what happened here."

"Now?" Mendez shuddered.

Adams moved closer, until he stood in front of Mendez.

"Where will you go to hide, Admiral?" Kirk asked. "Klingon space? Certainly, you wouldn't be too welcome in Romulan territory."

"What a fool you are!" Adams grinned maniacally. "Don't you realize that once you take me with you, all I have to do is *this?*" He pressed the control unit at his waist;

the field faded away. "I won't be your scapegoat, Mendez. We're going down together."

"No!" Mendez cried. "Get him away from me! He's infected."

He cringed, using the doctor as a shield. As Adams neared, Mendez pushed McCoy forward. Adams laughed and stepped to one side as the doctor went sprawling off the edge of the platform.

The admiral sobbed as Adams reached forward and touched his arm; the phaser clattered to the transporter pad, and Spock scooped it up.

Adams' smile faded. "A damn shame"—he shook his head with real regret—"that I'm no longer infectious. I've been wanting to do that for a long time."

Epilogue

Lisa stood in her quarters, looking at her two friends. Her long black hair was down on her shoulders, and she was dressed in civilian clothes, a powder-blue jumpsuit that was almost a perfect match for Lamia's complexion. She held a lightweight beige suitcase in front of her with both hands.

"They said your replacement would be here tomorrow," Lamia said, after an awkward silence. She was staring at Nguyen's stripped bunk and at the painting on the wall above it. Lisa suddenly realized that the Andorian would be spending the night alone, and was overwhelmed by pity. She set the suitcase down and hugged Lamia fiercely.

"I'm going to miss you." She drew back and looked at her friend fondly.

"Maybe you'll be back." Lamia's blue lips were stretched in a shaky smile.

"Maybe I will," Nguyen said. Tomson had convinced her to try six months' personal leave instead of resigning altogether. It made sense; she could have Colorado for a time, and know that if it didn't work out, the Fleet would still be there for her. Besides, she owed Tomson a favor.

"Take care of yourself," Stanger said, and reached out to give her a quick hug.

"You too," she answered, smiling up at him. "Thanks."

"For what?" He raised his eyebrows slightly, as if he were surprised.

"For what you did on the observation deck."

"Oh, that." He shifted his weight as if the memory made him uncomfortable. "It was nothing."

"Oh, that," she mimicked teasingly. "You just saved my life, that's all."

"You would have done the same for me."

I've gone one better, she thought smugly, but she said nothing. He would find out soon enough this morning, when he reported for duty. She had half expected Tomson to ignore her suggestion, to make some comment about not wanting to make a character judgment based on the ravings of a sick man. But to her surprise, the lieutenant had listened. The fact that Stanger had just saved Lisa's life and the fact that Tomson was willing to bargain to keep Lisa in the Fleet probably had something to do with it.

They had both agreed that little would be served by questioning Rosa. If Stanger wanted to protect her, then that was his business. But at least they could do something to help him out.

"Well." Lisa made an effort to sound cheerful. She had already decided that she was not going to cry; at least, not here, in front of them. "I guess I'd better get down to the hangar deck before they decide to leave without me."

"I'll write." Lamia's antennae were starting to droop.

"I will too," Lisa answered. She looked at them both and then picked up her suitcase.

Stanger's brown eyes were moist; he cleared his throat. "Guess we'd better report for duty."

A halfhearted attempt at a smile flickered across Lamia's face. "That's true. You certainly can't afford to be late, can you?"

"No, you can't," Nguyen answered. Not today, of all days. She took a deep breath and forced herself to walk out of the room without glancing behind her.

She was very sorry she wouldn't get to see the look on Stanger's face when he found out.

"Well." Stanger was consciously trying not to fidget. "I guess we ought to be leaving." He kept wanting to say, *but,* and couldn't quite bring himself to.

"Yes." Lamia avoided looking at him with those bright green eyes. She made a sharp move toward the door.

"Wait . . . " He stepped in front of her. "I was wrong, what I said to you before. About friends being a complication."

"Maybe you were right," she answered. He tensed defensively at that, but she had a point: she had trusted him, and he had hurt her. But there was no hostility, only sadness, in her voice. She tilted her chin up at him and looked him square in the eye, her cap of silvery hair swinging gently. She was not the slightest bit aware of her beauty, and that made her all the more attractive.

He hesitated. "I'm sorry, Lamia. I was . . . hurt by someone I cared for very deeply, once. I admit I was bitter. It's taken me awhile to get over it."

"Are you over it now?" Her manner was serious.

"Yes." And he noted with quiet amazement that it was true. However badly Rosa may have hurt him, he had survived; and there was nothing she could take away from who he was now.

"I didn't want to be anything more than your friend, Jon. It's normal on Andor for people of the opposite sex to be friends . . . and I thought it was normal here. But I kept thinking you misunderstood—or that I'd somehow inadvertently given the wrong signal."

"N-no," he said. The room seemed suddenly overheated. Oh, hell, what was the point in avoiding it? He hadn't been completely truthful with her before, and where had it gotten him? "It—it wasn't that I thought you were—well, felt that way . . . " *Look at you, stuttering now. Smooth, Stanger. Very smooth.* "I knew it wasn't you, Lamia. It—it was me."

"You?" She cocked her head quizzically for a moment, and then her complexion began to take on a deeper hue. *"Oh,"* she said. Her antennae rose and drew so far forward on her scalp that he came very near to giggling nervously. She beamed at him. "I don't suppose we could just try being friends for a while, first?"

Stanger grinned. "I'd like that."

They smiled awkwardly at each other all the way to the security office.

Tomson was waiting for him. Stanger arrived a full minute early, and she seemed to sense it; she got up from her desk and peered out into the security lounge. To her surprise, he and the Andorian ensign were simpering at each other like fools. Odd. Before Stanger's illness, the two of them had seemed mortal enemies. But then, Tomson had always been confounded by the intricacies of personal relationships.

Maybe in his own way, Stanger was just as good at making friends as Lisa Nguyen; maybe it just took him longer. Tomson sighed. Nguyen better have been right about him. Of course, there was the indisputable fact that he had saved Nguyen's life.

If it was all true, he would make an excellent second-in-command.

A shiver of resentment passed through her at the thought, but with time she would get over it. *All right. Admit it and be done with it. You don't like anyone taking al-B's place. But he's dead, and there's nothing you can do about it.*

She closed her eyes briefly and opened them again. Stanger and Lamia were too occupied with each other to notice her. She leaned further out her door and cleared her throat. "Stanger." She intentionally avoided using his rank. "Come into my office. Please." The "please" was an afterthought, a conscious attempt to seem more approachable. It was good for morale, she supposed. Otherwise, she would not have bothered.

He and Lamia jumped up as if they had been electronically prodded. "Yes, sir," Stanger answered swiftly. It was clear he expected a reprimand, and was trying to puzzle out exactly what he had done to deserve it. *Is my expression that unpleasant?* Tomson wondered. She had not meant it to be.

Stanger followed her inside. The door closed, blotting out the view of Lamia's curious face. He waited stiffly at attention while Tomson walked behind her desk and sat down. She gestured at the chair next to him. "Sit."

257

He lowered himself cautiously into it. "I was on time this morning, wasn't I, sir?"

"Yes, yes. It's nothing like that." She fastened her gaze on him intently, so as not to miss his reaction to what she was about to say. "Good news, actually. Your promotion to lieutenant, junior grade, came through."

She was slightly disappointed. Not a muscle twitched in his strong, dark face, but he stared at her hard for a full minute, and with each passing second, she could see more and more of the whites of his eyes as they grew rounder. "But I'm not up for a promotion," he said blankly, like someone who has just confronted an impossible reality.

"I know that," Tomson replied with contrived irritability. "But it wouldn't be seemly to have an ensign as a second-in-command."

That shattered his composure completely; Tomson fought the urge to rub her hands in triumph. "B-but . . ." he began, and trailed off, confused. "But . . ." And then he gave up and grinned like an idiot. It was all she could do to keep from smiling herself. Perhaps the corners of her mouth were turning up just a bit.

His smile faded as something occurred to him. "Was this the captain's idea?" His eyes narrowed defensively. "Because if it is, I want nothing to do with it. I won't be forced on a superior who doesn't—"

"Enough." She waved him silent. He closed his mouth and studied her coldly. "It wasn't the captain's suggestion at all. Quite frankly, you have Lisa Nguyen to thank for this. She was the one who convinced me to do it."

"Lisa!" he exclaimed, frowning.

"You saved her life, after all. And I need someone to replace her. You've got more security experience than anyone else on the *Enterprise,* probably more than anyone I could bring in from outside.

"But I should let you know that there are conditions: if Nguyen decides to return to duty at the end of her six-month leave of absence, she'll be my new second-in-command. If you don't like that, you can transfer out. Either way, the promotion to lieutenant is permanent."

258

"You made a bargain, then," he said disapprovingly. "I'm not sure if I want to accept this, if Lisa talked you into it."

She felt heat on her face and knew her cheeks were turning red. "You forget yourself, Stanger." She leaned over her desk at him, her face level with his. "No one talks me into anything. I only do it because *I* want to do it. I gave you the promotion because after listening to what Nguyen had to say, I decided you deserved it. Is that absolutely clear, Lieutenant?"

He drew in his breath at the sound of his new rank. "Understood, sir."

"Good." Tomson sat back, mollified by the respect in his tone. "Your new assignment is effective immediately. I'll brief you outside, along with the others." She nodded to let him know he was dismissed. Stanger rose, still looking dazed, and started out the door. "Oh . . . and Lieutenant—"

"Sir?" He turned his head to look back at her, his eyebrows raised in an inverted V.

"Nguyen asked me to give you a message." She folded her hands on the desk and paused for effect. "Don't ask me to explain it. She said to tell you that we're not all like Rosa." It was all she could do to pretend she did not understand.

For a moment he looked like he would keel over in front of her. His mouth opened and closed a few times.

In the end, when he had control of himself, he gave a small, rueful smile and said: "No, sir, I suppose not."

"Come," Kirk said, at the sound of the buzzer. The door opened, and McCoy stepped inside from the dim corridor.

"Feeling up for some company?" The doctor smiled and lingered in the entrance, sounding apologetic for the intrusion.

"Come in, Bones. I won't bite." *Though I would have if you'd tried this yesterday.* Jim glanced down at the dust-covered bottle McCoy held down by his side. "What's that? Is it what I think it is?"

McCoy wiped the label on his tunic and held the bottle of Saurian brandy up so Jim could read it.

He whistled. "My God. That's older than the two of us put together." He took the bottle from McCoy and cradled it in his hands, admiring it.

"Obviously, you've never read my personnel file," McCoy joked. He went behind the desk and opened the cabinet where Jim stored his liquor. "What's that?" He nodded at the package sitting out on the desk. "Another early birthday present?"

"Package from home," Jim answered noncommittally.

"Let me guess. Your mom's home-baked cookies. So how come you never share them with the rest of us?" McCoy took out two crystal glasses and set them down on the desk. "For your information, this brandy is *almost* as old as the two of us put together. I was saving it for your birthday. Pour."

Kirk shook his head, aghast. "I can't open this now. What's the occasion?"

"Quince Waverleigh," McCoy answered briskly, without an ounce of gloom or pity. "Don't worry, I'll find something else for your birthday. Now, will you pour, or do I have to?"

"I'll pour." A dull heaviness took hold of Jim at the mention of Quince's name, but McCoy's consideration touched him. He broke the seal on the bottle and, with considerable effort, pulled out the stopper. "I take it you're going to suffer along with me? Didn't bring along your own private stock?"

"I'll risk it this time. I figure anything that old can't be too bad—even if it *is* brandy." McCoy waited expectantly while Jim filled the glasses and set the bottle down.

"To Quince Waverleigh." McCoy raised his glass.

"To Quince." They clinked glasses and drank.

"Not bad." The doctor smacked his lips. "Tastes kinda like a well-aged bourbon, doesn't it?"

Kirk didn't answer. "Thanks, Bones."

"What for?"

"Quince deserved a decent wake. And for trying to cheer me up."

"Is it working?" McCoy took another sip and peered at Jim over the rim of his glass.

"It's funny." Jim sat down at the desk and rested his hand on the bottle. McCoy took the chair across from him. "I was angry as hell about it at first. Angry at Mendez, of course . . . and at Quince, for not watching out for himself. Most of all, I was mad at myself."

"As if you could have done any differently," McCoy said impatiently. "When are you gonna learn to quit doing that to yourself? When will you stop taking all the blame?"

Kirk shook his head. "I'm not as bad as I was yesterday. I tried to figure out what else I could have done to trap Mendez without Quince's help, but without that message, I wouldn't have been convinced enough to return to Tanis. I would have followed Mendez's orders, turned Adams in."

"Seems to me the Romulans owe you two a big thank-you." McCoy drained his glass. "Not that you'll ever get it. But you and Quince really did save the Empire."

Kirk wasn't listening. "But all that could have happened without Quince having to die. I feel like I marked him for death."

"Philosophy was my worst subject," the doctor said softly. "All that damnable logic. All I can say is, it happened, Jim, because you *didn't know*. Both of you figured Quince could take care of himself. Maybe if either of you had been more careful, he wouldn't have died. But how are you supposed to know everything that should have been done? I know Mendez did it intentionally, but in a way, Quince's death was a sort of accident, a senseless thing, and that's the cruelest thing of all to have to face."

Jim took a deep swallow of brandy and felt the fire crawl from the back of his throat all the way down into his chest. "Quince had been down lately. His wife didn't renew their contract, after eight years."

"Poor devil," said McCoy. "I know what that's like." He held his empty glass out.

Jim poured another drink for both of them. "When I'm able, I like to think that—it's crazy—I somehow made life easier for him, by giving him something to do."

"You have to admit, espionage is more exciting than paperwork. I think you're right, Jim. I didn't know Quince

261

all that well, but from the way you described him, he didn't sound like the kind of person who wanted to die in his sleep."

"No." Jim set the bottle down, unable to say anything more. He wanted very badly to be able to believe it.

"And look at it this way: maybe it wasn't senseless at all. After all, he helped to bring Mendez down. He may have even kept the galaxy from a biowar."

"I thought about that, too. Apparently, Quince tried to get in touch with Admiral Noguchi the night he died, so an investigation into his death has already been launched. It seems that they've already found four other admirals involved with Tanis base."

"That's hardly the whole Fleet," said McCoy. "For a while there, I thought you were afraid you were the only one who wasn't in on it."

"I did. I was beginning to think I was some kind of naive Boy Scout not to believe it." Kirk shook his head, remembering. "I wonder what they'll do with Mendez."

"He'll probably be assigned to psychiatric counseling and a penal colony for a while. That's if the prosecuting attorney is worth anything."

"If the attorney's worth anything," Jim repeated bitterly. It hardly seemed fair. "And if not . . ."

McCoy shrugged. "I've already figured out how Adams will try to get out of his confession. Of course, there's no way he'll get out of the fact that he and Mendez were in this thing up to their eyeballs. And Mendez must be sore enough to testify against Adams, what with his turning traitor and trying to sell the virus to the Romulans. I'm sure that bothered the admiral more than Adams' spilling the beans."

"So how will Adams get off?" Jim asked.

"Oh, he'll claim that his insanity was only temporary, that he only killed because of the H-virus. I was afraid for a while that if he lived to stand trial, he'd have no problem going free. But the fact that Stanger was ill, yet protected Ensign Nguyen from Adams, says a lot. It says that the homicidal effects can be resisted. We owe Stanger a lot for that." He looked questioningly at Jim. "I hope you gave the man a commendation."

"Promotion. He's Tomson's second-in-command now."

"Glad to hear it." The doctor rose to his feet. "Well, I don't mean to drink up all your expensive brandy, Jim, even if I did bring it myself."

"You don't have to rush off, Bones."

McCoy grinned smugly. "Oh, yes, I do. I promised to buy Christine a drink. I don't want to be drunk before I even get there." He nodded at the desk. "I'll let you open your mystery package. 'Night, Jim." He nodded and walked out.

"Good night, Bones." The door closed over McCoy, and Jim sat watching it for a minute.

He had been dreading opening the package from Quince Waverleigh's lawyer. It took him twenty minutes and another glass of brandy before he could bring himself to do it.

At last, he put his hands on the package. It was not particularly heavy; knowing Waverleigh, it probably contained a bequeathed bottle of tequila and a taped good-bye from Quince. He peeled the thin, crackling paper away easily and slowly eased the lid off the box.

Old Yeller's beady, dead little eyes stared up at him. He lifted the armadillo out gently, though Yeller felt stiff and unyielding as a wooden plank. Jim pulled the packing from the box in his search for the expected good-bye tape, but there was nothing else inside.

Quince hadn't even bothered to say good-bye . . .

For no good reason, he felt crushed. He'd half hoped to find something in Quince's last message that would ease his suffering conscience.

Disconsolate, he stared back at the little animal on his desk, then ran his fingers over it. It had a curious feel to it . . . spine-hard in some spots, soft-skinned and bristly in others. Jim felt self-conscious and silly talking to it, but he wanted to hear Quince's voice again. "Hello, Old Yeller."

Old Yeller came alive under his hand. The creature writhed and opened its long, narrow muzzle. Waverleigh's cheerful voice came out. "Hi, Jimmy."

"Hello, Quince," he whispered, feeling morose.

But the little animal kept talking . . . and the tone in Quince's voice made Jim sit up in his chair and listen.

"Look, Jimmy, if you've got Yeller with you, I reckon

you're feeling pretty bad right about now. I hope you got my message okay—"

Jim held his breath. *Hope you got my message* . . . Good Lord, Quince must have programmed the message right before he died. "But I just wanted you to know . . . no regrets. This is the most fun I've had since my promotion! So lighten up, Jimmy. You were always too damn intense and too quick to take the blame. Have a drink on me. And give Yeller a pat now and then, so he doesn't get too lonely.

"Waverleigh out."

Yeller's jaw stopped working. Jim reached out and stroked the armadillo's hard outer shell.

He didn't stop when the intercom whistled, and Sulu's placid face appeared on the screen.

"Leaving the Sagittarian arm, Captain. Awaiting your orders."

"I see." Kirk looked up from petting Yeller. "Well, Lieutenant, it seems that Command has finally taken pity on us after all that star charting. Lay in a course for Star Base Thirteen. Maybe shore leave will be somewhat more fun than our last assignment."

The corners of Sulu's eyes crinkled. "Yes, *sir.*" He paused. "More fun, maybe, Captain, but certainly not more *interesting.*"

"I can tell you're in need of leave, Lieutenant. You're beginning to sound like Mr. Spock." Kirk was surprised to find himself feeling faintly amused. "Kirk out."

He sighed and looked back at Old Yeller, who once again stood stiffly.

Jim picked up the bottle and poured himself another brandy. He had the glass to his lips when an oddly Quince-like notion seized him. He got a small shot glass from the cabinet, set it next to Yeller's front paw, and put a thimbleful of McCoy's brandy in it.

He raised his own glass. "To Quince Waverleigh," he said, and smiled for what seemed like the first time in a very long while.

Prologue

A TIME BEFORE stardates. And a captain's privilege to go there.

Even with the unchanged cornfields lying beneath sprawling blue skies and the barn smell all around him, Jim Kirk discovered he couldn't quite get away from reality when the communicator in his pocket suddenly chirped. His hand automatically went for the utility belt that usually held his phaser and communicator when he wasn't on board the ship, and only then did he remember he wasn't wearing a uniform.

"Mind your own business, Bones," he muttered as he found the device inside the lightweight indigo fabric of his sailing jacket. He snapped the grip open with too much ease—not something he ordinarily perceived in his movements—and spoke firmly into it. "Mind your own business, McCoy. I'm on leave."

"On leave and suddenly psychic, too, I see," the familiar voice plunged back.

"Who else has the gall to disobey direct orders?" Kirk shifted the communicator to his left hand and used his right to wrench open a sliding panel in the barn's loft wall. Not easy; it hadn't been open in—no, he didn't want to count years right now. The eddies of time weren't his best friends at the moment. The backwashes . . .

"What do you want?" he asked as he reached into the metal cubbyhole behind the panel of century-old barnwood. He was quite aware of the guilty hesitation on the other end of the frequency when McCoy didn't answer right away.

"I thought you might want company for dinner."

"That's the best excuse you've got?"

"Well, it's hard to come up with a shipboard emergency hanging here in spacedock, you know. Dangling a juicy stuffed Cornish hen dinner in front of you was all I could come up with. I'm a surgeon, not a . . . not a . . . damn, I can't think of anything."

"Then you have something to keep you busy," Kirk said sharply. "There are some days when a man doesn't want to be cheered up. Kirk out."

He flipped the grid closed and stuffed the communicator and everything it represented back into his pocket. In his mind he saw McCoy's squarish face skewered with helpless empathy and knew he'd been unfair, but everything was unfair. Where was it written that a starship captain always had to be the exception? This wasn't his day to be exceptional. Today he wanted to be what he remembered himself as—a tough curly-haired blond kid with big aspirations and a painfully realistic edge to his imagination. He knew that if he looked out the loft door he'd see his mother peeking out the farmhouse window like she had during his entire boyhood, wondering what her son was thinking and not having the nerve to come out and ask. Either that or she just had more respect for his privacy than McCoy did.

No surprise. Bacteria had more respect for privacy than McCoy did.

Kirk shook away an urge to glance over his shoulder and reached into the hidden metal box inside the loft wall. Carefully he pulled out an uneven bundle of letters, ragged and yellowed, a bundle of Starfleet notepaper preserved only with a child's obsessive care for something particularly precious. His lips curled up on one side as he ran his thumb across the discolored ink of a handwritten line.

"Stone knives and bearskins," he murmured. His throat closed around any further comment, embarrassing him in front of himself and making him glad he was alone. He straightened up—certainly one thing that had been easier twenty-five years ago—strode through old hay to the loft door, and sat down in a wedge of sunlight with the bundle of notepaper.

The sunlight on his face, real sunlight, made the natural ruddiness rise in his cheeks again. He could feel the color seep back into his skin, aware of how pale starship duty sometimes made him in spite of special whole-spectrum artificial lighting with all its pretense of sunlight. Like pills instead of solid food. The same, but not. Maybe that was because starship lighting had no warmth.

Starship . . . how could a word so beautiful seem so sinister to him now? It hadn't been the ship's fault, this tragedy that crushed him to the Earth's surface like sudden gravity. It hadn't been McCoy's fault, though McCoy felt otherwise. It hadn't been Spock's fault, though Spock hadn't been able to help no matter how much he wanted to. *So, it must be my own fault. My fault, because I earned command. And for my reward, I pay.*

Squinting in the bright daylight, he divided the pile in two, just for the sake of mystery, then picked up a letter and started reading.

May 10, 2183

Dear George and Jim—

This letter is going to be late reaching you—sorry. Your letter had to find me after being delivered to the wrong starbase. That's Star Fleet for you — we can patrol a galaxy, but we can't get a letter through.

I feel bad about last month, troopers. I know I promised to be there, but there's a problem with promises and you might as well learn it. Even fathers have to break them sometimes.

George, I want you to know I'm proud of that green ribbon you won at the science fair. You already know more about biology than I ever could. I hung the ribbon right on the door of the base recreation deck, so everybody who goes in has to look at it. I'm getting congrats for you from *all over the starbase.*

*About the other idea, Jimmy—
probably not. Space isn't really
very pretty when it's all you
have to look at. Someday
you'll appreciate having
a planet under your feet
when you look at the stars.
Okay, so it's not much of
an answer.*

"No," Kirk sighed, "it's not. But I probably wasn't listening anyway." He leaned back on the gray barnwood and crossed his ankles, then indulged in a sip of the coffee he'd brought out here with him. Doused with honey and milk like his aunt used to make for him when she thought he was too young to take coffee black, it was more of a liquid candy bar than coffee. The taste of nostalgia.

He tipped the crusty letter away from the sun and spoke to the handwriting.

"Keep talking. I'm listening now."

Chapter One

THE SECURITY COMMANDER set his pen down and spun the sensor camera roller, then gazed up at the row of monitors. Each monitor was carefully positioned so that he got a clear view of his own reflection, and it was a damned annoyance to always have to be looking past that fellow with the rusty red hair and the stern expression that reminded him of bleached-out dreams. He blinked to clear the reflection from his mind, and looked past it to the views of the monitors, each of which showed a different compartment, lab or lounge on the starbase. At two o'clock in the simulated night, things were quiet. At least temporarily.

The officer set the computer sentry on automatic survey,

picked up his pen, and went back to his writing while he had the chance.

Of course there's no reason you can't visit here when school's over, boys. But living on Starbase Two is out of the question. After all, your mother has her own career to consider, and even as Chief of Security here, I wouldn't have enough free time to make it worth your while to give up the life you have on Earth. There aren't any meadows here, or any lakes, or frogs, or race tracks, or anything. Just labs, classrooms and simulators, and a couple of gyms not even big enough to throw a baseball in.

"Don't make it a sad letter, George."

George looked up into Lt. Francis Drake Reed's eyes, eyes shaded by an awning of umber hair that reflected his West Indies heritage. Drake was doing his priest thing again, but this time it was no sham.

"How do you know it's a sad letter?" George asked, burying the sudden shiver that ran down his arms.

Drake sat on the console and gazed down at him. "I see your face."

George's complexion, normally peach-pale, flushed russet. "Hang you."

"End the letter before it gets sad, George," Drake pressed.

For a moment, George's eyes grew cold as rocks, and his brows flattened over them. *Don't tamper with my privacy,* they warned. *It's all I have.*

"Love . . . Dad," Drake prodded. He pointed at the paper.

Beneath the smoldering indignation and the embarrassment he felt at being so thoroughly interpretable, George felt the sting of regret. If only he could allow his family to know him so well. If only . . .

Before the rage boiled, he broke his glare away from Drake and dragged his attention back to the paper. His fingers were stiff as he wrote the final words.

*George, look after the family.
You're my second-in-command.
I'll write to you both when
you get to Georgian Bay.*

*And Jim, don't get mad
when Aunt Ilsa calls you
"Veemee."*

*Signing off,
Dad*

He folded the paper immediately, then again, as though the folds would seal out any invasion. Knowing Drake was watching, he slipped the letter into a Starfleet envelope, slid his fingers along the pressure seal, addressed it sloppily, then opened the communications chute and dropped the letter in. The sound of automatic suction told him it was gone. Two weeks from now, his boys would be reading it. And it was too late for him to snatch it back and change anything. The commitment made him nervous. He closed his eyes for a moment and covered his mouth with a bloodless hand. Strange how just writing a letter . . .

"You always get surly when you write to your puppies, Geordie," Drake said as he folded his arms and shifted against the console. "You have the temper of a resting alligator, you know, and I'd like to hear you admit it freely."

George glanced at him briefly and let the indignation flow

away, disguising the change in fiddling with the monitor equipment. "I'd rather sleep with a Romulan."

"You might. You don't even know what a Romulan looks like."

"I don't have to."

"George, you are a bigot."

"I know."

Without the slightest announcement, the office door slid open. That in itself was a surprise; the security office doors weren't supposed to open except for cleared personnel, and the people who entered, two men and a woman, didn't seem to be wearing any of the coded clearance badges needed for reading by the computer sentry. George swiveled around slightly in his chair, just enough to get a good look at the woman, who was in the lead. The only thing that he had time to register was her grape-green eyes and the color of her shoulder-length hair—like a wheatfield just after dawn. Biscuit-blond.

She took two measured steps into the office, followed by the two nondescript men, and without a pause she asked, "George Kirk?"

The answer was automatic. "Yes?"

The two men lunged around her, one heading for George, the other for Drake.

Drake was taken by surprise, training or not, and his attacker managed to pinion his arms before he could draw his hand cannon. The woman moved in instantly and pressed a moist cloth over Drake's nose and mouth. Drake's eyes widened in terror and disgust at the stifling medicinal odor in the cloth, and his arms and legs turned to putty in the grip of his attackers.

George had had that extra second necessary to raise his feet and kick off the other man's first lunge, and by the time he rolled to the floor and came up, he had managed to draw his weapon. Lacking time to aim and fire it, though, he simply brought it upward in a sweep and butt-stroked the stranger's jaw. Had he not been startled by Drake's sudden collapse at the hands of the woman, he might not have been overtaken. But when Drake went down, the second man moved in on George and kicked him hard across the pelvis. Stunned, George fought the numbness and tried to keep his balance, but the only way to do that was to lean on the hand that held his cannon. The two men grappled his arms and held him as he writhed and tried to kick back, and the woman moved in.

George bellowed an animal protest as the cloth closed in on his mouth, and the woman had a fight just getting near his face. Something about her told him she was a professional. She seemed to know the moves he would make as he twisted and tugged against the two strong men, and she anticipated him enough to force the odorous narcotic into his nostrils. His muscles jellified. The room turned to sizzling colors. A tunnel began to close around his vision, snuffing out the colors. He felt himself sinking. The cloth pressed tighter over his mouth, and the heavy drug drowned his universe. A black, black universe.

"Hello, children."

The bridge of the cramped little runabout brightened at the sound of its master's voice in such a manner that seldom accompanies the reappearance of a captain on a bridge. True to the greeting, it was as if Dad had returned from a fishing trip. This wasn't their usual assignment ship; that was plain from the sparseness of crew and their unfamiliarity with the design. This was nothing more than a getting-from-here-to-there ship, and this time the "there" was top secret. No one but the captain himself seemed to have any concrete idea of where they were going or why.

The young man on helm turned immediately and said, "We have warp, Captain. Our e.t.a. is thirty-nine minutes."

"Ah! Good," the captain responded in his reassuring Coventry chant. "Thank you, Carlos. You always do such a magnificent job." Clad in a sloppy Irish wool cardigan that hid much of his mustard-gold Starfleet uniform, the captain was a one-man destruction zone for the hackneyed image of Englishmen as stuffy and passionless. That was evidenced as he dropped his hand on the helmsman's shoulder. "Have you had your lunch? This is a good time."

The helmsman looked up for confirmation and found it in the captain's offhand nod. "Thanks, sir . . . thank you."

"Not at all. Off you go." He waved a hand at the thickset communications officer and said, "You too, Claw. Off you go. Dr. Poole and I can handle things up here for a short while, I 'magine."

The two junior officers gratefully left the bridge under the affectionate gaze of the captain. On the port side, a woman with dark blond hair folded her arms and said nothing, but merely watched the captain.

He was a gentle-faced man in his early forties, with brown hair sloppily palmed to one side, a slightly hooked nose, and powder blue eyes pouched with experience. Given to hanging his hands in the pockets of that non-regulation cardigan, he looked out of place on the tight little bridge. She remembered the time she'd pecked at him about the sweater, only to be informed by another officer that the captain suffered a rare blood deficiency that made him slightly chilly most of the time. While any other officer in Starfleet would feel obliged to wear a thermal layer *under* the uniform, this man simply slipped the sweater on and called it solved. Over several years of service, the sweater, like its master, had acquired a slight sag and a lot of respect, not to mention a professorlike image that smothered any vestige of his Starfleet accolades—considerable ones.

When the juniors were gone, the captain settled into the helm chair instead of his command seat and lounged back, shifting his gaze to the woman. She was still looking at him as though he needed looking at.

With a deep breath and an easy grin, he said, "Rolf tells me you knocked them out straight away."

The woman shrugged with her eyes. "I didn't want to have to explain anything to them. I don't have the answers."

The captain stuffed his hands into his old knitted friend. "I could give you the details of the mission—"

She held up a defensive hand. "No, thanks."

"You'll have to find out sooner or later, Doctor my dear."

"No, I don't. The less I know, the less involved I have to get, and the sooner I can get back to the colony I've been assigned to. The one I *requested* and was *granted* by the Federation."

The captain's thin lips curled in unmistakable amusement. He tipped his head. "It's a compliment."

The woman leaned forward. "It's an intrusion. I have other work to do in another place."

"Can't you see that you must be the most qualified person? You'll be the first, you know."

"I'm sure there've been doctors on big boats before," she responded dryly. "I don't know how you arranged to get my orders changed, but I intend to log a formal protest as soon as we get back."

He chuckled. "Orders do change, Sarah. And this is an emergency mission, after all—"

"You're not going to admit it, are you?" she accused.

The captain tossed his head and laughed. "In my experience, it's wisest never to admit anything to a pretty woman who's also smart."

She grimaced, her ivory face made pasty by the poor lighting and given a green cast by the medical services smock. Only her dark brown eyes, as she narrowed them at him, seemed to have any substance in the unflattering light. She gave her head a shake as though to call attention to what she had once described to him as uneventful hair. "Don't smooth me, Captain. I'm over thirty. I've heard it before."

"Obviously not sincerely enough." He rolled back still farther in the wobbly helm chair and watched space stretch by at warp two. "At least I managed to convince the authorities to let me select my own command crew. And there was barely time for that. Well," he said, giving the ship's navigation console an affectionate slap, "I'll explain it in full to you as soon as Kirk gets up here."

Dr. Poole settled into the science station seat and told him, "He's not going to get up here. I locked them in the hold."

"Oh, *that* won't make any difference."

She blinked. "Houdini?"

"Stubborn."

His rueful nod ushered in a silence that lasted several long, quiet minutes. Through the wide main portal, they watched space peel by with the kind of speed it takes time to get used to. It never ceased to be startling, or beautiful, or even a touch frightening, and none of it was natural. This speed was the accomplishment of inventive minds. In all the wonders of the natural universe, this wonder belonged to intelligence alone. It was nice for something to be marvelous because it didn't know any better, but to be marvelous by *design* . . .

The captain sighed and contemplated the miracles he would see in the next few days. Inside the pockets, his hands clenched with foresight and the quaking thrill of participation. In his eyes was reflected the passage of hope's foothills.

When the bridge entry panel opened and the floor vibrated, he knew the contemplation was over for a while.

"On your feet!"

The captain and the doctor turned and stood up to face the two men, the russet-haired one armed with a particle-cutter from a ship's emergency kit. Though Dr. Poole froze, the captain swung his arms out wide and said, "George! How good to see you! You look strapping. How're the boys?" He strode to them and gave George a pat on the arm, then turned to Dr. Poole. "I told you they'd be right along." He gave George a little shake and drawled, "Ingenious fellow."

George Kirk let his breath out in a gasp and sucked in a new one, staring fiercely at the captain, then the doctor, then the bridge, then the captain again. "R—" He took another breath and tried again. "Robert!"

Behind him, Drake brandished the bent lighting panel they'd used to break out of the hold, still not quite convinced of the captain's jovial greeting.

The captain rocked on his heels, devilishly pleased with his reunion. "Didn't think I could be so clandestine, did you?"

"You . . ." George began, *"You* kidnapped us?"

"Well, there simply wasn't time—"

"There'd better be time now!"

"Oh, yes, plenty. A good eight or ten minutes yet, I'm sure," the captain said, glancing at the chronometer.

George took a few uncertain steps around the bridge, his head still swimming with the ricochet, and demanded, "Where is everybody? This ship's practically empty. Where's the crew?"

"In the mess hall, I suppose, having a good lunch. There are only a few on board. Security reasons, you see."

George narrowed his eyes. "Security . . . what are you up to?"

"I want you to volunteer for a mission."

"What mission?"

"I can't specify."

"To where?"

"I can't tell you."

"For how long?"

The lopsided grin appeared. "Sorry."

"After I volunteer, then you can tell me?"

"Right."

"And I'm supposed to just trust you?"

"I'd be so grateful."

"All right. I volunteer."

The captain's grin widened and he looked at Sarah. "Didn't I tell you?"

Sarah shrugged her innocence. "It wasn't my idea to drug them."

"Yes, would you care to explain that?" George demanded, glaring at the captain.

"Well, you see, this mission is the ultra-top-secret response to an emergency situation, and decisions had to be made quickly. They finally allowed me to choose my own officers, so—"

"Who did?"

"Starfleet Command."

"You got Starfleet Command to authorize you to knock us out and kidnap us?" George shook his head. "I'd like to see that memo."

The captain held his hands out wide. "It was the *only* way they'd agree to it." Amused by Kirk's dubious expression, the captain suddenly touched his lips with one finger and said, "Oh, forgive me. I'm being inhospitable." He gestured gallantly between them and the woman. "May I present Commander George Kirk, and over there is Lieutenant Francis Drake Reed. Gentlemen . . . Dr. Sarah Poole."

George stared rudely at her, quite aware of the rude part, and once his memory adjusted for the sickish bridge lighting and the green smock she wore instead of the unmarked lab jacket she'd been wearing before, he recognized her. "We've met," he snapped.

Sarah bobbed her eyebrows and requested, "Don't look at me like that. He did the same thing to get me here."

George snapped back at the captain, "You did that to her? And why pull Drake into this?"

The captain shrugged and strode a few steps to the upper bridge for a long look at Drake. "While it would be easier if you'd just drag around a teddy bear or suck on a blanket, I knew you'd want him along." The hands went back into the pockets, and the captain suddenly looked as though he was hovering in front of a blackboard, waiting to see if his students comprehended a new hypothesis. He was so innocuous and self-assured that he was almost impossible to dislike. With that tolerant grin, he nodded. "Well, then.

This is a good time for explanations. Gather round, children." He moved to the computer bank and tapped the access. "Computer on," he said.

"Working."

"This is Captain Robert April. Request security access, Starfleet Command authorization, graphic tape one."

The console buzzed to life, and its raspy fake voice responded, *"Authorization accepted. File on screen."*

Above them appeared a series of diagrams and photographs of a familiar colonial transport ship, one of the Seidman Class long-distance movers. Old, but time-proven. It meant nothing at all to anyone except, of course, Captain April. He nodded at the diagrams. "This is the United Federation Colonizer S.S. *Rosenberg*. She was off into space to colonize a newly discovered planet in the space just recently charted by the Federation. Five days ago we received a distress call from the *Rosenberg*. They don't, of course, have an advanced sensor system and weren't able to realize the severity of an ionic storm cluster they encountered until after they were already too deep inside it to stop the damage and reverse course. They're adrift. No engine power, and heavy radiation leakage in their storage compartments and engineering areas. Most of their foodstuffs has been contaminated. Actually, even if they did have the food, there's radiation leakage into the inhabited parts of the ship. It's only a matter of time, and not much time at that. To make the long story tolerable," April said with a sad sigh, "they're going to die out there."

George was the first to break the heavy silence. "How many?"

April half turned. "Fourteen families. Fifty-one people. Twenty-seven are under fifteen years old. Young families with babies, and without experience. And without food."

"God . . ." Sarah breathed, then caught the breath with the knuckle of her thumb and kept herself from uttering her anguish.

"Of course, a shuttleplane was dispatched straight off," April went on, "but no conventional ship can risk going through the ionic storms until they've dissipated, and that could take years. The rescue ship is going around the storms, but even at warp three that'll take four months. The *Rosenberg* only has about three weeks' worth of supplies on hand, and, of course, I mentioned the radiation leaks." He gazed at the graphic screen. It cast its pattern of lights on his face. "Fifty-one people who think they're going to die in space, hopelessly out of range. And the really tragic part is that we can communicate with them quite nicely, with communications at warp twenty. All of the Federation is listening to them die out there. Journalists are having a field day, you can well imagine."

His gaze dropped as he stepped off the upper deck, past the three pained faces of his chosen crew, only to find himself yanked around to stare up at George Kirk. Unmistakable in the Vikinglike hazel eyes was the image of two little boys in a cornfield on a planet suddenly too far away for peaceful memory.

"You've got something planned," George snapped. "What is it? We'll try it."

April's light blue eyes filled with affection, and he grinned at the fierceness he knew he would need at his side. He opened his mouth to answer, only to be interrupted by the beeping of the ship's auto-nav. He turned as though responding to a dog barking outside his door. "Ah! We've arrived. Drake, do you know how to take the ship out of warp?"

Drake blinked out of his trance and recovered his usual false humility. "I shall die trying, sir." With that, he moved to the helm and pecked at the controls.

April moved toward the bridge viewing portal and watched in wonder as the ship smoothly fell out of warp drive and approached what appeared to be a spacedock behind a little cluster of asteroids. He breathed deeply, as though he could nearly smell the fresh air of reassurance.

George left the upper deck, his eyes never leaving his former commander, all the details of their mutual past flashing through his mind. He came to April's side and saw unshielded resolve in the captain's expression. It was infectious. And confusing. He shouldered his way into April's periphery and quietly prodded, "What is it, Robert? What are you planning?"

"Think of it, George," April murmured. "An impossible rescue. A way to turn a four-month journey into a three-week epic triumph in the name of life. Think of it."

Now George moved around to face him, and to force April to look at him. In the upper edge of the viewscreen, unnoticed, the spacedock moved closer.

"Why all the cloak and dagger?" George pressed. "Why didn't you just ask me?"

"Couldn't take the chance, old boy."

"Why?"

April stepped closer to the helm, placed his hands on the console, and looked out, upward, at the looming spacedock. He nodded out, up. "That's why."

Soft lights from the spacedock played in his eyes.

George stepped closer, leaned over the console, and looked out. The lights bathed his ruddy cheeks and drew him on, into astonishment.

"My God . . ." he whispered. "What is *that?*"

"That," April breathed, "is a starship."